JANET PYWELL

Broken Windows

A Mikky dos Santos Thriller

First published by KIngsdown Publishing 2020

Copyright © 2020 by Janet Pywell

This novel is entirely a work of fiction. The names, characters and
incidents portrayed in it are the work of the author's imagination.
Any resemblance to actual persons, living or dead, events or localities
is entirely coincidental.

Janet Pywell asserts the moral right to be identified as the author of
this work.

Janet Pywell has no responsibility for the persistence or accuracy of
URLs for external or third-party Internet Websites referred to in this
publication and does not guarantee that any content on such
Websites is, or will remain, accurate or appropriate.

Designations used by companies to distinguish their products are
often claimed as trademarks. All brand names and product names
used in this book and on its cover are trade names, service marks,
trademarks and registered trademarks of their respective owners.
The publishers and the book are not associated with any product or
vendor mentioned in this book. None of the companies referenced
within the book have endorsed the book.

First edition

This book was professionally typeset on Reedsy.
Find out more at reedsy.com

Foreword

Broken Windows – A Mikky dos Santos Thriller

MIKKY IS DETERMINED TO MAKE A DIFFERENCE. LIFE CAN'T STAY THE SAME. NOT AFTER WHAT HAPPENED.

Buckle up – this rollercoaster of a thriller will leave you breathless!

Mikky's task is simple. Find out who owns the valuable dagger, the talisman and symbol for a cult-like group in London's underworld – a drugs gang led by the Asian, who controls the streets with ruthless violence. He recruits children: befriending them, grooming them, and controlling them through fear, as they package and sell drugs.

The Dixon Trust provides a safe house and haven for these unprotected and extremely vulnerable kids. Run by Matt, an ex-convict, and supported by a local politician, Raymond Harris, these men are determined to rescue and protect the children, and save lives.

Given another chance, and taught by Matt, the *Parks* become experts in freerunning and parkour. It gives them a sense of worth and purpose, and when they're asked to participate in an action-packed movie, their self-esteem knows no bounds.

None of them expects – death.

Mikky gains access and insight into their world as she films a documentary. But devastated by shocking events, she is determined to find the dagger, and to flush out the cult leader and hold them all to account – even if it means risking her own life.

The story weaves around the mesmerising parkour kids – the *Parks*. They will have you hooked – their stories are captivating and heartbreaking, and they will have you gunning for each of them until the final twist.

Set in London (England), Ouarzazate (Morocco), and Basel (Switzerland).

Acknowledgement

When I began *Masterpiece* – the first Mikky dos Santos thriller – in 2016, I had no idea where the talented art forger and sometimes morally wayward protagonist would head. All I knew was that Mikky would be different, and over the years – along the way – I've had to keep up with her skills and all the useful technology and gadgets that have been used in the series. I've had the help of experts and friends, and this book is no different – so I'd like to thank Carrie Breed, Katie Hicken, Mark and Sally Rogers, Tracey Falcon, Matt Maguire, Mark Swift, and Amanda Gerrard.

Chapter 1

"Drugs are a waste of time. They destroy your memory and your self-respect and everything that goes along with your self-esteem."
Kurt Cobain

PROLOGUE

I'm running for my life. The staircase is steep and dark. I smack the button for the light, leaping in the air, narrowly missing a curled-up body in the doorway. It groans and moves.

The stench is oppressive.

My breath is in raspy gasps. My knees are growing weak.

Another floor, higher and higher, up the tower block.

A gunshot echoes over my head and instinctively I duck. I've lost count of the number of floors – maybe twenty, more?

Breathlessly, I turn another corner, and up more stairs, conscious of my assailant's steps behind me, looming closer.

There's a glint of light at the end of the passageway, and I'm halfway along the corridor when another shot rings out, pinging off the metalwork.

I throw myself at the emergency exit, pushing the bar, careful not to drop the prize wedged under my arm.

The door flies open. I blink. Suddenly, I'm in natural light, but it's dusk. The December sun is fading, and the bitter wind bites at my ears and nose.

Gasping lungfuls of air, panting heavily, I glance across the rooftops, getting my bearings: London. More specifically, Islington, and in the distance, Regent's Canal.

Another gunshot ricochets off the steel railing. I duck and run for cover behind a giant pipe, probably heating ducts. The man following me slows his pace and approaches cautiously. He knows I'm trapped.

I peer over the edge. We're twenty-five storeys high.

I have vertigo.

My head swims.

My mouth is dry.

I raise my right leg and swing it over the wall, dangling it into the empty void and hugging the bag to my chest.

'There's no way out.'

His Asian accent is strong, and his voice is loud across the open space between us, drifting in the breeze. 'Give it to me!'

I'm not armed. I wish I was. I swallow hard, staring down at the drop below; my head swims, and my hands begin to shake. I'll never survive.

My pursuer takes a step closer; his dark almond eyes are devoid of emotion.

'Put the bag on the ground, or I will kill you.' He points the Smith & Wesson, a powerful handgun, designed to stop any game animal, at my chest.

I hesitate.

He takes a step closer.

'It's not worth it.' He grins. 'I *will* kill you.'

I'm astride the low wall, probably over seventy metres above the ground. My assailant is six metres away, not close enough for me to charge at him or to throw the bag at him. There's no way out. Sweat breaks out on my forehead.

He's a professional.

I swing my leg back over the wall, face him, and lower the bag to the ground, conscious of the vast open space behind me.

'Open it!' he demands, waving the gun at me.

I bend down and unzip the bag, and show him the dagger that still has traces of my blood on its blade.

He smiles.

I shout, 'We can come to some sort of agreement! Make a deal. Work together. I'm on your side.'

I raise my arms wide, stretched out like I'm Jesus on the cross, wearing only my hoodie. My coat was torn from me, and I lost my phone. I know Peter won't be able to follow me.

I call out, 'I can pay you—'

'You're a liar, Mikky. You tried to fool me once, but you won't do it again. I'm the Asian. No one messes with me – and gets away with it.'

'I didn't, I—'

I turn to my right, distracted by the noise of a helicopter, its motor humming, whining and growing closer.

'You hear me? I'm the Asian,' he shouts. 'They're not going to save you, Mikky. No one can!'

That's when he fires his gun, and the shot hits my chest. Air explodes from my lungs. The powerful force of the bullet lifts me backwards and up into the air. I fall back over the concrete ledge, and I'm suddenly spiralling head first, from the twenty-fifth floor, toward my fate and certain death below.

Chapter 2

"Crime has always been a regrettably consistent element of the human experience."
Mark Frost

TWO WEEKS EARLIER:

The Ivy Brasserie on London's South Bank overlooks the bright blue and red towers of Tower Bridge. It's one of London's most iconic landmarks, that crosses the River Thames toward the Tower of London. The imposing bridge towers are joined at the upper level by two high-level walkways forty-two metres above the water, and a movable bridge that is, on this mid-November evening, busy with vehicles and pedestrians. I'm contemplating the Tower of London, north of the river, wondering how it would feel to be incarcerated in the cells before being executed.

'Mikky?'

'Sorry, yes.' I return my attention to the two men dining with me. My handsome, dark-haired Spanish boss, Inspector Joachin García Abascal, and his friend, Chief Inspector Mulhoon from London's Metropolitan Police.

'Quite frankly, I welcome Joachin's involvement in this

case.' The chief inspector rubs his palms together slowly, but it's also the intense expression in his green eyes that gives away his nervous demeanour. 'And yours, of course, Mikky. I don't know what else to do. In the past year, I've lost two outstanding undercover police officers, and we're still not getting anywhere.'

It's mid-November, we've finished an early supper, and although it's barely eight o'clock, I'm sipping a brandy, with black coffee.

'So, you want me to look for a sword?' I ask.

'It's not just *any* sword,' the chief inspector replies. 'It's a specific one that we believe the gang members swear allegiance to; it's a special one that—'

'But you have no idea what it looks like?'

The chief inspector shakes his head. 'No. The two undercover officers didn't get close enough to find out. You have to remember this gang is professional, and they're recruiting young kids, vulnerable people, and press-ganging them into selling drugs on the street. In the past few months, we have managed to break up a few drugs rings, working across counties with different forces, but this one is different. It's operating independently and multiplying. It's a cult-like environment; the kids are fanatic, they're sworn to secrecy, and we can't break through to get to the cult leaders ...'

'But you've managed to rescue a few of them, Mulhoon?' Joachin leans his elbows on the table, his dark Spanish eyes regarding his friend's reaction carefully.

'Yes, but we can't prove they were part of this particular group. They won't say anything. Although we work with social workers, and we've managed to arrange for some of them to go into specialist foster care, they still fear for their lives.'

'But you think they were in this cult-like group?' Joachin asks.

'We believe so. We definitely know they were involved in selling drugs, but it's not worth prosecuting the children; we need to get the organisers – the leaders, the guys at the top. One of our guys – undercover – was friends with Ali; he's one of the *Parks*.'

'The *Parks*?' I query.

'Parkour – it's a discipline, a sport, a thing that the young kids have started to do; they often use these skills to run from the police. But this is run by an ex-con who wants to turn his life around, so he trains these kids specifically, to keep them out of trouble. So many of them lack a father figure in their lives and Matt is making great progress with them. He's organised a group of *Parks* to go to Morocco, where they're making a film. There are a couple of action scenes where they want these kids freerunning – their stunts are amazing, and as far as I'm aware, there'll also be a couple of scenes set in London – it's one of those action movies by Sandra Worthington.'

'Didn't she get the Oscar last year?' Joachin asks.

'Yes, finally a black woman – an English woman – won the award for best director,' I reply. 'I remember reading an article about her.'

'So, let me get this straight,' says Joachin. 'You want Mikky to go to Morocco, make friends with this group of *Parks*, gain their confidence and see if she can find out about this cult?'

'Yes.'

'In the hope that we can find this sword—'

'Well, we're not sure what it is; it's a trophy of some sort,' the chief inspector interrupts me.

I continue, 'This trophy, which – you think – may be a sword, and once we find this, we can trace back ownership of the sword to the cult leader?'

'Yes.' The chief inspector nods seriously. 'It's not dangerous. You won't be in England, so there's no conflict with the Met and Europol, and, after what you told me, Joachin, Mikky is an expert in cultural artefacts.'

Joachin looks at me and raises an eyebrow, barely hiding his smile. 'Mikky has an appreciation of all art forms, isn't that right?'

I grin back at him. 'Absolutely.'

The chief inspector washes his hands in an imaginary fashion, then leans back in his chair and folds his arms.

'I want to stress, Mikky, this isn't dangerous. Your life will not be threatened. We just need the information, and when you know what the sword is like, then hand that information over to us and it's job done – you can go home.'

'And Sandra is cool with this?' ask Joachin. 'She doesn't mind Mikky going onto her film set?'

'Yes, following our last conversation and your advice, Joachin, Mikky can travel to Morocco under the guise of a photographer making a documentary about the *Parks*. Sandra's happy about it, as it may even give more credence to her next film.'

'So, Sandra Worthington is happy for me to go over there?' I double-check.

'Yes.' The chief inspector nods vigorously. 'She has no idea that you are part of Europol. She thinks you're a photographer and that you've approached the Met police and social workers here in London. The documentary will be focused on the *Parks* and their skills, and how they have turned their lives around.'

'Mikky can do that, can't you?' Joachin looks at me.

I nod and drain my brandy.

'There is one other thing,' the chief inspector says. He lowers his voice in the busy restaurant. 'The prime minister will be very grateful for your involvement.'

'The prime minister?' repeats Joachin, raising his eyebrows.

'Yes, as you know, the election is coming up next month – on the 10th December. The prime minister wants to spearhead his election campaign knowing that the cult leader is under arrest, and that this particular drugs ring has been exposed, then he will have more, how shall we say, kudos with the voting public. He will have delivered on his last election promise to make the streets safer, and he will be extremely grateful.'

'And so will the public,' adds Joachin.

Chief Inspector Mulhoon looks at me. 'This is a grave matter, Mikky. This affects not only London but the whole of the UK. This gang seems unstoppable. It's growing at an alarming rate. Two of my guys have been discovered and killed. There's no one on the streets willing to reveal anything – they're too scared. It's a long shot, but we need more details about the sword they swear allegiance to. Someone must perform the ritual or whatever it is they do. We can't get anyone close enough here to get more information, but with your background, asking questions, under the guise of a self-employed film-maker in Morocco – I feel it's a risk worth taking.'

'What happened to the undercover officers?' I ask.

The chief inspector gazes out of the window before answering quietly, 'They were executed.'

'How?' I insist.

'They were shot from a very short distance.'

'Okay, well, there's one condition for me going to Morocco,' I say.

'What's that?'

'No one else must know I'm going. It's just between the three of us.'

'I'm not happy about that,' replies Mulhoon.

'That's how it has to be,' I insist.

Joachin stares at me. 'If you leave tomorrow, you'll be in Morocco for four nights, and you'll be home by Friday. And, after that, you can go back to travelling the world with Marco.' He looks at the chief inspector. 'Mikky is right, Mulhoon. No one else needs to know about her visit.'

'Who's Marco?' asks Mulhoon.

'Mikky's getting married,' Joachin explains.

I hold up my hand and laugh. 'Steady on, Joachin. We haven't set a date yet, and besides, we're not in a hurry; it might not even be for a couple of years.'

Joachin smiles. 'If you leave tomorrow, a couple of days won't interrupt your schedule too much, will it?'

I shake my head. I know I'll go to Morocco.

'I'm looking forward to it already.' I smile.

'I'll organise your flight for the morning.' The chief inspector picks up his phone that had been lying on the table and begins searching through his contact details. 'They're filming over there now, they have a couple more days left, so we haven't much time. You must leave in the morning. Will Marco be alright with that?'

'It's not Marco I'm worried about.' I stare at Joachin and smile. 'I'm staying with my mother so, Joachin, I suggest you explain to Josephine why I have to disappear so quickly.'

Joachin grins. He knows my birth mother well and he can

already imagine her reaction.

The chief inspector raises his phone to his mouth and I hold up my hand.

'I don't know who you're phoning, but you're not to tell anyone who I am and that I'm going to Morocco. That's my condition. You tell absolutely no one.'

The chief inspector places his phone back on the table. 'Of course. You have my word.'

'Not even the prime minister,' I add.

* * *

'But Joachin, this is such short notice,' Josephine wails an hour later.

'Mikky has only just come back from travelling around Europe with Marco in his yacht. I haven't seen her for six months, and besides, I wanted her to look at wedding dresses.'

'Wedding dresses?' I say with a laugh. 'There will be plenty of time for that when I get back.'

Josephine and Simon's penthouse loft is large and minimalist, situated on London's popular Bankside, and it has floor to ceiling windows with panoramic views of London. Outside, the Thames is bathed in darkness, and the red and blue lights of Tower Bridge catch the moonlight. We are within walking distance of Borough Market, Tower Bridge, and City Hall, and it's barely a five-minute stroll from the Ivy Brasserie, where Joachin and I had dinner with Mulhoon.

Joachin is sitting on one of the white sofas drinking coffee. On the walls, there are original paintings by a couple of local London artists who I vaguely know, and photographs of London streets.

'I thought we'd have time for shopping,' Josephine complains. 'We haven't had this opportunity for months.'

'I'll make it up to you when I get back,' I reply.

Josephine stands up and wanders around her large penthouse apartment, and stares out to Bankside, which is the historic area south of the City of London, on the river opposite us.

'It's only for three days, Josephine.' Joachin's voice is friendly, and like me, he's nursing a generous measure of brandy and waiting for Josephine to accept our change of plan. 'It's an opportunity we can't turn down. It's with Sandra Worthington, the film director who won an Oscar.'

'I've heard of her,' Josephine replies, and as she frowns, there's beauty in her deep eyes, full mouth, and dark hair. 'Glorietta knows her sister. She's a soprano, too.'

My birth mother was once a well-known opera star, also a soprano, famous around the globe for her incredible range and timbre. After an unfortunate incident – a gunshot that punctured her lung, and the death of her partner – Josephine no longer sings, but her best friend Glorietta Bareldo is regarded as the greatest in the world. Fortunately for me, they are all part of my chequered family.

'And it's a documentary?' Josephine asks.

'Yes, it's about some local kids from London who have turned their lives around by learning parkour ...' I reply vaguely.

'But this isn't police business – it's not dangerous?'

'No!' Joachin and I reply together.

'So, why are you here, Joachin?'

'Mulhoon and I have been friends for years, and he was looking for someone to make a documentary, and I thought of Mikky.' He doesn't meet my gaze, but I can't help but think how easily the lie flowed from his lips.

11

'You will be good at making a documentary, Mikky. Besides, it will get you away from all that other dangerous business.' Josephine's previous reference to my involvement with Joachin and Europol makes me smile, so I turn away.

'Don't worry, Josephine. You know I'll always look after Mikky; she's like a daughter to me, too.'

Josephine stares hard at him but doesn't reply.

I say, 'I'll be gone four nights at the most. I'll be home on Friday, I promise, and then we can go shopping on Saturday.' I pull out my phone to check flights.

'Simon and I are flying to Miami on Friday, or had you forgotten?'

I smile. 'It had slipped my mind.'

'What does Marco say about all this?' she asks.

'He understands,' I lie, not willing to tell her that I haven't yet been able to get hold of Marco, who is currently at sea and sailing his yacht between Croatia and Italy.

'But I wanted to spend some quality time with you.' Josephine has always been persistent and used to having her own way; however, I seem to have the ability to thwart her plans regularly.

'We can do it when you get back.' I check my phone to see where Marco will be and how easy it will be to speak to him.

'Mikky!' At the sound of my name, I look up sharply.

'Yes?'

'You're not running away again, are you?' Josephine moves toward me.

A few years ago, after a surprise marriage proposal, I'd rushed away from New York to Rhodes on an errand for Simon. I smile.

'No, not this time, I promise. I love Marco with all my heart.'

Josephine seems satisfied, but her direct gaze unsettles me, and I realise, not for the first time, just how similar we are – both in looks and character.

'Is there a flight to Marrakesh?' she asks, and by her tone, I can tell she's hoping there are none.

'Yes, first thing in the morning.' I scroll the flight times and availability.

'Book two seats,' Joachin says.

I glance up at him, surprised. 'Two? Are you coming with me?'

'No, but Peter is on his way over here tonight. He'll meet you at the airport first thing in the morning.'

'I can manage on my own,' I complain. 'I don't need a chaperone.'

'I'm not sending you alone,' Joachin insists. 'Josephine isn't the only one who wants you home by Friday.'

* * *

The following afternoon, I'm on another continent and in a different country when I finally get hold of Marco, who is currently somewhere in the Adriatic Sea between Italy and Croatia.

'Morocco?' he asks.

'It's pronounced War-zazat. It's only for a few days. I'll be back in London on Friday.'

'I want to look after you,' Marco says over the phone.

'Peter is with me.'

'You're so precious to me, and I don't want anything to happen to you.'

'Stop worrying, my darling. I'm on a film set in Morocco, not

13

in outer Mongolia!' I glance around at the imposing sandstone buildings in the Kasbah around me. 'I'll be home soon, my darling, and we can spend Christmas together.'

'I'm looking forward to it, Mikky. It will be my first Christmas in England for years.'

'Then we'll just have to make it extra special,' I reply.

'I miss you; it's not the same out here sailing without you.'

'I know, but Joachin needed me, and I have taken six months off already. I have to work!' I say with a laugh.

'I understand, but it seems like you left me longer than four days ago. Besides ...' I hear the smile in his complaining tone, 'you haven't answered my proposal.'

'I did,' I reply, laughing happily. 'You know I will. You seem to have told everyone anyway – even Joachin knows, and Josephine. Of course I'll marry you.'

'Let's set a date.'

'When I get back from Morocco.'

'No, now.'

'Are you always this impatient?'

'Mikky, the past few months sailing around the Greek islands with you, talking and making plans for the future and Blessinghurt Manor, have been the best months of my life. I'm not letting you go ...'

'They were the best months for me, too,' I whisper truthfully.

'Then marry me. Let's set a date.'

'Surprise me,' I reply.

'You wouldn't mind?'

'I'd love it.'

'Mikky?' Peter calls out from behind me, and I turn around. 'They're going to start shooting in a minute,' he whispers.

I wave in acknowledgement and say into my phone, 'Marco, I must go, my darling. Let me know when you've sorted out the yacht and you're heading back in England.'

'It'll be a week or so, by the time I've sorted everything out.'

'Then I'll be back in England before you.'

'I'll meet you at Blessinghurst Manor?'

'It's a deal.'

* * *

It's our second day filming. I'm on the set, and although I'm enjoying the drama of the film set, and have taken millions of images, hours and hours of videos, and I've used my drone to monitor the *Parks*, it's tiring just standing around.

'They're going to do the aerial shots now,' Peter explains. His chestnut eyes are alive with excitement, and he takes my arm and guides me to stand beside one of the canvas chairs. 'Look!' He points to a drone circling high in the cloudless azure sky. It's eighteen degrees and almost sunset, and I loosen the cream silk scarf at my neck.

Ouarzazate is 200 kilometres, and a road journey two and a half hours in duration, south-east of Marrakesh. The citadel sits on a plateau 1,160 metres above sea level. To the north of the town, the Atlas Mountains stretch into a hazy backdrop, and to the south of the Kasbah lies the desert. Its nickname, 'the door of the desert', is apt, and I can imagine the intense heat of the summer.

The drone hovers overhead, but its whine is faint against the Berber voices babbling around us, as orders and instructions are barked, translated, and then shouted in American.

The film set seems chaotic and busy, but everyone appears

to have a defined role and seem to know what they're doing. I've been impressed with the slick way the filming is being directed and the calm manner of Sandra Worthington.

After a brief introduction, and a promise to catch up later, Keith, the producer, has explained and helped us find our way through the maze of the set, crew, location, and hotel.

Now, outside and staring up at the sandy-coloured Kasbah of Taourirt, presumably one of the most beautiful in Morocco, it reflects the fading sunlight and glows majestically like a lost kingdom. I'm left with the image painted on my mind as Peter pulls me into its belly; a labyrinth of intricate passageways, steep steps, and narrow rooms where colourful carpets, paintings, and ceramics are on display.

We step over cables, pass camera operators and their assistants, and I'm conscious of Peter's grip on my arm as the set falls still.

'Keith said to stay here.'

'Can I film?'

'Not right now,' Peter whispers excitedly. 'You took enough pictures this morning. Just enjoy this.'

I pull my scarf over my head and cover my dyed-blonde hair, that seemed so natural on Marco's yacht in Greece but now seems out of place.

Peter's face is covered by a dark hooded cloak and his head is wrapped in a grey turban. My heart begins to race. I too am in disguise. He could be anyone, and so could I.

I hear them before I see them; a shuffling, then soft, bare footfall. The *Parks* appear, freerunning quickly, five lithe bodies leaping gracefully, something between a dance and acrobatics, serenely controlled and breathtakingly perfect. Their hands and bare feet use the simple structures of the

Kasbah; running, jumping, overlapping, at once precarious and tangled, landing on railings, roofs, and ramps, flipping, vaulting in imaginative and elegantly polished ways. I remember the terms they've mentioned in practise, like the quadrupedal, where they run quickly on all fours like dogs; and wall running like a super hero; or the safety vault, with a one-handed cartwheel and then a side flip. Every obstacle is a challenge as they spring, coil, leap, or use a barrel roll before stretching up and wall running, tic-tacking up the side of impossibly high floors, scuttling over the rooftops, and then they're gone.

A voice shouts, 'CUT!'

'Wow!' I exhale in a gasp, not realising that I'd been holding my breath.

I pull the scarf from my face and turn in wonder to look for the *Parks*. But they've disappeared, leaving me in awe of their short performance.

Peter's face is alive, and he's laughing with me. We've witnessed the performance several times this afternoon, and I've taken pictures and even used a drone; now I'm happy to have just seen the experience again, so close, without having to record it.

Sandra and Keith study the footage, share a discussion with Matt and another stunt advisor, then Keith shouts.

'AGAIN!'

'My goodness, that was breathtaking. What I'd give to be able to do that.' Peter squints up at the high walls of the Kasbah that the *Parks* scaled with ease.

'It's just practise,' I reply, grinning. 'You could try it!'

'And you need the proper equipment.' He taps his artificial foot against the wall, and it kicks up a plume of dust.

'You're full of excuses.'

'You could do it,' he suggests.

'Nah! I'm too old for parkour. Maybe ten years ago I'd have loved it. Besides, these are kids. How old are these guys?'

Peter frowns. 'Some of them are as young as fifteen. Matt is trying to recruit more of them, but he says it's difficult. He told me that there's too much temptation on the street – but this filming is a way for the kids to make money—'

'Come on, quick! Let's get ready,' I urge.

'QUIET ON THE SET!'

I hold my position, watching and waiting for the five *Parks*. This time, Ali, the leader, arrives ahead of the others and he leaps up the wall, runs along its narrow side, swings from a window ledge, and throws his weight up and onto the roof.

It's a spectacular feat, and the drone, operated by one of the film's camera crew, hovers in the sky, its lenses capturing the agility in this boy's natural physical ability.

'CUT!'

'Wow!' I whisper. 'That was so impressive!'

Peter nods and grins. We walk companionably back to the square where the crew on the film set have set up camp, and I'm excited to be here making a film documentary.

'Did you get it all?' Peter calls.

Keith, the producer, replies, 'I'm not sure; Sandra is checking it, but it looked good from where I was on top of the wall. We've had enough cameras rolling all day. So, it should be a wrap for today.'

Although he has narrow shoulders and hips, his ginger-red Viking beard gives him an authoritative and commanding presence.

'It was awesome,' I say. 'It was as good, if not better, than the earlier stunts.'

Keith smiles at me. 'They've been rehearsing really hard, but they do make it look so effortless.'

'Did you get all the footage you need?' I ask.

'I hope so, but there are more scenes tomorrow.'

'You're also filming a few scenes back in London, aren't you?' Peter asks.

'Yeah, we're setting up a few action scenes in North London – Islington.' Keith strokes his beard, thoughtfully brushing it with the back of his fingers. 'That will be next week – hopefully – or the week after, tops.'

The square is now awash with people milling about – not the local Berbers, but a mixed international crew, busy looking at cameras, moving cables, and checking monitors.

'It's great you managed to make it for the last few days of the shoot. It's an important documentary that you're making, Mikky, and that guy over there deserves a medal for everything that he's doing.'

I follow Keith's gaze that rests on Matt – a man probably in his early thirties, with a shaved head and muscled arms, with a web of violent inky tattoos; guns, knives, skulls, and serpents.

'We'll crack open the beer, shall we?' Keith says. 'Are you guys coming back to the hotel?'

'Sounds a great idea; all this filming makes for thirsty work,' agrees Peter.

Over Keith's shoulder, I can't take my eyes from Matt, an ex-convict, who has turned his life around and is now acting as a role model to the five teenagers at his side. The experts in parkour, the *Parks*, are laughing, exuberant and breathless. Although Peter and I have met them all, we still haven't yet been able to break through their natural reserve.

* * *

The following morning, I'm in one of the Bedouin tents, in Ouarzazate, especially erected for the crew. It's where they leave drinks and snacks for us, and I'm sitting cross-legged on a cushion with my DJI Phantom 3 drone upside down between my knees when Ali appears. He's a short-haired Muslim boy with a round cherubic face. His hair is cut in a popular style, the fohawk taper. It's buzzed around the ears and dropped down to the neck, making it a clean-cut look. The hair on top is spiked, styled forward, and it makes Ali look dashing and handsome, apart from his sallow cheeks – which are dented with pox marks, old spots that have healed poorly.

'Having a break?' I ask.

'Yeah, we can only film for three hours a day.'

'Is that a legal thing?'

'Yeah.' He watches me from a distance while he checks his phone.

I remove the screws, one screw per arm, then I remove the eight 5mm screws with a different screwdriver, and then the four 10mm screws. I'm searching for a T8 screwdriver when Ali asks, 'What you doing?'

'I'm changing the motor. There's a screw on each arm near the landing gear.' I undo them, then flick the Phantom back over with the motors facing up, and I peel back the silver strips.

I'm conscious of Ali stepping closer.

Using a plastic spudger, I separate the two halves of plastic shell of the drone and when it clicks loudly, I smile.

'Yay, success!' I carefully remove the upper half; following the ribbon cable to the control board, I locate the connector. I pull out the cable, separating the two halves of the drone. 'The next part is harder,' I say, working in silence, removing the glue that covers the three wires connecting the motor to the flight controller for each arm of the drone. Then carefully I desolder the black, yellow, and red wires where they connect to the flight controller and I remove the old motor.

I'm conscious of Ali kneeling beside me as I install the new motor, and then I follow the same procedure in reverse to put the drone back together.

He picks up the old motor and turns it in his hands. 'You've actually replaced the motor?' He grins.

'Yes, and now,' I say with a smile, not able to resist showing off, 'to recalibrate.'

'What does that do?' he asks.

'When I film you, I want the horizon levels to stay fixed. So, I need to calibrate the sensors.' There, I say, watching the screen. 'Calibrating in progress, it will take a few minutes.'

We wait and watch the screen.

'Now I need to adjust the gimbal roll.' I know I have his attention and I'm enjoying his silent interest.

'Do you want me to show you some of the film I took earlier of you?'

'Yeah.'

We sit companionably on the floor while I find the video footage of the *Parks*. On the first day there were stunts in the desert, and the last two days have been in the Kasbah and the hotel, jumping, running, and climbing over the balconies.

'Impressive,' I say. 'That's an amazing J-step kick. It's almost as good as your butterfly kick and front hand spin.'

'Cool,' he replies, impressed that I've mastered some of the parkour steps.

We laugh at some clumsy moments and how one scene had

to be re-filmed. My legs are cramped so I stand up, leaving him with the consul, watching the images of the *Parks*.

'How did you get so good at this?' he asks.

'I used to kitesurf and snow-ski with my ex. We used drones all the time.' I'm helping myself to a mint tea when he stands up and follows me to the table.

'What's that, Mikky?' he asks, placing the consul on the table.

'Mint tea, would you like some?' I offer him mine. 'I've only just poured it out.'

He takes it doubtfully. 'What's that in it?' He pulls at the fresh mint and slides it with his finger to the edge of the glass.

'Mint.'

He smells it and stares at me. 'What does it taste of?'

I laugh. 'Mint. Try it and see if you like it. It's Maghrebi mint tea, green tea with spearmint leaves and sugar.'

He shakes his head. 'I'm thirsty. I want a cold drink.'

'All Moroccans drink this,' I reply.

'Some guy in a shop in the Kasbah wanted me to go inside and drink it with him ... but I didn't.'

'By offering you mint tea, it's an expression of their hospitality,' I explain.

Ali looks doubtful, and when I laugh, he grins ruefully.

'Come on, Ali, take a sip, it won't kill you!'

He brings the small glass to his lips, and I watch his expression change; his nose wrinkles and he grimaces dramatically.

'It's not bad. A bit sweet.'

'It can calm you, or it can be refreshing, awakening, and enlivening. It could give you the energy, Ali, to do what you do ...'

Ali grins and continues to sip the mint tea while I pour one for myself.

We stand companionably under the shade, watching the crew outside in the Kasbah, and the action going on around us.

'You know about a lot of stuff, Mikky.'

'Do I?' I'm surprised.

'Yeah, drones and stuff. You even changed a motor. It's all technical ...'

'It's what I do, Ali. It's quite easy really.'

He focuses on Keith and Matt chatting on the edge of the sprawling Taourirt Kasbah, a suitable and convincing backdrop for filming in places like Somalia or Egypt.

'Are you enjoying this filming experience here in Morocco?'

'It's very different. I don't know how to ... The people are—'

'The Berbers can be quite intimidating?'

'Yeah.'

'But it's fun, no?'

Ali's brown, watchful eyes are suddenly alert and happy. 'Yeah. I love it. I never realised it would be this good.'

'Is it very different to Islington?' I ask with a smile.

His laugh reflects the irony in his tone. 'A million times different.'

'Is this better?'

'It's like a holiday.' I'm watching his expression, wondering if my camera could capture the excited emotion in his eyes when he says, 'Mikky, can I ask you a favour?'

'Of course.'

'Will you come into the Kasbah with me? I want to buy a leather jacket, but I don't know how to bargain – and they all tell me I have to do that!'

'Of course I will.' I smile, pleased that he trusts me and

23

wants me. 'You could ask Matt; he'd take you.'

'I know, but he's not as savvy as you; you know stuff about this place and you're comfortable here.'

I grin. 'I spent months here once, travelling through the Atlas Mountains taking pictures.'

'Yeah, so you'll know what to do in the Kasbah. I don't want to look stupid.'

'You won't, Ali. It will be fun.'

* * *

The next day, after we finish another twelve-hour day filming, it's past eight o'clock in the evening when I follow Aziz, our guide, and Ali back into the Kasbah. Past the rich-smelling spices, and the camel slippers, the colourful Berber robes, the handmade jewellery, and finally to the leather stalls selling handbags, wallets, and coats and jackets.

Aziz leads us into a small shop and then leaves, waiting outside in the shade, unwilling to get involved in the financial negotiations. I know the stall owner will pay him a commission or small percentage for bringing us to his stall, but I don't mind.

'It's how they survive and make money,' I explain to Ali.

He nods, but he's not listening; he's walking through the rows of jackets, all colours and designs; goatskin, sheepskin, and calfskin.

The musty smell is overwhelming, and I stroll around on my own for a while, admiring leather shoes, male and female purses and wallets, handbags and travel bags, pouffes, and finally I'm back to Ali, where he's looking confused and worried.

'Are you okay?' I ask. 'Seen anything you like?'

'There are so many, Mikky. It's hard to choose.'

'Many, many many.' The shop owner flutters around us. He has a missing front tooth, bleary eyes, and he wears the long robe of the Berbers. He begins pulling one jacket out and then another, and then another, and Ali becomes more and more confused.

I grin at him and pull a blue bomber jacket off a hanger.

'So much choice!' he moans.

'Try one on,' I insist.

Ali slips his arms inside, marvelling at the soft lining.

'Do you like it?' I ask.

He shakes his arms inside the sleeves and looks at himself in the mirror.

'Do *you* like it, Mikky?'

I laugh. 'You have to like it, Ali. You'll be wearing it.'

'I know, but—'

'Maybe you'd be better in a flying jacket?' I suggest.

'Ah, pilot's jacket!' The shop owner pulls out a tan soft, vintage leather jacket with a sheepskin collar.

Ali pulls off the blue bomber jacket and stares at the one the shop owner is holding out.

'Mikky, look, that's a proper pilot's jacket,' he says with awe.

'Try it on; I bet you'll look fab.'

It fits him perfectly. He stands in front of the mirror, facing the front, and then from side to side, posing, preening, and smiling. I can't help myself. I pull out my camera, and while I snap a few shots of Ali preening, the shop owner disappears.

When he appears a few minutes later, he insists we go to the back of the shop where we sit, cross-legged on large cushions on the floor, drinking mint tea.

'Moroccan hospitality,' Ali says with a grin, raising his glass at me. 'I might start making this at home.'

'Cheers!' I say, smiling back.

Ali poses with his mint tea, and I ask the shop owner's permission to take a photograph of them together. They both beam happily at my camera.

'Do you like this jacket?' I ask Ali, already knowing the answer.

'Mikky, I love it. I've never worn anything like this in my life.'

'Can you afford it?'

'With what they're paying me for a week filming, and then I'll get more in London next week, I can easily afford it.'

'Okay, so now you have to negotiate.'

Ali's eyes turn dark and severe, and I laugh. 'This is the fun bit, Ali. Start with offering him two-thirds of the marked price.'

'Really?' Ali looks shocked.

'It's a game. Go with it. And pretend you mean it.'

Ali steels himself, takes a deep breath, points to the label with the price, and shakes his head, offering a new price.

The shop owner pretends to look offended and comes back with another higher number.

Ali looks at me, so I say, 'Increase your price but don't meet his price.'

Ali grins and then he gets the hang of it, and the price between them gets shorter, and then suddenly Ali puts out his hand, and the shop owner shakes it.

I wait, snapping photographs and talking to Aziz, who magically reappears, while Ali concludes the financial transactions.

Back out in the Kasbah, we're heading back to the hotel, and Ali is smiling. His usually sad eyes are now the colour of flecks of golden chestnuts; rays of light and happiness.

'I did it, Mikky! I've never bargained before.'

'You did really well, Ali!'

'Thanks for coming with me.' He grins, and I laugh back at him, delighted that his new jacket could make him so happy. 'It's the best thing I've ever bought.'

'Stand there, and I'll take a picture of you with the shop in the background – so you'll always remember this moment. You'll be able to tell your children about it one day.'

'I'll never forget this, Mikky. I've never owned anything like this – ever.'

He poses with his hands in his pockets, while I snap his smiling face.

'But you will have to take it off when you shower,' I say, knowing it's a scene I shall never forget.

Chapter 3

"*Marijuana is self-punishing. It makes you acutely sensitive, and in this world, what worse punishment could there be?*"
P. J. O'Rourke

At our last dinner in Ouarzazate, I sit beside Sandra Worthington, and I have the opportunity to study her up close. She's a handsome woman, in her sixties, with long, silver-grey hair that contrasts with her dark skin. She has an enigmatic smile and a southern counties British accent.

'I believe your sister is a soprano,' I say.

Sandra looks at me in surprise, so I add, 'A very good friend of mine, Glorietta Bareldo, knows her.'

'You know Glorietta?'

I smile. 'Yes. Very well.'

'Now, that's a surprise.'

I laugh. 'I know I don't look the opera type – and I'm not, really – but Glorietta and Bruno are like family to me.'

I can see Sandra assessing me in a different light, and in the yellow hue of the illuminated hotel courtyard, I notice how the crow's feet at the corner of her green eyes crinkle in delight.

'How wonderful!'

'Bruno and my husband get on very well.'

She tilts her head to one side when I ask, 'Has this been the perfect location for your film?'

'Perfect. It's been amazing, and we've been lucky. We didn't go over schedule!'

'They're long days filming,' I say. 'Over twelve hours sometimes.'

'Yes, it's been gruelling. We're lucky that it's not the height of the summer − that could be a disaster in the heat, but we won't have that problem next week when we return to the lovely British winter.'

'Do you live in London?'

'I travel a lot, often filming.'

'There must be a lot of pressure on you as a director now?' Peter sips his wine. He's sitting opposite me.

'Yes, you're right. Once you've won an Oscar, there's even more pressure on you, but to be honest, I don't take any notice. I'm lucky I can make the films I want to make. There are not enough women directors, and even fewer women who make action movies. They don't like us doing that − they see it as a man's job.'

'I can imagine,' Peter replies. 'What made you choose to film here?'

As Keith leans forward and explains, I notice a small diamond stud in his ear.

'Well, you see, we could have used Aït Benhaddou − it's an UNESCO world heritage site − but Sandra didn't want that. Ouarzazate is perfect. So many films have been made here − Atlas Studios is one of the biggest in the world. Films like ...' He ticks them off on his fingers. '*Game of Thrones*, *Gladiator*, *The Living Daylights*, even *Lawrence of Arabia*. But Sandra wanted something different—' He looks at Sandra.

'This had to be original, exciting, and daring.' Sandra smiles. 'I wanted somewhere thrilling and original, and like the *Parks*, it's all about risk-taking.'

Keith sits back and sips his wine, then says, 'Exactly. The film is about a London property dealer who goes to Egypt to visit his archeologist brother, but by mistake, he becomes embroiled with the murky underworld and an illegal drugs ring.' He takes a deep breath, then says meaningfully to Matt, 'You've all been so wonderfully enthusiastic about this project, it brings a different dimension to the film. The *Parks* have done a fantastic job.'

'I agree,' adds Sandra. 'They are a credit to you, they've been amazing.'

Matt leans forward and places his thick arms on the table, which emphasises his giant biceps.

'It's not about me. It's about these poor kids. You don't know what it's done for these guys to come over here and get this experience. They have a purpose now. They have hope. They see they're worthwhile and they can do something useful. They have *talent*.'

I find Matt fascinating.

Chief Inspector Mulhoon said he was an ex-con and I've watched him for four nights with the five teenagers. They clearly respect him, and they appear to have a special bond with him. They trust him, and I wonder why the chief inspector hasn't asked Matt for more help. He would be in a perfect position to find out about the talisman, the sword, or whatever it is that the cult uses to initiate people into their sect.

Peter nods; he's enthralled by this company and conversation. 'They have talent in abundance, but what will happen to them now?' His enthusiasm for the *Parks* is evident. 'Is there more work for them?'

'That's the problem,' Matt says, lowering his voice. 'I don't want them to go back to what they did before. I want to keep them safe. I want to keep them happy – they've had a terrible time. They have no experience of what a normal family life is like. They are from broken homes – maybe one of the parents is an addict, or where their parents don't even bother to turn up to the police station to help them out. There are no male role models for them to follow or to look up to, and they have little or no support at home. Some of them were junkies – they were running drugs for the gangs in London. I can't let them down now.' He scratches his chin thoughtfully; his eyes are deep-set and dark.

I'd like to photograph his face and capture the distress in his eyes.

'Well, we're filming in the next week or so with them in London,' says Sandra, and she says to Peter, 'And as you and Mikky are making a documentary about the *Parks*, that will involve them even more in something worthwhile.'

Matt makes eye contact with me.

'They're thrilled about the documentary, Mikky, but they are quite shy, as you've noticed. They're not used to people taking an interest in them for anything good or positive. They don't open up easily.'

I smile. 'They've been fine. We've got some good footage from them. I know it will take time for them to open up more, and they love talking about the parkour.'

'You've been a hit with Ali,' Matt says. 'Thank you.'

'It's a leather jacket.' I grin. 'He was amazing when he bought it. He did very well. We even had mint tea in the back of the shop. It's a different culture here, and they've adapted to it quite well. I hope that when we get back to London, we can follow up on the interviews and filming?'

'That would be great.' Matt returns my smile, holding my gaze for a fraction of a second longer than necessary.

I turn away and survey the scene around me.

We're sitting on the hotel's terrace, at one end of a long table, under the moonlit sky studded with stars. But it's colder now in the evening, and I tuck a red silk scarf into my worn black leather jacket and sip my red wine.

Matt says, 'They're very health-conscious, and now they are in a film – it's the beginning of becoming rich and famous.'

Keith complains, 'It's not just the *Parks* – they're too young, but hardly any of this crew drink.'

He nods at the crew and assistants further down the table, all with names and titles I've long since forgotten.

'They're all vegan, vegetarian, or pescatarian,' he moans.

'But they are passionate and enthusiastic,' Sandra chips in. 'It's their youth that I most admire, and their vitality. They're an interesting group; some are talkative, and others are quiet. It's a good mix.'

At the end of the table, the parkour and freerunning experts – three boys and two girls – are drinking soft drinks. Their faces are alive, shining, smiling, and happy. They know we're making a documentary and they appear to be enjoying the attention, and when Ali raises his fingers in a victory sign, we all laugh.

'He's the comedian,' Matt says.

'He's also a good leader,' Peter adds. 'This is an experience I'll never forget.'

'Do they work out regularly?' Keith asks Matt. 'Isn't it risky what they do?'

'We think of it as a challenge,' Matt replies. 'We self-challenge; it's about being entrepreneurial and self-sufficient. That's how we train. It's a life lesson for them.'

'What's the difference between freerunning and parkour?' he asks.

'Freerunning is an expression of one's self in the environment without restrictions, and parkour is how they get from A to B in the most fluid – fastest and efficient – manner. These kids do both. It's about managing risks and developing skills to test one's limits.'

'It was incredible. It had the precision of a ballet,' I say, and they all turn to look at me.

Sandra smiles. 'I agree. It was beautiful to watch them.'

'So, when are you filming next?' Peter asks.

Sandra replies, 'It will be back in London – Islington. Some of the crew left earlier to set up, and we'll join them tomorrow. We're on the early flight.'

'I was hoping to have a more detailed chat with some of the *Parks*.' I look at Matt. 'But the filming days have been so long, and they're exhausted by the evening.'

'Time will be tight in the morning. We're also on the early flight; perhaps you could speak to them tonight?'

'Or back in London?' asks Peter. 'The flight was full, so we're on the later flight tomorrow.'

Matt nods. 'Of course. Come to Dixon House.'

'I loved watching them today,' I reply. 'I've never seen anything like it. I'd like to film it all again.'

'We can let you have some footage for your documentary,' Sandra says. 'Keith can arrange it.'

'Thank you.'

'How did you get these kids involved in this film?' Peter asks

Matt.

'Keith introduced me to Sandra, and it seemed like such a good idea to get them over here. It is, after all, an action movie.'

'You're brave to make action movies,' I say.

Sandra shakes her head. 'It's a male territory, but that won't stop me.'

'Not enough women are directors,' Keith interjects. 'But then, not many women are like Sandra, either.'

'How did you meet Matt?' I ask Keith, but neither of them meets my gaze, and it's Matt who replies eventually.

'We met a while back at a mutual friend's party.' He stands up. 'I guess if you want to speak to these kids, you should do it now ...'

Keith agrees, 'Yeah, they'll probably want an early night.'

* * *

I move with Matt and Peter to sit with the *Parks*. We've already explained that we'd like to make a documentary about their skills, and Matt arranged all the legal permissions with their guardians.

'Do you want to film us tonight?' Joe asks.

'Are you getting a taste for being interviewed?' Monika replies with a laugh.

'Would you mind?' I ask.

'Nah, I don't mind.' Ali grins, and I notice again his pox-damaged skin and hurt eyes. The excitement of filming on location, as well as buying the leather flying jacket that he proudly wears, has loosened his tongue. He holds court, responding to my questions, for our documentary film.

I use my iPhone to record some of the conversation and video their reactions, but I'm careful not to intimidate them.

They speak comfortably about their talent and their skills, but then I turn the conversation to try and make it more personal.

'Do you think training in parkour helped you escape from the difficulties on the street?' I ask.

'Difficulties?' Ali frowns.

'Drugs, gangs, poverty ...?' I reply slowly. It's the first time that I've been able to broach the subject of their past, and it's a risk I know I have to take. Tonight is possibly our last chance to address the topic.

'My brother's been smoking crack for fifteen years. He's not thirty, but he looks almost forty.' Ali rubs his nose with the back of his wrist.

'Crack cocaine?' I ask, and he nods gravely.

'Once you start, you can't stop till your money's gone.' Ali's eyes, ringed with dark circles, are now severe and unblinking. So different from the teenager who I went shopping with yesterday.

'Where is he now?'

Ali shrugs. 'I dunno. I haven't seen him for a while. He had to disappear ...'

'That must be frightening,' I say softly. 'Do you know where?'

'No. It's best not to ask—'

'It's not the drugs,' says a thin, pasty-faced boy called Adam, who rarely speaks. His light-blue eyes are eerily translucent. 'It's the gangs.'

'Drugs are evil, but the gangs trap you,' agrees Monika.

She looks barely sixteen. Her afro hair, now scraped back

35

and tied in bunches on her head, makes her cheekbones appear sharp under her thin face.

'They train you into getting your own gang. You go to a place and find a crackhead, give him some stuff, and get him to give your number to his friends – other users. That way, you build up a client list.'

'My sister is twelve, and they tried to recruit her.' Joe scratches his crew cut. 'She wasn't happy at school, she started playing truant, but I wouldn't let her join them. I made her go to my auntie's house in Reading.'

'Do you know who "they" are?'

'Nah. You don't want to get involved with them. They're not good people.' Ali pauses and looks around at his friends. 'We're gonna stick together. Matt helps us, and we're gonna look out for each other.'

'You all live in London?' I ask.

Ali raises his glass and gulps his orange juice quickly before saying, 'Yeah, but I don't know what we'll do now – you know, in the long term, once this is over.'

'We'll think of something,' Matt replies. 'You're safe with me. We're going to carry on with our training, our parkour, and then we'll see ...'

'Are you frightened of the gangs?' I ask, but it's Matt who replies on their behalf.

'Of course, everyone is frightened, Mikky. You've got to be careful. But I've lived through it all and I managed to stay alive and come out the other side, just as these kids are doing. Once I got clean, I was determined to help others, but it's not enough just to get the kids away from the area and place them with a foster family. We've got to offer them more. They need a future where they belong – a job, money, security, and more

36

importantly, somewhere they feel safe.'

'My foster family didn't want me to leave,' Ali says. 'I was safe with them.'

'Did you have to leave them?' Peter asks, as I video Ali's face.

'My mum wants me back home.'

'Where's home?' Peter asks.

'Brentwood.'

'But your mum's an addict,' Monika says to Ali, clearly concerned at the thought of him going back to her.

Ali frowns. 'It's not her fault.'

'But she's gotta get clean,' says Joe. 'You won't be able to do nothing until she wants to help herself.'

'I thought you were going to live with your dad,' says Monika.

'I stay with him sometimes, but he works nights on the trains.'

'Does he make you feel safe?' I ask.

Ali grins at the camera, but the smile doesn't reach his eyes.

'Nah. He's never there. He doesn't want me with him really. He walked out on me and Mum when I was four. She started taking drugs, and that's when I was put into care.'

Lisa leans forward, across the table, nearer to me, and when she speaks, she has a lisp.

'You can film me if you like.' Then she turns to Ali. 'You were lucky. My foster mother doesn't like me. I think sometimes she hates me, but she gets paid good money to look after me.'

'And does she look after you?' I ask, as I film Lisa.

Lisa shrugs. 'She doesn't hit me, if that's what you mean.'

'Is she kind?' I insist.

'She's alright, she's happy I'm doing this – she wants me

to get into the movies, so I make good money.'

'She wants you to get famous.' Joe's eyes are serious. 'She wants you to be a rich actress.'

'Yeah, she says she'd move to Hollywood with me.' Lisa grins.

Joe sniggers.

'Do you want to work in films?' I ask Joe.

He's Albanian; watchful and serious.

'Nah. Parkour is what we do. We're the *Parks*.' He bangs the table with his fists.

Monika sniggers and covers her full mouth shyly, with the back of her hand.

'We belong together,' he adds.

'It's like the army, isn't it, Peter?' Matt says. 'You know, where you all look out for one another.'

'Army?' asks Ali, looking at Peter.

Matt explains, 'Peter was in the SAS. He went to Afghanistan.'

There are gasps and nods of approval, while I contemplate the level of conversation that Matt and Peter must have had over the past few days.

'You're a war hero?' asks Lisa.

'No, I'm not a hero.' Peter smiles, and I see the young kids looking at him for the first time, taking in his dark hair and short beard.

'You limp,' says Monika.

'What happened to your leg?' asks Ali.

'A roadside bomb in Afghanistan blew off my foot.'

'Wow!' says Monica, covering her mouth. 'That's serious shit!'

'Yeah.' Peter grins.

'Ignore him. He *is* a hero,' I say, smiling.

Peter looks embarrassed.

'Look, this isn't about me. This documentary is about you guys. You're a good bunch of people. That's why we want to make this film. It's about you. And, you're right, you just have to stick together. Matt's right, too; it's about taking care of each other.'

'We'll stay together. We're training all the time, and we're getting better.' Joe nods seriously.

'I'm gonna buy new trainers with the money we got for making this film,' Ali says. 'They're over a hundred quid.'

'I'm getting a hoodie,' says Joe.

'You should get a jacket like mine,' Ali says.

'I wanna get a new iPhone,' Monika says with a grin.

'Did you earn that much?' Peter asks in surprise.

'Yeah, it's decent money, and they paid for our flight—'

'And this posh hotel—'

'I'm getting new trainers, too,' adds Joe.

'Has this been a good experience for you?' I ask, looking around at their excited faces.

Joe nods. His eyes are like shining lumps of coal.

'I'd never been away before. It was my first time on a plane – I want to be a pilot.'

'Really?'

'Yeah. I love flying.'

'I want to be a nurse,' says Monika. 'I'm going to look it all up when I get home.'

Joe teases her, 'You said this morning that you want to be an actress like the one in the film.'

Monika thumps his arm.

'Leave her alone, Joe. She's alright – nursing is good,' Ali says.

Joe laughs and bangs the table with his fist, and repeats it as if it's the funniest thing he's heard.

'A nurse!'

Monika looks affronted, but she says, 'There's nothing wrong with changing your mind.'

'And what about you?' I ask the quiet, dark-haired girl Lisa. She's leaning her head on her arm, listening to everyone.

'I'm seventeen,' she replies.

'What do you want to be?'

'I don't know. Who would want me?'

'What would you like to do?' I ask gently.

'I think I want to be a teacher.'

'That's a fantastic idea.' I smile.

Peter asks, 'And what about you, Ali, what do you want to do?'

He straightens up and pushes out his chest.

'I'm going to work with Matt. I'm going to be a policeman.' He looks around smiling, looking for their approval.

They smile, but only Joe laughs aloud and bangs the table.

'A policeman!'

'And you?' I ask Adam, the pasty-faced boy with the light-blue eyes, who has remained silent and watchful for most of the time, but he ignores me and continues to stare silently at something invisible on top of the table.

* * *

'Do you want to film us some more?' Monika asks, nodding at my idle iPhone on the table.

'Maybe another time?'

'I don't mind.' Ali smiles. 'I can show you some parkour

steps.'

I grin. 'Thanks, but no!'

'I do.' Joe looks at me. 'I don't like being filmed.'

'That's why I want to talk to you, and get to know you. I think that's more important, don't you?'

'Yes.' Joe smiles, but his tooth at the front is brown and rotten.

'I like your tattoo – this is really cool.' Monika trails her finger along my forearm. 'It's like a work of art.'

'It is Edvard Munch's *The Scream* – it's a famous painting, do you know it?'

She shakes her head.

'Mikky's an artist,' Peter says. 'Her body is a complete work of art.'

'Are you two married?' Lisa asks.

'No, we're not. Peter is married to a lovely Polish lady, and they have a three-month-old baby called Zofia.'

'Really?' Monika smiles at him.

Peter takes out his iPhone, and Monika leans closer to look at the baby pictures.

'Do you have any tattoos?' I look at Ali.

'Yeah, look!'

Ali raises the sleeve of his T-shirt to reveal an Aztec design.

'I'm getting a serpent, like Matt's, next month – right across here.' He points to his shoulder and the back of his neck.

Matt shakes his head and laughs. 'We'll talk about this back in London.'

Joe lifts his trouser leg to reveal a picture of Taylor Swift tattooed on his calf. 'I'm getting another one,' he adds, 'on my back.'

'How many tattoos have you all got then?' I challenge, then

I sit back and watch as they count.

'Seven,' says Ali.

'Five,' says Joe.

'Three,' says Monika.

'None.' Lisa shakes her head. 'I don't like them.'

'And you, Adam?' I ask.

But Adam turns away and shrugs, as if he's suddenly not interested in our conversation. Still, I want to keep him involved, so I say, 'Would you believe me if I told you I've got the severed head of John the Baptist across my breasts and chest, and Salomé's seven veils wrapped around my waist? I've also got a painting of the Last Supper and the Garden of Eden ...'

Adam glances up to look at my breasts and then gazes suddenly back at the invisible spot on the table.

'Can I see them?' asks Monika.

I laugh. 'Not this evening, but maybe another time we can all share our body artwork?' I glance around at them all.

'Why are all yours religious?' she asks.

'I had a tough time growing up, pretty much like you all. I was adopted, but my parents didn't want me.'

'So, your birth mum gave you away; then your parents didn't want you either?' Ali clarifies my situation.

'That's how it was.'

'That's a bitch,' he says.

'Yeah,' I agree. 'See this scar?' I point to the ragged skin on the back of my hand. 'My mum tried to slash my face, but I lifted my hands just in time.'

There are gasps, and I demonstrate, by covering my face with my hands, and the table falls silent.

'That's sad,' says Monika. Her eyes look pained and she

takes my hand. 'But you're just like us, Mikky. You've had a rough time, too. You're damaged.'

'Yeah,' I say quietly. 'That's why I want to make this documentary. It's important to tell people what we've been through so that it doesn't keep happening. We all want a better life for ourselves and our kids, don't we?'

* * *

Some of the crew members leave the long dining table and Ali jumps up; within minutes, the *Parks* are all sitting at another table, nearer the bar, with a deck of cards between them.

As I walk to the bar with Peter, Monika is perched on the arm of Ali's chair. She's trying to give him advice but he pulls away, shielding his cards, laughing good-naturedly.

At the piano bar, my mood has turned sombre.

'It's the haunted expression in their eyes when they're reminded of their lives in London,' I say to Sandra. 'They're too young to have gone through so much.'

'I agree with you, Mikky. It's unfortunate. That's why you must make this documentary,' she replies.

We're distracted when Joe slaps down his cards and bangs the table before raising his arm in mock triumph.

'This is helping them,' Matt says, sipping a beer. 'It's been good for them. It's giving them a sense of value – a sense of belonging.'

'We will use them in London ...' Keith says, nodding knowingly at Sandra, and she smiles back.

'We can talk about it on the flight in the morning, Matt,' Sandra says. 'We'll work something out. We're aiming to use one of the high-rise buildings in Islington, but we need the right permissions first.'

'Raymond Harris might help,' suggests Matt. 'He's been invaluable to us at the Dixon Trust.'

'The politician?' asks Peter.

'Yes, he's our local councillor.'

'That's who we are working with,' Sandra replies. 'Isn't it, Keith? He's been very accommodating, liaising with the council and the local residents.'

'Isn't Raymond Harris standing in the local election next month?' asks Peter. I glance at him in surprise. He's clearly been doing some background homework.

Matt nods, and I imagine how his life has changed from once being a criminal to now being a valuable carer of these kids.

'Yes, without him on our side, I don't know what we'd do. He's been instrumental in helping us. I started a Trust – the Dixon Trust – four years ago. It provides a place where we can keep these kids safe. The problem is, these kids are innocent, but drugs gang members have groomed them, and sometimes it's been over a long time.' He shakes his head. 'They pick on the troubled kids. Some of them are loners, others have been abused, or they are from broken homes; some – like Adam – are probably even autistic.'

'Adam didn't speak to us when we were chatting earlier,' I say.

'It's normal, Mikky. Don't take it personally. Some of them are really troubled and on the spectrum. It takes them a long time to confide in or to trust anyone.'

He doesn't elaborate, so I ask, 'How do the drugs gangs get them involved?'

'Very often they befriend them. They see the kids are alone. Maybe in a park, sitting on a swing, on a bench, watching other kids playing, and they ask if they want to play football or go to the shops, and they make friends with them. They make them feel as though they have a friend, someone to share things with, and they get hooked into doing things together. They groom them into running errands. These kids don't have a normal life. They're often from broken families, or their parents may be addicts. They have no stability and they live on the poverty line.

'So, these gang members tell them there might be an *opportunity* for them, *maybe* to earn money, do something *they* want to do, and they make them all sorts of promises. They get to know them. They hang out together, and they find out the kids' backgrounds and who, if anyone, will miss them. You see it on the TV and in the news – these kids go missing from their homes after they get them hooked on drugs. They put them in a decaying flat somewhere, and they live in squalid conditions, and they're forced to bag up crack to sell on the street. They live off junk food, they're malnourished, and sometimes don't see daylight for weeks. It's a slow process grooming them – but a dangerous one; they build smaller gangs, and then there are drug wars, county lines and all that stuff. Knife crime is on the increase, as they're forced to prove themselves – to prove that they are worthy gang members ...'

He picks up his beer.

'Is there no support?' asks Sandra.

Matt wipes his mouth with the back of his hand.

'Very little; I work with the police, but what can you do? When I met these guys – the *Parks* – they were in a terrible state. Some came to Dixon House because they felt safe and others were encouraged to come by friends or people in the community. We've even picked some of the kids off the streets.

I thought parkour would be a good discipline for them. It's healthy, disciplined, and exciting. It's something different they can improve on, and it helps them mentally, too.'

'You've done an amazing job.' Keith smiles.

'We work with local residents in the high-rise blocks; for example, we organise a gardening community – a project to keep the area clean and tidy. We try and work with the council and community groups to put on performances by local artists or exhibitions, and we try and incorporate dysfunctional families into the wider community.'

'Not an easy job,' I say.

'No.' Matt scratches his arm; the tongue of a vicious serpent is wrapped around his bicep.

'And these kids know that Dixon House is there for them?' I ask.

'They do now. But it takes time. A year ago, when I met Ali, he was sixteen, but he had closed down. He couldn't speak. He was mentally exhausted. He'd spent two years with the drugs gangs and he was drained, but now look at him,' Matt says with a smile. 'He won't shut up.'

We turn to look at them playing cards and laughing.

It's a safe, calm, and relaxing evening, and I'm suddenly happy that I've come here with Peter. He must see the expression in my eyes, as he leans toward me and whispers loudly.

'I told you it would be an amazing experience, didn't I?' He's playing his role to perfection, and he adds, 'I knew this documentary would be a good idea.'

I smile back and try to hide the sarcasm from my voice. 'You were right, Peter. I've loved being here, and especially in the Kasbah, that was such an amazing feeling watching these guys dancing, weaving, and jumping in unison like a shoal of fish or a murmuration of starlings. They were incredible. I'm surprised they didn't hurt themselves.'

'We worked out a routine, and we challenge ourselves before they begin filming. We've practised it over and over, and they've loved it,' Matt says.

'They were excellent; we had to change some of the choreography.'

'Will it be very different in London?' I ask Sandra.

'It's not so easy to film action scenes in a high-rise building, but I have a few ideas. I'm not sure if they'll work. I've some different stunt guys on board, and they're looking into it all, too. Safety is our number one priority, and some of the scenes take time to set up. We have a couple of locations that we're considering, but if we can use the *Parks*, then we will.'

Matt smiles but his face, now in the half-shadow, looks tired and worn. Dark circles devour his eyes, and the stress of his previous life appears etched on his face, and there's a weariness to his demeanour. He's looking as if he has the world balanced on his shoulders and he doesn't know which way to turn, for fear of it falling off.

Chapter 4

"Rape is a more heinous crime than murder since the rape victim dies throughout the period she lives."
Amit Abraham

It's late by the time I get to my bedroom, and I close and lock the door behind me. The Moroccan lamps cast a warm glow over the patterned rug, matching curtains, and bed cover.

I strip off my clothes, brush my teeth, and flick off the bathroom light. I listen to a message from Marco, conscious he's probably now sleeping, when there's a light tap on my bedroom door.

'Hello?' I whisper, but there's no answer, just a persistent tap.

'Hello?' I call louder.

'Mikky?'

I quickly pull on a bathrobe and open the door. I have a fleeting glimpse of Monika as she pushes me by the shoulders back inside my room and up against the wall, and very firmly, she plants her lips on mine in a wet snog. Gasping, surprised and shocked, I manage to grab her shoulders and push her away.

'Monika, stop!' I say urgently. 'Stop!'

'I want to see your tattoos,' she whispers. 'The bloody head of John the Baptist.'

She leans forward to kiss me again, but I manage to dodge her embrace. She kicks the bedroom door closed and, ignoring me, she walks in and sits on the edge of my bed with her hands in her lap, gazing at me with a defiant brown-eyed stare.

She has changed into boy's blue-and-white-striped pyjamas, and very slowly, she begins to undo the buttons.

I stand beside the door with my arms folded, assessing her and the situation, knowing I must tread carefully. Rejection is a massive theme for these teenagers, and I must handle it well.

'How old are you, Monika?'

She stares at me. Her eyes are dark and hurt. 'Nineteen.'

'Tell me the truth.'

'Almost seventeen.'

'You're sixteen?' I walk over and sit beside her on the bed and, very deliberately, I pull her pyjama top closed. 'I'm in my mid-thirties – old enough to be your mother.'

'So?'

'So, I'm sorry if I've given you the wrong idea.'

She places her hand on my knee, and I leave it there while she says, 'But you're so lovely. You understand me, Mikky. I know you do.'

I remove her fingers but keep hold of her hand.

'I *do* understand you, Monika. Just like you, I've been through a tough time, but also like Matt, we've come out the other side. You are doing the same. You're on the right path …'

She holds my hand, and when her tears begin to fall, she lifts my palm to her cheek.

'I was raped ...'

I place my arms around her shoulder.

'He came to our house. He knew my stepdad. I was twelve. He said I was aloof and unresponsive, but I wasn't interested. I wanted them to leave me alone, but they said I needed to be taught a lesson. They called me a snobby cow.'

'Oh, Monika. I'm so sorry ...'

She shakes her head. Her sobbing muffles her words. 'It's like they thought I'd enjoy it; they even told me I was asking for it, but I was wearing a dress as I'd been to my friend's birthday party. I was crying, but he blamed me. He made me smoke pot. He said it was my fault and that I'd led him on, but I didn't, Mikky. I promise you.'

'I know. I know.'

I hold her in my arms while she cries.

Monika pulls away from me and blows her nose, and eventually she continues, 'One guy told me he was *entitled* to do it to me and, after that, my stepdad brought them home regularly. The first one was an addict. The second one made me ...'

I pull her against me and I stroke her hair as she tells me what happened in a haltingly sad voice. She talks, and I hear her pain as I listen silently to her child-like voice.

I don't tell her about ITs – the set of Implicit Theories that underpin the cognitive process of rapists, skewing the perception of their victims. Unfortunately, this is how rapists rationalise their sexually violent behaviour.

'Then, they came to our house to buy crack, and when they saw me, I was part of the deal. They weren't really his friends. He hardly knew them, but they gave me cannabis and then stronger stuff. It deadened the pain, but then I didn't know what I was doing most of the time, and then this guy came along ...'

'Matt?'

'No, this was before Matt. This guy was Asian. I think he's Chinese. He speaks quietly, and he has a presence. You know you want to please him.'

'You had sex with him?'

'No, it wasn't like that. The Asian was the boss, in charge, and you did what he told you to do. My stepdad was frightened of him. It's weird, but I trusted him; I thought he'd look after me. He stopped the men from touching me. He took me to a safe house but then I was forced to bag up coke and sell it.'

'How did you get out?'

'The police. They got my stepdad – he's in prison now. They caught some of the other guys, too.'

'When was this?'

'Last year.'

I'm thinking of the two undercover police officers who were also killed last year and wonder if the events are related.

I ask, 'And the Asian, what happened to him?'

'He disappears all the time, but he keeps coming back. The thing is, I can't forget him.'

'Does he frighten you?'

'I never want to see him again.'

'So, were you in a gang or a cult?'

'Yeah ...'

'How many were in it?'

She shrugs and wipes her eyes on a tissue that I give her.

'Did it have a name?' I persist.

'It didn't need one. You just knew you were in it ...'

'How?

'I got a tattoo.' She points at her chest. 'We all have one. It's like a ceremony sort of thing.'

'What sort of tattoo?' She doesn't answer me, so I ask, 'Who is *all*? Is it like a gang and the Asian is the boss?'

She wipes her eyes, then concentrates on her hands in her lap, and won't reply.

'Does the Asian have a name?' I ask.

She shakes her head. 'I hate men.'

'You don't have to hate men. You like Ali,' I say gently, 'and Joe, and Matt. They're kind to you, aren't they? They treat you kindly.'

She nods and wipes her eyes with the back of her hand. 'Yeah, they wouldn't hurt me. Neither would Peter,' she adds quietly. 'Would he?'

'No, Peter is kind. He's a protector.'

'Like Ali and Matt.'

'Yes.'

'Can I stay here the night with you? I could sleep right here.' She pats the side of the double bed. 'I promise I won't kiss you.'

'I don't think that's a good idea. Don't you have your own room?'

'I'm sharing with Lisa, but Joe's in bed with her.'

'Joe?'

'They're together, but no one knows, so it's a bit awkward for me with them both, you know ...'

'Okay,' I say, checking my watch. 'But on the condition that you go straight to sleep. You have an early flight. We have to be up at five-thirty.'

* * *

Monika falls asleep almost immediately. I lay awake, staring up at the ceiling and listening to her rhythmic breathing getting deeper and deeper. I turn on my side and study her profile. She's lying on her back, angelically, her parted lips giving a small shudder as she exhales.

I lie on my back thinking of the *Parks* and their complicated lives. I'm lying to them about the documentary, but it's crucial we find out about the talisman and take this information back to Inspector Mulhoon.

These kids need people they can trust and respect, but I feel like I'm just another pimp, using them for information with no intention of making a film.

It's just a pretext to get them to open up and to trust me.

Monika trusts me. That's why she came to my room and confided in me. Now all I can do is think about the tattoo that she pointed at under her left breast.

What sort of symbol did they all have?

I couldn't ask her to show it to me. I couldn't alert her to my real aim.

I watch the rise and fall of her chest, and in the semi-darkness of the bedroom, I can see the outline of her breasts. Her pyjama shirt is still undone; she didn't bother to close the top buttons. She'd fallen asleep almost immediately, exhausted from the exercise and filming, and then afterwards by her sad confession.

I wait, unable to sleep, for the room to grow lighter, for the light to stream in through the light curtains, but I doze off, and when I open my eyes, Monika is lying on her back with her arms over her head, and she's snoring quietly. Her pyjama top has fallen open, and her pale brown breasts and chest are exposed.

I throw off the bed covers and tiptoe across the room to get my camera.

In the half-light, I adjust the settings on my Canon 5D and stand over Monika. I adjust the lens, focus, and snap several images, then I remove the camera from my eye and check the results; when I look back up, Monika's eyes are open, and she's staring at me.

'What are you doing?' she mumbles.

'I'm going outside on the terrace to photograph the sunrise. I was just going to wake you. It's a beautiful morning. Come on!'

I wave my camera in the air and pull open the curtains, flooding the room with the early morning sunrise. 'It's going to be a beautiful day.'

* * *

We all have an early breakfast in the hotel, and while we wait for the minibus, I take a quick film of the *Parks*, who are sleepy but good-naturedly wave and grimace in the early morning.

'Are you always this lively?' Ali complains.

'Can you show us any of the stuff you took yesterday?' asks Joe.

Lisa stands beside him, very close, and I believe Monika's excuse for visiting my bedroom.

She returned to her room where she showered, and now she's dressed in camouflage track pants, and her hair is tied in colourful ribbons. She smiles shyly at the camera.

I show Joe some of the drone footage I took yesterday on set, but I notice how Adam hangs back until I hold out the screen.

'You want to look?'

'No.' Adam shakes his head.

'Let me take a picture of you all together,' I suggest.

We're standing around while the *Parks* throw their luggage on the minibus. They pose quickly, hanging out of the door, grinning on the step of the bus while I snap some pictures. They're happy and copy each other, flicking V-signs.

I show Keith the photographs, as they board the bus.

'You're an outstanding photographer, Mikky. Maybe we should use your images. How did you get so good at this?'

'I've filmed kitesurfers and skiers, lots of action stuff, so I'm used to filming people moving at speed.'

I flick the camera to video.

'It's incredible,' agrees Sandra, looking over our shoulders. 'You're an excellent photographer.'

'Thank you.'

'It's an amazing thing that you're doing, Mikky. Filming this documentary is very important. The world needs more people like you, and I hope it won't stop here.' Matt is looking at the images over my shoulder, and I tilt the screen for him to have a better look. His breath smells of mints, and when he grins, he holds my gaze.

'What do you mean?' I ask.

'Well, I hope you'll come and see us at Dixon House. It would be great to get some publicity about the work we do. We might even get more funding.'

'What's the name of that politician that helps you?' Sandra calls. 'Keith, what's the name of that politician who's helping us with the film location in London?'

'Raymond Harris,' Matt replies.

'Maybe you could interview him, Mikky?' Sandra suggests.

Keith scratches his Viking beard. 'If you start getting

55

testimonials from people in the public eye, then that could gain a lot of weight for your documentary. You want to get it on national television. Especially with the election coming up next month.'

'That's true,' says Matt excitedly. 'Sandra, maybe when you've finished the film, Mikky could interview you and talk about your experience working with these guys. You could perhaps say what a contribution they've made to the film and how dedicated and hard-working they are?'

'Your testimonial would make a big difference,' I agree, smiling at Sandra while feeling appalled that I've lied to them all.

'Let's arrange something back in London. I'd love to help you,' she says to me, and then adds, 'Besides, if your best friend Glorietta Bareldo and my sister are friends, then we must look after each other!'

She hugs me warmly, and Keith risks two continental kisses to my cheeks.

'We're filming at Dixon House next week,' I say.

'What a splendid idea. I hate the idea of saying goodbye to you guys.'

Peter holds out his hand, but Matt pulls him closer into a bear hug.

'Thanks mate,' he whispers, slapping Peter's back. 'I appreciate all that you've done to help these guys.'

'Right, come on, you guys, say goodbye.' Matt pushes the five teenagers awkwardly forward, and with a mixture of hesitant hugs, high-fives, and knuckle-bumping, I laugh with them, as they finally climb into the van.

Monika blows me a kiss, and Ali salutes us from the window. Joe grins excitedly, and Lisa wipes away a tear. Only Adam remains stony-faced and aloof, preferring to stare out of the front window.

As we wave them off and watch the minivan disappear, I can still hear Monika's soft voice whispering as she hugged me in parting.

'I love you, Mikky.'

* * *

Peter and I are on the evening flight, and so we spend the morning sightseeing, and at lunchtime, we find a small restaurant where we sit under the shade of an umbrella enjoying a lunch of delicious lamb couscous.

'You've enjoyed being here, haven't you, Mikky?'

'Yes, but I feel I'm a fraud,' I reply. 'The *Parks* trusted us, and I can't let them down.'

'You won't let them down. They like you,' Peter says. 'But it will take a little longer for them to trust us. Joachin seemed to think it would happen in a few days, but these few days haven't been enough. These kids are very reserved. I think we have to go back to London and follow up on our documentary—'

'They did trust us, Peter. I'm surprised at how much they did speak to us, but I feel like I'm using them. Look at this ...' I reach for my camera. 'I didn't want to tell you earlier, but Monika came to my room last night ...'

Peter's hand, holding a fork of couscous, pauses halfway to his mouth. 'She went to your room?'

'She stayed the night.'

'For God's sake, Mikky! What happened?'

'Lisa and Joe were having sex, and she didn't want to be in the bedroom with them.'

He tosses the fork on the plate and, when I turn the screen of my camera in his direction, he wipes his mouth with a napkin.

'What the ...?' He glances at me and then back at the image. 'That's a sword?'

'It looks more like a dagger to me,' I mumble.

'You mean, Monika has a tattoo of a dagger under her left breast?'

'She said there was an Asian who made her get it, and she says they all have one.'

'Like in a cult?'

'She didn't want to speak about it. She was abused. She wanted to talk—'

He shakes his head and exhales loudly. 'Oh my God, Mikky ... that's awful.'

'She's very affected.'

'Did she specifically mention the Asian?'

'I think she is a cult member, Peter. Or she was. She told me how her stepfather's friends raped her and then she was groomed by the Asian into selling coke. Chief Inspector Mulhoon seems to think there is a cult – it's a gang. But I'm thinking maybe all the members have this tattoo inked on their skin. She mentioned a ceremony.'

'So, what now, Mikky? Are you sending this image to the chief inspector?'

'No, I can't tell him that Monika has this tattoo. He'd take her in for questioning and harass her. I can't take the chance that they would potentially put her life at risk. She's been through so much. I can't betray her trust when she's trying to make a new life for herself. We must tread gently.'

'But they have trained police officers. I'm sure that they—'

'No! We must go slowly with her. With all of them,' I insist.

'Then what do you want to do?'

'I'm going to find out more about the dagger – that's what he wanted me to do. He wanted me to find out what sort of talisman it was—'

'And then what?'

'And *then* I'll tell Mulhoon.'

'So, we'll catch the flight this evening to London, as we planned?'

'Yes, but this afternoon I've asked Aziz to take us through the Kasbah to a specific shop – I want to find out how easy it is to make a replica of this dagger.'

* * *

'I googled swords and daggers like the one that Monika has under her left breast,' I explain after lunch to Peter, as we walk through the Kasbah with our guide Aziz.

'There are loads of valuable swords. There's the Sword of Mercy that once belonged to Edward the Confessor. There was a carved sabre in a museum in Brazil, and a thirteenth-century Japanese sword used by a Samurai. There's also Napoleon Bonaparte's gold-encrusted sabre, worth $6.5 million, and finally – if you believe in coincidences – an eighteenth-century Boating Sabre belonging to the Chinese Qianlong Emperor, with an estimated value of $7.7 million.'

'A Chinese dagger?'

'Well,' I say, teasing, 'there is a fascinating one that looks like the Shah Jahan's personal dagger, worth $3.3 million.'

Peter whistles softly.

'The problem is, Peter, none of them – as far as I know – have been stolen.'

'So, you think the dagger Monika has tattooed on her chest looks like the Japanese sword used by the Samurai? An Asian dagger?'

I shake my head.

'No, Peter. It looks exactly like a replica of the Shah Jahan's dagger, valued at over $3 million.'

'Really?' He stops to look at me.

'Yes.'

'So, could the design of the tattoo be based on this dagger?'

'Hypothetically, if they use a dagger in a specific ceremony, like Monika hinted at, then it doesn't have to be an original. Who would know the difference? These street kids are probably drugged to the eyeballs and so terrified. If it looks expensive, then they'll believe anything.'

'So, it could be part of an initiation ceremony?'

'Maybe,' I reply.

As we pass the stalls, local merchants call out, and one even pulls on my arm, but Aziz steps between me and the stallholder and angrily admonishes him.

'They like lady blondes.' Aziz gives me a dazzling smile.

'Little do they know,' Peter adds, 'the Rottweiler bites.'

I grin at him before falling back into step behind Aziz.

We weave our way through narrow alleyways, past large shops selling luxurious carpets and rugs, and smaller stalls displaying handmade jewellery and souvenirs. The stench of cured leather and exotic spices fill my senses, making me both heady and tired.

It's been a gruelling few days and with little sleep. I'm emotionally exhausted; caught up in the euphoria and excitement of the *Parks*, I'm beginning to feel guilty.

I want them to trust me but I've lied to them.

Aziz comes to an abrupt halt, and I almost walk into him. He stands aside at the entrance to a small workshop. Peter lowers his head and enters first, and I follow him into a stifling room filled with a small wooden worktop, anvils, assorted rusty tools, and metals. It smells of burning metal and cannabis.

Inside, a man with one arm is bashing an iron rod held tightly in a vice attached to the wooden bench. His forehead drips in sweat. His Liverpool football shirt is stained and grubby. He barely looks up as Aziz explains what we need, but he continues hammering rhythmically.

I pull out a piece of paper, a copy I sketched of Monika's tattoo.

Aziz lays it on the bench, and when they converse with each other, they ignore me. Instead, they look to Peter for confirmation on price.

Peter nods in agreement and pulls out a cash deposit.

Aziz translates the blacksmith's short answer. 'He'll deliver it to the hotel in two hours.'

* * *

We arrive back in London to a cold, dark, and damp November night. I shiver dramatically, missing the African heat, and I don't feel warm until we're back in Josephine's penthouse apartment, enjoying a brandy nightcap before going to bed.

'Three hundred euros,' Peter says, turning the dagger carefully in his hands. 'Do you think it was worth it – and the hassle of declaring it at customs?'

'It's alright. It's not *that* good.'

'Well, we can turn it over to the chief inspector. Job done!' Peter says.

61

I hesitate.

'What is it, Mikky? What's troubling you?'

'What about the documentary?'

'Forget that! You've done what Mulhoon wanted you to do, which was to find out about the dagger; you can give him the photos of Monika's tattoo – you don't have to say who she is – and your sketch and now this replica. We can get on with our lives.'

'What about the *Parks*?'

'Forget them. Think of Marco. Go to Blessinghurst Manor, go shopping with Josephine and relax.'

'She's a bit miffed with me for pulling out of our planned shopping trip this week, and besides, she's gone to Miami with Simon this weekend.'

Peter laughs. 'Does she think you arranged to go away to Morocco on purpose?'

'Probably; let's have another drink.' I hold out my glass and Peter fills it for me, and I savour the brandy on my throat.

'Are you keeping your blonde hair for Christmas?' Peter grins.

'I'm dying it next week.'

'What colour?'

'Marcos likes a brunette.'

'He should find one then.' Peter laughs.

'He's been talking about our wedding.

'Marco's already asked me to be his best man.'

'Really?' I pause with my drink at my lips.

Peter grins. 'You didn't know?'

I shake my head. 'We haven't really talked about the wedding.'

'But he proposed?'

'Yes, but we didn't go into details. I didn't expect him to go ahead and ask you—'

'Don't you want to marry him?'

'Of course I do, I just thought he'd be more ... um—'

'What?'

'Reticent.'

'Why?'

'I haven't exactly had the best of lives, have I? I've got a past, Peter – as you well know.'

'Look, Mikky, we all know about your past, but that doesn't stop us from loving you.' He reaches over to where I'm lying curled up on the sofa and refills my glass.

I sigh and stare out over the London skyline, suddenly remembering that it was only last night when we were with the *Parks* and film crew in Morocco.

'Thanks, Peter. Cheers!' I raise my glass in a toast.

'What's wrong?'

'I'm not sure if I feel worthy of Marco.'

'Worthy?' Peter explodes laughing. 'Why?'

'He's inherited Blessinghurst Manor and—'

'And what? Don't you *want* to live there?'

'Yes, I love it. It's lovely to have somewhere to call home finally.'

'But it isn't Spain?'

'No, but that doesn't matter. I can live anywhere with him, and besides, we can sail to Spain or wherever we want to go. There's freedom on the yacht, and that suits us both,' I reply.

'Well, you'll be near to Josephine and Simon when you're here in England.'

'That's true. We'll be able to spend more time together, even if we meet here in London.'

'I know how close you are to Josephine now.'

'I know I am. I feel fortunate, especially when you think I've barely known my birth mother for five years.'

'That doesn't matter. She loves you and would do anything for you. You're very similar, Mikky. Besides ...' He drains his glass. 'She's crazy about you. And, she's sworn me to guard you with my life.'

'Everything is practically perfect, then.' I can't hide the sarcasm in my voice.

'Mikky, what's *really* troubling you?'

I ask quietly, 'Am I good enough for Marco?'

Peter leans across the coffee table, and he takes my hand in his.

'Mikky, you are more than good enough. Marco loves you and he wants to spend the rest of his life with you. Now, to be honest, you might not get many more offers. You're knocking on a bit, and you're almost past your sell-by date. So, if I were you, I'd make the most of it, or you'll be doomed to a lonely life of solitude and masturbation.'

I explode laughing, and that's when Peter's phone rings.

It's past midnight, and we're still grinning when he checks the caller ID.

'Matt? Hi. It's good to hear from you. I'm here with the lovely Mikky. Did you have a good flight back? What?' He pauses and I watch the colour drain from Peter's face. 'Dead?'

* * *

Peter swallows hard and stares down at the table, concentrating on Matt's words that I can't hear. His jaw's clenching and unclenching, and when he eventually looks up at me, there

64

are glassy tears in his dark, bewildered eyes.

I unfold my legs from the sofa and lean forward, a sense of dread speeding through my veins.

'I'm so sorry, Matt. No, it doesn't matter. I know it's late. Thank you for letting us know. I'll call you later in the morning.' Peter pockets the phone and clears his throat before meeting my eyes.

My heart is beating erratically. There's a stone lodged in my heart, paralysing me as I wait for Peter to find the words. The silence stretches between us, then his voice cracks.

'It's Ali.'

'Ali?' I whisper, conjuring up the round, cherubic smiling face and the hurt, soulful eyes. 'Ali?'

'He's dead.'

'Dead? But that's impossible. He wants to be a policeman.'

Peter shakes his head and grips his hands tightly.

'How?' I ask.

'They think it's suicide.'

'Suicide? That's impossible.'

Peter's eyes fill with tears. He whispers, 'They just found his body in the river. He threw himself off Tower Bridge this evening.'

'But he had so many plans. He wanted to be a policeman. He wanted to work with Matt ...'

Chapter 5

"All crime is a kind of disease and should be treated as such."
Mahatma Gandhi

The following morning, in Josephine's London loft apartment, we have spread out: Peter's computers, two monitors, and a couple of other gadgets already cover the dining table.

You can see Tower Bridge from Josephine's penthouse, but when I stand at the window, there's nothing to suggest that Ali has taken his life. I begin to hope, if not think that Matt is wrong, and he's made a mistake. Perhaps it's all a dream. It couldn't have happened. But the inevitable question haunts me – why?

'I can't believe it,' I say to Peter, as we lock the penthouse and take the lift down to the street, and I'm still trying to make sense of it when we take the tube train to Islington.

'It doesn't seem possible that Ali has taken his own life. It doesn't make sense,' I whisper.

Peter is unusually quiet. He links his arm through mine as we make our way to the address Peter found on the Internet.

We're looking for answers, and there's only one place we can think of visiting.

The building consists of two old Victorian houses, refurbished and knocked into one, and is ten minutes from the Angel tube station. Inside, it's decorated cheaply with colourful, plastic, and practical furniture. Dixon House is a haven and refuge for many.

Matt doesn't seem surprised to see us.

'Sorry, we didn't want to phone first. We both wanted to see you in person.'

'How are you?' Peter asks.

Matt grips Peter's hand and then pulls me into a tight hug. I can feel the strength of his shoulders through his tight T-shirt.

'Come on, let's get some coffee, but not here.' Matt pulls on a leather bomber jacket and indicates for us to follow him down the street into a cosy café.

Matt looks exhausted, as if he's been awake all night. The smile he had yesterday when they left us in Morocco has been replaced with a worried frown.

'The Dixon Trust opened the Crash Pad last winter,' he explains. 'We'd seen how other charities had done something similar, and we wanted to provide somewhere for homeless people to go in a crisis.' Matt rubs his shaved head. His hands are massive, and he has a tattoo on each finger – spelling out the words *died* and *live*.

'We wanted to provide a safe and secure environment for them. Sleeping rough on the streets is dangerous, but here we can give them clean bedding, towels, access to hot water, and a decent meal. They can wash their clothes, and there are people here who will listen to them and, more importantly, support them.'

'Are they all homeless?' Peter asks.

'Most of them are sleeping rough. They've been thrown out of their homes, and some might be as young as twelve or fourteen.'

'Did Ali come here?' I ask, leaning on the table between us in the small café a few streets behind Islington High Street and around the corner from Dixon House.

Matt nods.

'I found him on the street. He was hiding. His stepfather beat him, his mother is a junkie, and his father had disappeared. He had nowhere to go, so I brought him here the first time, when things got terrible – just over a year ago. I couldn't let him go through any more, the poor lad. Social services got involved, and we found him a foster family – but he was always torn. His mother kept coming for him and wanting him to go back and look after her, but then his stepfather would beat his mother again, and—'

'What about the police?' I ask.

'She wouldn't admit that anyone beat her or him. She said she fell or banged into something, something like that.' Matt shrugs and rubs his eyes. 'Then, about three months ago, his father turned up in one of the flats near here, and he agreed to take Ali back.'

'So, Ali was happy?' I ask.

'His father wasn't around much, but afterwards I got Ali away from the gang – he was interested in parkour. He used to hang out here, with me, and help out. I feel so helpless, Mikky – as if I've let him down.'

I reach out and squeeze Matt's hand, conscious of his strength and the size of his fingers.

'You didn't, Matt. It was the opposite; you gave Ali hope and something to feel good about.' I remove my hand.

'Thanks for meeting us.' Peter sips his coffee, and Matt nods in appreciation. 'I wish we could do something. Can we help,

Matt?'

Matt bites his lower lip. 'It's the others I'm worried about.'

'The other *Parks*?' I ask.

'I phoned them but haven't seen any of them yet.'

'And Monika,' I whisper, 'how did she take the news about Ali's death?'

Matt shakes his head. 'They're all devastated.'

'Ali wanted to join the police force and work with you,' Peter adds. 'He had a lot of respect for you, Matt.'

'Why would he have killed himself?' I ask. 'It doesn't make sense.'

Matt shakes his head. 'I don't know, but I can't prove that he didn't.'

'Can you tell us what happened yesterday?' Peter's voice is grave.

Matt pauses then says, 'We flew into England, got the train, and it was about lunchtime when we got off the tube at Islington. We all went our own ways, but we agreed to meet up on Sunday – for some parkour training. Sandra seemed to think she'd be able to confirm a role for them in another scene by then. Keith is checking the building and permissions, and health and safety, but they seemed optimistic, and the kids are excited—'

'Was Ali looking forward to it?'

'Yes. You know Ali. You know what he is – was – like. He was the ring leader.' Matt rubs his head.

'Where did he go when you came back?' I ask.

'He said he was going to see his foster family in Camden.'

'He wasn't going home to his father?'

Matt shakes his head.

'Did you check with the police that he got there?' asks Peter.

Matt stretches his shoulders, and his muscles ripple under his white cotton shirt.

'Presumably, he went back and had tea with them, and he then headed out. He told them he was meeting up with friends.'

'Who?'

'They didn't ask, and he didn't say.'

'What about his mother?' I ask.

Matt shrugs. 'She's in pieces. She's an addict but ...'

Peter and I wait, and the silence stretches between us.

'She's devastated,' Matt continues. 'She accused the stepfather of intimidating him, but he was in the pub. He has a room full of alibis.'

'What about CCTV?' asks Peter.

'The police are checking for other witnesses. There was one guy who said he saw him jump. He was driving across the bridge at the time. He couldn't stop. He called 999, but then it was too late.'

'There should be webcams,' Peter says.

'Maybe, but I can't believe he jumped off Tower Bridge.' Matt grips his hands tightly, and his fingers lock together in a firm grip.

'What time was it?'

'About seven o'clock.'

'Do the police suspect foul play?' Peter insists.

Matt shakes his head. 'I don't know. I don't know anything anymore. It just doesn't make sense.'

I place my arm over Matt's massive shoulder in a comforting hug; he's built of solid muscle. I say, 'If there's anything we can do ...'

* * *

The newspapers and TV news channels are full of the upcoming election. Politicians are canvassing, making speeches and promises in equal measure, and Ali's death goes almost unnoticed.

'I won't see you now,' complains Josephine when she phones me later that morning.

Peter and I are travelling by taxi to a cafe near to Scotland Yard.

'That's fine, Josephine, if you and Simon want to stay on longer in Miami.'

'I was hoping to have some quality time together shopping. Do you forgive me—'

'We'll do it when you get back,' I reply, secretly relieved. 'So, tell me, how is everything in Florida?'

'It's warm, thankfully.'

'And your mother?'

'You mean *your* grandmother?'

'That's the one.'

'She sends her love.'

'Thank you. Send it back.' I wink at Peter, who appears oblivious to my phone conversation and seems happy to gaze out at the London sights.

'She wants to come over and see you. She wants to meet Marco.'

'She will.'

'Where is he?'

'He's sailing and hard to get hold of at the moment.'

'You need to set a date for your wedding.'

'Marco will arrange everything.'

71

'Not your wedding dress. He can hardly try that on!' she replies.

'Of course not, but it won't be until next year – there's plenty of time.'

'What sort of dress would you like – white?'

'Too virginal, Josephine. Even I wouldn't get away with that.'

'Something pretty?' she insists.

'I want to show off my body art. Maybe black, muddy brown, or boring grey ...' I tease, raising my arm to look at Edvard Munch's *The Scream* tattooed on my skin.

'It's not a funeral. It should be the happiest day of your life,' Josephine admonishes me, and I imagine her frowning.

'Well, it won't be, Josephine – *that* was the day that you walked into my life – my darling mother.' I smile.

'I'm not taking any notice of you. You're being facetious.'

'I'm really not. Sorry, Josephine, but it's been a difficult few days.'

'I know, and I'm sorry one of those children have killed themselves. I really am, but you haven't got too involved with them, have you?'

'What do you mean?'

'Well, your life can move forward, can't it? It's over now, isn't it?'

The taxi pulls to a screeching halt.

'Of course.' I glance at Peter, but he's focused on the red traffic lights.

'And Marco, when will he come home?'

'He should be back in England in a couple of weeks ... Look, we will have a lovely spring or summer wedding next year, and you can make all the arrangements and invite all the guests you like. We have plenty of time. Stay in Miami as long as you want.'

'Then let's go shopping when I get back. We can—'

'Pop into John Lewis?' I suggest.

'No, I was thinking about my friend Jemma. She makes dresses. She often made mine when I was on stage.'

'But you were an opera singer, Josephine – or did she make your wedding dress?'

'Don't be ridiculous, Mikky! It was far too long ago. I lived in Ireland then. But she did make the pretty turquoise one I wore for Glorietta's private charity concert with Prince Charles and Camilla, at the palace, a few years ago.'

I yawn.

'I'm thinking off-white, cream, and perhaps long ... with a lace ruffle at the collar.'

I explode laughing. 'And, if I have a choice, I'll wear my biker boots and a golden Cinderella dress.'

* * *

Our meeting with Chief Inspector Mulhoon is brief. He's agitated and clearly busy, fielding calls and interruptions as we sit in his office.

I take ten minutes bringing him up to date with our trip to Morocco, and how the *Parks* were enthusiastic, happy, and engaging.

'Did Ali seem worried about anything?' he asks.

'No, he was very animated and spoke more than anyone.'

The chief inspector shakes his head. 'And you found out nothing about a sword or a talisman?'

'It's early days yet,' I lie. 'These kids are damaged. They

73

don't speak easily. They've been hurt, let down, and abused by just about every adult they've met, so they are hardly likely to trust me or Peter that quickly.'

'But we did make some progress,' Peter adds, giving me a hard stare. 'They liked us. I'm sure of that.' He smiles.

The chief inspector rises from his desk to stand and stare out of the window.

'You think this will take much longer? I don't – didn't – want you to be involved in anything here in England.'

'We're not, but we went to see Matt at Dixon House this morning, and he seems to think that continuing with the documentary is a good idea.'

I observe Mulhoon, waiting for him to explode.

'But there is no documentary. There never was!' Mulhoon replies angrily, turning from the window. He bangs the table with his fist. 'One of these boys has died!'

'I know,' I say softly. 'We got to know Ali and the other *Parks*.'

'I don't want you getting involved, Mikky. Or you, Peter. Go back to Spain or wherever it is that you live ...'

'It sounds as if you're angry with us.' Peter holds my arm to keep me seated and calm, and continues speaking. 'Ali showed no signs of wanting to kill himself. He told us he wanted to join the police force and work with Matt. He had everything to live for ...'

The chief inspector sits down, tugging his jacket over his ample waist. 'I told Joachin, a few days in Morocco, that's all you would need and—'

'You also told Joachin that the prime minister would be grateful for any help – especially with the election coming up in a few weeks.' I lean forward across the desk and push

Peter's hand off my arm. 'It's not our fault that we didn't find anything out, and it's not *our* fault Ali killed himself. We've offered to help you, but quite frankly, I can make a documentary with or without your help. These kids need support, and even Sandra Worthington agrees with us. It's a good opportunity for them to tell their side of the story – and besides, you never know, it might flush out the real criminals.'

The chief inspector glares at me. 'This isn't sanctioned by the Metropolitan Police or me. I can't have you getting involved. It could be dangerous. I'm going to speak to Joachin. You can't make a documentary – not now.'

I stand up and stare down at him.

'Speak to who you like. You won't stop me from making this film. And if I don't owe it to Ali to finish it, then I certainly owe it to the *Parks* and other kids who are managing to survive out there.'

* * *

'Joachin isn't going to be happy.' Peter limps beside me, and as I walk quickly along the embankment, he tucks his arm through mine. I slow my pace, and my breathing calms as I gaze out across the river, watching a small craft negotiating the strong current.

'Why not? It's no longer a police business. It's a private documentary project.' I take a deep breath before replying, 'Mulhoon had no right to involve us and then tell us to back off.'

'He's doing his job, Mikky. He's already lost two police officers.'

I stop and turn to look at Peter.

'You know I have to make the documentary, right?'

Peter shakes his head. 'I'm not sure, Mikky …'

'What? Oh, don't tell me you're bottling out.'

I turn on my heel and walk quickly away, but Peter catches me and spins me around to look at him.

'Listen, Mikky, wait! You saved me. You barged into my apartment eighteen months ago, and you gave me a good reason to live again. I love Aniela, and our daughter Zofia is the most precious thing in the world, but I also love you – I'd never abandon you. I will be here to help.'

'I don't need you here.'

'I promised Joachin and Josephine – we work as a team, and if you're making the film, then I'll do it with you. But I just wish you'd shown the chief inspector the dagger you had made in Morocco. You should have told him about Monika's tattoo. You *must* share that information with him.'

'But if I do, then he might want to know how I knew about it. I can't put Monika's life at risk. She's already devastated about Ali.'

'I know.' Peter places his arm around my shoulder, and we walk companionably in the cold mid-November drizzle.

'Give me a couple of days, Peter. Let me speak to Monika and the *Parks* and make sure they're all okay, and then we'll go back to Mulhoon and tell him. What do you say?'

* * *

It's late afternoon by the time we return to Dixon House.

One of the volunteers, Claudia, is of African descent – third generation from Ghana.

'But I've never been there,' she says, smiling happily. She's dressed in a pretty, flowing multicoloured dress and matching yellow and gold turban. Her high cheekbones, red-painted lips, and dark eyes make me think she wouldn't be out of place as an African princess in a Disney film.

Matt explains, 'Claudia has been incredible; she talks to all the kids. They confide in her, and they have done since the beginning.'

'They trust me,' Claudia says, her voice as deep as her cleavage, and I risk a smile. 'Even the boys,' she adds smartly, and winks at me.

'So, what did this girl say to you?'

'Her name is Kiki. She is a friend of Ali's. She said she saw him yesterday after he came back from Morocco at about six o'clock. He was full of their trip, and about the filming, and how he was going to spend the money – a few days shoot, maybe a couple of hundred pounds. Kiki said he was happy and excited. She also said there was no way he'd kill himself.'

'Did she tell the police?' asks Peter.

Matt sighs and grips his hands in a tight lock.

'This is the problem. Kiki made a statement, but it takes the police ages to get witness statements and all the facts together, and to then process the information. They're *still* waiting for the CCTV from Tower Bridge.'

I glance at Peter, knowing what a whizz he is with technology, but he won't meet my hard stare.

'The police are more concerned with protecting the politicians in their silly election,' Claudia says. 'The police don't have time, and they don't care about the gangs, the drugs, or the Asian.'

'The Asian?' I sit up with interest. 'Who's he?'

'He's no good. There's always trouble when he's around,

isn't there, Matt?'

'What do you know about the Asian?' I turn to look at Matt.

The sorrowful and emotional countenance that he had when we met this morning has now changed to one of frustration, and he frowns as he speaks.

'We try and avoid him. I tell the kids. I try and warn them. He's evil. You see, he controls everything – all the drugs gangs. They work independently, but he's like the main cog in the wheel, and he keeps it all together.'

'Do the police know this?'

'I suppose they do,' replies Claudia.

Matt continues, 'The *Bics* are disposable – that's what the drug runners call the children. They use *Burners* – disposable phones – to set up a line of drug users.'

'They have their own language,' Claudia explains. '*Clean skins* or *tinys* are children with no police record, and they use them as *Runners* and *Shooters*—'

Matt interrupts her. 'They make friends with the kids, and they're normally between twelve and fifteen years old, and they get them to move the drugs around and sell them.'

He cracks his knuckles, and they crunch loudly in his small office. 'They use trap houses, that's where they keep the kids – where they prepare bags of crack or coke, and then they send them out to sell the drugs. When they go outside of London, they call it going country, going lunch, or OT – Out There!'

'My goodness,' I say with a sigh. 'That's no life for these kids.'

'Plugging is worse.' Matt's voice is low, and his tone measured. 'That's when they have to conceal the drugs inside themselves; either in the vagina or the rectum. Sometimes they hold wrapped drugs in their mouth just in case they get stopped by the police, and sometimes they swallow them. The results can be catastrophic.'

Claudia nods her head in agreement. Her shining eyes now seem dull, and her eyes are troubled. 'But it's the capping – the shooting – or the cheffing that's worse.'

'Cheffing?' I whisper.

'That's when they stab someone with a long knife or a machete.' Matt exhales loudly. 'It's called splashing – when they stab someone repeatedly until they're bleeding heavily. They make the kids do it to prove themselves, and it makes them fearless. The danger of getting killed or going to prison is nothing to them. They're more frightened of the Asian.'

'They're so young, sometimes fourteen or fifteen.' Claudia toys with the large decorative rings on her fingers. 'Knife crime is on the increase, and it's all drug-related – and it all comes back to the Asian.'

'And it's getting worse,' adds Matt.

'Do you think Ali was involved in his gang?'

'He *was* involved, but I got him away. But now I've got a feeling that they caught up with him last night.'

'Who? The Asian?' asks Peter.

Matt replies, 'He's the most vicious. They brainwash these kids. They make them believe they are invincible, but it's all false bravado ...'

'Until they kill someone,' adds Claudia.

'Do the police know about the Asian?' I ask.

'They can't find anything about him. There's no evidence. Nothing to link back to him. He's very clever.'

'And you think the Asian killed Ali?'

Matt looks at Claudia and then at Peter and I. 'Yes, somehow he did. But I don't know how to prove it,' he whispers, cracking his knuckles and making me shudder.

* * *

'You know they're asking for our help,' I say to Peter. 'They need us.'

We're driving Peter's white van that he uses when he travels across Europe.

Joachin had told me Peter was flying to England when he came to Morocco with me, but Peter must have a sixth sense. He drove overnight from his home in Wrocław, leaving behind his beautiful wife – my friend – and their baby daughter Zofia, who I have yet to meet.

We've left Dixon House, and we decide to stop for dinner, south of the river, near Tower Bridge.

I have a morbid feeling of wanting to see where Ali killed himself.

'We'll park near London Bridge or Borough Market and then walk to the Ivy Brasserie on the Embankment,' Peter replies.

I don't tell him that's where I met Chief Inspector Mulhoon and Joachim for the first time, last Monday, just five days ago. It barely seems possible, so much has happened since.

Peter continues speaking as he reverses into a parking space in the basement. 'There was a brief mention of it on the local news, an eyewitness saw Ali; he said he jumped into the river, yet there's no reason why he would do that or, perhaps, more importantly, no note or anything at all to substantiate that it was suicide.'

'But there's also no evidence that the Asian or anyone else killed him.' I open the door and climb out.

Peter locks the van and links his arm through mine as we

walk, and I'm conscious of his loping gait and false foot. It's a heavy price he paid to serve his country in Afghanistan, but heavier still is his PTSD. I'd found him, broken and hiding from the world, in an apartment in Wrocław, but now he's a happily married man with a beautiful baby daughter, and my heart eases a little at the enrichment we have brought to each other's lives with our close friendship.

In the restaurant, we ask for a table by the window, and I gaze out at Tower Bridge illuminated against the night sky while we wait for our gin and tonics to arrive.

'Peter. Why *this* bridge?'

'Nothing makes sense,' he agrees. 'There must be CCTV cameras everywhere.'

'If the Asian did kill him, then why would he take that risk, coming here? Surely he'd have known there are cameras on the bridge?'

Peter shrugs. 'If it weren't for a witness seeing Ali jump, I wouldn't believe it.'

The waiter suddenly appears at our side. We order fish, and I wait until we are alone until I say, 'Who was the witness?'

'A tourist, from Portugal. That's what the police report says.'

'The police report? How do you know?'

'I had a quick look.'

'How?'

'They write everything up on the computer.'

'You *hacked* into the police system?' I whisper, leaning forward in my chair.

'No, I just had a little wander through their system.'

I stare at Peter, thinking about the implications of his actions.

'What would Joachin say?'

Peter grins. 'I won't tell if you don't.'

'But we can't get involved in this—'

'What?'

'Ali's death ... it's not what we do.'

'What *do* we do?'

'We trace valuables – things of cultural and historical significance; books, documents, paintings, statues, that sort of thing ...' I spend the next ten minutes telling him unnecessarily what we do, how we have recovered stolen property and returned it to its rightful owners, and how we protect items of cultural value.

'We work for Europol,' I end with finality. 'We return valuable items to the rightful owners.'

'There's nothing more valuable than life – especially a child's life.' He holds my gaze, and I'm still staring at him when the waiter places our plates of fresh fish on the table between us.

'Are you telling me that you *want* to get involved in this?'

'It's not that I *want* to, Mikky, but nothing seems to be happening, and if you don't act quickly, as you well know, the trail goes cold.'

'What trail?'

'The Asian,' he replies. 'Could he be Japanese, Chinese, Thai?'

I eat slowly, thinking, and then I say, 'You have to tell Joachin you looked at the police report.'

'Why?'

'Because it's illegal.'

'Since when did that bother you, Mikky?'

I shake my head and look out of the window, gazing at Tower

Bridge, my appetite faltering. I put my knife and fork together, thinking about Ali and what he must have gone through in those final hours.

'Do you think he suffered?' I ask.

'I hope not, but the thing is ...' Peter eats sparingly and, like me, doesn't finish his meal. 'It's only since our little one, Zofia, was born that this type of thing has started affecting me. I never thought being a father would change me, but it has, Mikky. Seeing Zofia's vulnerability scares me sometimes. I want to look after her. I never want her to be sad or upset, or hurt, but I know that I'm being unrealistic. It frightens me. I can't look after her the way I would like to – like making sure her friends are kind, or that her first boyfriend is gentle, or that her heart is never broken.' He leans forward earnestly. 'In Morocco, I felt very protective of those kids. I tried to imagine what sort of life they'd had. My experience with this injury is awful.' He nods down at his prosthetic foot. 'But I chose to be in the army and to go into the SAS. I wanted to be a part of something good and true. I had a purpose, and I saw that in *their* eyes that night when we spoke to them, Mikky. I saw them as a group, a team helping each other – and, like Ali said, it was as if they were in the army ... and I can't imagine what he must have gone through with a mother who's a crack addict and a stepfather who beat him. Let alone what Monika and Joe and Lisa – and that quiet lad Adam, who is too scared to speak – have been through. That boy Adam – he didn't even speak. He couldn't say a word, whether through fear or insecurity, or the fact that he's been so hurt. These kids are seriously damaged, Mikky. They need help.'

'Matt is very good for them. He's devoted to them.'

'I've looked at Matt's record.'

'You have?'

Peter nods. 'He was a runner for different gangs from the age of twelve. He went to prison on his eighteenth birthday – for possessing drugs and GBH – for eight years, but he got out after four. After he came out of prison, he turned his life around. He's been clean for over six years.'

'He's only twenty-eight? I thought he was older.'

'He looks almost forty,' agrees Peter. 'It's frightening what that life does to you.'

I place my head in my hands, and when I close my eyes, I see Ali's face beaming with excitement and pride.

'I can still hear him saying he wants to be a policeman.' I remove my hands from my face and stare at Peter.

'We have a responsibility.' He stares at me.

'What will we tell Joachin?' I ask.

'Well, we could tell him the truth. We'll say that it does appear the Asian has started a cult of some sort, and they swear allegiance to a dagger.'

'You're joking? Tell him the truth?'

'Maybe all the members have a small tattoo under their left breast – like Monika.'

'How would we find out?' I ask. 'Do you think I should ask her?'

'But why that dagger, Mikky?' Peter asks. 'There was a rationale in Mulhoon's thinking when he set you that task to find the original dagger – and I think he's right.'

'You think that finding the dagger will lead to the Asian?'

'Perhaps. The Asian might be the tip of the iceberg.'

'What do you mean?'

'Well, I think he might not be the main person.'

'Why?'

'In my experience, the top person is normally well removed from the grubby action.'

'Like a field marshal and a soldier?'

'More like the president and a soldier.' He grins.

I sit back and think about the impact of his thoughts.

'You could be right,' I say. 'I think we should tell Joachin that we're going ahead with finding the dagger as agreed, and that the documentary is a cover.'

Peter signals to the waiter for our bill.

I gaze through the window at Tower Bridge. 'We will find the Asian. I promise you.'

* * *

As we leave the restaurant, the November wind is chilly across the Thames. Peter and I lean on the river wall, watching the headlights of the cars crossing the famous suspension bridge, and I tuck my scarf inside my parka.

'I'll let you speak to Joachin,' I say.

Peter nods, and we walk in silence toward Josephine's loft apartment, until I ask, 'What else can you hack into?'

'It's not about hacking, Mikky. The only way we will stand a chance of getting close to the Asian is to be one of them. It's about integrating ourselves.'

'You'd stand out, you're too old,' I say.

'I know,' he replies quietly.

'You mean me?'

'You're fit, Mikky. You kitesurf, you run, you're as fit as they are.'

'Oh my God, you want me to learn parkour? Are you nuts?'

He grins. 'No, but you can take an interest in it – for the

film.'

'I think we need to talk to Monika, Joe, or Lisa—'

'I agree, but we can't be seen to be talking to them. We might put them in danger.'

'How can we communicate with them, then?'

'Through the charity – Dixon Trust?' he suggests. 'We'll tell Matt that you want to spend time at Dixon House – filming, asking questions, that sort of thing, just like any other regular investigative journalist. Claudia and Matt will understand, so that it won't be dangerous. You'll be safe there, and you'll have the opportunity to speak to the *Parks*. They trust you, Mikky. They loved your tattoos, and you had their respect. That's why Monika came to your bedroom that night in Morocco. She trusted you.'

I sigh. 'You think that's the best way forward?'

'Don't you?'

'I feel as though I'm betraying them, using them to get information about the Asian.'

'Well we are – but if you tell yourself something good will come of it, then you'll feel better.'

'Something good?'

'We'll find the Asian.' Peter squeezes my arm. 'You can chat to anyone, Mikky. They believe that you're a freelance journalist making a documentary, and after that, you can do what you like with it; show it to the police, make it public, nothing – whatever you like. You'll be in a position to ask if any of them have a tattoo and if they're in the cult or sect or whatever it is – and if they are, then they will lead us to the cult leader.'

'The Asian?' I say, mulling over the imaginary face of this monster in my mind, while I gaze at the blackness of the

Thames. 'The Asian ...'

But Peter's voice is quiet beside me. 'Not just the Asian, Mikky. My money is on someone else, someone at the top, but we have to find the Asian first.'

* * *

That night, after speaking to Marco on the phone, I'm lying on my bed thinking. Marco had been full of sympathy and love. He'd understood when I'd told him about the *Parks*, and he'd also agreed that we should make the documentary.

'Promise me, you'll be careful?' he whispers.

'I promise. I'll be at Dixon House most of the time, with Claudia and Matt.'

'Okay, my darling.'

We say goodnight and agree to speak tomorrow.

I'm restless. I can't stop thinking about Ali, and now I reach for my camera and play back the video. Ali is sitting at the table on the hotel terrace in Morocco on the last night, wearing his flying jacket.

'My foster family didn't want me to leave,' Ali says. 'I was safe with them.'

'Did you have to leave them?' Peter asks.

I video Ali's face, keeping a still hand.

'My mum wants me back home.'

'Where's home?' Peter asks.

'Brentwood.'

'But your mum's an addict,' Monika says.

Ali frowns. 'It's not her fault.'

I rewind that scene to capture the hurt in Ali's eyes.

'But she's gotta get clean,' says Joe. 'You won't be able to do nothing until she wants to help herself.'

'I thought you were going to live with your dad,' says Monika.

'I stay with him sometimes, but he works nights – on the trains.'

'Does he make you feel safe?' I ask.

Ali grins at the camera, but the smile doesn't reach his eyes.

I freeze the screen and lay the camera on the bed beside me, then I gaze up at the ceiling thinking of Ali.

I will find out what happened.

Although all the evidence points to it and there was a witness, Ali couldn't have killed himself.

Chapter 6

"Violence is a crime against humanity, for it destroys the very fabric of society."
Pope John Paul II

I'm at Dixon House for most of the week, hanging around, asking questions. I take innocuous photographs with the consent of the people there; homeless, dropouts, addicts, volunteers, and visitors, in the hope that someone will reveal something. Anything that will become useful and lead us forward in our investigation.

I also check the image of Monika's tattoo, but against her ebony skin it isn't clear, and when I check it against the dagger made in Morocco, it's a poor imitation of a knife. I can't match it with any certainty against any well-known or famous weapon, but that isn't to say that the cult didn't have one made especially for initiating these young kids.

It's frustrating, and my mood darkens as the week progresses. I haven't seen any of the *Parks* – none of them have come near Dixon House, and I haven't spoken to anyone who knows or admits to knowing the Asian.

I've been discreet, bringing it up and hinting at a cult-like environment on the streets. I've tried to talk about the drugs gangs and county lines, and I've helped the volunteers to prepare fresh produce donated by local shops for the food bank for some local residents, in the hope they will confide in me.

This morning, I've even helped prepare coffee for Elevenses – a social club that attracts the older population. I've filmed some of the martial arts programmes, which consist of eight young kids who live in the high-rise blocks nearby, between the ages of eight and twelve, who giggle and play fight, while being shown basic self-defence moves. They pose for us and it's funny when they pull faces and push each other. I find their humour and good nature reassuring and wholesome.

Today, Claudia is standing beside me, shouting encouragement, clapping and cheering them when they get their moves right, and I'm caught up with her enthusiasm.

'It's just one of the activities that we provide,' she explains. 'There's also an open mic night next week, a book club, and art classes. There's an art class starting now, in fact.'

I follow her to a smaller room, where the walls are bright blue and orange. It's an activities room, where tables have been pushed together in the centre, reminding me of a school classroom. Occupying the chairs are a few teenagers and a couple of adults, hunched over sketch pads, drawing still lifes of a tall green fern next to a white coffee mug displaying an elegant light-blue lily. A young man who appears to be teaching sits quietly sketching and occasionally offering advice.

I pause at the edge of the room, recognising Adam – he was in Morocco with us, but he hadn't spoken much. I remember how his haunted eyes had absorbed every detail. When I'd watched the parkour scene on playback with Sandra, I'd been surprised that he'd been the most elegant and natural of them all.

Adam doesn't seem to notice me. He doesn't look up, so it gives me the chance to study his features in more detail: thin face, blue eyes, pale skin, short, hay-coloured hair. He hasn't begun to shave yet. Adam, I remember, is sixteen and from Serbia.

'Mikky is an artist,' Claudia explains. 'This is Ben – the teacher.'

'Hello, Ben.' I smile.

He grins at me. 'Hi, Mikky. Great! We need all the help we can get. I'm not really a teacher. I'm in my second year studying fashion. Grab a piece of paper and give us all some advice.'

Claudia leaves, saying she needs to make some phone calls, so I wander around the room, taking an interest in the drawings, spending time engaged in random conversations. I explain that I'm an artist, but I won't elaborate that my talent lies in painting forgeries of old masters. I spend a few minutes pointing out areas in their sketches that could be improved, either through shadow and shade or the angle. They're simple tricks but effective.

When the person in the chair beside Adam leaves, I sit beside him, but he doesn't look up or acknowledge me, and to my surprise, his drawing is exceptional. The detail is incredible, and when I tell him, he acts as if he hasn't heard me.

'That's amazing. You've done well to capture the angle of the fern's leaf, at the edge here, and that's excellent shadowing on the mug.'

Undeterred, I reach for an empty sketch pad on the table and pick up a pencil. I draw quickly from memory. I sketch

91

Adam running, jumping, somersaulting, and using the railings and the steps in the Kasbah to gain elevation. I fill in the background, the backdrop of Kasbah in Ouarzazate, but in the foreground, I focus again on his body; his arched back, thin arms, and the balance of his feet. I create several mini-sketches, and I'm so totally absorbed in my art that when I feel his breath touching my cheek, it's like a sweet breeze. I look at him, and our eyes lock. His pale blue eyes now show a glimmer of interest, or is it curiosity?

I turn the drawings for him to see, and he takes the sketch pad from my hand to study it closer. He remains speechless, as if the pictures are precious works of art.

'Do you recognise yourself?' I whisper.

He's slow to respond, but eventually, there's a slight nod of his head. He continues to stare at the sketches.

'Good!' I laugh. 'I thought you were going to say they were crap!'

He shakes his head. His nails are chewed, and the skin around his fingers is red and raw. He has teenage spots across his forehead and neck, and his hair is thin and straight.

'Did you like Morocco?' I ask, conscious that the other people in the room are beginning to pack up and leave, but I'm in no hurry, so I smile and say, 'I loved Morocco. My favourite part was when you all came running at me in the Kasbah. I was terrified.'

He flicks a glance at me, and he frowns. His eyes are puzzled and unsure.

'Not terrified frighteningly ...' I add quickly. 'More of in an exciting way. It was wicked. You were so quick, and the way you scaled the wall ... that was amazing.'

His head barely moves in a nod, and I remember Matt saying

how some of the kids can barely speak. They withdraw into themselves. But now, I'm at a loss. I have an urge to pull this boy into my arms and reassure him that everything will be alright, but I can't. I know for sure that he'd push me away.

I'm just a stranger.

'You can draw really well, Adam. This sketch of the fern is excellent.' I lean forward to study his work, but he waves my sketch pad in my face.

'You can keep them if you like, Adam. I've been drawing for years. As a child, it was my way of escape. I was brought up in Spain, and I used to hide from my parents in churches; my mother was jealous, and she used to beat me, and my father was an alcoholic,' I whisper.

He reaches out, and his fingers are gentle when he strokes the ragged scar on the back of my hand.

'My mother did that. She was aiming for my face, but I covered it with my hands.' I show him how and he watches me silently. 'I was terrified ...'

'I remember, you told us that night in Morocco,' his voice is barely a whisper. 'Does she still hurt you?'

'No. She's dead now. She was drunk, and she wrapped Papa's motorbike around a tree.'

'Good.' He rips my drawings out of the sketch pad, tucks them into his pocket, stands up, and leaves the room without looking back.

Later that afternoon, Matt makes me a coffee, and we sit in his office. It's stark, newly painted but informal. There's a worn couch, a rickety desk, and a couple of mismatched hard chairs. He places the mugs on a Formica table between us.

* * *

93

'I saw Adam in the art class,' I say.

'Adam's autistic,' Matt explains. 'A gang recruited him over a year ago, and they had him running errands at first, and then drugs to Suffolk. The police broke up the drugs ring, and it wasn't worth prosecuting the children. They weren't criminals – they were victims – and Adam went back to live with his grandparents. We try, through Child Services, to return the kids to their families. Adam's grandparents are old.'

'Where are his parents?'

'His mother died of an overdose when he was ten, and his father, well, we don't know who he is or where he is. The grandmother said the daughter never told them. She was pregnant at seventeen, and they threw her out. They knew nothing about her or Adam until we knocked on the door fourteen years later. Adam had been living with a guy – a stranger – who was a real nasty piece of work. He got Adam involved in the drug-running, but after this drugs bust, the guy went to prison.'

'At least the police are catching some of them.' I sip my coffee. 'They seem active.'

'It was a big police operation last year. Rumour had it that there were undercover cops involved – unfortunately, they were killed and the Asian disappeared, but now he's back.'

'Do the police know?'

Matt shrugs. 'I assume so. I try and stay out of getting involved with the police and the gangs. We have to remain neutral. Dixon House has to be a safe place for the kids around here to come.'

'Do they live near here?'

'Adam lives in one of the flats on the estate. You might have seen the three high-rise blocks behind here? It's not ideal, but his grandparents are quite old, and they took him in, so they're doing their best. At least they let him come here, and they know that parkour means a lot to Adam.'

'He's very talented.'

'He's incredibly gifted,' Matt agrees. 'He's one of the best.'

'He doesn't speak much.'

'No, he won't speak about what happened, either. He won't tell us what happened to him or who was involved. We've tried to help, to offer counselling and friendship, but he stays completely silent.'

'Do you think he's frightened?'

'Maybe. I think he knows that the bad guys are all still out there – and when something happens as it did to Ali, it's a warning to them all.'

'But the Asian's not the one in charge?' I ask Matt deliberately as a question.

Matt shrugs. 'In my experience, it often goes much higher than the thug on the street who intimidates the kids.'

'Peter thinks the same,' I reply. 'So, if the Asian is the enforcer, then who is it? Who makes the rules? Who's in charge?'

Matt cracks his knuckles.

'I don't know, Mikky, but if I did, I'd go after them myself. I'd hunt them down and kill them with my bare hands for all the lives that they have destroyed.'

'So, what *do* you know about the Asian?'

'Nothing, Mikky. Absolutely nothing. No one will risk their lives talking about him.'

* * *

Half an hour later, Claudia joins us. She brings a strong-smelling herbal tea into Matt's office and places the mug on the table, and wraps her green, yellow, and orange dress delicately under her bottom as she sits down. She wears a matching turban that emphasises the deep colour of her beautiful skin, and the gold bracelets on her arm jangle as she sips her tea.

'How does this place keep going? How is it funded?' I ask.

'Volunteers run it and we have some funding from the government, then there are private donations.' Claudia's African voice is melodious as it goes up and down on the musical scale.

'Is there a lot of support from the government – or is it the city council who helps you?' I ask.

Matt finishes his coffee and sits back.

'We're a registered charity. The local politician Raymond Harris has been incredible. He's a local councillor, and he's working hard to improve the estate. The council flats are in a terrible state. Some of them are filthy, with rats and cockroaches, and there are no locks on the main doors, and there are robberies all the time ...'

'Is that near here?'

'The estate consists of the three high-rise tower blocks, two roads behind us, walking toward Regent's Canal. They're old buildings now, and they're in a bad state of neglect. The residents are lobbying for more investment and support, and we're hoping that with the election next month, there will be more money injected into supporting the local people here. The problem is,' Claudia explains, 'that if the buildings aren't looked after, then they quickly become infested with rats and things. It also means that people have no respect for the property, and they do awful things; robberies increase, and they become a den for the drug users.'

'The problem isn't just the drugs, Mikky,' Matt explains. 'It's poor social housing, unemployment, *and* drug abuse, which all have a knock-on effect with the kids' lives and their education—'

'Domestic violence is also a big problem,' interjects Claudia. 'As well as sexual assault on young people; boys and girls. We do our best to provide help and support here, and we work closely with the police and social services, but sometimes it's a losing battle ...'

Matt cracks his knuckles. 'It's worse when we lose one of our own – like Ali. It affects us all. That's why I won't believe he committed suicide. He had too much to live for – he had plans, and he would have turned his life around. I know he would have.'

'Have you spoken to his family?'

'He lived with a foster family for a while. I spoke to them on the phone. His mother's an addict, but more recently, he lived with his father. He's a train driver. I spoke to him last weekend.'

'Does he live on the estate?'

'Yes.'

'In one of the high-rise flats?'

'Yes.'

'In the same one as Adam's grandparents?'

'No. There are three blocks of apartments, two with fourteen floors and one with twenty-five floors.' Matt flexes his shoulders.

'Sometimes the lift doesn't work, and homeless people are sleeping on different floors, in the hallways,' adds Claudia.

'Sometimes it reeks of drugs or urine, and it's not healthy, especially for the families who have young children.'

'What can be done?'

'Well,' Matt says, crunching his knuckles. 'Raymond Harris is doing his best, and the police are doing what they can do with limited resources – and we do what we can here. We try and give them shelter and a safe place to be.'

'Let's see what the election brings.' Claudia smiles brightly. 'I'm an optimist, and I'm hoping the new government will give us a windfall. They have to turn this around when you think of what all those businessmen and banks earn while these poor people live in poverty, waiting for help from the government because they can't get a job.'

Matt shakes his head. 'I doubt the government will change, Claudia. That's wishful thinking. I think we'll be stuck with the same capitalists, who only line their own pockets without a thought for the poor and the homeless.'

'Thank goodness we have Raymond Harris.' Claudia folds her arms across her generous breasts. 'Without him, we couldn't survive.'

* * *

I'm walking out of Dixon House when I spot Adam sitting on a low wall, a few metres down the road, on his own. He's looking at something in his hands – probably his phone – and I wonder if I should join him, but I decide against it. Instead, I check the address in my hand, hastily scribbled by Matt, and head toward the buildings they refer to as the estate.

The wind is cold on my face. It's four o'clock, and already the low cloud and the threat of more rain has brought darkness to the streets.

I sidestep a puddle, leap over dog poo by the lamppost, and avoid the addicts with bleary eyes and grubby fingers rolling joints and loitering in the doorways.

All around me, life goes on; a young girl with fake eyelashes, enhanced lips, and a fake tan pushes a buggy. An older woman tugs the hand of a screaming toddler, pulling him angrily along the street, and from an alleyway, a dog barks.

Beside a small park with a patch of green grass, three grey buildings rise into the sky and seem imposingly tall. I have vertigo. When I look up, it causes my knees to tremble and my palms to sweat.

I check the address and, using Google Maps, I find that each block of apartments is named after a saint: Luke, Thomas, and John.

Luke and Thomas have fourteen floors, and John is the tallest, with twenty-four. I swallow hard, and my mouth is dry.

The address is like the verse of the Bible.

Luke. 12. 24.

Matt and Claudia are right – the locks are broken on the main door. I walk in through the front entrance and there's no security. The lift is honking of urine, so I opt for the stairs, climbing two at a time, deciding it will keep me fit. Twelve floors, apartment number 24.

Some of the floors are not illuminated. The lights are broken, but I move on instinct, quickly, and I call out, shocked and surprised when a bundle in the corner unfurls and groans.

I hurry, climbing higher, wondering about fires and security.

A door bangs. A voice shouts and curses, so I jog up to the twelfth floor, scanning the door numbers: 24.

There is chipped paint on the front door and a new lock.

I knock and wait.

Eventually, a round-shouldered man with a walnut head and brown eyes behind round tortoiseshell glasses opens the door.

Ali's father, Mustafa, looks more like an accountant than a train driver.

'I'm Mikky dos Santos.'

'Matt phoned to say you were coming,' he says. 'Come in.'

'Thank you.'

'Mustafa.' His grip is warm and his fingers soft. 'Go straight on to the living room.'

Inside the small flat, I can see he's made an effort to make the apartment homely; there's a large L-shaped black sofa, a big television on the wall, and a few ferns and house plants on the floor. But there are no pictures, no framed photographs of Ali or him, or anyone.

'Do you want a drink?' he asks.

'No, thank you.'

I perch to where he points, on the edge of the sofa, and he sits at right angles to me. His elbows rest on his knees, his fingers gripping his hands, as if he's in prayer.

'I met Ali last week, in Morocco,' I begin.

'Ah, good. I think he enjoyed it there. It sounded like he had fun.'

'He and his friends – they're very talented.'

'They are good at parkour,' says Mustafa.

'Did you ever see them?'

He shakes his head. 'No, but Ali showed me the video thing he took on his iPhone.'

Silence falls between us until I say, 'I'm so very sorry ...'

Mustafa removes his glasses and wipes his eyes. 'It's so pointless ...'

'What?'

'His short life.'

'Was he unhappy?'

'No!' He sounds surprised at my question, and he replaces his glasses on his nose. 'The opposite. Things had just started going well for him. Matt had organised this trip to Morocco, and they were supposed to film again ...'

'He had a lot to live for.'

'Yes. He wanted to join the police force.'

'Were you happy with this?'

'Yes, of course. Anything, so that he didn't waste his life. It hasn't been easy – our life here – there's a lot of bad influences out on the street, and he fell in with the wrong crowd ...'

'Do you know how that happened?'

He barely pauses. 'His mother, she was a bad influence – she had no strength of will, and she took the easy way out.'

'The easy way?'

'Drugs,' he spits disgustedly.

'Was that easy for her?'

'It is around here. This place is rife ...'

'And what about your influence?'

'Mine? What do you mean?'

'Well, Ali is – was – your son, too.'

He glares at me. 'My parents didn't come over from Pakistan for me to live like this—'

'Where is your wife from?'

'She's English – from Brentwood.'

'So, you met, fell in love, and then ... what?'

He removes his glasses and polishes the lenses with the

corner of his shirt, then tucks it back into his trousers.

'I work hard.' He places his glasses back on his face and he focuses on me. 'I always have. But my wife didn't have the same work ethic. While I was out every day, she was playing bingo or in the pub, and then she met these ... these scumbags ... and they ruined her. You have no idea what it's like around here. I couldn't stand it, so I left.'

'But you came back?'

He looks away and concentrates on the new TV on the wall.

'I was off work with stress and anxiety. There was an accident – a body on the train track – not my train, but the one before me ... it's nerve-wracking going at that speed, and you don't expect that a body ...'

I wait while he composes himself.

'I didn't even bring up my son as a proper Muslim. I'm ashamed. It took me a while to get myself sorted out, but I lost my home – I couldn't pay my mortgage – and eventually I moved back here. Then Adam came to live with me. He'd been in foster care, and I felt guilty that I hadn't been able to look after him when his mother had let him down. He was my responsibility, but then I failed him, too ...'

'Did he ever mention the Asian?'

Mustafa frowns. 'I think I've heard the name. I don't know who he is. I've never seen him, but I know he preys on the kids around here and gets them to do jobs for him.'

'Like what?'

'Drugs and stuff.'

'Do the police know?'

'I think so, but no one sees him. They can't seem to catch him.'

'Is he the big guy – the man at the top?'

'I've no idea.'

'Was Ali involved with him?'

Mustafa scratches his head. 'I don't know.'

'I've heard there's a cult, and that the Asian has a following and some of the kids swear their allegiance to him ...'

He doesn't reply, so I continue, 'Was Ali a member of this cult?'

Mustafa shrugs.

'Did he have any tattoos?'

Mustafa looks surprised. 'He had an Aztec symbol thing on his arm, like a lot of boys do.'

'Was there a sword or a big knife?'

Mustafa shakes his head. 'He didn't show me anything.'

'Were you two close?'

Mustafa regards me carefully before replying, 'I work shifts – you know, on the trains – so sometimes I'd be asleep when he went to school.'

'Did you do things together?'

'Sometimes we watched TV.' He nods at the screen on the wall. 'But we have different interests. He likes sport and music, and I like films.'

'Did you know his friends?' I ask gently.

'He didn't bring anyone home.'

'A girlfriend, perhaps?'

'No, no one came here.'

Our conversation ends. There is nothing left to say. There is no more information that I can get out of this sad man. He's suffering, coping with his grief.

I reach into my bag and pull out a large envelope and offer it to Mustafa.

'What's this?'

'It's a photograph I took of Ali in Morocco. I thought you might like it.'

Mustafa pulls out the photo frame and gazes at Ali's smiling face, with his modern and popular haircut.

He's posing with his hands in his pockets, outside the shop in the Kasbah. While Mustafa studies his son's image, I'm reminded of Ali's shyness and inexperience in bargaining, and how he asked me to accompany him to buy the leather flying jacket.

Mustafa places it on the coffee table. 'Thank you.'

'Don't be afraid to get some help,' I say, as I walk to the front door. 'There is bereavement counselling available, and it might help you.'

'I'll see.'

I pause to look at the lock. 'Did you have a burglary?'

'That was a few months ago.'

'Did they steal anything?'

'Of course, the television and an iPad.'

'You sound as if it happens all the time.'

'It does. This is a council estate – it always happens.'

'Not all council estates are like this. Sometimes the residents have groups to support each other, and to improve things.'

'I don't get involved. I work too many shifts, and I'm too tired.'

'I'm sorry, Mustafa,' I say, but he doesn't answer, and as he closes the door behind me, I hear the lock scrape back into place.

* * *

I'm downstairs and back out on the street when I phone Peter.

I need to hear his reassuring voice in this crazy place.

'What did you hope to achieve?' asks Peter.

'I don't know,' I wail with my iPhone against my ear. 'I guess I wanted him to tell me he knew all about the Asian and where to find him.'

I'm standing outside the apartment block, and I gaze up at the other blocks; three tall towers – concrete, ugly buildings – filled with apartments and people with their individual human stories; tales of tragedy, heartbreak, poverty, and fear.

'But he couldn't tell you anything about Ali?'

'No.'

'So, what now?' Peter asks.

'I'm not sure ...'

I'm distracted by a grey Audi that cruises through the car park. It's getting dark, and the headlights sweep the brickwork before stopping at the entrance to Thomas's, on the far side of the parking.

I slow my pace as the car screeches to a halt. The passenger and driver's car doors open simultaneously, and two dark hooded figures emerge quickly. They leave the car engine running and the headlights aimed at the front door.

I can't see their faces, but instinctively I duck back into the shadows with my back pressed against the wall.

'Mikky?' Peter says. 'Are you still there?'

'I'll call you back.'

I pocket my iPhone, pull up the collar of my leather jacket, and plug my hands under my armpits to stay warm and retreat further into the dark shadows. Within seconds, the two figures return; I see them through the glass, moving inside the building, half-pulling, half-dragging a body between them. The person between them seems to have given up struggling but suddenly, outside, the prisoner's foot catches on the car door in a final attempt to break free, but they're rewarded with a heavy blow in the middle of their back and their knees buckle. The two hoodies bundle the limp body into the back of the car and slam the door.

'HEY!' I shout. I begin running, pulling my phone from my pocket.

The hoodies jump into the front of the car, reverse quickly, and drive off, brakes squealing.

'STOP!' I shout.

That's when I'm taken out from behind. A body comes flying at me, shoving me hard against the wall, leaving me winded and gasping. A hand covers my mouth and my phone flies out of my hand.

'Don't,' he hisses. 'Don't shout, Mikky!'

He lets me go, and I rub my throbbing arm, watching in disbelief as the Audi drives off. I turn my attention to my attacker, who is now standing quietly beside me with his hands in his pockets, still watching the tail lights of the car disappear.

'Adam?' I pick up my phone from the floor.

He doesn't reply.

'Christ! Why did you do that, Adam?' I complain, rubbing my arm, surprised by his strength and the force that he used to smack me against the wall.

He turns away, but I grab his hand and pull him back toward me.

'You owe me an explanation,' I hiss.

'Not here,' he whispers. He checks to make sure no one is around, then adds, 'Follow me.'

* * *

Adam walks, and I follow, as per his instructions, on the other side of the road and some ten metres behind him. He turns west, walking for fifteen minutes, heading toward Regent's Canal behind King's Cross and St Pancras stations.

Here it's well-lit. People are heading home after work, or out for a drink or a meal, and I feel my breathing return to normal, and my body calms and the tension begins to leave my shoulders.

There are bars, restaurants, and commuters. It's safer here.

Adam slows his pace, and I catch him up. We walk side by side, occasionally moving out of the path of a jogger or cyclist alongside the canal.

'What happened back then?' I ask, moving out of the way of a dog walker and a Labrador, but Adam doesn't reply.

Like most of the young population, he's wearing a dark hoodie and trainers, and I remember how capable he is of running and getting away.

'Look, Adam, this would be far more helpful if you were to speak to me. I understand it isn't easy for you, but I want to help ...'

'You can't.'

'How do you know?'

'I just do.'

'Do you want to get a drink or something to eat?'

He shakes his head, and we pause to lean on railings, where colourful houseboats are moored against the quay.

'Who were those guys?'

Adam shrugs.

'They took someone against their will. Do you know who?'

Adam shakes his head.

'We should tell the police,' I say.

'There's no point. It's too late.'

'Too late for what?'

Adam shrugs and walks on, so I follow him.

'Did they take you, like that?' I ask.

He doesn't reply.

'Why did you stop me from helping whoever they took?' I persist. I stop and shout, 'ADAM!'

He turns to face me. His pale blue eyes are almost trance-like.

'Talk to me,' I urge. 'Who is the Asian? Why have they taken someone? Where are they going?'

'You can't do anything.' He turns and walks away.

'So why did you bring me here?!' I shout at his retreating back.

'To get you off the estate!' he shouts over his shoulder.

'You're wrong, Adam! You are so, so, very wrong. I want to know what happened to Ali – and *you* can't keep hiding forever.'

I'm conscious of a couple turning to stare at me, and I realise my behaviour is inappropriate, but I'm frustrated.

Adam disappears like an elusive shadow into the blackness of the night, leaving me wondering how I can get through to him.

How can I make Adam understand that it's not in my character to give up?

* * *

I phone Peter and tell him what happened on the estate, and how I was leaving Luke's, but I witnessed two hoodies entering Thomas's and leaving a few minutes later dragging someone into the back of a car.

I give him the registration number I've memorised.

'Is there any chance you can track it?' I ask.

'There might be—'

'Can't you hack into CCTV cameras?' I complain.

'It's not always easy.'

'Did you speak to Joachin?' I ask.

'He's away and not back until later tonight.'

'Raymond Harris is the local councillor for Islington. Can you find out where he lives?'

'Why?'

'I want to pay him a visit.'

'You can't just turn up at his home.'

'I'm making a documentary, remember?'

'Mikky, slow down. You're not thinking! We need a plan.'

'We have a plan,' I argue. 'We've been doing our plan for a week, and I've been going to Dixon House, and nothing is happening, apart from more bad things. We have to stop it!'

'Listen, Mikky, that isn't what we said we'd do. We agreed that you'd hang out at Dixon House for a few days until Joachin is back. You are there to watch and observe – and see what you can find out. That's all.'

'I am watching, and I don't like what I'm seeing.'

'Europol have no jurisdiction over here – not since Brexit,' Peter argues.

'Look, Peter! Adam knows more than he's letting on, but he won't speak to me. He's frightened. I want to speak to the other *Parks*, the ones who came to Morocco, but they haven't even come into Dixon House since we came back. I have to speak to Monika.'

'Mikky, be careful. Adam must have been following you, so

109

anyone could be watching what you're doing. Besides, I've been looking at a few things ...'

'Like what?'

'Ali *was* in the cult.'

I stop suddenly, conscious I'm standing outside King's Cross. 'He was? How do you know?'

'I read the coroner's report.'

'What? Oh my God, did you *hack*—'

'I wish you'd stop using that word – I read it.'

'On the coroner's computer?'

'Well ... yes.'

'And Ali had the same tattoo?'

'Yes, and like Monika, it was under his left breast, near his heart.'

'What else did the report say?'

'The result of death is inconclusive. Ali drowned. But there was a blow to the left side of his skull, in keeping with being hit with a heavy object. He also had bruised knuckles and a blow to his right cheek.'

'As if he'd been in a fight?'

'Maybe.'

'Or he escaped – and he was running away?'

'Perhaps.'

I check my watch. 'How long will it take you to get me an address for Raymond Harris?'

'That won't be necessary.'

'Why?'

'We've been invited to a special event – drinks tonight. It's a fundraiser for our esteemed councillor.'

'Raymond Harris?'

'The very one.'

Chapter 7

"Crime takes the pulse of a culture. It tells us the truth about us as a species."
Andrew Vachss

A few hours later, Peter and I are dressed in our most elegant clothes. He's wearing a black dinner jacket and bow tie, and I'm wearing a black cocktail dress borrowed from Josephine's wardrobe.

'How did we get invited to this?' I ask, as we make our way through the crowd of strangers hovering in the foyer holding glasses of wine. Some groups are laughing loudly, others are standing nervously, but we make our way up the formal sweeping staircase of the prestigious hotel opposite London's Hyde Park.

'Matt said that two of the guests had to cancel, their flight is delayed, and it was an opportunity I didn't want to turn down.'

'Good idea, Batman.' I grin and take a glass of red wine from the passing waiter. 'Cheers! I need this after today.'

'Cheers.' Peter smiles and raises his glass, and we scan the room companionably, realising that many couples are doing the same thing. 'It's full of bigwigs.'

'It is? How do you know?'

'Because I read the papers.' Peter then proceeds to nod and point out different people to me across the room. TV celebrities, politicians, a few actors, and a couple of musicians. I scan the room, allowing my brain to capture the images of the people in their conversations and laughter while they think they're unobserved.

'That,' says Peter nodding, 'is Raymond Harris.'

My gaze rests on a man in his late fifties with hazel brown eyes, short hair, and a winning smile. On his arm is a much younger woman, in her late thirties, with enhanced lips, long glossy wavy hair, and perfectly pert breasts.

'His second wife, I assume?' I say.

'Definitely. His first wife lives in Devon. Their three children are all grown up.'

'Hello, you two.' Matt suddenly appears beside us and grins. 'You made it, then?'

Like Peter, he's dressed in a tuxedo and he looks remarkably handsome. With him is Keith, and Sandra Worthington and her husband Julian. After we all greet each other, Matt takes us to one side of the room, where we have a greater vantage point of the small stage. I'm conscious that people recognise Sandra and she greets those she knows, rather like Josephine, with this star quality that is both naturally charming and agreeable.

'I didn't expect to see you,' I say to her a little later. We are standing slightly away from the men.

'I'm supporting the cause,' she says with a giggle. 'We've got the permission through to film, and I owe it to Raymond to support him in this campaign.'

'Ah, be nice to the men in high places.'

'Exactly.'

'Did you meet him?' I ask.

'Only once briefly, but I've spoken to his wife a few times. Fortunately, she likes my films.'

'Who doesn't, Sandra? She'd be nuts not to.'

Sandra rewards me with a deep throaty giggle as I watch Raymond Harris walk across the thick dark carpet, toward the podium, under the magnificent crystal chandelier. The crowd hushes as he begins to speak.

Firstly, he thanks us all for attending, then he pledges to support the Borough of Islington. He swears to change the government and to introduce fairer schemes for Universal Credit and vows to eradicate poverty and the homeless people sleeping rough on the streets. He is rewarded with enthusiastic applause. He stresses that change is coming to our country. The election is built on the will and the trust of the people, and men like him will get the job done. He pauses before explaining there'll be a charity auction, then, quite openly, asks for donations by cash or cheque, before concluding with an uplifting plea that we all enjoy ourselves this evening.

Before resounding applause, he tells us to enjoy the canapés and wine, thanks us for our support, and steps away to a full kiss on the lips from his dutiful and adoring young wife.

'You're smiling, Mikky.' Sandra nudges my elbow, teasing me. 'You're enjoying yourself?'

'Just the originality of it all. I find it very moving.' I can't hide my sarcasm, so I drain my wine glass and look around for another.

'Will he appear in your documentary?' she asks.

'Raymond? Perhaps, do you think he will talk to me?'

'Maybe. You should ask him.'

'I'd be lucky to get within two metres of him, judging by all those people flocking around him, hanging onto his every word.'

Sandra chuckles. 'Maybe I could speak to Arlene for you.'

'Arlene?'

'His wife.'

'That would be lovely of you.'

'It might be a foot in the door – before everything kicks off in the next weeks.'

'You're right!' I add sarcastically. 'I guess Raymond might be busy with the election in a couple of weeks.'

A waiter pauses beside Sandra. She takes two glasses and hands one to me with familiarity. 'Cheers! I hope you're coming on set this week, Mikky?'

'I'd like to. And I'd like to see the *Parks* again – I haven't seen them since Ali died. They must be so shaken.'

'That was a shock.' Sandra stares at me. 'I couldn't believe it when Keith told me.'

'Keith?'

'Matt phoned Keith that evening. He was devastated when it happened.'

'Do you think the other *Parks* will be okay filming?' I ask.

'Well, Matt seems to think the *Parks* need to have a point of focus and it might do them good, but to be honest, the building we're using is very high and open, so we're mostly using a stunt team.'

'Really?' I tremble at the thought of going on the film set.

Sandra continues, 'It's very dangerous but exciting – I hope you both come and see it.'

'I'd like to, but I get vertigo.'

'Oh? So, you hate heights?'

I grin. 'Yes, probably as much as I dislike political fundraisers.'

* * *

'I've seen your films. I'm a fan! I'm delighted to meet you finally.'

'Thank you,' Sandra replies. 'And may I introduce my friend Mikky dos Santos – she's a journalist, and she's making a documentary.'

'Interesting,' Jeffrey Bonnington replies. His rakish thick white hair sits on the collar of his white dinner jacket, his goatee is neatly clipped, and he regards me carefully through round black glasses, then turns his attention back to Sandra.

Keith pulls me aside and whispers, 'You'd never believe he's seventy years old and he's a billionaire,' he explains. 'He's probably funding this evening.'

'He looks good for his age. Maybe he'll bankroll one of Sandra's films?' I whisper back.

'It looks like he'd like to.'

'Do excuse us. I'm going to borrow your friend for a few minutes.' Jeffrey Bonnington places his arm possessively around Sandra's back and guides her away to a group of people on the far side of the room.

Keith grins, and we turn to speak to Peter and Matt, but that's when a tall man with a thin face takes his turn at the podium to announce the start of the charity auction.

'That's Raymond's assistant,' Keith whispers, his breath sweet from the wine.

I watch for the next forty minutes as the crowd bid excitedly for the various donated prizes; a spa weekend in the country, dinner in the Shard, afternoon tea in Harrods, and a helicopter ride across the city of London.

'That's my friend,' Peter whispers to me, and when I look

at him quizzically, he adds, 'He's donated a sightseeing helicopter tour of London. We were in Afghanistan together.'

'Are you still in touch?'

'Sometimes.'

Sandra Worthington wins the bid for dinner in the Shard, and I notice that Arlene Harris graciously misses out on the bid for the spa weekend and that, like me, Jeffrey Bonnington doesn't bid for a thing.

I suppress a yawn and Matt catches me and grins.

'I'd love to see Monika again,' I say to him, once the bidding is over.

'I'll tell her when I see her. You do understand, Mikky, that I can't give out her number?'

'Can you give her my number and tell her I'd like to chat.'

But Matt doesn't hear me; he's distracted and ushered away by the tall thin man who did the charity auction, toward a group that includes Raymond Harris, Jeffrey Bonnington, and Sandra Worthington.

I lean against Peter's arm. 'I can't stand any more, can we go home?'

'You tired?'

'I meant I can't stand *it* any more. No one will notice if we slip out of here. Unless you want to stay?'

Peter replies, 'I was rather hoping we might meet Raymond.'

'No chance,' I say. 'Although if you donate a large sum of money to his political party, then he might give you some of his precious time.'

A tall lady with a pinched face standing in a group nearby turns to look disdainfully at me.

Peter takes my arm.

'Come on, Mikky. Let me take you home before you have a

tantrum and cause a fight.'

* * *

Back in Josephine's penthouse apartment, I toss my evening bag onto the couch before disappearing into the shower. When I come out, I pull on comfy joggers and thick socks, and lie on my bed.

I spend a few minutes checking my messages and then call Marco, hoping he is not asleep and will pick up my call.

'Marco?'

'Hello, my darling,' he calls cheerily down the line. 'I left you a few messages.'

'I've been out to a charity auction, then I took a shower. It's freezing here.'

He laughs. 'I've just pulled into Messina – I've had a fabulous view of Mount Etna today, and it's been beautiful. The only thing missing is you.'

'I miss you, too.'

'I spoke to Stella. She's not coming back from India. She's hoping to spend Christmas with her family in India now. Is that alright with you?'

'Oh! I was looking forward to seeing them all and spending Christmas together.'

'I know, but we will be together, Mikky.'

I think how lucky Marco's sister, Stella, had been after the attempt on her life by her nephew last year. His attempt to place a homemade bomb on the top of her car had left her face slightly scarred, but she had made a full recovery. Astonishingly, her ex-husband had been incredibly supportive, and now they were back together, living most of the year in his home in India, where he is now a surgeon.

Marco continues, 'I can't tell you how excited I am to be coming home. Home for Christmas, with you – it's going to be amazing. The best Christmas ever.'

'I'm so pleased, Marco. It will definitely be the best. But I was looking forward to spending time with Stella and the family. I wanted us to all be together.'

'Are you okay, Mikky?'

'I'm fine.'

'What's wrong?'

'Nothing. I'm tired, and I miss you, that's all.'

'How's Peter?'

'He's good. I think we're going on the film set with the kids who are doing the parkour next week.'

'That will be exciting. I loved the film clip you sent me that you took in Morocco. I'm sorry about Ali.'

'Thank you. It's still a shock.'

'What about the documentary – are you still going ahead with it?'

'I'd like to, but I haven't seen the kids at all.'

'I can understand that. They're probably frightened. Be careful, Mikky.'

'I will.'

'So, what's next?'

'I'm currently looking for a specific dagger, so I'll do some Internet research.'

'Great. Look, sorry, Mikky – I've got to go; the Harbour Police are here, and they want to check the boat over.'

'Is everything alright?'

'It's just a formality. They do it all the time to make sure I'm not smuggling anything. Don't worry. I'll call you later and remember – I love you.

'I love you, too,' I whisper, and then the line goes dead.

* * *

Peter is in the living room.

'Do you want wine?' I call out from the kitchen.

'Please.'

'Cheese?'

'Please.'

I prepare a tray of biscuits, cheeses, and wine, and carry it through to the open plan lounge/diner and push aside Peter's gadgets; I sit at the dining table opposite him. He's changed into jeans and a T-shirt.

'Aren't you cold?' I ask.

'Not anymore. You look fed up,' Peter says, reaching out and cutting a slice of Gouda. 'Are you okay?'

'I don't feel as though we're making any progress.'

'None at all?'

'No.' I gulp my wine. 'That was a complete waste of time this evening.'

'What about this?'

He slides a piece of A4 paper across the table toward me. It's a blown-up photograph of a small brown male nipple and underneath there is a curved dagger, about five centimetres long.

'Oh my ... what is this?' I whisper.

Peter holds my gaze and doesn't respond, so I say, 'Ali?'

Peter nods. 'Yes.'

There's something so deathly and final about the grainy

photograph that I feel as though I might cry. Instead, I bite my lip.

'It's the dagger,' I say.

I open my work bag and pull out my camera. It takes me a few minutes to find the photograph of Monika's tattoo from when she was sleeping in my bedroom in Morocco. I print out a copy – the same A4 size – then I lay the images together, side by side on the table, along with my sketch.

The image of Monika's isn't as good because of the light.

'It's just like this one. The daggers are the same.'

'Monika let you take this?'

'No, I told you, Peter. She was sleeping. Her pyjama shirt was open, so I photographed her.'

'That's illegal, and it's not ethical.'

'Wouldn't you have done the same?'

'That's not the point.'

'No! The point is, Peter, that we now have evidence that there is a dagger *and* it would appear there is definitely a cult-like gang. We can actually link two people with the same tattoo.' I smile. 'Ali and Monika were – or are, in her case – cult members.'

Peter refills our glasses and stares at the images laid on the table.

'Can you leave a cult?' he asks.

'I wouldn't think so when you think of the Moonies and Scientology. They make it very difficult for people to leave. Impossible, even.'

'So, do you think Monika must still be a member of the cult?'

He lifts the photographs closer to his face and frowns, analysing the detail.

'Probably, and that's maybe why she won't speak to me.

It might be why she hasn't gone to Dixon House. She's frightened.'

'But how do they control these kids? What's the attraction to join the cult in the first place?'

'Matt seems to think it could be a parental influence; you know the fact that the Asian provides for them – money, food, shelter. Think about it: Ali and Monika are both from families where the parents have separated and, worse still, they were already involved with drugs ...'

'So, there's no family cohesion,' Peter agrees. 'No stability. The kids have no role models.'

'Matt reckons they have no *male* role models. Ali's father wasn't around, and neither is Monika's – they both lacked stable male influence in their lives.' I lean my elbows on the table and say, 'Peter, what if ... maybe Ali tried to leave the gang, and that's why they killed him that night. Perhaps he wanted out ...'

'According to Matt, he'd already left.'

'What if they wouldn't let him go?'

'I think you're right.'

'Really? You actually agree with me that Ali was somehow killed?' I pause with my wine glass against my lips. 'Why do you say that?'

'I've found CCTV from Tower Bridge the night Ali died.'

* * *

'Found?' I query. 'You found CCTV?'

'Acquired,' Peter mumbles.

'You acquired it?'

'Well, not me, exactly – a friend helped me.'

'How come you have so many friends who help you in these shady dealings of yours?'

'Not shady,' he replies sulkily, and I ruffle his hair and laugh.

'Show me, then. Come on!' I lean over his shoulder, conscious of his familiar aftershave as he brings the computer screen to life, and we watch the film on the screen in silence.

Cars are driving over Tower Bridge. A hooded figure emerges from the bottom left of the screen, hunched over and running like a dog on all fours – quadrupedal coronation in parkour. There's a gap in the traffic. The figure jumps effortlessly – a safety vault – then precision jumping to land on the balls of his feet, wall running up the illuminated steel structure, bar swinging, then there is a butterfly kick, quickly and with practised skill. It's a balancing act, bar kick over swing, looping, overarm and underarm – rehearsed and perfect parkour – and a jump spin, until he finally reaches the high-level glass walkways.

Peter switches CCTV for a better angle of the hooded person, and I can make out the leather flying jacket. It's a shadow, an outline. The traffic continues moving below. No one appears to have noticed Ali's graceful athleticism.

He stands, breathless, while he contemplates the scene below.

'I've compared Ali's movements with the ones we filmed in Morocco, Mikky. I'm convinced it's the same person.' Peter taps a few keys.

'It *is* Ali,' I whisper, watching the screen intently. 'I know it is.'

Inside my heart, I'm screaming – *wait, don't do it, Ali* – but the figure doesn't hear me.

He pauses, kneeling, hunched over his sneakers, and I

imagine the cold and biting wind on his face. Then, he seems to turn slightly in our direction – does he see the CCTV? – before turning his back and almost defiantly, with his arms stretched wide, jumping into the darkness of the icy water below.

I slump back into my seat, shocked.

'Do you want to see it again?'

'Not right now.'

Peter tops up my wine glass, and I know he's looking at the clip again, but I can't. I've seen enough.

'It *was* suicide,' I mumble. 'Ali jumped.'

'It looks like it.' Peter focuses on his screen, tapping the keyboard with his stunted fingers, blown off by an Afghanistan bomb.

'But then why did you agree with me? Why did you say that you think they killed him? It doesn't make sense.'

'No, but this does.'

He turns the computer screen in my direction, to where there's another CCTV in a dark street. It's an almost empty car park, when suddenly the back door flies open, and a figure bolts from the parked car.

'Is that a supermarket car park?'

Peter nods.

'Is that Ali?'

'I think so.'

'He's escaped.' I wait, holding my breath, watching as he's followed by two hoodied men leaping from the car to chase him. 'Where is this?'

'Islington.'

Two men give chase, but Ali is quick. He uses his acrobatic skills to escape, sliding down the railing of a steep flight of steps, and they all go out of view.

'Is that it?' I ask.

'It's enough for me to think that whoever they are picked him up. Perhaps they were going to kill him, but his leap off Tower Bridge is almost an act of bravery. When you look at it again, you'll see that he's up on the high-level walkway. I think he's looking for CCTV. It's an act of defiance, Mikky. I'm convinced of it.'

'I can't look again, Peter.'

I walk over and stand at the patio doors, looking at the illuminated Tower Bridge. I think of Ali running for his life, in fear, and running from what? Running from who?

It takes me another glass of wine before I can sit with Peter again and go through all the action, piece by piece.

'That car – is it the Audi that I saw that night?'

I'm desperate to link the hoodied men who chased Ali with the men who I saw in the grey Audi, after visiting Ali's father.

'No, I think it's a different car, but I can't see the number plate. I think they probably steal a vehicle for each different job they do. Maybe it's a coincidence they were both Audis.'

'Fingerprints?'

'Nothing.'

'Police report?'

'No, I think the owners are just happy to get their car back; they think it's joyriders – and if the car isn't damaged, they're grateful they don't have to claim on their insurance. And for the police, who are swamped with paperwork, they just want to tick the boxes that the car has been returned to the owner with no massive damage done.'

'So, Ali did kill himself,' I muse. 'But he had so much to live for – they must have put the fear of God into him.'

'Well, certainly fear,' agrees Peter, and I remember that Peter is agnostic.

'I think they put enough fear in him for Ali to take his own life.'

'It might seem that way, but we can't prove it, it's suicide.'

'And the coroner's report matches all this?' I ask.

'It's consistent with Ali being involved in a fight. He has bruised knuckles and a blow on his cheek.'

'But no marks around his wrist, as if he's been held captive?'

'No, none.' Peter looks at me. 'But it doesn't mean that he wasn't snatched, beaten, and then escaped.'

* * *

I can't sleep.

I toss and turn in bed, not getting comfortable. I have images of Ali in my head; having held his arms wide, it reminds me of the Art Deco statue – *Christ the Redeemer*, created by the French sculptor Paul Landowski. The figure of Jesus Christ in Rio de Janeiro stands at almost thirty metres high and the arms stretch twenty-eight metres wide. Completed in 1931, it's famous throughout the world and recognised as a significant landmark.

In the end, although it's barely three o'clock, I get up and make black coffee, and sit in the lounge, in the dark, curled up on the sofa, wondering why Ali killed himself.

What could have frightened him? Why would a boy who had so many dreams of turning his life around kill himself?

When Peter gets up and wanders through to the lounge at six-thirty, he's not surprised to see me, and I say quietly, 'Ali knew something. That's what gave him the power. He knew something important, and he wasn't going to let them have that information. *That's* why he took his own life.'

I swing my legs off the sofa and wait for Peter to reply.

He sits down at the dining table without speaking and fires up his computer before saying, 'Okay, Mikky. If you want to use that assumption – what could he have known?'

'He might have had information that he wanted to tell someone.'

'The police?'

'Maybe – he wanted to go into the police force, remember?'

'Then why not go to a police station and ask for protection?'

'I don't know ... well, maybe he was frightened ...'

'Of the police?'

'Maybe.'

'I'm not convinced.' Peter shakes his head. 'He could have gone to Matt. He knows Matt would have helped him and protected him.'

'This is bigger than Matt. Whatever Ali knew was very important.'

'How did he find out about it? He only came back from Morocco at lunchtime – so what happened between when he left Matt and the *Parks* at the tube station to when he killed himself just before seven o'clock?'

'We know he had tea with his foster family, saw his father, and then he met Kiki around six o'clock. Let's assume Ali was in this cult or gang – whatever its name is – and then he left it. He was relocated and put into foster care. He'd only recently gone back to live with his father. Maybe they caught up with him again when he moved back to the estate?' I suggest.

'Okay, I'm going with this theory.' Peter taps his keyboard. 'So, let's assume Monika has the tattoo because she is or was in this gang.'

'I doubt you're allowed to leave.'

'I agree. I wouldn't think so. You think of all the cults you read about. Their members are brainwashed, and they've been encouraged to have no contact with family or friends ...'

'I looked it up, and I think that there's a level of deception. They don't realise they're joining a cult and it's only when you want to leave that there are threats and intimidation. A cult leader uses psychology to get a person to distrust themselves – and very often they encourage them to take on a new personality – like an identity where their thoughts, feelings, and actions are marshalled and controlled ...'

'Through the cult leader?'

'Yes – now assuming it is the Asian – cult leaders are often charismatic, inspirational, and noble. They're motivated by a higher purpose—'

'Money?'

'No, I don't think so. It's not about personal gain; it's something more important – something more difficult to attain.'

'Power?'

'So, the cult leader, if it is the Asian, could be recruiting these kids by telling them that people need drugs because ...?'

'Because their lives are so crap – and by providing to the addicts, they're helping them get the drugs they want ...'

Peter looks doubtfully at me, and I shrug. 'It's just a suggestion.'

'What about trust?' Peter says. 'Isn't it all about trust and providing a place of safety?'

'Dixon House is a place of trust and safety. Matt and Claudia told me how the Asian and his team recruit these young and vulnerable children – they take them to houses and feed them while they bag up the drugs to sell on the streets. They promise them money and clothes and status, and the kids believe in what they do. These kids are tested – with chaffing, remember?'

'Yes. It's a test.'

'How often do you hear on the news that young kids have gone missing, and that knife crime is on the increase or a body of a young boy has been discovered stabbed? Knife crime is growing, as are the drugs gangs and the county lines.'

'You're right, Mikky.'

'Matt said there was a police raid last year and I think that's when Mulhoon's undercover officers were killed, but they don't prosecute the kids – that's how Matt can step in and help them. Dixon House is a safe place for them to go.'

'So, Ali and Monika had help. They had Matt and Dixon House.'

'Yes, but what if something else happened?'

'Like what?'

'I don't know.' I stare at him, my mind a blank.

'Okay, so if they got to Ali – which it looks like they did – did he pass on this information he had to anyone else? Did he tell Monika, for example?'

'I don't know. I wonder if they were in the cult together.' I get up and stand at the window.

'Would Matt know?' asks Peter.

'Maybe. We need to know how long ago they were relocated to foster homes. Did they know each other in the cult or did they meet at Dixon House – afterwards, after they were rescued?'

'Perhaps they were lovers,' suggests Peter.

'They're kids.'

'Mikky, don't be naive. How old were you when you had sex for the first time?'

'I'm not answering, but it wasn't pleasant or comfortable.'

'Maybe you should speak to Matt or Claudia again, or someone down at Dixon House. Find out what you can about their relationship.'

'What about you, Peter?'

'I'm seeing Sandra today, and a couple of stunt doubles. They're looking at the safety of the building for freefall diving. They're shooting later this afternoon and tomorrow.'

Rain begins pounding heavily against the glass and London is covered in dull, heavy mist, and I feel the weight of the low cloud on my shoulders.

'Mikky, are you alright?' Peter asks.

'I'm frustrated, Peter. Monika doesn't want to know me, nor do any of the *Parks*. I just don't feel we're getting anywhere.'

'What do you suggest?'

'We need a catalyst. We need to stir them all up and get a reaction.'

'That would be like stirring up a nest of vipers, Mikky. These people are dangerous, and you don't want to get involved with the Asian. We're not doing that. Let's just tread softly ...'

'*Tread softly because you tread on my dreams ...*'

'Pardon?'

'W.B. Yates – The Cloths of Heaven. *But I, being poor, have only my dreams ...*' I quote, just as a thunderclap rips open the sky.

129

Chapter 8

"Punishment is not for revenge, but to lessen crime and reform the criminal."
Elizabeth Fry

An hour later, after I've showered and dressed, I'm sitting comparing the photograph of Monica's tattoo and the close-up image that Peter managed to take from the picture of Ali's body he hacked from the coroner's records.

I've also placed the iron dagger, made in Morocco, on the table beside me.

It's not much of a match, but it's something. It's a rough sample, so I spend a while sketching the dagger, amalgamating the images, noting the smaller details and trying to analyse the short inscribed text.

When I finish, I scan the Internet, looking at images that resemble my sketch. There is a substantial similarity to my sketch and a dagger that once belonged to Shah Jahan, who lived from 1592 to 1666 and who was probably most famous as the Mughal emperor who built the Taj Mahal, constructed as a memorial to his wife.

The original dagger was sold by Bonhams in 2018, for $3.3 million.

I check some more sites, official records, and my favourite – the Art Loss Register (ALR), the world's largest database of lost and stolen art, antiques, and other valuable collectables. The ALR is London-based and part of the New York-based non-profit International Foundation for Art Research (IFAR). The database, created in 1991, is used by the art trade, collectors, insurers, and law enforcement agencies worldwide.

It's my bible, and I know enough about the artwork, and priceless artefacts, to understand that the original dagger would be a collector's dream.

I call my contact at the London auction house, and I ask for some information, but none is forthcoming. He tells me, off the record, that the sale was recorded as 'owned by a private collection'.

I hang up, discouraged and thoughtful.

The original dagger is beautiful and quite unlike the iron weapon made for me in Morocco. The carved jade hilt is just over eleven centimetres long, and the curved watered-steel blade almost thirty centimetres. And, according to my contact at the auction house, it was more of a ceremonial weapon, with scrolling designs inlaid with gold at the top of the blade.

More importantly, it appears to match the tattoos that Monika and Ali have on their bodies.

'But why this dagger?' I ask aloud. 'If this is the original dagger that Monika and Ali's tattoos are based on, why hasn't it been reported as stolen. Or could it be a replica?'

I show Peter the images of the shah's dagger downloaded from the Internet. 'I wonder what happens in the initiation ceremony?' I ask. 'Who is there?'

Peter checks his watch, then stands up. 'Sorry, I have to go, Mikky. I'm meeting Keith and Sandra on set, do you want to come with me?'

'No, thanks. Call me later,' I say. 'Let me know how you get on?'

'Okay, and you let me know if there are any developments this end,' he replies, grabbing his coat and hobbling out of the door, while I'm left to ruminate the questions of the dagger on my own.

It's almost lunchtime when my phone rings.

'Are you coming in today?' asks Matt.

'I thought you were on the film set with Peter,' I reply. 'He left a while ago.'

'No, the *Parks* aren't filming until tomorrow. They're checking health and safety today, and maybe changing some of the stunt routines with the stunt team. Freefalling, I think ...'

'How awful.' I laugh.

I hear the smile in his voice. 'Aren't you interested?'

'Only if it was off the edge of my sofa. That's the highest for me. I have terrible vertigo.'

He laughs. 'So, will you come to Dixon House?'

'Do you need me there?'

'Monika's here.'

I sit up straight, pushing the iPhone closer to my ear. 'How is she?'

'Quiet. But you said to let you know if she showed up.'

'I'm on my way.'

* * *

Monika looks exhausted, and her eyes are devoid of any emotion. Her sharp features shock me; her face appears thinner, and her cheeks more prominent. Although she's sixteen, she looks like a small child, vulnerable, alone, and defeated.

I fetch us drinks and slide onto the sofa beside her at Dixon House.

'How are you?' I ask.

The canteen has machines that dispense lukewarm coffee and hot chocolate, and a tray of assorted wrapped biscuits, and it overlooks the outside interior patio, where two men are smoking. I recognise them as the homeless ones eating dinner last week. The one wearing matted, filthy gloves says something, and they both laugh loudly, expelling smoke and warm air from their mouths. The other one experiences a coughing fit.

Monika holds the mug of hot chocolate between her hands.

'Did you know there are more food banks in this country than there are McDonald's?' Her voice is soft and raspy.

'No, I didn't.' I sip the tasteless coffee.

'Half a million people need help and turn up at food banks regularly.'

'Really?'

'Our government's crap. They feed the rich and penalise the poor.'

'Probably.'

'Don't you know anything?' Her scornful brown eyes rest accusingly on me.

'I haven't spent much time in England, but I'm sorry – it's no excuse for my ignorance.'

'There's a five-week wait for Universal Credit, so it means most of the time we haven't got money. It's cash flow. Don't you realise? Everyone needs money to pay bills.'

I nod and hold the Styrofoam cup balanced in my palms as I listen.

'That's why it's so easy to get hooked. That's why you get into it and do what *they* ask you to do ...' Monika's voice is a whisper, and I lean forward with my elbows on the Formica table.

'Who's *they*?' I ask.

'The gangs. Isn't that what you want to know? They prey on us. They watch the lonely ones. They look out for the kids who are unhappy and who don't fit in.' She taps the table with her index finger, a stirring, rhythmic, angry beat. 'They trap us.'

'Did they prey on you?'

She looks away, and her gaze rests on the two men outside. One puts out his cigarette and pockets the stub in his shabby coat pocket.

'Mum thought we'd stand more of a chance if we stayed here. She's from Ukraine originally, and she was a baby when she came to live here in England. She met my dad; he's from Barnet, but his parents are originally Jamaican – that's why I've got this hair. It's his hair and this skin is from dad's side of the family. I hate it. I've got his flat nose, too.'

'I like your hair – and colourful beads. You look beautiful.'

She gazes scornfully at me. 'What do you know—'

'What does he do, your dad?'

'I don't see him. I haven't seen him since I was six. Mum threw him out.'

'Why?'

'She said he was abusing me, but I don't remember. I've got a vague memory.' Monika shrugs. 'I told you about my stepdad and his friends, and what they did to me. I told you everything – you know, that night.'

134

'Yes, you did.' I remember our conversation in the hotel in Morocco vividly. 'Do you live with your mum now?' I ask.

'Nah. She's in and out of rehab, so I stay with my dad's sister – my auntie.'

'Do you like that?'

'She's got three sons. They're not always nice to me.'

Her eyes grow darker, and she puts the chipped nail of her thumb in her mouth and chews. 'She doesn't want me training no more. I can't do any more films. I've got to leave the *Parks*.'

'Did you tell Matt?'

'He said he'd speak to her. He said he'd explain. It's not just a physical thing; it's mental, too. It helps me.'

'Does it make you stronger, as a person?'

'Sure, it does.' She grins without happiness. 'I'd be dead without it.'

'Why do you say that?'

She pauses and looks at the two men outside. The one sitting down is coughing and rolling another cigarette.

'Look at them. They'll be dead by the time they're thirty. Drugs kill – but I won't take drugs.'

'Do you now?'

'For a while, I did. I had to. It numbed the pain.'

'Then you stopped?'

'I met Matt.'

'How did you meet Matt?'

'I was watching them. They were in the park on the estate where I live. They were doing these jumps and leaps. Joe had a skateboard then, and he'd board down the handrail of the steps. He was so cool.'

'Was he the best?'

Monica grins. 'Nah, Adam's the best, but Ali used to pretend

135

he was. Ali was the gobbiest. He talked the most, and in the end, we would believe everything he said. He always sounded so convincing.'

'I'm sorry about Ali. It was a terrible shock.'

Her eyes darken. 'Ali's not here now.'

'You must miss him.'

'He killed himself.'

'Do you know why?' I ask gently. 'Why would he do that?'

She shrugs.

I persist and lean forward. 'He didn't appear unhappy in Morocco. That last night we all sat talking, he said he wanted to be a policeman. Like you, he had plans for the future.'

'You can't have plans here.'

'Where – at Dixon House?'

'No, outside, out there.' She flicks her thumb at the window. 'Why?'

'Because they come along and spoil them. You have to do what *they* say.'

'The drugs gangs?' I lean forward, nearer to her.

She nods.

'Listen, I need to ask you something, Monika.' I wait until she makes eye contact with me, then I continue, 'What do you know about a group – maybe drug dealers – who ask you to swear allegiance to a group, like a cult?'

'Nothing.'

'I know you get a tattoo of a dagger, so they know you're part of them, and you can be trusted.'

Her eyes don't leave my face, and she doesn't reply.

So, I insist. 'You can trust me,' I whisper.

'How do you know about this, this dagger tattoo?'

'Ali had one.' I reach for my bag and pull out the sketch of the dagger I made earlier, and I turn it around for Monika to see.

She glances down at it and then looks away, out of the window. I can see her thinking as she bites the skin inside her cheek.

'What about Joe and Lisa? Are they in it, too?'

Monika continues to look at the sketch of the dagger, but her eyes appear unseeing and unfocused.

'What about Adam?' I persist.

'Adam, he doesn't speak – in case you haven't noticed.' She pushes my sketch aside.

'Were you and Ali lovers?'

She shakes her head. 'We slept together sometimes but nothing serious.'

'Did you buy that new iPhone?' I nod at the pink one lying on the table beside her elbow.

'Yeah, with the film money. They said they'd still pay me for the next scene even though I won't be able to do it tomorrow. My auntie says I can't. I would have taken them to court if they didn't pay me. I've got a contract.'

'Life is short. There's no point in haggling over money. But it's good that they will pay you. Sandra is a decent person.'

Monica shrugs, as if she's unconvinced.

'Why won't your auntie let you do the film?'

'She don't like it. She wants me at home.'

'The other *Parks* will miss you.'

'Yeah. Poor Lisa is the only bitch in the team now. She needs looking after.'

'You need to look out for each other.'

'Yeah.'

'But what about Ali? No one could help him, could they?'

She won't look at me, so I speak slowly, staring at the top of her head.

'Monika, this is serious; I think he knew something. I think he knew something important and that someone might have wanted to stop him from telling anyone else. I think that caused him to jump off Tower Bridge. Do you think that's possible? Do you think he had any information that could damage the cult or the Asian?'

'The police asked me, and I said no.'

'I'm not the police, Monika. I'm your friend.'

She runs her hand across her tight curls and then rubs her eyes with the back of her hand. 'It's dangerous. He'd kill me if he found out.'

'Do you mean the Asian?'

She doesn't reply.

'If he found out that you're talking to me, then the Asian wouldn't be happy?'

'If we spoke to anyone. And yes, he'd kill you, too.'

I look around the room to make sure no one can hear us before I lean closer to her ear.

'I need to know about the dagger, Monika. Is this it?'

'Yeah. It's expensive. It's a real proper one. Sharp.'

'What sort of initiation ceremony is—'

Monika is looking over my shoulder and her face turns rigid with fear. Her eyes widen, but she's not looking at me. I turn around, and Adam is standing in the doorway, staring at us both with fury in his eyes.

* * *

Monika doesn't hang around. She grabs her phone and runs,

and I don't attempt to stop her. Within seconds, she and Adam have disappeared. I clear the table and go looking for Matt, but his office is empty, and Claudia has already left.

In the hallway, there's a young bearded fellow with a bald head, wearing a striking purple shirt, who introduces himself as Sam.

'I'm on duty,' Sam says. 'There's a card game going on, and the homeless are arriving for something to eat, so if you want to help out, I'll see you in the kitchen.'

Sam disappears with a small wave, and I chat to a few volunteers before heading into the kitchen where Sam is washing dishes. I pick up a tea towel and begin to dry the plates.

'The dishwasher is buggered,' he explains.

'Have you worked here long?'

'About two years ...'

'You do a magnificent job. I was with the *Parks* in Morocco. I'm making a documentary.' I let him digest this, then I add, 'Matt said that some of them have had a terrible time and that this is a haven for them.'

'They're like family.'

'Some of them are just kids like Ali.'

'Yes, poor Ali.' Sam wipes his moist eyes on his shirt sleeve.

'Do you know who his friends were?'

'Kiki was close to him. They were friends. She saw him the night he died.'

'How can I find Kiki?' I ask.

He nods his head toward the dining area.

'Kiki's in there. She's the one with the green hair. It's the first time she's been here since ...'

I glance through the open door.

139

Kiki, a small untidy girl who I haven't seen before, is unsmiling and wiping tables. A few minutes later, she comes into the kitchen, and I smile at her.

'Hi, I'm Mikky.'

'Hi.'

She throws the cloth into the sink and is about to leave the room when I say, 'I met Ali in Morocco.'

I have her attention. She turns and looks at me. 'So?'

'So, he was good at parkour. Did you ever watch him?'

'Yeah.'

Sam glances at Kiki and moves past her. The washing up is done, and he moves away to put the pans in a cupboard.

'Ali didn't strike me as the sort of guy who would jump off a bridge.' I fold my arms and meet her stare.

'Nah.'

'He told me he wanted to be like Matt. He wanted to be a policeman; did he tell you that?'

'Yeah.'

'The night he died?'

'Yeah.'

'What else did he say?'

Kiki rubs her nose and looks at Sam's back. 'Nothing.'

'What did you chat about?'

'Nothing.'

'Do you think he killed himself?'

She shrugs. 'Dunno.'

Sam pauses near me and says, 'A witness saw him jump.'

'Yes, I know, but it doesn't make sense. Why make plans about the future if you're going to kill yourself.'

Kiki stares at the floor.

Sam clatters pans into a deep drawer.

'Was he in any sort of trouble?' I ask.

Kiki looks silently at me and shakes her head. 'There's always trouble. You can't get away from it. I'm going now. Bye, Sam.'

'Bye, Kiki.'

'Wait!' I reach out, but she pulls her arm away from my grasp. 'Did Ali belong to a sect?'

'Get off. I don't know what you're talking about.'

'Kiki, this is really important.'

'Well, it isn't anymore. Ali is dead, and no one gives a shit.' She pushes past me and storms out, and I'm left looking at her retreating back and green hair.

'I care!' I shout.

* * *

'Kiki is saying nothing,' I say to Peter.

'These kids are closed up, and they don't know who to trust,' he agrees. 'You're a total stranger to her.'

I move to the window of Josephine's penthouse, to study the Thames and the illuminated London skyline.

'Was it a good view on location?' I ask Peter.

'Yes,' he says shortly, not looking up from his computer.

'How many floors?'

'Fourteen, but it was freezing.'

'And the stunt guys?'

'Very professional. Sandra also wants to do a couple of stunts on the estate near Dixon House.'

'The three high-rise blocks of social housing?' I ask. 'Where most of the *Parks* come from?'

'That's right. Luke, Thomas and John but we were at another

building today behind that – nearer to the canal. It used to be social housing, and it's undergoing some renovation; hence all the scaffolding and building materials and equipment. It's almost an empty shell up to the first five floors, so it's all open and drafty. That's where we were today.'

'Who gave her permission for that?' I ask.

'The construction company, I suppose.'

'Or the government – the local authority?'

'I'm not sure. Do you want me to check?' He looks up.

'I don't know if it's important – probably not.'

The computer bleeps; it's a familiar ring, and we both look at each other.

Peter waves at me to sit beside him.

'Come on, that will be Joachin. I said I'd wait for you, and we'd speak to him together when you were here.'

I stroll over to the dining table, sit down, and focus on the computer screen.

Joachin looks handsome, tanned, and relaxed.

'A week in the Canaries,' he says with a smile. 'You should try it, Mikky. You look exhausted.'

'But we did go to Morocco,' says Peter, and he proceeds to tell him about our film-making and the *Parks*.

Joachin listens attentively until the part where Ali is found dead; then his face visibly seems to crumble. He shakes his head in sympathy but says nothing until I finish telling him how I visited Ali's father, Mustafa, and then witnessed the kidnapping of an unknown person bundled into an Audi.

'So? What does this have to do with us?' Joachin asks.

'I think it's all part of this cult,' I interject before Peter can respond. 'They use a dagger as their talisman, and they each have a replica tattooed under their left breast upon their induction.'

Joachin says nothing but continues to stare at us both.

'I believe the dagger was stolen, and I also believe it's very valuable,' I lie.

'Who has the tattoo?'

'Ali and Monika – two of the *Parks*.'

'What evidence do you have?'

I don't dare glance at Peter as I speak.

'I'm waiting for an image of Ali's tattoo. Once I have that, then I can begin to identify the dagger with certainty – once I know what we're looking for, I can give you more information, and that may lead us to the Asian.'

'The Asian?'

'He's the head honcho on the street who intimidates everyone.'

'The head of the drugs gang?' asks Joachin.

'We don't know for sure,' Peter responds. 'But in my experience, there's normally the guy who does the dirty work and then the head guy at the top who doesn't get his hands dirty.'

'The cult leader?' asks Joachin.

Peter scratches his cheek. 'We believe the Asian is the link. Once we find him, then we can set a trap for the big boss.'

'Have you liaised with the police – with Mulhoon?'

'Not entirely.'

'Good.' Joachin runs his hand through his hair. 'Good. That's a relief. Well, let's leave it there. We're not getting involved. It's a street crime and nothing to do with us – especially as it's now out of our jurisdiction. Just in case you haven't noticed, the UK is no longer in the EU.'

'That's irrelevant,' I argue.

'Haven't you heard of Brexit?' Joachin sounds fed up, as if he's been repeating the same mantra for a long time at meetings all over the continent.

'It's the dagger that we're after, Joachin. That's what you wanted us to find. You wanted us to get to know the *Parks* in Morocco, and we have. Now one of them is dead—'

'Mikky, forget that – we can't get involved!'

I lean nearer to the screen. 'You wanted the dagger, Joachin, and I can find it.'

'Okay, so tell me about the dagger.'

'What if I can prove it's been stolen? What if it's from a museum in Europe – then that will involve us, and Europol, won't it?'

'That's a very tenuous link, Mikky, and besides, I doubt you'd find the dagger without getting into danger. I fear that these ... thugs ... these drugs gangs, are extremely dangerous. If your friend Ali is anything to go by – I don't have to spell it out. I don't want either of you involved. We must leave it now. Tell Mulhoon what you know and let's draw a line under it.'

I can't reply, and Peter is struggling to support me.

'I want to make the film,' I say stubbornly.

'What film?'

'The documentary.'

'That was your cover, Mikky. It was a pretend scenario to get you to Morocco and to see if there was a possibility of you gaining the trust of these kids. There isn't – and never was – a documentary.' Joachin's voice is firm and determined.

'I want to make one. The *Parks* deserve it.'

'I forbid it.'

'There's no harm in me looking for the stolen dagger, either,' I say.

'How can you do that without getting involved, Mikky? It's dangerous. Far too dangerous for you to be over there and getting personally involved. I know what you're like.'

'I'll look after her,' says Peter.

'That's not the point, Peter. You of all people should know better. We have no jurisdiction, no backup at all. It's not Europe. This is English street crime, and it's not for us to be involved.'

'I'm only looking for a dagger, nothing more.'

Joachin shakes his head.

'I forbid you to do anything, Mikky. These gangs have no regard for human life. They'll put a bullet through you before they even bother asking you a question. Stop it, now!'

* * *

'So?' I say to Peter, an hour later, over a plate of home-made tuna pasta.

'We'll have to be careful. Joachin is right. We can't be seen to be getting involved with police business, but I think the dagger is the right starting place. You've made some headway, Mikky, and it appears that you've found a match to the tattoos. Do some homework on cults and see what you can come up with—'

'What about Adam? He frightened Monika.'

'You have to forget that. Concentrate on the dagger.'

I shake my head. 'What about the Audi I saw that night? I gave you the number plate. Can you trace it?'

'I have a friend who is working on it.'

'Good.' I munch on the pasta, suddenly very hungry.

'Mikky, I want you to wear a wire. I need to be able to protect you.'

'I'll be fine. I know you track my mobile anyway.' I grin.

'That can be taken off you, at any time, and then I'd lose you. You need a wire or something else, something more trustworthy.'

'What do you have in mind? A bar code?' I joke, but Peter's face is serious. 'No way. You're not putting a chip in me.'

'It's a new technology.'

'I don't care – I'm not having it – I'm not a dog.'

Peter sighs. 'I've never met anyone so difficult in all my life. I really don't envy Marco at all. Doesn't he realise what he's marrying?'

'Don't you mean who he's marrying?'

'No – you're a force. You're headstrong, rebellious, challenging, and immensely—'

'Gorgeous?' I suggest.

'Frustrating.' Peter finishes his dinner and wipes his mouth with a paper napkin.

'Don't tell Marco. He hasn't worked it out yet. We're still at the honeymoon stage in our relationship – you know the bit – where he loves me, and I can't do a thing wrong.'

'You can't risk your life, Mikky. It's not worth it.'

'I'm not risking my life. I'm looking for a stolen cultural item.'

'I thought you were making a documentary.'

'I am, but I'm also looking for a dagger.'

'How do you know it's stolen?'

'I don't, but it will be when I find it.'

'What do you mean?'

'I intend to steal the Asian's dagger – then he can come and find me.'

Peter pauses with a glass halfway to his lips. 'Are you completely fearless or just stupid?'

'Neither. But I'm not going to let the Asian get away with this – someone has to stop him. We can't protect Ali, but we can certainly protect the others. Consider it a duty of care.'

'Oh, Mikky. Poor Marco, if only he knew; you'll make a great mother one day – to tiger cubs.'

* * *

The following morning, I'm sharing Matt's office and staring at my computer, googling the top fifteen most valuable daggers in the world.

'If there is a cult,' I explain to Matt, 'and they swear allegiance to it, then we must find out more details. Someone who heads a cult is remarkably and notoriously charming; they have this grandiose idea of themselves and what they can achieve, you know – unlimited power or success – but they often demand blind obedience and admiration from their followers. So, how do you think they get the kids to believe in them?'

'Power, fear?' he suggests. 'Maybe intimidation?'

'I think it has to be more than that. Normally with a cult, there's belief – they're brainwashed.'

'Drugged?' Matt suggests.

'Sometimes. But I'm thinking about what you said – a father figure. These kids are very often from dysfunctional families. They have no male role models – look at Ali. His father disappeared, and then his stepfather beat him.'

'You think the Asian is a role model?' Matt says disbelievingly.

'He could father them, protect them, look out for them, provide for them – food, shelter, money.' I'm trying to provoke a reaction from him.

Matt flexes his shoulders. 'If they're not obeyed, a parent can get angry, and they can punish their children.'

'But would the Asian do his own dirty work? Is he the cult leader or a step removed? Would the Asian defend the cult leader?'

Matt frowns. 'I don't know.'

'Is there any chance that you can contact Lisa or Joe? I need to interview them for the documentary.'

'It's taken me a long time to build up their trust, Mikky. I'm getting uncomfortable with all the questions that you're asking. I don't want them going through anything else. They've been through enough. They're still in shock about Ali.'

'I know. I do understand, but I need to ask them a few more questions.'

'I don't want you to stir up trouble.'

'I won't—'

These kids are safe here. They feel protected—'

'Ali wasn't safe, was he?'

Matt tenses his fingers into fists – spelling out *died* and *live* tattooed into his skin.

'I'm not happy, Mikky. I thought you were a photographer but—'

'I am – and an artist – but look. I didn't want to say anything, but I also advise the police on missing cultural items.'

'Cultural?'

'Yes,' I lie. 'There have been enquiries about a valuable dagger that's been stolen, and I'm wondering if the two things could be related. The dagger that is used by the cult and this stolen dagger.'

I give him the benefit of my wide-eyed innocent look, and I don't blink.

'What sort of dagger?'

'I'm waiting for more specifics on that,' I lie again. 'In the meantime, if I can talk to one person who is in the cult, or has been rescued, then the chances are that they will have seen it. They will have been through the induction ceremony, and they will have a tattoo of it under their left breast.'

Matt looks doubtful. 'And then what?'

'Then I find out what the dagger looks like, and I can track it back to the original ownership, and find out where it was stolen from, and it might lead us then to the cult leader.'

'So, the kids will be in danger?'

'No, I just need information, Matt. A picture, an image of the tattoo, and once I have that, I will be gone.'

'Is this part of the documentary?'

'Not necessarily, but I promise you that when I finish the documentary, you can view it first and make sure you're happy with it, and if not, then we can edit it together.' I smile. 'We can also dedicate it to Ali.'

'I don't know if this documentary is a good idea.' Matt cracks his knuckles.

'Okay, then I won't make it.'

Matt sighs. 'I'm meeting the *Parks* tomorrow. Sandra wants us to look at the building site where she wants them to perform in a new scene. Keith is working out the details, and I'm waiting for him to phone me back.'

'Great! Can I come with you?'

* * *

The following morning, I'm standing inside the empty shell of a fourteen-storey building, in Islington, north of the River Thames.

Peter was right. It's cold, wet, and draughty on the fifth floor. All around us, the plastic covering is flapping noisily, and the building seems to creak and groan.

Keith, Matt, and the *Parks* are assessing the location and facilities for them to practise their stunts; scaffolding, iron bars, wooden planks, bags of sand, cement, and concrete steps are used as props and moved accordingly.

'They've paused the building work today and over the weekend while we film,' Keith explains to me, 'so we don't have long to film what we need.' He shouts to one of the crew members, 'Has the Freedrop BMX Mattress arrived?'

Behind us, the film crew, technicians, and runners are carrying cameras, cables, camera tracks, and mechanical arms, as well as setting up monitors and drones.

I watch all the activities, wrapped in my thick parka, a scarf, and beaney hat, stepping out of the way as required, watching Joe, Adam, Monika, and Lisa as they huddle around Matt. They're talking techniques and I hear the familiar names carried on the wind: quadrupedal, wall running, tic tacs, precision jumping. Matt is demonstrating feet placement and jump spins while the *Parks* appear nervous and excited.

Earlier, Joe and Lisa nodded at me, and even Adam looked in my direction, but Monika wasn't friendly. It was as if she didn't know me or even remember visiting my bedroom in Morocco.

I turn to Keith. 'I thought Monika wasn't allowed to film

with the *Parks*. She told me her mother wasn't happy.'

'Matt spoke to her. He managed to persuade her that it would be good for Monika to be a part of this and to be with her friends.'

'They're thinking of starting from the bottom floor and running up,' Peter says, coming over to stand with me. He's hunched in a grey trench coat and a woollen hat. 'They might also use that yellow crane.'

He points to the far side of the buffeting plastic sheet that has been pulled aside. 'But the health and safety guys aren't happy, so it's taking a while to figure out. They've also employed stunt doubles for the lead actors for the more dangerous—'

'I hate heights,' I say, peering down over the edge. My knees begin to wobble, and my palms break into a sweat.

Peter grins. 'This is only the fifth floor, Mikky. Wait until you're up there.' He nods at the open staircase. 'It's Baltic on the roof.'

'Why did they leave some of the building as a shell?'

'The company who was doing the refurb ran out of money, and now the local government want to take it over to build social housing.'

'Is that Raymond Harris who is doing that?'

'He's a popular politician.' Peter grins. 'It could be.'

'The *Parks* are not friendly like they were in Morocco, Peter,' I complain. 'Maybe if I buy them lunch they will talk to us then.'

'You have to tread carefully, Mikky. Matt is anxious that you might do something to put their lives in danger.'

'I'd never to that.'

'I know you wouldn't do it intentionally, but if certain people find out that you're asking too many questions, then it might not bode well for them – or you.'

'If there is a cult, Peter, then these kids are being coerced into belonging. A cult leader is most often a sociopath by nature and will be incapable of showing any genuine empathy for them. The leader will have no remorse for destroying their lives. They'll be so delusional that they'll believe they're giving them a better chance in life, and the opportunity to have a career within their drugs empire. It's what they do, they exploit and abuse—'

Peter places his hand on my arm.

'I know, Mikky. I know. I do understand, but we must be careful.'

'What about the Audi, did you manage to find anything?'

Peter shakes his head. 'Not yet.'

I sigh and dig my icy hands further into my jacket pocket.

'This is ridiculous, Peter. We need information, and quickly, before someone else dies.'

Chapter 9

"To have once been a criminal is no disgrace. To remain a criminal is the disgrace."
Malcolm X

Lunch consists of us huddling around the table in a local deli. The *Parks* have worked up an appetite, and they devour wraps, sandwiches, and cake with a teenage hunger I haven't seen in years.

They speak excitedly with their mouths full, except Adam, who barely looks up from staring at the table.

'It's wicked, up there,' Joe says, his bright eyes brimming with excitement. 'It's the nearest I can get to flying. I want to go all the way up.'

'Did you go up to the twenty-fifth floor?' I shudder.

'Yeah, you coming up with me later?' he asks with a laugh.

'You're joking! I have vertigo. Wild horses wouldn't drag me up there.'

'They won't let us,' Lisa lisps. 'Health and safety say only the first five floors.'

Joe scoffs at the restriction. 'The stuntmen are doing the best stuff; running along with the crane and leaping onto the twelfth floor.'

'What about the roof?' asks Peter.

'Nah, it's a no-go area. They say it's too high and too dangerous,' Joe replies. 'But I'd do it.'

Matt grins. 'No, you won't. I won't allow it!'

'Maybe I'll become a stuntman.' Joe swallows the last of his chicken wrap and reaches for his juice.

'Not a pilot then?' I tease.

'This is more exciting.' Joe laughs.

Monika grins. 'It's an amazing feeling.'

'It's great you're here with everyone.' I push fruit cake in her direction. 'Eat up. You must be starving after all that exercise.'

Monika doesn't reply, but she smiles and accepts the cake.

'Cold,' lisps Lisa. 'It's so cold. I can't seem to get warm.'

She hasn't taken off her gloves, and she wraps her fingers around the hot chocolate.

Matt wipes mayonnaise from his chin. 'It's perishing for the end of November.'

'I'm going on a holiday,' Monika announces. 'After this is all over.'

'Where?' asks Lisa.

'Haven't decided, but with the money we're earning, I might get a job in a bar in Spain or Greece.'

'Weren't you thinking of nursing?' I bite into my cheese and tomato sandwich.

Monika shrugs. 'Nah.'

'You did say that,' Joe says quietly. 'You said in Morocco, that's what you were going to do.'

'I changed my mind,' Monika replies defensively.

'You're allowed to change your mind,' Lisa says. 'But I'm still going to be a nurse.'

'I want to feel warm. I want some sunshine—'

'You're lying. You're just frightened.' Joe stares at Monika. 'I'm not.'

'You want to run away,' he insists.

'Frightened of what?' I ask.

'It's not like that.' Monika throws her unfinished cake on the table and glares at Joe. 'Besides, it's got nothing to do with you.'

'What hasn't?' asks Matt.

'Nothing,' she replies, still making eye contact with Joe. 'Absolutely nothing at all. Joe's got a big gob, that's all.'

'Has this anything to do with Ali?' I ask.

Joe stares at me, and Monika picks up her hot chocolate. Then Joe slurps his juice and Lisa looks away at a couple on the far side of the room. Adam doesn't lift his gaze from an invisible spot on the table. He eats his sandwich, screws up the wrapper, and tosses it onto the table.

'We don't want to talk about it,' Joe says.

'You don't want to speak about your friend?' I ask gently.

'No,' agrees Monika. Her face is resolute and unreadable. 'We don't.'

I let the pause linger before asking, 'Why not?'

It's Joe who answers quietly, 'He's dead, and that's it. He's gone.'

'Do you think he killed himself?'

They share surreptitious glances, which are beginning to infuriate me. I need answers, and they need to help me.

'Look, I think Ali was involved in a cult.'

I take it in turns to look at each of them all, trying to make eye contact and ignoring the angry stares of Matt and Peter.

'I think it's a cult where there's an initiation ceremony involving a dagger, where you swear allegiance ... and I think

155

you have a tattoo inked here on your breast.'

I point to my jacket and space just under my heart.

Joe, Monika, and Lisa follow the direction of my finger, but Adam refuses to look anywhere other than the invisible spot on the table.

'And the thing is, I want to find the dagger. I need to know what it looks like.'

'Why?' asks Lisa.

'Is this to do with the documentary?' asks Joe.

'Sort of ...'

'I don't want to be in the film you're making,' says Monika.

'I need to find it because it's been stolen, and we think it's very valuable,' I lie.

'Are you police?' asks Joe.

'No, I'm a cultural expert. I look after the heritage of cultural possessions, like artwork and—'

'Paintings?' suggests Adam, looking up for the first time.

'Yes.' I gaze at him, remembering how we sketched together, wondering if he kept the drawings I made of him.

'But you're not the police,' insists Joe.

'No.'

I let that sink in before adding, 'I just want to find the dagger and make sure it isn't the one that's been stolen and I've been asked to find.'

'By who?'

'By a private owner,' I lie again.

Peter is glaring at me. He's annoyed I've broken our cover.

The silence continues until Matt begins grabbing the rubbish together.

'Right, come on, guys. We've got some moves to bust on the fifth floor.'

* * *

I spend the afternoon hanging around, watching and waiting.

All film sets are the same. It takes so long to set up the action scenes and to have everything and everybody in place, and it's quite dull and icy cold. Initially, I was interested, but now, it's getting dark, and I'm frozen.

While the crew continue to set up lighting and camera angles, Sandra Worthington checks the film monitors and discusses techniques with the stuntmen. She's wrapped up in a woollen scarf, and only her nose and eyes are visible. Although we chat quickly, she's in a hurry to finish the filming for the day before the light is completely gone.

'Coming to the roof, Mikky?' She takes my arm laughing, and I unhook my arm from her hand.

'Not today, but thanks for the offer.' I grin.

Peter takes it all seriously. He hobbles elegantly beside Keith, who's taking advantage of Peter's SAS knowledge for the fight scenes, and once they decide to venture up to a higher floor, I decide to leave.

'I'll see you later.'

Peter takes me to one side. 'You've blown our cover; you've worried Matt and the *Parks* don't know what or who to believe.'

I sigh. 'I'm sorry.'

'Come on, Mikky.' Keith beckons me to follow them all.

'No way.' I back off.

'Coward,' Peter says with a grin.

I give him the middle finger and Joe and Lisa laugh.

Monika is playing on her mobile phone. Any intimacy of our chats or the night she stayed in my room has been forgotten. I walk over and crouch down beside where she sits on a concrete step.

'You'll get a cold,' I say.

'I'm fine.'

'Look, Monika, if you ever want to speak to me, I'm here for you.'

'I'm fine.'

'Do you want my number?' I ask. I scroll through my contacts, find my number, and I hold it up for her to see. 'I won't ask for your number. I'm not hounding you. I just want you to know I'm your friend and if you need to speak or you want to meet up or hang out and have a chat, then give me a ring.'

I'm relieved when she adds my number to her contact list.

'Thank you,' I say. 'Now, I'm getting out of here before I freeze to death.'

'Yeah.' Monika grins. 'It's cold, alright.'

As I stand up and stretch my legs, I notice that Adam is sitting alone, secretly watching us. I walk toward him, but he jumps up and moves quickly away from me.

I give up.

I wave to Peter, Keith, and Sandra, but they're heading upward, too busy to notice me leaving.

This block is only ten or fifteen minutes from the train stations in the north of London, and Regent's Canal. It's a busy area, and it looks prosperous – more prosperous than the other side of the estate, where the Luke, Thomas, and John blocks stand like three pillars sprouting up from the earth.

I pause at the news-stand to pick up a copy of the *Evening Standard*.

There's been another stabbing in West London, and the headline is a quote from the prime minister, promising that more police will be deployed under his government. Millions will be spent on the NHS and the police forces across the country. In the rest of the article, he vows to break up the drugs gangs and to hold those responsible to account. His election promise is clear: *I will clean up and we will win!*

* * *

The following morning, I arrive at Dixon House early, and I'm surprised that Matt and the *Parks* are having breakfast in the canteen together. I greet them casually with a wave and Matt comes over to me holding his coffee.

'Come with me,' he says, taking me by the arm and guiding me toward his office. His desk is stacked with documents and paperwork.

'Legalities, insurance, and paperwork – it's a pain.' He pushes it to one side and sits down. I sit down opposite him.

'Monika says she can't do any more filming,' he says. 'Her auntie is very difficult, so I'm having to replace her and Ali, of course, with a couple of other guys. They're not as good, but they'll be fine.'

'Do you know her auntie?'

'Of course, they come to the food bank most days.'

'She has children?'

'She has four boys.'

'Do they work?'

Matt considers the question, frowns, and cracks his knuckles. 'They've done some bar work, stacking shelves, cleaning cars – they left school without much of an education. The system fails people like them – they're expected to go to university, but quite honestly, they'd be better off as apprentices.

You know, a mechanic, or a butcher, plumber, or electrician.'
He sighs. 'There's so much wrong with our country, Mikky.'

'Maybe the election will solve it.'

'A change in government won't change anything. The system has to change, and how we do things, but from my experience, no matter who is elected, they only serve themselves. You never see a poor politician – in any country in the world.'

'That's true,' I reply.

'There's poverty everywhere, Mikky. And, like many people with her background – education, family, and lack of support – Monika falls between the gaps. On the estates around here, it's normal. They are second- and third-generation unemployed, and they're bored. They have no job and no money. They go looking for fast money, which is invariably in drugs, and it gives them kudos and status in the community. And if they have to cheff someone to prove themselves to the gang bosses, then they do. They have no regard for human life, and they don't even care if they go to prison. They're desperate to prove themselves. To rise higher up in the gangs – and that means more money and better status.'

'And more violence?'

'Very often, yes.'

'It's an ever-spiralling circle,' I say.

'It's so easy to hook these kids in – that's the frustrating thing. I know, Mikky, because it happened to me. At first, I thought I was the big guy; you know, I had money in my pocket, and the girls were easy. I had new trainers, I could afford a hoodie, the best iPhone, and I had a decent place to live with regular meals, but then—' Matt breaks off.

'Then what?' I ask gently.

'Then they want more from you. The police start watching you, following you, and searching your body. It isn't enough to plug yourself with drugs, because other gangs know you, and suddenly you've got to protect yourself. You shove the drugs up your arse in case you get stopped by police or robbed by thieves, but they have eyes everywhere. There are risks and constant danger. The pressure builds. You've got to deliver and get paid. Half the junkies are stoned, so you've got to squeeze the money from them and run. Timing is everything, but then you have to prove you can look after yourself. You've got to keep the peace between the addicts and the gangs, and you've got to clean up. Then when you're told to stab someone, a traitor, or someone who's turned rogue, there's no backing out, Mikky. I know ...'

'And there's no one to talk to ... to turn to for protection – not even the police?'

'You can grass them up, but they'd kill you and your family.'

'But the police need to—'

'Mikky! It's terrifying – and worse, it's the Asian.'

'Did you know Monika and Ali were part of the gang?'

'I guessed. It isn't rocket science.' He sighs and cracks his knuckles, and the sound echoes in the confines of the small room.

'You were brave to get them away.'

'But it doesn't last. They got to Ali again. Look at what happened.' Matt grips his hands.

'So, what now?' I ask.

'What did Monika say to you?'

'Nothing. She clammed up. Adam is around, and she seems frightened.'

'Adam,' he repeats thoughtfully.

Matt is holding back on me. 'Do you know if he's in the cult, too?' I ask.

Matt shakes his head. 'It's hard to know what's going on, Mikky. Look at me. I'm just trying to run this place and get funding to look after as many people as I can. Can you believe I'm trying to sort out our Christmas fund-raising activity? Christmas carols and an auction for children's Christmas presents. Most of these kids won't even know or care it's Christmas.'

'Who's the main sponsor, the main fundraiser?'

'Raymond Harris and his wife.'

'His wife? Arlene?

'Yes, she's great. She helps out here sometimes. She and her friends do sponsored marathons and stuff like that to raise money. Why?'

'I'd like to talk to her.'

* * *

I spend the next few hours researching daggers and Arlene and Raymond Harris, then after Matt phones me, I find my way to a leafy suburb in Islington's upmarket area. It's a two-storey, white-painted brick house with warm, yellow lights on the front porch.

I ring the bell and wait.

I had thought Raymond Harris's wife, Arlene Elizabeth Harris, was younger. But today she looks in her early forties. She's well made up and wearing a printed patterned dress. Her doll-like face has been surgically enhanced, leaving her with a permanent expression of pleasant surprise, and when her lips curl in a smile, the skin on her face doesn't move.

I give her the benefit of a broad smile and hold out my hand.

'Hello, I'm Mikky dos Santos, I've been at the Dixon Trust working with Matt. Thank you for seeing me.'

'Come in; Matt called me.' She takes my outstretched hand, and her fingers are strong and boney.

'I'm a freelance journalist. I'm making a documentary on the *Parks*. I've been looking at the amazing work that Matt, and you, and your husband, of course, have been doing at the Dixon Trust. You know, all the parkour and the filming in Morocco – I was thrilled to be asked over there.'

'I don't do much at Dixon House.' She smiles vaguely. 'It's Raymond who you need to speak to. He's amazing. He has been extremely forceful with his stance for better housing conditions.'

'Well, quite frankly, I'd be delighted to be able to interview him. But I think he must be swamped with the election coming up. I'm thrilled to be here now with you.' I shiver dramatically on the cold doorstep, and pull my collar closer to my neck and hike my photography equipment higher onto my shoulder. 'Would it be possible for me to come inside? I'm frozen.'

Arlene opens the door, and I follow her down a polished oak floor to a kitchen, which appears to be the social hub of the house.

'I won't be able to tell you very much,' she calls over her shoulder.

'Matt says you and your friends have been amazing raising money with sponsored events.'

'Oh, that! That's nothing.'

There's a small red sofa, and an exercise bike pointed toward the terrace window, and a TV showing the BBC lunchtime news. There's also a crystal glass of white wine on the central island.

She sees me eying the glass with appreciation.

'I suppose with the election coming up that Raymond is working flat out?' I grin.

'I don't normally drink at lunchtime ...'

'Me neither. It is a rare luxury.' I rub my hands.

'Would you like some wine?'

'Well, I'm not driving. I'd love to, thank you. You're really kind.' I smile and place my camera case on the counter, watching her lithe, neat body as she moves toward the massive double-door American fridge in the corner of the room.

The bottle of expensive Chablis she pulls out is half-empty, and she pours a generous glass for me and slides it across the counter. I guess she's a fitness fanatic and a drinker.

'Cheers! This is lovely, Arlene – thank you.' The wine glides down my throat as smoothly as my lies glide out. 'Goodness, that's delicious.'

'Cheers.' She indicates for me to sit on the sofa and waits for me to speak. 'I only drink Chablis.'

I smile. 'Well, perhaps you could help me fill in the gaps about your husband?'

'Have we met before?' she asks.

'I was at the fund-raiser last week – the charity auction?'

'Oh yes.' She smiles and crosses her legs, clearly pleased. 'That was fun, wasn't it? We raised over £200,000 that evening. I paid for afternoon tea at the Ritz but then I donated it back again – we can eat there any time.' Her ringed fingers catch the light, and I spot a genuine and large diamond, as she waves her glass before sipping its contents.

I get straight to the point. 'I'm particularly interested in what drives Raymond – why is he so prolific – he's certainly trying to stand up against the criminals on the street. He's got *cojones.*'

'He believes in social justice – as I do.'

'He's got the support of the home secretary,' I say, winging it, after reading an article in the *Evening Standard* and other online sources. 'And, if you don't mind me saying so, he's very popular in the area – especially with all the work he's done with the young kids at Dixon House.'

She sighs. 'Raymond works hard. He's often late home for dinner. He works all hours. He's passionate about providing a safe place for the children. They're all victims, you know.'

'The Dixon Trust is amazing. I've been speaking to Matt and Claudia, and they sing his praises and say how remarkable he is. None of it would be possible without him.'

'Ah yes. They're also amazing. He couldn't have done it without Matt. They've drummed up lots of support within the local community and are achieving great results. I raise money for them, too, you know, finding sponsors when I run the marathon, and things like that.' She pauses, then asks, 'So, Mikky, what is it that you want to speak to Raymond about?'

'I'm making a documentary on some of the *Parks*. In particular, the ones I met in Morocco that were filming over there. Do you know the *Parks*?'

'Ah yes.'

'Do you know them personally?'

'Not particularly.'

'They're incredible, such talent.'

'I'm familiar with some of their skills.'

'It was such a shame about Ali,' I say. 'I can't believe it.'

She blinks hard, but her face remains pleasant.

'Did you know him?' I ask.

'I met him. I volunteer down there sometimes. I know some

of them at Dixon House – Ali used to come by quite often.' She toys with the stem of her empty wine glass. 'It's hit everyone very hard.'

'It must make Raymond more resolute to take a stance against poverty and the drugs gangs.'

'It does.' She takes a sharp intake of breath and stands up to fetch the wine bottle. She offers to refill mine, but my glass is still full. She shrugs, but fills hers and leaves the bottle on the floor by her feet.

'You're right. It was a shock. Ali was a lovely boy.'

'Do you think he committed suicide?'

She looks surprised. 'Of course – that's what the police said. Why?'

'He had so much to live for – he had plans. He told me in Morocco that he wanted to be a policeman.'

She smiles fondly. 'Ali was always a planner. He always had some new idea, and he was so full of enthusiasm. It was contagious. He was always upbeat and positive.'

'Do you think someone might have killed him?'

She appears to consider my question carefully before answering. 'He'd been mixed up with the drug runners, a few years ago, but we'd got him away from all of that. Matt has been brilliant with him, he'd done a fantastic job, but I don't know ...'

'Do you know who these bad guys are?'

She shakes her head. 'They work in small gangs, and you never know who is in the other ones. They're like small pockets that work independently.' She moves the wine glass in circles, rotating it in the air. 'They're very clever. Street smart.'

'But there must be someone in charge,' I insist. 'There must be someone who controls them all. Someone who masterminds it all, and decides on where and who they'll target with drugs.'

She nods in agreement, but her face remains unmoved with the same surprised, polite smile.

'I suppose so. The police are active – and the prime minister is eager to show results, especially before the election. The new home secretary is deploying even more officers to break up the drugs gangs. They used over 120 police officers last year – and twelve people were arrested in the north of England and went to prison.'

'They were shutting down the county lines,' I say, as if I know what I'm talking about. 'Apparently, they recruit young children and use them as drug mules to traffic drugs to addicts in other counties, so it makes them harder to catch. It often means that the different local police forces have to work together to catch them. But this gang in London – Islington – is controlled by the Asian.'

'The Asian.' Arlene mulls the name over, as if it's a disgusting and despicable flavour affecting the taste of her wine.

'Have you heard of him?'

'I've heard his name, yes, but I know nothing about him.'

'They think he's Chinese.'

'Really?' She gazes at me, and I imagine her in a few hours with a few more glasses of Chablis inside her and wonder if Raymond comes home to a drunk wife every night.

'Do you know anything about a cult?' I ask.

She shakes her head and pours the remaining Chablis into her glass.

'Nothing.'

'Have you heard about a tattoo some of the kids have?'

She shakes her head.

167

'Ali had one.'

'Did he?'

'Presumably,' I reply.

'I've never seen it.' She appears lost in thought, then she asks, 'How would I have?'

'Have you ever seen them doing parkour or freerunning?'

She looks up and appears surprised I'm still in her house. She's in a trance-like state, and I imagine her in the gym or on her exercise bicycle, in the early morning, without her make-up on and with her hair tied up.

'Do you go to the gym, Arlene?'

'Yes. Every morning.' Her lips appear slightly lopsided in a smile. 'Why?'

'I can see you really look after yourself.'

She squares her shoulders and almost slips off the sofa, completely unaware of the irony in my voice, and that's when I decide it's time for me to leave.

* * *

My phone rings and I reach into my bag to retrieve my iPhone.

'Where are you now?' Peter asks.

'I'm in a taxi heading to Bond Street.'

'What for?'

'There's a weapons specialist who knows a lot about swords and daggers and things. But guess what? I just went to visit Arlene Harris.'

'How did you manage that?'

'Matt arranged it for me. I went to their house.'

'Sandra was going to do that—'

'I know, but she's too busy.'

'So, how was Arlene?'

'Drunk.'

'Really?'

'I think she's bored. Raymond is out all the time, and she's paraded out when he needs arm candy.'

'Okay, I've got to go. Let me know how you get on.'

'What are you doing?'

'I'm with Sandra and Keith still on location – at the site. They're setting up the stunt landing mats. It's the minutiae of the details. We've got to make sure the *Parks* are protected, or they might hurt themselves – and we can't let that happen.'

'Peter?'

'Yes.'

'I'm not sure how else we can drive all this forward. There's no news on the person who was bundled into the Audi last week. No one is reported missing, and short of hanging around on street corners or becoming a drug addict again, I don't know how we can get through to the cult.'

'Stop worrying, Mikky. Everything will work out. It always does. You have to let things take their course. By the way, Aniela and Zofia are coming over next weekend, but we're going to have to cancel our visit to Blessinghurst Manor.'

'Why?' I reply.

'My uncle has been driving her mad with so much work since the baby was born. She needs a break and we have to visit my aunt in Scotland.'

'Scotland?'

'I'm picking them up at Edinburgh Airport.'

'Oh.' I'd been looking forward to seeing Aniela again and meeting Peter's baby daughter.

'Sorry! I can hear you're disappointed.'

'These things happen, I guess.'

'I'll see you later?'

'Yes. Perhaps you could speak to Adam? Try and get him away from the others – I think he knows something, Peter.'

Peter breathes heavily down the phone.

'Look, Mikky, if he won't speak to you, then he certainly won't speak to me. At least you've had a conversation with him, and you sketched him. Hang out at Dixon House, let them get used to your face, and they will trust you eventually. It's a waiting game.'

'Do you think?'

'With your gorgeous face, of course they will. It's just a matter of time.'

* * *

The taxi drops me outside an expensive shop in Bond Street. The Christmas lights have been switched on, and they are ribboned across the road, shining brightly. Instead of feeling Christmas cheer, I'm disappointed. Stella and her family not coming over from India, and now I won't get to see Peter's wife and new baby.

Inside, the shop is unusual. It has a mixture of expensive antiques, furniture, paintings, and book collections. Apart from a miniature Christmas tree in one corner, there's no evidence of the winter holiday looming on the horizon.

'Good afternoon. I'm Martin. How can I be of assistance?'

Martin is suave and dapper, dressed in a three-piece grey suit, with neatly gelled spiked hair.

I pull out the sketch of the images I made from Ali and Monika's tattoo.

'I want to purchase a dagger, like this. It's for my husband's birthday,' I lie.

I spend ten minutes talking to him about the original one made by Shah Jahan, the Mughal emperor who built the Taj Mahal for his wife.

'I believe the original dagger was sold by Bonhams in 2018, for $3.3 million.'

'This is very specific,' the expert Martin replies, studying my drawing. The Rolex on his wrist glistens under the bright lights. 'I'm not sure we can find anything similar—'

'I can go up to a million dollars, if necessary.'

He stares at me, and I wonder if he can smell alcohol on my breath.

'Well, I could check.'

'I'd appreciate that.'

'I'd need a deposit.'

'No problem.' I pull out my credit card.

He straightens his shoulders and smiles. 'Well, I can try and source something similar. May I take a copy of the drawing? A photograph?'

He places the sketch on the counter, lining it up in the light to study it more carefully, before taking a picture. He seems to take forever, and I fear my journey across the city has been wasted.

'I'm not sure of the price,' he says, handing me back the sketch.

'As I said, it's for my husband. If you could find something similar? Have you sold anything like this before?'

He flicks his head in denial.

'Never?' I persist.

'No.'

He's lying.

'But you might be able to source something similar for me?' I ask.

'This seems quite specific. And if it's something like this ceremonial dagger that you want, then you could get one made.'

Now he has my attention. 'Do you know someone who makes replicas?'

'Of course, there are specialists who could make something like this to order ...'

'Have you done that before?'

'I believe we might have done.'

'Very long ago?'

'I wouldn't know the date.'

'For a fraction of the price?'

'Yes, well,' he says with a cough, 'it depends.'

'My husband doesn't need to know.' I smile back at Martin.

'Perhaps not. Replicas can, I believe, be quite ... authentic.'

'Where can you—?'

'I'd have to investigate the matter.'

'Of course,' I reply, wondering what percentage he'd make on the transaction.

'Leave it with me. Let me have your number, Ms dos Santos. I'll give you a ring in a few days.'

* * *

I take the tube, and when I come out at the Angel Station, I'm surprised that it's already dark. The nights are drawing in, eleven days until the election on the 10th December, and only four weeks until Christmas.

It's a fifteen-minute walk from the station to Dixon House, but it clears my head. A replica dagger … and then I'm wondering what I will buy Marco for Christmas; something special, something momentous and deliciously exciting.

I turn a corner and Adam jumps out from a dark alleyway.

My heart races.

He whispers, 'Follow me.'

I duck into single file behind him, back down the alleyway, conscious of the high wall and barbed wire around us, as he leads me away from the estates and Dixon House. We pass houses, apartments, and business offices via a route of narrow alleyways, until finally we reach Regent's Canal and I'm reminded of the last time he brought me here.

Reassured by the quiet calm oasis of the canals amidst the busy noise of London traffic and cars, I call out, 'How far are we walking?'

'The canals are over eight miles long,' he replies over his shoulder, his hands dug deep into his pockets, but he slows his pace, so I catch him up.

'I love these painted houseboats.' He doesn't reply, so I ask, 'Do you still paint?'

'Paint?'

'Sketch, paint, draw? You have serious talent, Adam. This would be an ideal place to sit.'

He ignores me and pulls his hoodie further forward to cover his head. I glance around, noting the CCTVs, and pull off my hat, just in case Peter has to look for me.

'How did the filming go today?'

'Fine.'

'You finished early?'

'It was dark.'

173

'Where are we going?' I ask.

'Just keep walking.'

'No.' I stop and he turns around to face me. 'I'm not going any further until you tell me what's going on.'

'You want information, Mikky. I'm giving it to you.'

'What information?'

'I'm going to let you meet someone.'

'Who?'

'Badger.'

'Who is Badger?' I'm conscious of dog walkers, cyclists, and joggers dodging around us, and I stare up at the CCTV on the lamppost, as if I'm looking at Peter himself.

'Come on, Mikky. He's in the group.'

'In the cult?'

'Yes. He'll tell you what you want to know.'

* * *

Adam leads me away from the lights again, through more alleyways and backstreets, and I have no option but to follow him until I'm quite lost. We arrive in a quiet street, filled with garages and lock-ups. He pulls back a corrugated steel door and we step inside.

He fishes out his iPhone and switches on the torch.

'Mind where you step,' he says.

In the darkness, I can make out vague shapes. It's the inside of a garage. It smells of grease and oil, and there are various cars in different states of repair. I squint in the light, but there are no Audis.

Adam moves forward, and so I follow him cautiously, occasionally tripping over a stray hand tool discarded by one of the mechanics.

'Sit here,' Adam orders.

The iron seat, like one from an old school, is rickety and cold. I shiver. Suddenly, a light shines in my face, and I blink and turn away, shielding my eyes with my arm as they begin to water.

'What do you want to know?' a voice says out of the darkness.

'Um, can you please not shine the light in my face.' I mumble into my sleeve. 'This isn't an interrogation. I'm making a documentary – a film ...'

The light is switched off, and it takes me a few minutes to adjust once more to the small light that Adam holds on his iPhone. He's shining it at the floor between the stranger and me.

There's a vague outline of a figure that appears to be lean-ing/sitting on the bonnet of a car, and the room smells of weed. He's smoking a joint. When he takes a drag, I see the embers of the joint flame brightly, and he exhales slowly.

'Well?' he asks.

'Who are you?'

'Call me Badger.'

'Are you in the cult?'

'It's not a cult. We swear allegiance, and we look after each other.'

'Allegiance to who?'

'To ourselves. We're all brothers.'

'And sisters?'

'Of course.'

I strain my eyes to stare at him, but he's pulled a black stocking over his face to hide his features and to distort his voice. There's only a small hole for his mouth, where he inserts the joint and inhales.

'Does it have a name – this group?'

'It doesn't need one.'

'How many are in this group?'

He laughs as he exhales and spits on the floor. 'Loads.'

'How many?' I challenge him.

'Thousands.'

'All with a dagger tattoo.'

He laughs. 'Some.'

'What's the aim of your ... cu— brothers?'

'We're a pharmacy. The biggest pharmacy ...' He pulls out a knife over thirty centimetres long, and the steel blade shines under Adam's light, and Badger lays it beside him on the bonnet of the car, where it glistens menacingly.

'It's simple. It's business. It's supply and demand. They demand – and we supply.'

'Drugs?'

'Weed, coke, crack, heroin – you name it, we have it.'

'You sell to other addicts?'

His laughter is raw, and it slices across the darkness. 'Don't be stupid. Where have you been living? We sell it in clubs, bars, and restaurants. Everyone buys it.'

'Everyone?'

'Doctors, teachers, lawyers – pretty much everyone.' He steps toward me and my body tenses. 'It's quicker to order drugs than a takeaway pizza. Hold out your hand!' he orders.

I hold it out with my palm upward, trying not to shake, and Badger steps toward me. He drops a sugar cube into my hand, and I feel a surge of relief.

I sniff it. 'Crack cocaine?'

'Very good. It's yours for free.'

'No, thanks.' I offer it back to him. 'I don't use it anymore.'

He takes it from me and puts it in his pocket and laughs. 'You did use it?'

'Yeah,' I reply. 'A while ago. I'm clean now.'

'Respect!' he says, and moves away. 'But you're stupid!'

'Why?'

'I made $300,000 last year.'

'That's a lot of money.'

'You can imagine what my boss made.'

'Who is your boss?'

He laughs. 'Now, I'm not *that* stupid.'

'So, how does it work?'

His voice takes on a sense of pride, and he boasts, 'I train the kids. They've got to be young, maybe twelve or so. The younger, the better. They're easy to manipulate and easily impressed, and they like carrying knives; they think they're big when they carry a weapon.' He picks up the thirty-centimetre blade from the bonnet of the car and tosses it between his hands. 'You see, I've got to look after them. I train them to look out for themselves and each other. We've got to defend ourselves.'

'From who?'

'If you piss me off, step on my territory, you'll get shanked in the neck.'

'What if someone comes after you?'

'They've tried, but they don't come back a second time.'

'Because they're frightened?' I ask, trying to keep the fear out of my voice.

'Because they're dead.'

My mouth is dry. I can't form any saliva in my mouth, but I

can't show I'm scared.

'This is my life,' he continues. 'This is what we do. When you've watched a pregnant woman snorting coke, or a guy selling his arse for some weed, or an old man scratching about in the dirt to get his next fix, nothing bothers you. Sometimes, I kill them to put them out of their misery. Their world is shit anyway. I put my knife in their throat, or their heart, and I hear them cry out with relief when their body expires, gasping and sucking for air.'

It's Adam who next speaks quietly in the darkness. I'd forgotten he was there.

'Is that enough for your film, Mikky?'

I feel his hand nudging my shoulder for me to stand up, and I back away from Badger, who seems increasingly wired and erratic.

'You've got to be on your guard,' Badger says, spitting loudly. 'Anyone can come for you at any time.' He slashes the air with the blade. 'I'll cheff you, Mikky. I'll cheff anyone who comes near me ...''

I feel the blade in the air near my face and I duck backward.

'Come on,' Adam whispers, and he grabs my arm, pulling me quickly back toward the garage entrance. Behind us, the loud voice reverberates, punching off the corrugated iron as if it's a prophecy or a legacy that he believes himself, that he's genuinely invincible. 'No one messes with BADGER!'

Chapter 10

"There are crimes that, like frost on flowers, in one single night destroy character and reputation."
Henry Ward Beecher

Outside, I gasp in lungfuls of air. I'm wired, and my body is tense. We jog away from the lock-up, my shoulders hunched against the continuous rain and my hair soaking wet. I'm breathing heavily, and I'm shaking. We slow our pace, and I dig my hands into my pockets. I'm shivering.

'Was that what you wanted?' Adam asks.

His wet hair is plastered to his forehead, and his pale eyes look eerily translucent. 'Can you use it in your documentary?'

'Maybe.'

We walk in silence until we get back to the familiarity of Regent's Canal and my breathing returns to normal.

'Do you want a drink?' I ask him.

'No.'

'Aren't you cold?'

'No.'

'Aren't you afraid, Adam?'

'No.'

'Why not?'

'I'm not in their gang.'

'How come?'

'I'm protected.'

'Why?'

Adam doesn't answer, and we walk in silence.

'How are you protected, Adam?' I insist.

He stops outside the tube station. 'This is as far as I go,' he says.

'Why did you take me to meet Badger?'

'It's for your film.'

'What about Ali? Why wasn't he protected?'

'Take the tube,' Adam says. 'Go home.'

'Why won't you speak to me?'

'I don't know anything.'

'I think you do.'

He shakes his head and won't look at me.

'Are you filming tomorrow?'

'Yes.'

Without another word, he turns on his heel and walks away, disappearing into a flood of people carrying Christmas packages and heading home in the rush hour.

* * *

Peter is furious. He stomps around Josephine's penthouse, his prosthetic foot clanking on the wooden floorboards.

'What on earth possessed you to do such a stupid thing?'

'It wasn't stupid—'

'Do you know how dangerous these people are?'

'It was Adam who—'

'I don't care who it was, Mikky! You're making waves in the

community, and we're not supposed to be doing that.'

'I'm not making—'

'You are! Matt told me that you've been speaking to the *Parks* about the dagger tattoo. All it will take is for one of them to report back to their boss, or gangland head honcho, or the Asian, and you'll be dead!'

'I won't be dead—'

'Mikky!' Peter stops and stands in front of me. 'You're delusional. Joachin asked us to go to Morocco and investigate the dagger, that's all. Punto! Nada mas!' he emphasises in Spanish. 'We have no jurisdiction over here.'

'But what about you—'

'I'm helping on the film set as we originally agreed. We were making a documentary about the *Parks* and how parkour has turned their lives around, and I'm trying to keep our cover authentic, and you were supposed to be researching the dagger, but now I find that you're running off and you've disappeared with—'

'I don't want to be on set – I don't like heights.'

'That's not the point, and you know it!' Peter pulls out a dining chair and sits opposite me, our knees almost touching. He takes a deep breath and says in a quieter voice, 'We are not here to bust this cult, or this drugs gang or whatever they are. That's a matter for the Metropolitan Police, Mikky. All we have to do is to find out about the dagger, and we've done that.'

'We haven't found—'

'But you've hoodwinked me, Mikky. You said you were de-termined to make this documentary, but then you go charging off, down some backstreet canals to a warehouse to meet some crackhead with a knife, who by all accounts sounds like he was off his head …'

I attempt to speak, but Peter holds up his hand.

'I haven't finished, Mikky. This is dangerous territory. It's on the news every day; about the drugs, knife crime, kids disappearing into these houses where they're forced to do all sorts of things, and teenagers winding up stabbed on the street. You have to stop.'

'I trust Adam. He's not in the cult.'

'But he knows people who *are*.'

'He's protected,' I insist.

'Protected! There's no such thing! And now one of the cult members knows about *you*. He told you how much he earned, for heaven's sake!'

Peter hobbles over to the floor to ceiling windows and stares across London's skyline.

'You must promise me that you'll stay out of this, Mikky, or I will have to call Joachin,' he adds.

I rub my head. I'm tired. 'Okay.'

'Promise?'

'I didn't hoodwink you,' I growl.

'We have to tell the police what we've found.'

'Okay,' I reply meekly.

'Promise?' Peter frowns at me, and then his mobile bings. He pulls it from his pocket and reads the message. 'Oh no, I've got a feeling we're too late.'

* * *

Joachin insists on Skyping us. Peter and I sit side by side, staring at Joachin's face on the computer.

'I've received a complaint from Chief Inspector Mulhoon.'

182

Joachin's face is stern. He doesn't smile and there's no small talk or pleasantries. 'Mulhoon told me that Matt's unhappy. You're speaking openly to the *Parks* about this cult, and a dagger tattoo, is that true?'

'Matt's complained?' I ask. 'I don't believe it!'

'It doesn't matter who's complained, Mikky. Is it true?'

'Well, yes, I did mention it to them ...'

'Raymond Harris is also upset with you. He told the police that you went around to his house, without being invited, and started harassing his wife.'

'That's not true! She poured me a glass of wine. That's not harassment, and besides, she was drunk!'

'That's not the point, Mikky; I gave you clear instructions. Our jurisdiction only goes as far as Europe. In Morocco, you were supposed to get the *Parks* to trust you and to open up with interviews to find out about the dagger from a cultural viewpoint, on the off-chance that it had been stolen or was being used to initiate a cult ceremony—'

'And that's what I've done—'

'I told you not to get involved in police matters in the UK.' Joachin frowns at me.

Although we haven't always agreed, I've never seen him this angry before. I look at Peter for support, but he remains silent, and he won't look at me.

'What have you found out about this dagger?' Joachin asks.

So, I tell him the truth. I explain how we have compared a picture of Monika's tattoo, and one of Ali's, and how we were able to compare them. I also tell him how I had a poor replica of a dagger made in Morocco. 'Since then, through my diligent research, I've concluded that it's very similar to an original once owned by Shah Jahan, the Mughal emperor who built the

183

Taj Mahal.'

Joachin listens in silence until I finish.

'So, where is it?' he asks.

'The original was sold at auction for over $3.3 million.'

'Who bought it?'

'It's listed as a private collector, but I've asked a few friends to investigate for me who the private collector could be; my friend Marian Thoss might be able to—'

'Right, you must pass this information on to Chief Inspector Mulhoon first thing in the morning, and I want you as far away as possible from Islington and Dixon House. You must forget all this nonsense about making a documentary, and I want you to have no more contact with the *Parks*, is that clear?'

'Well,' Peter finally speaks up, 'they are filming tomorrow, and I have been instrumental in helping them with the action scenes. Sandra Worthington has been very appreciative, and she expects me there tomorrow ...'

'Okay. Well, take Mikky with you. Stay together at all times. Once the filming is over, I want you out of there, away from London. Is that clear?'

'Yes,' I reply.

'Yes, of course.' Peter almost salutes, but instead, he rubs his hand on his trousers.

When the screen goes blank, and Joachin's face disappears, I poke out my tongue. Peter catches me and says, 'Childish, Mikky. You really are so childish.'

* * *

As much as I'm impressed by the *Parks*, filming for me is a slow and tedious process. Everything has to be precisely 'in situ' – the actors, stunt people, equipment, and cameras – so I quickly lose interest.

Peter turns around regularly to make sure I'm still standing behind the cement column, which is my refuge and my protection against the wind. I return his smile and poke out my tongue.

I promised I'd stay with him today, but the novelty of filming is wearing thin.

I try Marco's mobile and realise he's probably at sea, but he will dock in a few hours in Split, Croatia – where we met last year and fell in love. I stamp my feet, impatiently wishing I'd thought to wear two pairs of socks.

I watch and wait, as the light fades to mid-afternoon, and although spotlights are erected, it's decided there isn't enough light to continue filming.

'We'll finish it in the morning,' Sandra cries out.

Peter rubs his hands together, and Matt nods at the *Parks* who wait to one side of the cameras, away from me.

There are murmurs of approval as the crew begins the process of packing up, and I wait, smothering a cold and tired yawn.

Matt joins us, smiling happily.

'It went well, didn't it?' he says.

'Brilliant.' I can't help my sarcasm, and he looks at me, not knowing what to say.

'Are you alright, Mikky?' he asks.

'Not really.'

I can feel Peter's heavy gaze on me.

'What's wrong?'

'I'm pissed off with you.'

'Me?' Matt sounds surprised, which makes me angrier.

'Yeah, you complained to Mulhoon about me.'

'The chief inspector?'

'Yes, the very one.'

'I didn't complain—'

'He said you did and that I'd been asking the *Parks* too many questions. You must have phoned him and—'

'I didn't phone him. He came to Dixon House.'

'Really? Why?'

Matt shrugs. 'I guess it's all to do with the election. He came with a couple of journalists yesterday after you'd gone.'

'And you complained?'

'Not exactly. I mentioned you were making the documentary and because Raymond Harris was with him, I thought maybe he could be interviewed—'

Peter interjects, 'We were told that you and Raymond Harris complained that we were harassing the *Parks* and Raymond's wife.'

Matt frowns. 'Why would I do that? I made the phone call for you to meet Arlene Harris, remember?'

I take a deep breath. 'True!'

Matt holds out his hand. 'Truce?'

'Yes.' I take his hand.

'You know I don't want you to ask too many questions, but I promise, I didn't complain.'

'We believe you,' says Peter. He slaps Matt on the shoulder. 'It's a shame we couldn't get up to the twenty-fifth floor – the wind is too strong – but tomorrow it's supposed to be calmer.'

'We're going to start at first light.' Matt rubs his hands; he's wearing a thick hoodie and cap. 'Come on, guys, who wants hot chocolate?' he calls out, and when the *Parks* appear, he adds, 'I'm buying!'

He winks at me, and they gather around him, and I'm conscious that Adam won't look at me. He's on his phone, and still sending messages as we all pile into the coffee shop and gather around the table.

Lisa is bubbly, and Joe is happily chatting to Peter, asking him about his experiences in the SAS. The two new boys aren't interested in speaking much, so I listen and watch Adam, who won't look up.

Matt returns with a tray of drinks and slides into the booth with us, sharing out the hot chocolate and coffee.

'I'm ready for this,' he says.

'Will we get paid for tomorrow?' asks one of the new boys.

'Sure you will, Mo,' Matt replies, blowing onto his hot chocolate. 'You get paid very generously, and they'll take it as a full day.'

'That's fantastic,' Lisa lisps, 'I'm going shopping next week.'

'What will you buy?' I ask.

'Clothes for our holiday.' She looks shyly at Joe but he just grins back at her.

'Where are you going?'

'Back to Morocco. We looked on the Internet and we've got a great deal, next week, at a hotel with all our food and stuff ...'

'Near where we were in Ouarzazate?'

'No,' Joe replies. 'It's somewhere near the coast.'

'Fantastic.' I smile.

Adam looks at me and frowns. His hot chocolate remains untouched, and he's gripping his phone tightly.

'Okay?' I ask quietly.

He doesn't reply. He sends another message on his phone.

187

'Monika didn't come today,' I say, throwing the comment out to them all.

Lisa shakes her head. 'She was meeting someone.'

'Oh? Like on a date?' I smile.

'No, it's one of her brother's friends ...'

'Stepbrother,' corrects Joe.

'Where were they going?' Adam asks, looking up from his phone.

Lisa looks at Joe, but he shrugs. 'Dunno.'

'Why?' I ask Adam. 'Is something wrong?'

'I haven't been able to get hold of her since last night.'

I glance at Peter, who toys with his coffee cup and doesn't say a word.

'She's probably out with friends,' Matt says cheerfully, tipping back his head and finishing his drink noisily.

Adam frowns and shakes his head.

I lean across the table and try and make eye contact with them all.

'Did you know the young guy they found in the canal last night?'

I can feel the anger in Matt's glare. He stands up quickly and gathers the cups together, keeping busy, brushing imaginary crumbs from the table.

'No,' Lisa says.

'It's nothing to do with us,' adds Joe.

One of the new boys, the Indian, says to me, 'Where are you from?'

The other new boy, Mo, says, 'Don't you get it, or are you stupid? You don't ask questions, or you'll be cleffed—'

'Or shot in the face,' adds Adam.

* * *

The call comes through to me just before midnight as I'm trying to sleep.

Marina Thoss, my friend and the daughter of Theo Brinkmann – the Belgian who trained me in forgery and selling on the black market – speaks quickly in English.

'Mikky? I've found the private collector.'

'Really?' I sit up in bed.

'Yes.'

'Great! Listen, Marina, I do appreciate you helping me with this.'

'You were always good to my father, Mikky. He said you were the most honourable thief and a pleasure to do business with—'

'I'm not a thief anymore. You know I'm with Europol?'

'Yes, I do, but I don't want to know anything else. It's no concern of mine.'

'Well, I do appreciate your help.'

'I know, we look after each other, you know that.'

'Yes.'

I know very well the unwritten code in the underworld of art theft and antiquities.

'Do you have a pen and paper?'

'Yes.'

'The shah's dagger was bought by auction from Bonhams for $3.3 million.'

'Do you have any pictures you can send me?'

'I'll email them to you.'

I hover the pen over the paper. 'I need to know who the private collector is – and where they live.'

'He's in Basel.'

'Basel – Switzerland?'

'Yes.'

'Do you have a name?'

'Jeffrey Bonnington.'

* * *

The Basel Christmas Market is busy as we cross Münsterplatz in the heart of the old city. We pass the massive decorated Christmas tree and weave our way through the small, rustic wooden chalets; stalls of waffles, grilled sausages, Swiss raclette, glühwein, and Basler Leckerli – a Swiss Basel spiced sweet bread similar to the British gingerbread.

I pause to look at some handmade jewellery, but Peter glances at his watch, so I hurry beside his limping gait, past the Basler Münster Church – Basel Cathedral – into Münsterberg and up to Freie Strasse.

The main shopping street of Basel houses all the luxury brands from Swiss watches to handbags, but I'm not tempted, as we're staying only a few hours in this beautiful Swiss city on the edge of the Rhine, on the French and German borders.

The cobbled streets and beautiful medieval and baroque architecture in Grossbasel, home to wealthier residents of the city, is south-west of the river, and we pause on the Mittlere Brücke to admire the towers of the Basler Münster Church before crossing into Kleinbasel, where it's trendy for young people to gather for food and drinks.

Our guest is waiting at a table near the bar. Peter recognises him immediately from our charity auction evening at the London hotel only last Tuesday. He marches over with his arm extended, and the older man stands to shake his hand. This gives me time to study the private collector, and I think that he now looks older than he did barely a week ago. He has long white hair, round black glasses, a neat goatee, and a crumpled green tartan jacket. He's a scientist and director of one of the world's leading pharmaceutical companies – Provartis.

'Jeffrey Bonnington,' he says, after we introduce ourselves. 'I'm delighted to meet you. Please sit here, and I'll order coffee.'

'Thank you.' I sit in the indicated leather seat, noting the colourful tropical birds painted on the wallpaper.

'I believe this is the "in" place to meet,' he says with a grin, revealing a gap between his front teeth. 'Did you know we're just around the corner from where Hermann Hesse wrote *Steppenwolf.*'

'I loved that book.' Peter removes his trench coat and crosses his legs. 'Thank you for meeting us.'

I slip my parka on the back of my chair, and we sit making polite conversation for ten minutes while we wait for our coffee to be served. While the men speak, it gives me a chance to watch the multimillionaire who so readily agreed to meet us at short notice.

'It's not a problem. I'm delighted. I've known Marina Thoss for many years,' Jeffrey says by way of explanation. 'I'm only too happy to help you.' He smiles and continues, 'You're lucky to catch me. I'm leaving for the Caribbean shortly. We spend a month there every Christmas to get away from the snow and cold – well, in my case, rheumatism and arthritis.'

'Do you have a big family?' I ask, as he pours coffee and cream for us. 'Thank you.'

'My wife, Stephanie, and our two boys and their wives and children.'

There are traces of damage on his skin, brown sunspots, but he doesn't look like he's ever been ill in his life and certainly not riddled with pains in his joints.

'Thank you for sparing us the time,' Peter says. He clears his throat. 'We won't keep you unnecessarily—'

'Let's cut to the chase,' Jeffrey says with a grin. 'You've come a long way to speak to me, and we can dispense with the formalities. You're interested in a cultural item that I have in my collection, I believe?'

He looks at Peter and then to me. His eyes are resting on my lips when he adds, 'It's no secret in the art world that I have a unique collection, but I don't broadcast it.'

'We're interested in a dagger that belonged to Shah Jahan,' I reply.

Jeffrey Bonnington's eyes narrow at the mention of the dagger.

I continue, 'It was the—'

'I know what it was,' he interrupts me, 'and I also know he built the Taj Mahal in homage to his wife.'

I ignore his sharp tone and say, 'Bonhams sold the original dagger ...'

'It was no secret that I bought it.' He bristles. 'It's not something that I brag about, but yes, I added it to my collection – my private collection.'

'Collection?' Peter leans forward.

'I buy artwork for the company and several banks, but this was for me. It's what interests me. I have a variety of swords, daggers, and knives. They're not to everyone's taste, but they are my, what shall we say, interest, passion, hobby?'

He shrugs and smiles, as if everyone was such an accumulator. His fingers are slim and well proportioned, and I imagine him in a laboratory bent over a microscope, analysing details of diseases, compounds, and remedies with the same intensity as reading the inscription on the shah's dagger.

'It's worth a substantial amount of—'

'Yes, I'm sure you know how much I bought it for; it was a few years ago, and it was an investment.'

'A valuable investment.' I'm determined to finish at least one sentence.

He stares at me. 'I'm sure you've done your research, and you have probably investigated my background, too, and you will know that I inherited a considerable sum of money from my father's property investments. In turn, I developed an interest in pharmaceuticals and my own company merged with Provartis in 1996, and to this date, I am still a member of the board and own a considerable number of shares.'

'You don't have to explain your finances to us.' Peter stirs his coffee.

'Where is your collection?' I ask.

Jeffrey Bonnington looks surprised but he recovers and answers quickly, 'My private collections are in various places. I'm not naive enough to have them on display in my house.'

'You mean they're in a bank vault or somewhere safe?' I persist.

He pauses before answering.

'If you're referring to the shah's dagger, then I can assure you that it is firmly in my possession.'

'In Switzerland?'

'You'll have to take my word for it.'

'May we see it?'

'That won't be possible.' He pulls back the cuff of his sleeve and regards his Rolex for a few seconds, long enough for it to be a hint. 'I am in rather a hurry.'

I lean forward.

'We just need to know that the original is definitely in your possession and that it hasn't been stolen.'

'Stolen?'

'Yes. I saw one a few days ago in London,' I lie.

He stares at me, then glances at Peter. 'That's impossible.'

'When did you last see the dagger?' I ask.

He doesn't answer immediately, and then he asks slowly, 'Did it have the nasta'liq inscription on the blade with the official title, date, and place of birth of Shah Jahan?'

'Yes,' I lie. But I've done my research, and I add, 'It also had the honorific parasol, and you know what that is ...'

'The ancient pan-Asian symbol of royalty and divinity.' He rubs his nose with his forefinger.

'Yes.'

He drains his coffee and places the small cup back on the saucer.

'Look, I can tell you that my dagger, the original, is safely locked away. Now, is that everything?' He looks around for the waiter to ask for the bill, but Peter raises his hand first to get the attention of the well-dressed barman.

I reach into my bag and I pull out two photographs, both A4 in size, that Marina Thoss had so thoughtfully emailed me last night. One image shows the dagger, and the second shows a close-up of the blade and the inscription is legible. I place them silently on the table.

'This is what you purchased at auction.'

Jeffrey Bonnington leans forward and, pushing his glasses

further onto his nose, he inspects the images, tilting the coloured pictures to see them better.

I then show him my sketch of Monika and Ali's tattoos.

'Where did you get this?'

'I was with the person who has this dagger.'

He places my sketch back on the table. 'It's not real. It's been tampered with.'

'I can assure you that—'

'If you are here to blackmail me, or to try and get money out of me, it won't happen. I have given you my time willingly, but this is too much ...'

He stands up and reaches for his coat.

Peter also stands up. 'We are not here for the money. We just need information. A lot of lives depend on it.'

Jeffrey pushes his arms into his coat. 'The dagger, the original Shah's dagger that I purchased, is safe—'

'Do you think this is a good imitation?' I stand up and face him.

'Perhaps,' he replies grudgingly. 'Perhaps.'

'Where is the original?' I ask.

'I can't tell you. It's safe. Good afternoon and thank you for the coffee.'

'Wait!' I say; he stops and turns to look at me. 'Where would you get a replica made?'

'I wouldn't. I don't need to.'

＊ ＊ ＊

He's at the door of the cafe when I catch up with him.

'Mr Bonnington, is it a coincidence that you were in London last week at a charity event for Raymond Harris?'

195

'What do you mean coincidence?' He pauses, blocking the entrance, and then steps aside as the door opens and another client enters.

'Let's go outside?' I suggest, and he stands aside to let me pass. I wait for him in the street, and Peter follows. I tuck my parka into my neck against the cold.

'Mr Bonnington, I know that you're familiar with Islington and that you support the politician Raymond Harris—'

'It's no secret.'

'But tell me something – don't you think it's more of a coincidence that the dagger you claim to have in your private collection is being used as a cult talisman to initiate children into drugs gangs in London?'

'What? I don't know what you're talking about.'

'Your dagger is a symbol of intimidation for young kids. These very children that Raymond Harris is determined to protect. He's involved in the Dixon Trust that is a haven for these children.'

Jeffrey Bonnington looks bemused. He replies, 'I think you've come a long way for nothing. You're certainly on the wrong track if you think I or Raymond Harris are involved in any illegal drug trade. I haven't spent my whole life fighting to improve the drug trade – legally developing antidotes to diseases and illness around the globe, fighting infections – only to be accused of being involved in a sinister underworld of illicit drugs involving children born into poverty. It simply isn't my style.'

Peter holds out his hand. 'Thank you. And I'm sorry that we have offended you. We just wanted to ensure that your dagger was firmly in your private collection where it belongs. You can see how worried we were when we saw this one. It's the image of the one you own.'

'It might be a replica. But I can assure you this has absolutely nothing to do with me, and if you want to take it up with anyone, then speak to Chief Inspector Mulhoon at the Met. He will vouch for me.'

'Thank you. I'm sure that won't be necessary.' Peter's smile is sincere as he shakes Bonnington's hand, while I keep my hands firmly in my pocket.

'Well, I'll be telling Mulhoon about your visit,' he says, tugging his collar closer to his neck. 'Good day to you both.'

* * *

We stop at the Christmas market for grilled sausages and glühwein. Although we've been awake and travelling since before dawn, I'm not hungry. But I do need fresh air. All around us, people wear bobbled hats, mittens, and scarves; they huddle companionably at barrel tabletops, enjoying the warmth of nearby fires.

'That was a waste of time,' I mumble to Peter.

He's ordering us a snack and drinks.

'What did you expect?'

'I don't know. He's a pompous ass, and on top of it, he's going to speak to Mulhoon, who in turn will get onto Joachin, and he'll know we were in Basel. He'll also find out that I lied about the dagger, telling him that I'd seen one in London exactly the same.'

Peter laughs and bites into the spicy sausage. 'It could only happen to us – well, to you, Mikky. It was a bit of a wild goose chase to come here.'

'He wouldn't even tell us where he keeps his collection. He's ex-directory, and even Marina didn't have a home address for him. He uses a Swiss bank as his secure address, which you couldn't hack into even if you wanted to—'

'You have to let it go, Mikky.'

'He was playing with us,' I complain. 'It was awful.'

'We didn't factor into account that he inherited lots of property, and although his main home is here in Switzerland, the dagger could be as far away as the Caribbean.' Peter raises his empty glühwein glass to the bearded man behind the stall for a refill.

'The dagger could be stashed away in a bank vault here in Basel,' I add.

'Based on all the collectors and people that you've met, what does your instinct tell you?' Peter asks.

I shrug and take the glass he offers me. 'Thank you. Erm, I'm not sure. It depends on how close Jeffrey is to his wife and family ...'

'In what way?'

'Well, if you were married to him, would you like a roomful of weapons on display? Or would you say, "Jeffrey, please ..."' I imitate a woman with an affected high voice. '"Go and put your toys in your room. Our guests don't want to play with those nasty, dangerous weapons"?'

Peter laughs.

'Do you think he's worth looking into?' I ask. 'Should we dig deeper?'

'To what purpose? What now? We know Jeffrey Bonnington owns the original dagger, but so what?'

'Well, Jeffrey says he has the dagger; do you think we've spooked him enough so that he might go and check his collection to make sure it hasn't been stolen?'

'Stolen? We can't spend days here following Jeffrey Bon-nington. He might make a phone call to someone to check. Besides, I don't think that the dagger used by the drugs gang in London is authentic. Maybe someone – the Asian – just modelled it on this dagger because he saw it on the Internet and he had a replica made.'

'Do you think Jeffrey will contact us if the dagger has been stolen?' I ask.

'I think he's more likely to contact his insurance company ...'

'How do we even know the Asian has a dagger?' I complain and drain my glass, looking expectantly at Peter, but he's ignoring me.

'I think we have a problem,' he whispers, and turns his back away from the crowds. 'We're being followed.'

Chapter 11

"Little crimes breed big crimes. You smile at little crimes and then big crimes blow your head off."
Terry Pratchett

'Who would follow us?' I ask Peter.

We both stand facing the food stall, with our backs to those around us. We've moved naturally close together, as if we're lovers, and I lean my head against Peter's shoulder so we can speak quietly.

'Who knows we are here?'

'What do they look like?' I ask.

'Beard, five-eight, brown coat, green cap.'

I reach into my bag and raise the iPhone to take a selfie of us, trying to gauge the people around us, but there's no one matching Peter's description of the man, so we move again, a different angle – another selfie – to survey the scene around us.

'Come on, let's go and get some waffles,' Peter suggests, taking me by the arm.

'I feel sick,' I reply.

'Play along,' he whispers, guiding me to a sweet-smelling stall, where he orders two waffles with chocolate.

'Hold these,' he says, passing the sweet chocolate to me, then he disappears, leaving me standing alone in a crowd of Christmas shoppers.

I wait, glancing around, my photographer's eye taking in the smallest detail, the fleeting glance, the subtlest of movements, and then I spot the bearded man.

He fakes interest in a ceramic dish on a nearby stand, then glances at me, but I move away. He follows me, very slowly, checking the distance each time, careful not to alert me.

I catch a glimpse of Peter, who has manoeuvred himself so that he's positioned on the far side of the man. I toss the waffles in the bin, then move quickly – the man appears to realise, and he turns around to run, but Peter blocks his path.

I grab the man's hand and press my phone into it.

'Thief!' I shout, holding my phone in his hand. 'He's taken my iPhone.'

The man's mouth opens in disbelief just as Peter takes a step forward. There's scuffling, someone shouts, I scream, and then Peter's reassuring voice says, 'It's alright. I've got him.'

Peter has the man's arm tucked firmly up behind his back and shouts in Swiss German, 'It's alright, I've got him. Police!'

And, without waiting, Peter marches the man securely from the market and into a cobbled quieter backstreet.

I linger awhile at the market, and I reassure people nearby that I'm okay and have my iPhone back, and because it's Christmas and it's a festive atmosphere, it's quickly forgotten and I make a swift exit.

In the backstreet, Peter has the man pinned against the wall while expertly patting him down.

'Who are you?' Peter asks first in English, then Swiss German, holding him against the wall, but the man doesn't reply.

'He's the kind one,' I whisper to the man. 'But I'm not so nice. You're following us – why?'

He refuses to answer, so I grab his balls and give them a gentle squeeze.

He cries out.

'Just tell us who asked you to follow us.'

'Herr Bonnington.' His voice is husky, and his eyes begin to water as I squeeze.

'Jeffrey Bonnington?'

He nods.

'Why?'

'He wanted to make sure you were leaving.' His accent is heavy.

'Leaving Basel?'

'Yes.'

'Why?'

He shrugs. 'He didn't tell me.'

I squeeze.

'Arrggg ...'

I stop and ask, 'Who are you, police?'

'Nein, nein, nein ... I'm his secretary.' He sounds breathless.

'Good! Then maybe you can tell us where Jeffrey Bonnington keeps his weapon collection?'

He shakes his head. 'Nein! I don't know. I don't—'

I squeeze.

'Arrgghh, not here. It's not here in Basel.'

I stop squeezing. 'Where?'

'I don't know, I promise, but it's not in Switzerland.'

* * *

On the train from London Heathrow into the city, Peter says, 'There's a message from Keith. Filming was delayed today because of the weather. So, they're filming in the morning.'

'Maybe we should check out where Jeffrey Bonnington has his homes. Then it's a process of elimination.'

'Mikky, what's the point?'

'To check the dagger ourselves, to see if the real one is in his collection.'

Peter sighs. 'I don't know if that will make much difference. You're not going to steal it. There's no point in going down that route.'

'Mulhoon's officers found out about a dagger, that's why he asked us to find it. Now, I'm sure there's a link to this dagger and the Asian. There's too much of a coincidence, you know, with Jeffrey Bonnington turning up at the charity auction in support of Raymond Harris.'

'You've forgotten the most important aspect, Mikky. Raymond is fighting street crime. He's hardly likely to be involved in supporting the Asian and increasing the drug war in his constituency.'

'Okay, that's true. You have a point.'

'So, what do we do now?' he asks.

'I think we have to go back and trace Ali's steps from the moment that he arrived back in London. We know he went to his foster family, he saw Kiki, and he also saw his father. But we need to know what he found out. If we are right in our assumption that he knew something and he was ready to tell the police, then we need to know what it was. Who else did Ali meet? He'd been with us in Morocco, and there was nothing to suggest he knew anything then.'

'We'll have to tread very carefully,' he says, just as the train pulls into the station. 'Very carefully indeed.'

'Can you ask your friends to help? Maybe he used a credit card, or can you track Ali's phone calls?'

Peter sighs. 'We can try.'

'I'm worried about Monika,' I add. 'She went off with Adam.'

'Adam is her friend,' Peter reminds me.

'Maybe we should pay a visit to Dixon House?'

'It's too late now, Mikky. Let's go home and get some rest.' Peter's phone pings and he glances at the message. 'Oh no, I think the proverbial mess has just hit the fan,' he says.

'Really, why? Who is it?'

'Joachin is in London. He wants to meet us in an hour.'

'Does he know about our trip to Switzerland?'

'Not unless Jeffrey Bonnington has complained already to Mulhoon.'

* * *

Joachin isn't happy. He's like a severe judge in a courtroom. He's scowling and his normal amenable affability has gone. We sit at a table in the corner of the pub, very near the Angel in Islington, ten minutes' walk from Dixon House and fifteen to the estate. I'm wondering if he'd like to see the area and meet Matt, but I don't ask Joachin. He's monosyllabic and uncommunicative, and he waits for Peter to return with our drinks.

'Gin and tonics all round, I got us doubles.' Peter beams at us both as if there's nothing wrong.

'Cheers.' I raise my bulbous glass and tap it against his and Joachin's, not waiting for them to raise their glasses. I relish the taste on my tongue and smack my lips as if it's the last drink before my prison sentence.

'That tastes good.'

Joachin leans forward and twists his wedding band around his finger. 'I made it very clear that we have no jurisdiction here in the UK. We're no longer part of what's going on in this country, and until the election is over next week, we have to be very careful and tread cautiously—'

'But—'

He holds up his hand to silence my interruption, waits, and then toys with the stem of his glass. 'The thing is, is that there have been complaints about your behaviour. You have put children's lives at risk—'

'But—'

He holds up his hand again. 'Mulhoon is seriously pissed off with you both. Matt has complained that you're using the children and working out of Dixon House, and now … and now it transpires you took it upon yourselves to fly to Basel and harass one of the world's most prolific and revered scientists.'

'Jeffrey Bonnington is hiding something,' I say.

Joachin shakes his head. 'It doesn't matter. He's out of bounds.'

'But he doesn't live in England — that's why we went to Basel,' I argue.

'Mikky! Stop! He's out of bounds because he is *not* involved in the seedy, gangland, county drug wars in England.'

'He might—'

'He might nothing!'

'He owns the original dagger that the gang here swears allegiance to, and we thought that perhaps his dagger – the original one he owns – had been stolen.'

I pull the pictures I'd shown Jeffrey Bonnington out of my

bag and lay them on the small round table between us.

Joachin glances down at the photographs.

'Is this important?'

'This is what we do, remember? We find fakes and forgeries. We thought we were doing him a favour, by alerting him to the fact that his dagger might have been stolen from his collection.'

It's a wild presumption on my part, but I play my role well.

Joachin inhales deeply. I can see him still glancing at the printed images on the table, not wanting to get hooked into my tale.

'Bonnington insisted that it hasn't been stolen,' adds Peter. 'Which is incredibly strange, considering he paid $3.3 million for it.'

'What's strange about that?' asks Joachin.

'He didn't even want to check,' I reply. 'Wouldn't you?'

'He wouldn't tell you if he did check, would he?' Joachin counters with a frown.

'It's a crazy sum of money for a dagger.' Peter sips his gin.

I know that Peter has no appreciation of collectors and the amounts of money they would pay and the lengths they would go to acquire something they wanted; call it greed, passion, desire – to him it's an illness, like alcoholism or drug addiction.

'Perhaps the cult members swear to a *similar* dagger. It can't be the original,' Joachin says. 'Although it may be an excellent fake.'

'I'm looking into that,' I reply.

Joachin glances down at the photographs again. 'You are?'

'Yes.' I think of Martin, the assistant in Bond Street, and make a mental note to call him tomorrow.

'How did Jeffrey report us? Through Mulhoon?' Peter asks. Joachin looks up, surprised. 'Yes.'

I glance at Peter and then back at Joachin.

'This seems to be a coincidence. Everything keeps leading back to Mulhoon.' Peter scratches his chin.

'He's the investigating officer.'

'He's not getting very far,' I argue. 'What if we have a problem with the police?' I whisper, glancing over my shoulder to make sure we are not overheard. 'What if, after Ali returned from Morocco, he wanted to tell the truth. What if he wanted to go to the police and tell them everything about the Asian and the drugs gang, and he set up a meeting, but the police betrayed him?'

Peter stares at me like I've gone crazy, and so I continue.

'What if whoever Ali spoke to – a policeman – sold him out and back to the Asian? The Asian knew where to find him. The Asian was going to kill him, but Ali wouldn't give him the satisfaction, so, unfortunately, he killed himself.'

'Mikky, this is ridiculous—' Joachin holds up his hand.

'What if someone or maybe even a few police officers are bent? What if they're on the same side as the Asian?'

'Mulhoon isn't!' Joachin argues. 'It's impossible.'

'Maybe not, but there is at least one person who betrayed Ali.'

'You have no evidence at all, Mikky. This is all guesswork. You're going from one theory to the next.' Joachin smacks his glass on the table.

'Mulhoon lost two undercover officers. Someone must have betrayed them!' I whisper urgently. 'It's Mulhoon who knows you, and Raymond and Matt.'

'How well do you know him?' asks Peter.

207

'Mulhoon? We met years ago at a European conference when the political climate was less tense; we have worked well together in the past, but now ...' Joachin's sentence trails off as he looks at Peter and then to me. 'You must stop with these ridiculous ideas. You have no evidence of anything and you're just stabbing at ideas in the dark.'

'That's not very appropriate,' I say, taking the moral high ground.

'You know what I mean.' Joachin shakes his head. 'Now, I forbid you to get any more involved with this business. Stay away. Leave London – go to Blessinghurst Manor or go sailing around the world with Marco. But you can't stay here.'

* * *

In the morning, when I wake up and shuffle into the lounge, Peter is at the computer.

'Have you been here all night?' I yawn and place strong black coffee for him on the table.

'I slept for a few hours.'

'You need to shave,' I suggest. 'Aniela doesn't like you with too much stubble, remember?'

Peter grins. 'Thanks for reminding me, but we just Skyped, and she seems to think I am still hot.'

'How's the baby?'

'Gorgeous, more and more like me every day.'

'A hairy little girl? Lovely.

Peter laughs. 'No, devastatingly handsome.'

'Umm, she definitely must take after Aniela or perhaps the baby isn't yours. What does the milkman look like?'

'We don't have a milkman.'

'Umm ... postman?'

'She's female.'

'Ah, well I don't know what to think – maybe it's a genetic thing. Are your mother and father attractive? I guess they must be, and the genes skipped a generation to your daughter!'

'Do you want some good news?' he asks.

'You've been away for a few weeks. Is Aniela pregnant again?'

Peter laughs. 'Not yet! Why don't you switch on the TV?'

'Why? Are you tired of speaking to me?'

'You might find it interesting.'

I pick up the remote and find the news channel, and it's filled with pre-election promises, political gaffs, and interviews with junior ministers. There's one person whose face is very familiar.

'Raymond Harris,' I mumble under my breath.

Peter stops tapping his keyboard, and we listen to the conversation on the screen.

'It's imperative that we have more social housing in our society. We need to provide for the homeless. We have far too many millionaires already—'

A female from the opposition party interrupts him. 'But we need foreign investment in the country. Just because we left Europe, it doesn't mean we don't welcome our overseas investors—'

Raymond's eyes darken. 'You mean Russian oligarchs—'

'I mean people who bring wealth to our city—'

'It isn't their wealth we need. We need a government who helps ...'

'If I can interrupt you both there,' the newsreader says with a smile. 'Thank you for coming on the programme today to

209

discuss the plans for the vacant building in Islington. It's an eyesore for the locals. Our politicians can't agree. Should it be a multimillion-pound high-rise investment for rich millionaires who want to invest in our country? Or a place for hundreds of British people who can't afford their own home – this could be a valuable opportunity for the local homeless people and those living on the breadline in north Islington. Send us a message on Twitter or contact us by email. Thank you for your insight today. I'm sure this will be resolved soon, perhaps even before the election. Meanwhile, let's see what's happening outside where you are. Here's Alan with the weather ...'

As the camera pans to the daily forecast, Peter reaches to mute the volume.

'That's the building where Sandra is filming,' I say. 'I didn't know there was such controversy about it.'

'Neither did I,' Peter says with a grin. 'But that newsreader certainly got under Raymond's skin. He appears very angry. He wants the building for the people in his constituency – and we both know why.'

* * *

It's mid-morning. I can't contact Marco as he's still at sea, so I'm comparing daggers – quality and engravings.

Peter stands up from his computer and walks over to the window, staring out across the London skyline.

'Are you okay?'

He scratches the bristles on his chin and then turns his attention to me. 'We've got a problem,' he says softly.

'What sort of problem?' I close the lid of my laptop, because when Peter is serious, I know there's trouble.

'I've been looking at CCTV from the night Ali died. Come and have a look.'

We sit at the table together, and I study the screen.

'Here's the grey Audi, with the same registration you gave me, the night you saw that boy abducted from the flats. Then here's Raymond Harris's office in Islington. It's a five-minute walk from the Angel, where we met Joachin last night. Look, the car is parked in the same street. You can see part of the front car number plate, so we can assume it's the same car. We can't see who gets in or out but look here ...' He points at footage from another CCTV camera.

'I recognise his walk and his mannerisms,' I mumble. 'He's also wearing his flying jacket over his hoodie.'

Ali is walking confidently in the same street as Raymond's office, with his grey hoodie over his head and his hands in his pockets.

'Did Ali go and see Raymond Harris after he came back from Morocco – the night he died?'

'We can't see that he actually goes inside Raymond's office. But Ali disappears for fifteen minutes between the CCTV camera at this end of the street, and this camera at the junction of the next road. It's 18:22 here, and 18:37 here.'

Peter pulls out a map.

'Here is the Audi.' He uses a stub of his finger to point. 'And here is Raymond's office.'

I stare at the map, imagining the street view in my head.

'Ali didn't take fifteen minutes to walk that short distance and there's no pub or other buildings he could have gone into, so he must have gone into Raymond's constituents' office.'

'Was the car following Ali?'

'I don't think so. It's facing in the opposite direction,' Peter explains.

'The occupants of the car didn't follow Ali?'

'It was already parked in the street.'

'The people in the Audi knew Ali was heading to Raymond Harris's office?' I ask.

'Perhaps.'

'So, I was wrong – it wasn't a corrupt policeman that tipped off the Asian and told him where to find Ali,' I muse, 'but Raymond?'

'Not necessarily, but it could possibly be someone who works in Raymond's office.'

While Peter and I sit watching the CCTV recording again in silence, I think about the implications of the possible involvement of one of Raymond Harris's employees in the drugs cartels.

'You know what this means,' I say.

'What?'

'Ali knew something.'

'What could it be?' asks Peter.

'I don't know, but I have to find the Asian quickly or none of these kids will be safe.'

'We should tell Joachin.' Peter taps his fingers on the table. 'It's the right thing to do.'

'His friend is Chief Inspector Mulhoon. None of them will want a political scandal before the election next Tuesday.'

Peter doesn't reply.

'We can't trust anyone,' I add.

'What do you propose?'

'Can you check Ali's phone record and see who he contacted? Who did he phone that afternoon? We need to find out how high this goes; Mulhoon said he lost two men – two undercover officers. Someone must be supplying information to the Asian.'

'But would Raymond Harris have known about them?'

'I doubt it – maybe – who knows? But it must be someone quite high up to have that level of information,' I say.

'Ali must have found something out – and that level of information cost him his life.' Peter looks at me.

'If the Asian is a paid employee, then there's someone higher.' I lean toward Peter and list on my fingers. 'We need to find out who Ali met, find the Asian, and if there's a dagger we have to steal it.'

* * *

The following day, the filming is finally over, and I'm walking down the road, arm in arm with Peter, heading for the tube station when I hear my name called. I stop and turn around. Adam has caught up with us, and although he's not out of breath, he's breathing heavily.

'I'm worried about Monika.' His pale blue eyes remind me of a frightened animal.

'Why?' replies Peter.

'She's not answering her phone.'

'Maybe she's busy.' Peter moves on and tugs my arm, so I walk with him.

'She still hasn't shown up, and it's the second day.' Adam's pale face is distressed.

'She probably wants to be on her own,' Peter replies.

'It's not that.' Adam places a hand on Peter's trench coat. 'We had a code. A signal – but she's not responding.'

213

'What's the code?' asks Peter.

Adam looks at me when he replies, 'She's to mention pizza in a message, you know, like ask me for a pizza. Then when I say, Four Seasons, she replies Margarita.'

'So?' says Peter.

'She hasn't replied.'

'Did you ask her for pizza?' I ask Adam.

'Yes, last night. I wanted to make sure she was okay. She was really pissed off with her auntie again. She said she couldn't film with us and couldn't be involved with the *Parks*. She was going home to speak to her mum—'

'So, you haven't heard from her at all today?'

Adam shakes his head. 'I called her first thing and then whenever we had a break, but she's not answering at all.'

'Maybe she's busy, or she's found another friend.' Peter attempts to pull me away.

'No! She would always talk to me. Especially—'

'Especially what?' I ask.

'Especially after what happened to Ali.'

'Come on, Mikky. Maybe she wants to get away from all of this.'

'Peter, stop!' I unhook my arm from his and stand glaring at him. 'What if they've taken her?'

Peter stares back at me and then replies slowly, 'Why would they do that?'

'Because,' says Adam, and we both turn to look at him, 'because she wants out, and she was ready to tell the police everything. She came up with this crazy idea that the police would give her immunity and a new identity, and that she could live somewhere else in the world if she told them everything.'

'Everything about what?' asks Peter.

Adam glances over his shoulder before he whispers, 'About the Asian.'

'Is that what Ali was going to do?' I ask.

Adam won't look at me, so I take a step forward.

'You must be honest with us, or we can't help you. Tell us, did Ali go to the police? Did he want to get out?'

'I don't know! Ali was different. He was braver.'

'If you know so much, why don't you tell us everything?' I ask.

'I don't know anything,' Adam protests. 'I'm not one of them.'

'You certainly risked Mikky's life the other night – with your friend Badger.' Peter snarls.

'Badger wouldn't have hurt her. Besides, I would have looked after her—'

'But we didn't know that, did we.' Peter walks menacingly toward Adam. He pulls his hands from his trench coat pocket, and in a nanosecond, Peter pushes Adam against the wall and is holding his arm across his throat. He pulls up his hoodie and tugs Adam's T-shirt from his jeans.

'Peter!' I shout, but he pushes me away with his elbow, and I realise what he's doing. Holding Adam securely across the throat, he scans Adam's chest for a dagger tattoo.

'There isn't one,' I say, leaning closer to look at Adam's chest.

Peter lets Adam go.

'Do you believe me now?' Adam tucks in his clothes.

'Not until you tell me who Badger is,' Peter replies.

Adam pauses before whispering, 'He's my brother.'

* * *

215

'Could this have anything to do with the body that turned up in the canal?'

'Mikky!' Peter admonishes me in front of Adam.

'We've got to save her,' I argue.

'No, Mikky. It's not happening! You're not going near Badger or any of the other gang members, I mean it. And that's final!' Peter says. 'Don't storm off, Mikky. That's what you always do; you walk away and then do your own thing and get into danger!'

'I don't!' I stop and turn around.

Peter walks toward me and says in a reasonable tone, 'Look, we can't get involved.'

'Says who?'

'Joachin.'

'Since when did you turn a moral corner? Where's the adventurous veteran I met last year?'

'He grew up. He has a family now.'

'Oh, so that's it? That's what's stopping you—'

'It's not stopping me—'

'Of course it is! What if that was your daughter they'd taken? What if it was Aniela or Zofia who was being held against their wish?'

Peter doesn't reply, so I press on.

'Monika doesn't have a father, mother, or sister to protect her – she has no one, and she'll end up at the bottom of the canal just like all the other poor kids who've had a rotten start in life—'

'This isn't about them, Mikky. It's about you, isn't it?' Peter holds my arms and squares me to face him.

'You had a shite upbringing, Mikky, I know that. Lots of people do, but you can't save them all. You can't be everyone's sister, mother, or best friend.'

'She came to me in Morocco, and she trusted me. She told me what they've done to her—'

'I know. I'm sorry.' He lets me go.

'Then help me, Peter. Please! Look, the police won't do anything now because there's no proof she's missing and her auntie won't report it, but if I can get into their gang, find her, and find the Asian, then you can call the police and come and find us. It's simple. Let's not overcomplicate it.'

'You think you can walk into their seedy place, wherever it is, confront the Asian, and ask for Monika to be set free? Are you I or stupid?'

'No, but I can threaten him.'

'How?'

'I'll wear a camera. You can view everything and relay it back to the police. I know you can stream it live on the Internet if you want to, we can video it all.'

'He'll shoot you.'

'He won't.'

'Why not?!'

'Because I'll tell him that I can get the real dagger for him.'

'What?'

'I'll tell him that I can steal the real dagger that once belonged to the shah.'

Peter laughs. 'He doesn't want a dagger! He deals drugs.'

I square my shoulders. 'If it's worth $3.3 million, you can buy a lot of drugs for that.'

Peter stares at me then says slowly, 'You're going to steal a dagger worth $3.3 million and give it to him ...'

'Yes, but he must let Monika free.'

'Her life is worth that much?'

'Everyone's life is worth more than that, but I can't save everyone.'

'So,' Peter says, sounding amused now rather than angry, 'you're not making sense! How are you going to steal the dagger? You don't even know where it is.'

'No, but I'm going to find out!'

Peter stares at me. 'You're completely nuts, Mikky. You'll never be able to do it.'

'Watch me.'

* * *

'I'm not watching you do anything. We're going to Dixon House.'

Peter pushes both Adam and I in the direction of the charity building, and we walk, in silence, until Adam asks, 'Why are we going there?'

'Matt will call Monika's auntie and find out if she is okay. We're not stormtroopers, and we're not going around to her house all guns blazing.'

Adam grins. 'That's a shame.'

If Matt is surprised to see us at Dixon House, he doesn't show it. His cheeks are still red from filming out in the cold, and he ushers us into his office and closes the door behind us.

'Adam has something to tell you,' Peter explains.

Matt listens carefully to Adam's explanation of the pizza code that he and Monika have, to make sure they are safe and well, and how Monika hasn't responded.

'So, rather than going to the auntie's house, we'd like you to phone and make sure she's okay,' Peter sums up our request.

It's clear that Matt doesn't want Adam – or us – in the room, so he suggests we wait outside in the canteen while he calls Monika's auntie.

Peter helps himself to coffee.

Adam plays on his phone, and I stare out of the window into the courtyard, assessing the small group of homeless smokers, wondering how their lives took such a dramatic turn and how easily mine could, and did, for several years. It spiralled out of control. The only thing that saved me was my art, and through that, I developed a love of paintings. I remember the countless hours I spent in churches, as I learned to appreciate the old masters, tapestries, and artefacts. It was, fortunately for me, my refuge, my safety net, and ultimately what saved me from a life of alcohol and drugs, as I travelled with my parents like gypsies through Spain.

'Mikky?'

I look up, and Matt is standing at his office door, waving us inside.

Once we're seated, Adam hovers by the door.

Matt explains, 'Monika was at home the night before last, but she went out yesterday morning. She hasn't come back yet.'

'She didn't come home last night?' I ask.

Matt shakes his head. 'Her auntie thinks she may have stayed with a friend.'

'They've taken her,' says Adam, pacing by the door. 'I know they have.'

'We don't know that,' replies Matt.

'They have, I just know it.'

'What can we do?' I ask Matt. 'Call the police?'

Matt shakes his head. 'I would call the police, but her auntie isn't worried. She's not ready to register her as missing.'

'That's because she's frightened,' Adam raises his voice. 'Her sons are all in on it. They abuse Monika ...'

Matt raises his hand. 'We don't know that—'

'You do, I'm telling you. Monika told me!' he shouts.

Matt replies, 'Yes, well, we don't have proof—'

'She told me as well,' I add.

Matt looks surprised, and Adam stares at me.

'Monika came to my room in Morocco, and we chatted. She told me everything ...'

'I didn't know that,' says Adam.

'Neither did I,' says Matt. 'They were supposed to stay in their rooms.'

'Lisa and Joe were together, so she didn't want to listen to them making out all night.'

Matt shakes his head and clenches his jaw.

'You should have told me—'

'There was nothing to tell—'

'Look!' says Peter. 'This won't help now. Where would they have taken her, Adam?'

We all look at Adam.

He looks at the floor and shakes his head. 'I don't know ...'

'Think!' I urge him. 'Would Badger know?'

'I'll find out,' he replies, reaching for his phone.

* * *

Peter disappears, leaving us at Dixon House, waiting for Badger to reply to Adam. He returns an hour later, driving his battered van. He slides back the door and Adam and I climb inside.

It's his VW that we used in the New Forest when we tracked

Roberto, Marco's brother, eighteen months ago. It's filled with computers, tracking equipment, and an assortment of gadgets. Fortunately, he'd driven it over to England the night before we flew to Morocco, and has kept it safe in the parking bay at Josephine's apartment.

Peter sorts through boxes of protective gear and we chat quietly as I get ready. Finally, Peter fixes the poppy pin to my parka and he hooks me up to the lapel camera, then checks his computer.

'That should be fine,' he says.

Meanwhile, Adam watches silently. He bites his nails, nibbling the skin at the corner of his cuticles.

I reach out and take his hand. 'It will be alright, trust me.'

Adam blinks but doesn't reply.

We test the microphone, and Peter says, 'We'll be able to communicate, Mikky. If there's any danger, I'll know.'

'And where will you be, Peter?' Adam asks.

'I'll be nearby. I've called in the help of a good friend, and he will help me track you – hopefully from Bill's helicopter.'

'Thanks, Peter,' I say, ignoring the feeling of fear that begins to ripple the inside of my stomach. I swallow the bile in my throat, hoping I won't be sick.

'Where's Badger?' I ask Adam.

He checks his phone. 'We're meeting him near the canal. We have thirty minutes.'

'Okay. Let's go.' I stand up.

'Look, Mikky.' Peter holds my arm. 'Marco, Josephine, Joachin, none of them will forgive me if anything happens to you.'

'It won't. I'm indestructible.'

'You're not, and I don't want to find your naked body, raped

221

and slashed and floating in the canal.'

I swallow hard and blink back tears.

'It's not me I'm worried about; God knows what they're doing to poor Monika.'

Chapter 12

"A crime is a crime irrespective of the birthmarks of the criminal."
Narendra Modi

Adam walks nervously and silently beside me, along the canal. 'Aren't you frightened?' he asks.

'No,' I lie, pulling the collar of my parka closer to my chin. The wind is bitterly cold, and I suddenly wish this were all over and I was sitting in front of the fire at Blessinghurst Manor with Marco, drinking brandy.

'Peter is watching over me,' I add, to reassure Adam, and self-consciously I hold my lapel so that the pin can see our route.

'I can't believe you'd do this for Monika. You barely know her.'

'I know her well enough. She trusted me. I also knew Ali. This is for him.'

'Are you sure you're not the police?' He glances nervously around us, but there are only couples, and people hurrying past us eager to get inside the warm. It's almost three o'clock, and it's already drawing dark; the days are shorter, and when it begins to rain, I pull my hood over my head and shove my hands deeper into my pockets.

'Positive. I'm not the police.'

Adam's phone rings. He pulls it out of his pocket, listens silently, and hangs up. 'Change of venue. They're not taking any chances.'

He slips his arm in mine, and we disappear down another alleyway and into the darkness.

At the end of the passage, a hooded figure is waiting for us. He's holding a Rambo knife with a thick blade, pretending to manicure his nails while he waits.

'Alright?' Adam asks, as we draw alongside the motionless figure.

Badger's face is covered with a stocking. 'Come on,' he says, nodding with his head for me to follow him.

'No!'

They both stop and look at me.

'Not Adam. This is as far as he goes.'

'What?' Adam protests.

'Go home. I'll call you later. You're not coming with us.'

'But I want t—'

'Piss off, Adam,' Badger says. 'She's right. Go home.'

* * *

My breath is rasping against my collar as we walk. I've lost track of where we are. We've walked down alleyways, dark passages, and streets that I don't recognise. Eventually, we come to a cul-de-sac, and we clamber over a building site to get to a disused warehouse. The light is fading, but just before we go inside, I glance up and recognise the building on my right. I'm momentarily pleased, yet confused. We've walked around in circles. My heart lifts.

We duck inside and wait.

Badger raps the steel door with the handle of his knife, and it opens. A man wearing a ski mask stands back and allows us through.

Inside, it's brightly lit with fluorescent strip lights. There are two parallel rows of tables, and on either side, children are sifting, packing, and placing small bags of white powder on scales. They barely look up, and when they do, they are glassy-eyed, tired, and lethargic. It's like a workhouse, a children's factory.

I follow Badger, past teenage guards supervising the children, to a room at the back, where three guys are gathered around a steel table. Behind them, on the wall, an array of CCTV cameras show the entrance to the warehouse and the streets nearby. They saw us approaching.

'What do you want?' The bald man could be a weightlifter.

Badger replies, 'She wants to join us.'

The guy grabs Badger by the throat and pins him against the wall.

'Why did you bring her here?'

Badger can't speak. He's gasping for air, choking, his eyes bulging.

'It was my idea,' I say quickly. 'I've got experience with this shit!'

He throws Badger aside and turns his attention to me. He's massive, Turkish, bald, and broad-muscled, with not an inch of fat. His eyes are glassy, and his breath is rank.

'Get your clothes off.'

'I want to speak to—'

He pulls at my parka, but I move instinctively and kick him in the balls. He doubles over, grabbing his crotch.

'Bitch!' He lunges at me.

I dodge him, but an arm comes between us. He suddenly backs off, but I feel his spit on my face when he hisses, 'I'll get you.'

'Who are you?' The man who's blocking his path faces me. He's dressed head to toe in black. He's small, wiry, and speaks with a Mandarin accent.

'Mikky.'

'What experience?'

'Drugs. I did all this in Spain, in Malaga.'

'When?'

'A couple of years back. Are you the Asian?'

He pushes the Turk out of the way and circles me.

'Why?'

'I need the money.' I bite my bottom lip. My heart is hammering.

'Money from drugs?' He sounds surprised.

'I can get you more money, much more money, but I need help.'

'Why would I help you?'

'For $3.3 million.'

His almond eyes smile at me.

I babble, 'It's about the dagger. I saw the tattoo. I know who owns the original.'

The Chinese man glances at the other two men. Then he regards me silently. He is circling me like I'm prey – a small mouse to his preying barn owl.

'I have the original,' he says.

'I don't think so.'

I straighten my back and look him in the eye. 'I'm an expert. It's what I do.'

'Maybe you want to steal *my* dagger.' He leans closer to me, but I don't flinch. 'Do you?'

The Turk steps toward me and the other man tenses, ready to spring. The atmosphere in the room is suffocating. It's hard to breathe.

I'm shaking when I say, 'The original is in Switzerland. And I can prove it.'

* * *

'Get out!' the Asian shouts suddenly at the two men. 'GET OUT!'

The Turk looks hurt and then confused, and he moves more slowly than the first man, not taking his eyes from me. He's my enemy, and I know he will want revenge.

After they are gone, the Asian opens the draw of his desk and pulls out a revolver. 'This is a 1935 Browning Hi-Power pistol. It's an antique. You might like it.'

He aims it at me.

My body goes rigid. My mouth is dry. I lick my lips. 'I'd prefer to see the dagger.'

'I'm sure you would, but it isn't an option. You were very stupid to come here.'

He steps closer to me, and I remember Adam's words:

He shoots you in the face.

'Look, I came here of my own free will, to work with you – I can get you the original dagger,' I bluff.

He smiles slowly. 'I told you, I have the original.'

'You don't. I'm an art historian, a cultural expert,' I lie. 'Or why would I have come here?'

'Why indeed? Maybe you're foolish, or perhaps there's

something else that you're after.'

'Like what?'

He grins. 'We both know you're not getting out of here alive. Badger should never have brought you, but he won't make that mistake again.'

'Don't hurt him. It was my idea. I forced him.'

'No one forces Badger. He's made a stupid mistake. You see, he thinks I don't know what goes on, but I have eyes everywhere. For example, I know you've made friends with that gang of kids who are filming. I know you want to make a documentary, and I also know you've been hanging out at Dixon House.'

'Did Matt tell you that?'

'Matt?' He laughs. 'Matt thinks he's in charge, but I know everything. You see, Mikky dos Santos – I even know that you went to Morocco.'

'I'm impressed.'

'You should be.' He taps the pistol against my cheek. 'It's my job to know everything.'

'Who are you protecting?'

'Protecting?'

'Yes, you're not the boss of all this.' I cast my arms wide. 'This wasn't your idea. You've been hired.' I glare at him.

'Like an assassin?' He places the cold barrel of the gun against my cheek and moves it slowly down my neck. The steel is cold against my skin, and I shiver involuntarily.

'You're too intelligent. Let me see the dagger, and I'll tell you if someone has tricked you.'

'Why would they do that?'

'You tell me.'

'I don't need to tell you anything.'

'Look, I'll join this cult, I'll get the tattoo, and I'll swear allegiance to it, if I have to; I just want to get some money.'

'By stealing?'

'Yes.'

'I thought you were making a documentary.'

'I am, but that was my way of getting information about the dagger.'

'Ah, so what do you want from me?'

'I came here from Spain. I've got nothing. I lied about making a documentary. I'm a thief.'

'How can I believe you?'

'I'll show you. I can prove it. Can I get my phone out of my pocket?'

He steps away and aims the gun at my chest. 'Move very slowly.'

I pull out my iPhone and google the theft of Vermeer's *The Concert* – from over five years ago. I turn the screen for him to read the article and see my photograph. 'I've changed a little, my hair is now blonde, but you can tell it's me.'

I watch him scan read, taking in the details while he occasionally glances at me. I have no intention of moving. He'd shoot me.

'There's more,' I say, flicking through the Internet.

I show him other articles; my involvement with a Book of Hours – an illuminated manuscript – and finally a valuable Torah that I returned to the Jewish Museum in Rhodes.

'I stole these and gave them back, but I'm sick of it. I rescue these valuable pieces of artwork and get nothing for it in return. I'm poor. I have nothing. So, I figure, there's nothing to stop me from doing it the other way around. I can steal the dagger for you, and we can split the money we make, or you can pay me money to steal it.'

'How much?'

'50-50 – halfway split.'

'But why do you need me?'

'Because after I've stolen it, selling it is the biggest problem. Not everyone pays the full market value if you sell it on the black market. Plus, I'll bring you back a trophy – the original dagger is far more precious and valuable than you could imagine.'

He turns his back on me and walks away to the far side of the desk. He lays the gun on the desk facing me, regards me thoughtfully, then he laughs. 'You must be crazy.'

'No, I'm serious.' My breathing is more relaxed. I part my legs, ready to run, break the door down, cause mayhem, but to my surprise, he reaches under the desk, opens a deep drawer, and pulls out a grey canvas duffle bag. He lays it on the table, pulls the string at the top apart, and pulls out the dagger. He places it on the table between us and nods at me.

'Take it!'

I lean forward; I'm about to pick it up and he grabs my wrist.

'Ouch!'

He quickly lifts the dagger and traces the blade down the inside of my thumb. It's as if my skin is made of soft silk. He draws a thin line of blood, and it drips onto the table.

I glare at him.

He releases my wrist and picks up the gun.

Wiping my hand on my parka, I hold the dagger, twisting and turning it in my hand, looking for the inscription that I know is on the original. The nasta'liq script on the blade of the official titles, dates, and place of birth of Shah Jahan.

When I lift it closer to the light, I'm also looking for the honorific parasol, an ancient pan-Asian symbol of royalty and divinity that Jeffrey Bonnington described when we were in Basel.

I point to the blade. 'See this – these dates are wrong.'

He leans toward me and knocks the dagger from my hand with the gun barrel. It falls to the floor, and he moves quickly to pick it up, but I bring my hands down as a fist and smack him in the middle of his back.

He's off-balance and he rolls to one side, dropping the gun. I aim to kick his face but he moves, and my boot connects with his shoulder, knocking him backwards.

I tip the steel table on its side and, using it as a shield, I push it at him, wedging him against the wall. He's barricaded behind the desk, so I pick up the dagger and whack him on the head with the end of the blade.

He slumps against the floor.

I shove the dagger into the duffle bag and sling it over my shoulder, walking quickly out of the room.

In the larger room, the Turk watches me cautiously as I move quickly past the child workers, and I'm almost at the main steel door when a shot is fired.

Someone shouts. Instinctively, I duck.

I kick out at the hooded teenager on the door, and he doubles over, but as I push him away, someone grabs my hood. I quickly unzip my parka and turn in one motion, wriggling my arms free, and then I'm running. I'm hugging the duffle bag with the dagger inside to my chest, aware of heavy footsteps behind me.

I hear gunshots, but I run.

I'm waiting for Peter to show up, and the maze of streets confuse me. I pause to catch my breath and get my bearings.

Suddenly, I catch a glimpse of the familiar building. I run.

I'm a fast runner, and I keep my head down, using the duffle bag as a baton, up and down, as if I'm in a relay, until I feel my pursuers falling behind.

I pause, but I hear a squeal of tyres, then running feet. I run faster and harder, climbing over parked cars, dodging people on the pavement, weaving in and out of the slow traffic and running in front of a bus.

I slow again to catch my breath, my heart pumping, and then a shot rings out. It pings the steel handrail of the staircase to the unfinished building block – the empty fourteen-storey building where Sandra and the *Parks* have been filming.

A white van appears. I expect to see Peter but the Asian steps out and, holding the pistol, he fires again.

I run up the stairs and into the empty, half-lit building.

The plastic is flapping, the scaffolding creaks, and I run, knowing the Asian is fast behind me.

'Mikky,' he calls out. 'There's no escape – I'm going to kill you!'

* * *

I'm running for my life. The staircase is steep and dark. I smack the button for the light, leaping in the air, narrowly missing a curled-up body in the doorway. It groans and moves.

The stench is oppressive.

My breath is in raspy gasps. My knees are growing weak.

Another floor, higher and higher, up the tower block.

A gunshot echoes over my head and instinctively I duck. I've lost count of the number of floors – maybe twenty, more?

Breathlessly, I turn another corner, and up more stairs,

conscious of my assailant's steps behind me, looming closer.

There's a glint of light at the end of the passageway, and I'm halfway along the corridor when another shot rings out, pinging off the metalwork.

I throw myself at the emergency exit, pushing the bar, careful not to drop the prize wedged under my arm.

The door flies open. I blink. Suddenly, I'm in natural light, but it's dusk. The December sun is fading, and the bitter wind bites at my ears and nose.

Gasping lungfuls of air, panting heavily, I glance across the rooftops, getting my bearings: London. More specifically, Islington, and in the distance, Regent's Canal.

Another gunshot ricochets off the steel railing. I duck and run for cover behind a giant pipe, probably heating ducts. The man following me slows his pace and approaches cautiously. He knows I'm trapped.

I peer over the edge. We're twenty-five storeys high.

I have vertigo.

My head swims.

My mouth is dry.

I raise my right leg and swing it over the wall, dangling it into the empty void and hugging the bag to my chest.

'There's no way out.'

His Asian accent is strong, and his voice is loud across the open space between us, drifting in the breeze. 'Give it to me!'

I'm not armed. I wish I was. I swallow hard, staring down at the drop below; my head swims, and my hands begin to shake. I'll never survive.

My pursuer takes a step closer; his dark almond eyes are devoid of emotion.

'Put the bag on the ground, or I will kill you.' He points the

Smith & Wesson, a powerful handgun, designed to stop any game animal, at my chest.

I hesitate.

He takes a step closer.

'It's not worth it.' He grins. 'I *will* kill you.'

I'm astride the low wall, probably over seventy metres above the ground. My assailant is six metres away, not close enough for me to charge at him or to throw the bag at him. There's no way out. Sweat breaks out on my forehead.

He's a professional.

I swing my leg back over the wall, face him, and lower the bagto the ground, conscious of the vast open space behind me.

'Open it!' he demands, waving the gun at me.

I bend down and unzip the bag, and show him the dagger that still has traces of my blood on its blade.

He smiles.

I shout, 'We can come to some sort of agreement! Make a deal. Work together. I'm on your side.'

I raise my arms wide, stretched out like I'm Jesus on the cross, wearing only my hoodie. My coat was torn from me, and I lost my phone. I know Peter won't be able to follow me.

I call out, 'I can pay you—'

'You're a liar, Mikky. You tried to fool me once, but you won't do it again. I'm the Asian. No one messes with me – and gets away with it.'

'I didn't, I—'

I turn to my right, distracted by the noise of a helicopter, its motor humming, whining and growing closer.

'You hear me? I'm the Asian,' he shouts. 'They're not going to save you, Mikky. No one can!'

That's when he fires his gun, and the shot hits my chest. Air explodes from my lungs. The powerful force of the bullet lifts me backwards and up into the air. I fall back over the concrete ledge, and I'm suddenly spiralling head first, from the twenty-fifth floor, toward my fate and certain death below.

* * *

I'm falling.

The building is a blur as I fall, spiralling, turning, screaming.

It ends quickly with a massive thud.

Whoosh!

Smack!

Then there's only blackness.

* * *

'Mikky?'

'Mikky?'

'Be gentle with her.'

'Slowly.'

'Is she hurt?'

'Is she alive?'

I open my eyes.

Peter is bent over me.

'Mikky? Can you speak? Say something.'

I groan.

'Is she dead?' Adam asks.

They have climbed onto the stunt jump airbag – a large mattress also used for fire rescue.

'She's alive.' Peter kneels at my side.

'That was awesome,' Adam says with a grin. 'I wish I'd

filmed it.'

'Be quiet, Adam.' Peter pushes him away. 'Can you sit up, Mikky?'

I lean against Peter's chest, and a man I don't know passes me a bottle of water. I take it gratefully and sip it slowly, looking around, getting my bearings, still reeling from the shock.

'Twenty-five floors.' Adam laughs. 'Wicked! They wouldn't let me do it. They said trained stuntmen only.'

'It's not funny, Adam.' Peter is clearly annoyed. 'That wasn't the plan, Mikky. You were supposed to find somewhere safe until I found you.'

'This is awesome.' Adam grins. 'So cool, the airbag has two chambers: the bottom chamber maintains stability for a realistic landing, and the top one is soft. It means the jumper will never hit the ground, since the bottom chamber is there to absorb the drop.'

I ignore Adam. 'They were chasing me,' I say, my voice weak; I cough, still winded by my experience. 'The Asian was chasing me.'

Peter unzips my hoodie. 'He shot you in the chest.'

Adam says, 'We were in the helicopter. It was awesome. We saw the Asian raise his gun and fire. You fell backwards, freefalling, and wow—'

'That's enough, Adam! Mikky, let me look.'

'Is she alright,' says a stranger, who is peering over Peter's shoulder.

'Who's he?' I ask, allowing Peter to examine the hole in my hoodie and pull at my clothes.

'This is Bill,' Peter replies, examining the hole in my protective vest, 'the helicopter pilot.'

'You were fortunate, Mikky, but we need to get you to a hospital.'

* * *

While I'm in A&E at Guy's Hospital, a police officer waits outside my room, and within twenty minutes, Chief Inspector Mulhoon arrives, looking tired and weary in a crumpled suit.

'The doctor tells me you were lucky. The vest protected you. It stopped the bullet, but you are bruised from your fall.'

'You look worse than me,' I say to him.

'Impossible!' he replies, sitting on the chair beside me. 'It's a busy time of year, with the elections, and now this silly stunt of yours is all over the news. We've got to sort out damage limitation with the press.' He sighs, and then continues, 'I told Joachin that I didn't want anything like this to happen. I didn't want you involved. I couldn't afford for you to—'

'Oh stop it!' I say angrily. 'Just tell us what's happened. Did you catch the Asian?'

Mulhoon shakes his head.

'No, but we have managed to break up that drugs ring. After Peter contacted us, we stormed the warehouse; we've made over ten arrests, and we've got social services involved to look after the children.'

'Did you find the camera I was wearing?' I ask. 'It was attached to the parka.'

'Yes.'

'Was it of some help to you?'

'Yes.'

'You can say thank you,' I add grumpily. 'At last, you have a picture of the Asian, and the dagger, and the Turk. Did you

237

get him?'

'No.' The chief inspector looks pensive. 'He's disappeared, too.'

'What took you so long?' I complain.

'You didn't tell us you were pulling this dangerous stunt. My officers are deployed all over London. I can't just summon officers from the NCA; these police operations take time to set up—'

'The NCA?' I ask.

'The National Crime Agency. There wasn't time. We have to plan this type of operation.'

'You mean the election is more important?'

'No. No, it isn't, Mikky, but—'

'But what?'

Mulhoon says grudgingly, 'Look, we are grateful for your help, but the press has information. They know someone fell off the top of the building and survived, and that it wasn't for a film.'

'Anyone who was in the area the last few days would know filming was going on.'

'Yes, but no one would have been that crazy to run to the top, pursued by an Asian with a gun.'

'I had no choice,' I whisper. 'Watch the film and tell me what you would have done.'

'I have watched it.'

'And?'

'You were very brave.'

'I was only like that because I knew Peter was backing me up.' I turn to him. 'How did you manage to track me after I pulled my coat off?' I ask.

Peter shakes his head and pauses thoughtfully.

'We were in the chopper. It was windier than we expected and then our connection was cut when the parka was pulled off you. I was hoping we would get to the roof on time.'

'Where is Adam?'

'Outside, he wants to make sure you're okay.'

'What about Badger? Is he alright?'

But it's Mulhoon who replies.

'He's missing, along with the Turk and the Asian.'

'And the dagger?' I ask.

'After speaking to Peter, we assume the Asian still has it.'

Peter says, 'Bill couldn't land the chopper on the roof but we could land in the car park beside the stunt mattress – it's been there for a few days for the stunt team. They were freefalling.'

Mulhoon rubs his shining egg-shaped head and sighs. 'They're trained and Mikky isn't. It could all have gone so horribly wrong – if the mattress hadn't been there.'

'Believe me, if the mattress hadn't been there and I hadn't been wearing a protective vest, I wouldn't be here today.'

'Did you know it was still there?' asks Mulhoon.

'I remember the film crew talking about taking it away. When I got to the roof, I looked over the edge. I couldn't believe it was still there.'

Mulhoon nods. 'You were lucky!'

My eyes feel heavy, and I guess the painkillers are kicking in. 'You have a lead now. You'll find the Asian, won't you?' I insist.

'You get some rest, Mikky. Let's meet up in the morning,' he says to Peter. 'I'll know more by then.'

'What about Monika? Do you know if she is alright?' I ask. 'She was one of the *Parks* who came to Morocco.'

'I'll check, Mikky. You need to rest now and leave it to us.'

* * *

I sleep soundly all through the night, and the following morning Peter and I are eating toast and drinking tea, watching the BBC News when Marco phones.

'I have a problem with the yacht,' he says. 'I won't be able to get back for another week.'

'That's alright, my darling,' I say, feeling suddenly teary.

'Are you alright?'

'I miss you.'

'I miss you, too, but don't worry, Mikky.'

'I'm sorry that Stella and her family aren't coming to England now.'

'Me too, but don't worry, we will have a lovely Christmas.'

'It seems so far away,' I moan.

'It's only a couple of weeks.'

'Peter isn't coming to stay with us now at Blessinghust Manor, either.' I look at Peter, and when he looks sadly at me, I poke out my tongue. 'He's going to visit his aunt in Scotland.'

'Sorry, Mikky, I have to go. I'll call you later. The boat mechanic is here. Bye, darling. Love you.'

'Love you too, Marco.' I toss my phone onto the sofa and glare at Peter.

'Who's Bill?'

Peter looks surprised. 'An old army friend.'

'The one who owns the helicopter?'

'Yes. He's the guy who runs the sightseeing tours.'

'The one who put up a prize at the charity auction?'

Peter grins. 'That's the one. He used to fly Apaches in Afghanistan with me.'

'He was a bit slow,' I say, grumpily.

'I know, Mikky, and I'm sorry. We were monitoring the SWAT teams gathering below and I thought they'd get there in time. I can't believe they took so long to get organised. Then when you shrugged off your parka, we lost sight of you between the alleyways and the buildings—'

'At least you had the chopper; you'd never have been able to follow me in the van.'

'That's why I asked for Bill's help.'

On television, the prime minister appears in a street scene canvassing for the election. Peter turns up the sound. He's in the north of England visiting other constituencies, trying to drum up support for another term in government. He's boasting how the Metropolitan Police successfully infiltrated a drugs gang and rescued twenty-five homeless children who'd gone missing. The video flips to the building which Sandra used for filming but which is now part of a crime scene.

There's no mention of me or the dagger. The journalist says that information is scant. They believe one of the gang members was pursued and managed to escape by freefalling onto a stunt mattress – part of the film stunt props which was fortunately still in place. It wasn't a secret that the empty building was used as a film set – and as such, geared up to filming action scenes.

The BBC switches to a journalist who interviews Sandra; the building is behind her and Sandra looks remarkably calm.

We spoke last night on the phone, but then Peter phoned her this morning. He suggested that she play the game, talking about her new action film, the *Parks*, and the health and safety protocol over the past days.

Sandra ends up reiterating that she's happy no one was

injured, and for her, it's back to work and another day of filming, but this time on location in South London. The screen cuts back to the studio and the interviewer, and Peter reaches to turn down the volume.

'That's lucky, we've managed to keep your name out of it.'

I swallow my toast as Peter picks up the phone; taking a call from Matt, he covers the mouthpiece.

'It's Monika. She's at Dixon House and she wants to talk to you.'

Chapter 13

"When crimes begin to pile up they become invisible. When sufferings become unendurable the cries are no longer heard. The cries, too, fall like rain in summer."
Bertolt Brecht

Peter insists on driving rather than taking the tube, and as we cross over Tower Bridge, I can't help but think of Ali and our trip to Morocco almost two weeks ago.

My head hurts more from thinking about the events rather than the soreness of my unprofessional fall yesterday. I was fortunate that Peter had been thorough in his preparation and insist I wear body protection.

I climb out of the van and wince; my body feels stiff and I ache. I smile at Peter when he looks concerned.

'I'm fine.' I link my arm through his. 'You're my hero, did I tell you?'

'Not recently.' He grins, but I can tell he isn't relaxed. His body is wired, and he glances continually over his shoulder.

Monika is in Matt's office, and when she sees me, she flings her arms around my neck and hugs me tightly. Then she pulls away, wiping her tired eyes. She looks exhausted and appears barely to have any strength to stand up.

She sinks into a chair and looks from Matt and then to Peter. 'Can I speak to Mikky alone?'

The two men leave the office. I pull another chair closer, so our knees are almost touching. I take her hands in mine, conscious of her rough skin and torn nails. 'You need a manicure,' I joke.

'And a haircut – look at it.' Her rough curls are a mess, and she tugs at the wiry strands with despair.

'Are you alright? Are they looking after you?'

'Social services took me to a place last night. It's a hostel where kids like me can hang out. I'm too old for a foster family.'

'What about your auntie?'

She looks up at me and her eyes grow round with fear. 'I can't go back. The boys – my stepbrothers – would ...' She shakes her head and looks away, so I squeeze her hands, more to control my own emotions than to help her.

'What can I do?' I ask.

She continues to look down at our entwined fingers and shakes her head.

'I don't know, Mikky, but I just wanted to see you. Adam told me you came to rescue me.' When she looks up, her brown eyes fill with tears. 'No one ever saved me before.'

'I wasn't sure you were in there. I didn't see you.'

'I was in a room.'

'Was it very awful?'

We hold hands and sit in silence for a while until she asks, 'Do you know what gaslighting is?'

'I know the term. I know it originated from the play *Gas Light* back in the 1930s – I think it was by Patrick Hamilton – and it was later turned into psychological thrillers on several occasions, the most famous version starring the old Hollywood stars Ingrid Bergman and Charles Boyer.'

She raises her head and looks confused at all this detail, and says, 'It's when someone messes with your brain. They make you feel like you're going crazy. They manipulate you and distort reality, then they blame you – so everything is your fault ...'

'The people that do that are often narcissists, sociopaths, or psychopaths. They exhaust you by running rings around you with crazy discussions, and they challenge and invalidate your thoughts, perspectives, and emotions until you doubt your own sanity.'

'My stepbrothers do it to me, Mikky. Sometimes I want to kill myself.'

I squeeze her hands. 'You can't let them do that to you. That's how they get away with it ...'

'They provoke me. They terrorise and threaten me, and then they laugh at me. I can't keep fighting them. I haven't any more energy.'

'Then you must stay away from them.'

'How?' She wipes a tear with the back of her hand. 'They come and find me – my auntie tells them she's worried about me and then they emotionally blackmail me into staying at home. They tell me I don't appreciate what I have, and how kind they are, and what they do for me, and that without them, I'd be nothing ...'

'We must find you somewhere safe,' I whisper.

'There isn't anywhere,' she mumbles.

I pull a packet of tissues from my pocket and offer her one. 'I wanted to do what Ali did ...'

'What's that?' I ask gently. My heart is sinking. 'You

can't—'

'He was going to the police, Mikky. After we came back from Morocco, you and Peter had given him hope and he said he wanted to do the right thing. He wanted to save us all from the Asian and those like him, but then *they* got to him. He told me if they found out what he was going to do, he knew they were going to kill him. But he wouldn't give them the satisfaction.'

'What was he going to do?'

'He thought he could do a deal, tell the police what he knew about the gang and the Asian – in return he thought they'd protect him, but it didn't work out that way.'

'He told the police?'

'He called me. He said he had a meeting and he was going to tell them everything he knew.'

'Who did he speak to?'

'He said there's no point in fighting them – even the ones you think are on your side –because they're not. He said everyone is corrupt.'

'Who did he speak to?' I urge. 'This is important, Monika. Think hard. Did he give you a name?'

Monika shakes her head.

'He wouldn't. He said he wanted to keep me safe. He said he had no choice. He had to kill himself. He wouldn't let them kill him.'

I sit holding Monika's hand, then I say, 'Monika, I'm sorry you're sad, and that this happened to Ali, but I want to help. Just clarify this – are you telling me that Ali went to the police, told them what he knew, and that they weren't interested?'

She shakes her head. 'It wasn't just that. I don't know who he went to see, but the Asian *knew* what he'd done. The Asian *knew* he'd gone to someone. The Asian went looking for Ali.'

* * *

Matt's office is quiet. Apart from a few voices in the hallway, we sit in silence. I know Matt was calling the social services and I wonder if anyone has arrived yet to look after Monika.

Her head is resting on her chest. She seems exhausted. She seems too tired to look up, so I lay my hand on top of her hair. She wipes her tears with the back of her hand, and when she finally looks up, her bloodshot eyes are the epitome of sadness, reminding me of the haunting images I've seen over the years of Mary the Mother of Jesus, holding her dead son.

'I'll speak to Matt,' I say. 'And find you somewhere safe to stay.'

'Mikky,' she says huskily. 'I'd tell the police anything, but I'm frightened ...'

'I know,' I whisper.

'I'd swap any information I have for a new identity some-where else, a new beginning, a new start – but I can't do that now. The Asian is still around, and it's only because you rescued me that I'm here now.'

'Why did he pick you up?'

'Because he knew Ali was my friend – he thought I might do the same thing.'

'Did you tell the police what he did to you?'

'No.'

'Why?'

'Because I don't trust them, either. The Asian is still out there.' Monika sits up straight, then lets go of my hands.

I stand up, and stretch my legs and my aching body. The fall from the twenty-fifth floor hurt even though I landed on a thick mattress. I walk to the window and move the blinds to one side, and see the rain lashing against the window. The courtyard is empty, but I can hear muffled voices; several people are huddled in the doorway, and occasionally a waft of smoke drifts past the glass.

'I'll sort it out, Monika.' I drop the blind and turn from the window.

Monika shakes her head. 'You can't. Look what happened to you. Adam told me what you did. The Asian shot you.'

'But he didn't kill me. He didn't win,' I say with resolve.

'But what can you do now? If the police are on his side?'

'Well, we need to look at this and see what our options are now.'

'Who's we?'

'Me and Peter.'

'But what will you do?'

'First of all, you have to tell us everything.'

* * *

Matt allows me to use one of the offices. He had gained permission for me to interview the *Parks* for the documentary and I'm taking full advantage of my privileged position to ask Monika questions. Claudia sits at the back, quietly watching.

Peter isn't happy with me speaking to Monika. He listens to her quiet, hesitant voice and he looks sad, but he remains tight-lipped and in the background, leaving me to gently ask her questions.

'Tell me about the initiation ceremony,' I suggest.

Monika speaks slowly. 'That's how I met Ali. They'd brought him from Barnet, picked him up off the street. There was a group of us – I'd been taken to this addict's house somewhere

248

in North London, and the leader of our group was ...' she pauses and looks at Peter.

'It's alright, Monika. Peter understands, but if you want him to leave the room, it's fine.'

She shakes her head and continues, 'He forced me to have sex with him, regularly, and he gave me drugs.'

'Do you know who he was?'

'No, but I saw him again. He was with the Asian in the warehouse.'

'What did he look like?'

'Gross! Fat, but it's muscle – he's Turkish.'

I suddenly know who she means. It's the man I kicked in the balls – the one who escaped with the Asian.

'So, did he take part in the ceremony?'

'He gave us the tattoos. We lined up. There was maybe twenty of us, all kids, all sworn to secrecy, and we took an oath, then they cut us with this knife – a big blade.'

I show her the picture of the dagger that I'd shown Jeffrey Bonnington in Basel.

'Is this it?'

'Yes.' She blinks, surprised. 'We all bled, then we had to lick each other's blood and that bonded us to each other.'

'Where did they cut you?'

'Here, under our heart. Then the Turk tattooed us, so it was a reminder that if one got caught or one betrayed us then everyone else would be caught.'

'Did you want the tattoo?'

She shrugs. 'It pleased the Turk, and when he was happy, he left me alone.'

'And Ali?'

'I think he was high. They gave us drugs to make it seem

like a great idea, and we'd chant.'

'Chant what?'

'I don't remember. It sounded like gibberish. Foreign …'

'Chinese?' I suggest. 'Mandarin?'

'Maybe.'

'Tell me about the dagger.'

'It was very sharp – I know a lot of the guys carry knives and some even carry machetes. But it's much more dangerous – its blade is so, so sharp,' she emphasises.

'Did it have any symbols or writing on it? Like this one?'

'I have it tattooed on my chest, remember?'

'Was there anyone else present at the ceremony?'

'I'm not sure. I think there may have been someone else.' She frowns.

'Like who?'

'I don't know, but the Asian seemed as if he wanted to impress. It was like a show.'

'A show?'

'He seemed aroused, if you know what I mean.'

* * *

I'm exhausted. It's been an emotionally draining afternoon, and my body aches. We're back in Josephine's apartment, and I lay on the sofa and close my eyes, thinking about Monika.

'We have a match on the dagger,' I say. 'But what would Raymond Harris have to gain by killing Ali?'

Peter shrugs. 'We're guessing.'

'How long do you think Ali was inside his constituency office for?'

'Probably ten or fifteen minutes.'

'That's a long time – long enough to confide in someone.' I get up from the sofa and move gingerly toward the table where Peter has set up the film on his computer.

We fast-forward the tape speed until Ali appears in the street. He's wearing his pilot's flying jacket. He pulls up the collar and disappears. Peter switches cameras to the far end of the same street where Raymond Harris's office is situated and he points to an Audi parked at the kerb. Ali appears and walking toward the camera, he passes the vehicle. But when the car pulls away a few minutes later, we can't see the occupants.

'Let's assume that the people in the car were tipped off by whoever Ali spoke to in the office – it might be Raymond or one of his staff. Then the Asian picked Ali up off the street and they stopped in a supermarket car park near Tower Bridge. Maybe they were going to kill him there – Ali had bruising associated with a fight. Let's assume that he managed to escape and he went to the nearest place he recognised – Tower Bridge – and once there, he realised his only way out was to kill himself.'

Peter replies, 'Imagine if you thought you could go to someone you trusted, someone who held a high office, someone like Raymond – a politician, someone who cares, and who is one of the principal board members for the Dixon Trust.'

'It makes sense,' I agree. 'Especially if he thought that whoever he spoke to was working with the police.'

'It would also explain the bruises found on his arms in the autopsy report,' adds Peter.

'He must have been so scared, poor Ali.'

'Not only scared, but he had nowhere to go. Where would he have been safe?' asks Peter. 'Not even Matt could help him. I think he must have lost faith in everyone.'

'So, can we conclude that the Asian works for Raymond or

someone in his office?'

'Therein lies the dilemma, Mikky. We need to find out if Raymond was in the office at the time. We need more CCTV footage.' Peter drums the stubs of his fingers against the table.

'But the police should have access to these CCTVs?'

'They aren't checking, Mikky. As far as they are concerned, Ali killed himself.'

'Assuming Raymond was in the constituency office – why would Raymond be working with the Asian?' I ask.

Peter places his palms face up, as if balancing weighing scales.

'He's the good guy on the one hand, in the public eye, helping the homeless and the poor. And, on the other ...' He tips one hand lower. 'He's working with the Asian to line his pockets with drug money.'

'To fund his political career?'

'To blindside everyone, I expect. Who would suspect a reputable politician working with the most fearsome drug leader?' Peter says with a sigh.

'It's like that Chinese book – *The Three-Body Problem* by Cixin Liu – where the Chinese encourage aliens to attack Earth, then when they do attack, the Chinese fight back and protect everyone. They become the Earth's saviour, and everyone is grateful. Never knowing that the Chinese started it all in the first place.'

* * *

I pour a whiskey and pass one to Peter.

'I have to go and speak with Raymond,' I say.

'And say what?'

'That we have evidence—'

'But we don't, Mikky. We don't have any evidence that he was involved in Ali's death.' Peter frowns. 'We can only assume Ali visited his office and that the Audi that you saw last week was parked outside in the street. The link is too tenuous.'

'We need to find out if Raymond told the police that Ali went to his office. He didn't tell Matt, or if he did, Matt didn't mention it to us.'

'We can't ask the police. We promised Joachin that we wouldn't get involved.'

'Can we ask Matt?'

Peter shakes his head. 'We can't go near Matt, either. We got away with going to Dixon House today because Monika wanted to speak to you. But if Matt thought we were doing anything to put the kids' lives at risk ...'

'You're right. We can't afford to let Joachin know we are still working on this until we've cracked it. Do you think we will?'

Peter grins. 'Definitely. When do we ever fail?'

I smile back. 'I need to visit Raymond. If we're going to rattle anyone's cage, then it might as well be the man at the top.'

'And run the risk that the Asian will come after you? I don't think so. We're not taking that risk anymore.'

'Why not?'

'Because the Asian knows who you are, and you won't be able to blag your way out of it again. He will definitely kill you.'

'I don't agree with you. Besides, what if it isn't Raymond? We are assuming it is, but what if it's one of the people in his office? We need to get a list of his employees. But in the meantime, I can ask Raymond if Ali went to see him – I can let him know we're onto him, shake him up a little.'

Peter looks doubtful.

'It's the only plan we have, Peter. We'll do it tomorrow, and you can wait outside in the van and listen.'

* * *

That night, Peter and I drink far too much whiskey and wine. I'm frustrated, angry, and upset. Peter's capacity for alcohol is far higher than mine. He keeps topping up my glass, and I knock it back as we argue. I rant about Mulhoon. I swear that Matt betrayed us, and how pompous Raymond Harris is, and how Joachin won't support us. And all the time, I drink more wine and complain that we've not moved forward in finding the Asian.

'Maybe I should steal the original dagger from the pompous Jeffrey Bonnington,' I suggest.

'How?' asks Peter, filling my glass.

'I'll find a way, you know I can do it,' I slur.

'You'll steal the real dagger?' Peter asks with a laugh. He's deliberately winding me up.

'You're a pain, Peter. You don't want to help me.'

I fill my glass, drinking recklessly, angry and frustrated, and when I eventually fall into bed, I'm very, very drunk.

I wake early. It's still dark outside and the bed covers are untidy. It was a deep but restless sleep. My body aches and I take a hot shower, allowing the water to wash over my hair and run down my back.

When I walk into the kitchen, Peter is preparing coffee and toast.

'Morning, sleepy!' he says, grinning.

'Why are you so bright and cheerful?'

'I just spoke to Aniela – and Zofia; I think she's growing so much. She looks much bigger than when I left.'

'Doting father!' I grumble.

'What's wrong?'

'I scratched my back last night,' I complain, rubbing a wound on the top of my hip. 'It was a mad night. I'm never drinking again.' I grin ruefully, knowing I will.

Peter slides a plate across to me with toast and marmalade. 'Yeah, yeah …'

I sit on the barstool at the kitchen island and reach for the coffee.

On the television, the BBC News is showing footage of the prime minister at an awards ceremony last night, pledging that more money will be invested into police services to fight crime. He laments the loss of a young boy, found yesterday, from the council estate in Islington, and I pause, staring at the picture of the boy on the screen.

The journalist reports, 'He's of Turkish origin and believed to have fallen foul of a criminal drugs gang. His body was found naked, raped, slashed, and dumped in the canal – probably as a lesson or a warning to others.'

'Another one,' I say, thinking of Badger, and Adam, and Monika, and I wonder where their lives will lead them.

My phone rings, and it's Josephine.

'Hello, sweetheart. Sorry to phone you so early, but we're not flying back today,' she says. 'They've asked Simon to stay on for some special dinner, so we might as well stay here for Christmas.'

'Really?'

'You don't mind, do you, sweetheart? Why don't you fly over and join us?'

'I was looking forward to— Oh look, never mind. That's fine.'

'You're not upset, are you? We'll be back in the New Year.'

'No, it's fine. I have to go. I'll call you later, Josephine.' I can't hide my disappointment as I hang up.

Peter sits beside me. 'Are you alright?'

'Josephine has cancelled Christmas, too. Everything is falling apart.'

Peter smiles. 'It will all work out.'

'She won't meet Aniela or Zofia, either,' I complain. 'You're buggering off to Scotland.'

Come on, Mikky. Let's plan.' Peter's tone is light and excited. 'Why don't we see Raymond, then go for dinner, or there's a new exhibition at the Tate – David Hockney, this evening.'

'What do you know about art?' I ask with a smile.

'You'd be surprised, Mikky. I'm not a complete philistine.' I laugh.

'Failing that, we could always visit the fictional home of Sherlock Holmes in Baker Street.'

'Now, that's more like it,' I reply. 'But first, let's get me a meeting with Raymond.'

'Only if you promise you'll be subtle. We don't want to get arrested and end up spending Christmas in prison.'

* * *

The following morning, Peter sits in the van listening through headphones. I'm wired with a pin of a sunflower attached to the lapel of my black leather jacket.

I enter Raymond Harris's political control centre – in Islington, only a few streets away from Dixon House – with curiosity and anger.

It's almost eight-thirty, but I'm left waiting in a shabby reception with a few homeless people; one is particularly aggressive. He is persuaded to sit down and wait by a calm and efficient male secretary. It's gone ten o'clock when it's finally my turn and I'm shown into Raymond's office. My patience and good humour have gone, and my hangover is blinding.

I smile. 'Would it be alright if I record our interview?' I ask.

Raymond smiles warily. He's immaculately dressed in a navy suit and white shirt. He's older than I thought he looked the last time in the hotel near Hyde Park. The election is clearly taking its toll.

He's in his late fifties, a good twenty years older than his second wife Arlene, and fleetingly I wonder if she awoke with a hangover this morning or if she's now at the gym.

'I didn't agree to an interview.' He tugs on his cuffs.

'For a journalist, I have a rotten memory, and I don't want the information to be inaccurate.'

'This is my morning for my constituents.'

'I understand that, but I am working with the Dixon Trust. I'm Mikky dos Santos. Matt and I have been working very closely together, and I wanted to get this finished to help with your election campaign. It's part of a documentary. I'm hoping I can get an angle on the injustices of the government, lack of policing on the streets, and how social housing is an absolute priority for our country.'

Now I have his attention. He frowns. 'You visited my home?'

I smile. 'Yes, I met your lovely wife, Arlene.'

'I don't like journalists visiting my home uninvited.'

'I wasn't uninvited. Matt spoke to her, and she agreed.'

I gaze into his eyes and smile. 'But if you're upset, then

257

I do apologise. Like you, I don't have a lot of time, and I thought you'd be supportive of my film. I want it to support your election campaign. If I can get it finished in time and maybe get it televised or on social media in the next few days, it might make a big difference. The prime minister might sit up and take notice. It will tell him you're not to be messed with.'

'How can I help?' His posture changes and his tone is almost affable. 'Record it if you like; you can take a seat here.' He indicates a rickety chair opposite his desk.

'It's not what I expected,' I say.

'What isn't?'

'I thought your office would be more salubrious.'

His laughter is light, and he doesn't take offence. 'No chance. This furniture has all been donated. All our funds go into the Dixon Trust.'

'But you are campaigning in the election?'

'Of course.'

'Do you think you'll get in again?'

He spreads his manicured hands on the table and smiles professionally into my camera.

'I'd like to think so. We've worked hard with the Dixon Trust to provide a safe place for the homeless, and for the kids on the street, affected by the drugs gangs. We're the only political party that is actively engaged in getting the homeless off the streets and helping those people living below the poverty level, and providing food banks. If it weren't for the Dixon Trust, some of these people would be starving.' He smiles professionally.

'What's your view on social housing?' I ask.

It's a question that I know will put him at ease. I pretend to take notes as he quickly reels off figures and statistics about the homeless, the number of food banks, and the general demise of social housing under this present government.

'Years ago, these buildings were full of asbestos and the tenants were never expected to stay longer than a few months. They were in a very poor condition and it was like legalised squatting, and the licence didn't pay rent. I believe everyone deserves a decent roof over their head,' he says. 'Many of the people on the estates are young and single; they were previously homeless or living on low incomes. If no new tenancies are granted, the flats become empty and squatters take over, and the blocks steadily deteriorate.'

'Do the community help to maintain the blocks?'

'They have made a remarkable improvement. Ten, even twenty years ago, there was more neglect and decay; windows were broken and smashed, and some of the flats were burnt out. There were cockroaches, pigeon mess, heroin users, discarded needles and other drug paraphernalia. You can't imagine the overwhelming rubbish chutes, or the graffiti, or the smell of urine in the stairwells. The lifts didn't work, robberies were a daily occurrence, as well as domestic violence.' He pauses. 'We've come a long way in a short time. We are making progress.'

'I'm aware of a solid community that cares for the area.'

'Well.' He puffs up his chest and takes a deep breath. 'Now you get hippies, anarchists, and all those types of festival-goers – who take cannabis and who believe they are excluded by society. Their poverty in this current affluent society only acts as further exclusion, which then reasserts their identity and ontology.'

I smile at his addition of metaphysics and wonder if he's

259

trying to impress. 'So, if the properties on the estate are neglected, then this contributes to increased crime on the estates?'

He stares at me. 'Broken windows may signal nothing more than increased criminality.'

'Do you think it's a sign of political resistance? Does the estate community aim for quality and affordable housing, and do they plead with you to have an improved environment for their families?'

'Of course.'

'How do you think social housing affects the drug culture in Islington, or is it the other way around?'

Raymond repeats some of his previous opinions and election promises, about lack of care from the current government, our vulnerable society, and our need to care for those less fortunate.

I smile. 'Islington, your area, has an increasing rate of drug-related crimes.'

'Is that a question or a statement?' His smile is tight at the corners, and he checks his watch.

'There was a big police presence just over a year ago, where they rescued twenty-five children and arrested over fifteen drug pushers.'

I know that Ali was rescued during this raid and that Monika's stepfather was one of those arrested. I continue, 'You must be pleased, unless you're upset that these drug-related incidents, involving the Asian, constantly happen in Islington – quite unusual—'

'I don't think that's necessarily true—'

'There is a group, a cult – a drugs gang – call it what you like, that is growing in numbers, through intimidation. They

recruit young kids and trap them in houses to bag up drugs –
coke, heroin, crack – to sell on the streets.'

He stares at me as I speak.

'You must have heard of the Asian, haven't you?' I insist.

He turns his attention to some papers on his desk, which he
begins to shuffle. 'It's not a name I'm familiar with.'

'It's a drugs gang operating in your area.'

'You can hardly call it my area. This city – this country –
has been under government rule that hasn't cared about social
welfare for years. I'm inheriting *their* problems. And drugs
are a national problem, the same as lack of welfare, job losses,
and Universal Credit.'

'Is that why you want that vacant building for more social
housing?'

'What do you mean?'

'There's a high-rise development near the Islington estates:
Luke, Thomas, and John's. But this building is where Sandra
Worthington has been filming. You've been discussing it on
television. Do you deliberately lobby for these buildings to be
turned into social housing so that there will be more voters
for you in your constituency?'

'What a ridiculous suggestion.' He checks his watch, frowns,
and stands up.

'Why? If you have an extra five hundred voters in one block
of high-rise apartments, then that will place you in a much
stronger position for any subsequent elections.'

'I have another appointment now.'

'Do you know that when children are forced to join the drugs
gangs and swear allegiance to a cult, they have a tattoo inked
under their heart?'

His eyes follow my finger, where I trace an invisible tattoo on the left side of my chest.

'Look, I'm sorry, Ms dos Santos.' He tugs on his jacket sleeves. 'I'm already late for another appointment, and as you can see, people are queuing outside to see me.'

'What would you do if it were true? If there was a cult?' I stand up and make a very deliberate effort to pack my notepad and recorder into my bag.

'I'd tell the police, of course.'

'Well, you'd be right. The police seem to be very capable of sorting out drugs rings across county lines in the north, but there's not much effort being made here in London – in Islington.'

'That,' Raymond snarls, 'is the fault of our prime minister.'

'Just one last question—'

The office door opens unceremoniously and the male secretary watches us suspiciously before announcing, 'The shadow chancellor is on line two for you.'

Chapter 14

"Only crime and the criminal, it is true, confront us with the perplexity of radical evil; but only the hypocrite is really rotten to the core."
Hannah Arendt

The following afternoon it is wet and grey. It's the day before the election and two weeks until Christmas. I glance out of the van window, ignoring London's Embankment and allowing myself to be hypnotised by the windscreen wipers' rubbery screeching across the glass.

'I'm so annoyed with myself for not asking him outright.'

'You couldn't do that, Mikky.' Peter checks the rearview mirror and overtakes a red double-decker. 'We can't afford to upset him, not at this stage, considering it's right before the election.'

'I'm going to nail him next time.'

'I know. Look, I've checked his schedule for today. After drinks in Westminster at five, he has an early evening appointment with senior ministers, followed by an evening reception at Tate Modern's David Hockney exhibition.' Peter drives, carefully negotiating the London traffic, past Westminster Bridge and Big Ben; I check my watch.

'Drop me off where you can.'

My phone rings.

'Hello?'

'Mikky? It's Adam.'

'Hi.'

'I need help.'

'What's happened?' I press the speakerphone so that Peter can hear.

'I've been waiting for you at Dixon House but you haven't shown up.'

'No.'

'Have you abandoned us?'

'No, of course not. What's happened?'

'I took Monika home with me to my foster family last night, but the Asian was waiting outside the house this morning.'

I glance at Peter.

'Did he do anything?'

'He's recruiting again. He's taking local kids and rumour has it that he's taking them out of London. He's setting up a new county line. A couple of local kids have already disappeared.'

'Did you tell Matt?'

'Yes, of course.'

'What will he do?'

'Tell the police, but they don't do anything. You did. At least you tried to stop him. We trust you, but I'm worried about Monika. She's really sad. She was crying all night. She's frightened.'

'You must ask Matt to help you.'

'It's only when we stay at Dixon House that he can protect us, but we can't stay there forever, and besides, Monika doesn't feel safe there, either.'

'So, where are you both?'

'We've been walking around, staying in busy places – Oxford Street, Soho, and places – but we can't keep walking, and I can't involve my foster family. I don't know what to do ...'

'Hang on.' I cover the mouthpiece with my hand and say to Peter, 'Can you go and pick them up, and I'll watch out for Raymond at Westminster. Then we can get help with social services?'

Peter nods.

'Where are you now?' I ask Adam.

'Near Covent Garden.'

'Okay, then walk down toward the Embankment. Peter is driving the white van, and he'll collect you.'

Out of the van window, I see Raymond Harris hurrying along the street. I cover the mouthpiece again.

'Look, Peter! There's Raymond. Let me out here, and I'll follow him.'

Peter pulls over to the kerb, and I say quickly to Adam, 'Wait on the Embankment. Peter will be there in a few minutes.'

'Okay, Mikky. Thanks.'

I pocket the phone and pull open the van door as Peter comes to a brief halt on yellow lines.

'Take care, Mikky,' Peter calls.

'He's not going to escape me this time.'

* * *

I pull up the collar of my jacket, and I'm about ten metres behind Raymond Harris when Peter's van passes me. I wave and give him the thumbs up.

Knowing my time is short, I lengthen my stride and quicken

my step, and within minutes I've caught up with Raymond.

I'm walking beside him when I say, 'Excuse me, Raymond?'

He turns and barely pauses. Although he smiles politely, there's a hint of irritation in his frown.

'Yes?'

'Mikky dos Santos, I interviewed y—'

'Yes, I remember.'

'I just wanted to ask you one last quick question.'

'I'm in a hurry.' He makes a big deal of checking his watch.

'I can walk with you. It will only take a minute of your time.'

He turns away and expects I will follow him.

'I didn't realise the old building they used for filming was so important.'

'Right.'

'You want to build social housing?'

'We discussed this yesterday. It's a disgrace. It's been empty for so long, and the longer it remains empty, the more the area becomes a breeding ground for drugs cartels and people who don't help our society. I know theories don't *prove* anything, but I've already explained the broken windows theory to you. It's symbolic.' He's sounding impatient.

'I know.'

'Broken windows create more broken windows. It's a criminology theory, proving there are visible signs of anti-social behaviour and civil disorder in these sort of abandoned places – that create an atmosphere for even more crime, sometimes even more sinister crimes that involve young people.'

'Like drugs gangs?'

'Potentially.'

'Cults?' I insist.

He sighs heavily. 'The theory suggests police patrol these areas to prevent further crimes such as vandalism, public drinking, drugs—'

'To protect society?'

'To improve law and order. But unfortunately, we have a prime minister who promises one thing and does another. And, because he dithers over the decision-making process for a building such as this one, and he – or his pathetic government – hasn't bothered policing the area, either, crime increases faster than you can snuff it out! Now, does that answer your question?'

'No.'

'Then get to the point! We're nearly there ...' He stops abruptly at the gated entrance to Westminster.

'Ali is the name of the boy who died a few weeks ago. He jumped off Tower Bridge. Did he visit you in your office the night he died?'

Raymond stares at me. 'What makes you think that?'

'Did he go to your office?' I insist.

Raymond shakes his head. 'I don't recall ...'

'What if I told you that Ali *did* visit your office – and that he was there for fifteen minutes.'

'I'd say you're very mistaken! Be careful you don't go making up slanderous stories.'

'I want the truth. What did he say to you?'

'He didn't say anything, because quite simply, I wasn't there.' He turns on his heel and disappears into Westminster.

'I'll find out!' I shout, but he's already disappeared.

* * *

I pull up the collar of my jacket and take the incoming call on my mobile, my head still firmly in my conversation with Raymond and his abrupt departure.

Where does that leave us?

Who was in the office?

Who did Ali speak to?

'Ms dos Santos? It's Martin McVey from Bond Street,' a clipped, well-toned voice says in my ear. 'You were asking about replica daggers?'

'Yes, hello. Thank you. I was.'

'I have found someone who will make a similar model to the dagger that you showed me, should you still wish them to do so.'

'Has he made one before?'

'I believe he has.'

'He's definitely made a copy of the dagger I showed you?'

'I believe so.'

'Who is he?'

'It's a private company.'

'Who is it?'

'I can't divulge that information. My client only works through reputable outlets, and he doesn't deal directly with the public.'

'Who commissioned the last dagger?' I'm walking along beside the road, keeping a lookout for Peter's white van.

'I can't tell you that, either. All our clients remain confidential.'

'If you don't tell me, the police will be all over your shop within a matter of minutes. They will raid your premises, and it won't look good in Bond Street. You're withholding important police information and—'

'You've shown me no evidence or documented proof that you're working with the police, Ms dos Santos—' His tone is equable and firm.

'I'm with Europol, and we're working on a case of this stolen – and precious – dagger.'

'I see.'

'Do you?' I reply tersely.

'In that case, perhaps you should come into the shop, with some appropriate evidence of your identity and position, and we can discuss it further.'

'Fine,' I say, wondering how I can get forged documents made so quickly. 'I'll call in later today.'

'I'm here until 5 p.m., Ms dos Santos. I look forward to seeing you – if you have the appropriate papers.' He hangs up, leaving me thoughtful and excited.

* * *

I call Peter.

'Did you find Adam and Monika?'

'The traffic is horrendous. I'm almost there.'

'Raymond denied that Ali had visited his office, so he's either lying, or someone else in his office has turned bad. Did you get a list of his employees?'

'Yes.'

'And Martin McVey from the shop in Bond Street has found a guy who makes replicas of the dagger we're looking for, but he won't give me any details unless I provide him with documentation that we're from Europol.'

'Is that what you told him.'

'Yeah, I tried to threaten him, but he wasn't having any of

it.'

Peter laughs. 'You should have been a mobster.'

'I wouldn't have been very successful.' And I grin despite myself. 'Can you hack into his phone records or something?'

'Mikky, do you think I'm a magician or something? I'm driving a van, and I can't just hack into everyone's records and phone calls at the drop of a hat.'

'You must know someone who can help. What about Bill, your friend?'

'He's a helicopter pilot.'

'Is there no one else who can help us?'

'I'll give it some thought. Look, I can see Adam and Monika. I'll collect you. Walk up to Westminster Bridge and we'll drop Adam and Monika at Dixon House, and make sure they're safe, before we do anything else.'

* * *

I pull out my phone and dial Matt's number. He answers straight away.

'Adam took Monika home to his foster family last night but the Asian was waiting outside their house this morning,' I say without preamble. 'Fortunately, Adam managed to get her out but they're not safe. We are just picking them up now. The Asian is brazen, Matt. He keeps showing up in Islington – why? What can we do?'

'I'd heard the Asian wasn't around anymore.'

'Well, he was this morning. He's back in Islington. He's recruiting and taking the kids out of London. Maybe he's setting up elsewhere, and he needs some vulnerable kids quickly?'

'I'll call the police,' says Matt.

'We'll bring Adam and Monika to Dixon House.'

'I'll also call social services,' Matt adds. 'They can't stay in this danger. We might have to relocate them to another area.'

'Good idea.'

'Are they with you now?'

'Peter is collecting them along the Embankment, then he's collecting me. These kids are in trouble—'

'Where are you?'

'At Westminster.'

* * *

I take Adam and Monika into Dixon House while Peter waits in the van. It takes me a few minutes, with Matt, to listen to their story, and when Matt lifts the telephone to speak to Chief Inspector Mulhoon and the social services representative, I'm ready to leave.

After hugging Monika and making sure she's drinking hot chocolate and feels she's safe, I promise Adam and Monika I'll see them tomorrow.

'Thanks, Mikky. I didn't know who else to phone.' Adam looks down at an invisible spot on the floor,

'Always come here to Dixon House,' I say. 'You're safe here and Matt will protect you.'

'I know we should, but—'

'I might not always be available. This is what Matt does. He takes care of you, and he will find a solution. He's on your side, and he will fight to keep you safe.' I want to hug him but I don't.

Adam nods at me, remains silent, and continues staring at

an invisible patch on the floor.

'Monika, I'll make sure we're in touch tomorrow. Stay here, and stay safe.'

When I get back to the van, Peter is smiling.

'You look like you've been speaking to Aniela,' I say.

'Wrong!'

'Okay, what's happened?'

'I've found the craftsman.'

'That was quick! I knew you could do it. How?'

'It was easy to check the Bond Street shop's records. Martin made the call to him this morning.'

'How did you know he's the craftsman?'

'Because he's listed in the directory. I cross-checked.'

'It's as simple as that?'

Peter grins. 'Yup! Oh, by the way, I'm meeting Bill for a drink at lunchtime, to thank him for his help.'

'Okay.'

'Do you want to come?'

'You're joking; I'm still getting over my last hangover!'

Jake Helmsdale, the craftsman, lives in Camden.

We park the van quickly and walk to his studio near the market, and as we enter, a small bell tinkles above the door like in the old shops of yesteryear.

Jake is in his mid-forties, with a shaved head and tattoos covering his head, neck, and arms. I'm trying to work out the designs; I don't want to stare, but I guess he's used to people reacting in the way I'm doing now.

He smiles. 'Hello.'

'Hi.' I walk toward him with my hand stretched out. 'Mikky dos Santos. This is my boyfriend, Peter.'

Jake wipes his hands on a dirty rag.

'I don't have any appointments today, I—'

'I know. I'm sorry, but we're heading home today, and we heard that you're a fine craftsman.'

'Home?'

'Yes, we live in Spain.'

'Hablas español?' Jake says.

I reply, lying in fluent Spanish, my native tongue.

'Claro, of course, I speak Spanish. I live in Mallorca – where did you learn the language?'

Jake replies in English.

'I lived there for a while; my parents had a place near Murcia.'

He doesn't seem to be in a hurry, so we talk about Spain, Brexit, and then London and living in Camden. He's friendly and relaxed. He's also clearly well-educated.

'I opened my studio a few years ago,' he explains. 'I've always had an interest in bronze, but I work mostly with steel and iron, and occasionally with rare gemstones and minerals.'

'It's amazing the number of people who commission items,' I say. 'In my experience, working in Madrid at the El Prado, many replicas could fool experts.'

'Was that your job?'

'Mostly; I catalogued the different pieces, but speaking to the range of experts, not all of them agreed.'

Jake nods seriously. 'I've seen it happen. A good forgery can fool many so-called experts. So, how can I help you?'

'I want a replica made of Napoleon's gold-encrusted sword ...' I lie.

Jake continues to stare at me, then he turns his attention to Peter, who leans casually against the workbench.

'Okay,' he replies quickly.

'How can you do it? Can we use photographs?'

'They would have to be detailed – if you wanted a replica.'

'Have you done anything like this before?'

Jake shrugs. 'I've done a lot of commissions.'

'Can I see the results?'

Jake is wary. I sense him weighing us up, and then he asks, 'How did you hear of me?'

'Through a friend of a friend,' I reply mysteriously, equally unwilling to share information.

'Unless I know your source, I'd find it hard to—'

'Trust us?' I finish.

'Yes.' He smiles.

'I don't need to know who you made things for – we'd just like to see some samples? Make sure your work is of a suitable standard.'

'I've made some serious pieces for considerable sums.'

'I'm sure you have, but I need to be sure that the recommendation has a foundation. I need to know, Jake, that you can handle this project with sensitivity and discretion.'

'I'd never betray a client.'

I smile. 'That's a good start, and that's what I like to hear.'

'I'll need some evidence about you, too.' Jake moves away from the table. 'A piece like this is likely to be expensive, so I will need a trustee or someone who will vouch for you.'

'Joachin Abascal is my boss. He's prepared to do that.'

'I'll also need proof that you have the funds.'

'We can provide that, can't we, cariño?' I turn to look at Peter, and in return, he nods his head thoughtfully. 'I can show you our bank details.'

Jake nods and writes down Joachin's name.

'The gold-encrusted sabre that was once owned by Napoleon

Bonaparte was last sold for $6.5 million,' I say.

Jake rubs his hand across the Aztec maze tattoo on his head. 'That's no problem.'

'How do you charge for your pieces?' I ask.

'I'll work out a price and give it to you.'

'Can I have your number?' I ask.

'Give me yours,' he says, the pencil poised in his hands.

'Do you want me to put it in your mobile?' I nod at the iPhone on the workbench beside him.

'No, I'll write it down.'

I give him my number then say, 'Can you show me anything that you've done on this scale?'

'No.'

'Nothing?'

He shakes his head.

'Then how will I know you can do it.'

'Trust me,' he replies, and when he smiles, I realise how attractive he is.

'I wish I could, but under the circumstances – and the amount of money I'm expected to pay – trust works both ways. I need a guarantee from you. So, unless you can prove that my contact was right and that you can do the work, I think I'll have to go elsewhere. Come on, cariño.' I take Peter's arm and pull him toward the door.

The bell tinkles.

'Wait!' Jake calls softly. 'Perhaps I could show you one thing.'

* * *

We wait as Jake disappears into a back room.

I don't look at Peter, and he doesn't make any signs to me. We're both aware that, almost certainly, there are hidden cameras focused on us.

It doesn't take Jake long to return with a massive black leather portfolio.

He lifts it easily onto the bench, unzips it, and folds it open.

Inside are two A4 photographs, one on each side, behind transparent paper to hold them flat. It's a presentation of Jake's most exceptional work, and I spend a while perusing the images, pausing to look at the details of replica knives, daggers, Samurai swords, and sheaths.

'Impressive,' I say, turning each page with care and caution, as if it's a valuable exhibit from a reputable gallery. 'And you made all these?'

'Yes.'

I turn the pages, my heart thumping, hoping I'll come across the shah's dagger, but when I get to the end of the portfolio, it isn't there.

Jake looks at me, expectantly.

'Well?'

'It's all excellent, but not what I'm looking for.'

His back stiffens. 'Why not?'

'They're not expensive items. The most they would sell for is a few thousand, perhaps one hundred thousand at the most. But I want something replicated that's worth millions. Thank you, anyway, for letting us see this.'

I glance at Peter as if to say let's go when Jake steps into my path.

'I am good. I can do it.'

'I'm sure you can. And I do appreciate that you can't give away clients' details, but—' I look at Peter and say, 'Will I tell him?'

Peter nods, but he doesn't know what I'm about to say. He trusts me.

I turn to Jake and say, 'You were recommended to us by the person who asked you to make a replica of the shah's dagger.'

Jake's eyes widen, and he turns away.

'I'm flattered, but quite frankly, I know nothing about it.'

'Okay, then I won't tell you that I'm willing to pay four times what they paid.'

'Four?' He spins around.

'Look, all I want to see is a drawing, a photograph, anything that will prove to me that I can trust you.'

Jake stares at me and our eyes lock, then he scratches his chin.

'Wait here!'

He returns a few minutes later carrying an identical black leather portfolio but smaller, half the size. He lays it on the table. One picture per page. The shah's dagger.

Bingo!

'Fantastic,' I say. 'This is more like it. This is the quality I want.'

The picture of the original dagger lies above the replica, and they are almost identical, but to my trained eye, the font is slightly too big. I know that Jake made the replica dagger. Now, all we have to find out is who commissioned the replica.

* * *

The atmosphere in the room is palpable. I know that Jake knows he's taken a risk by sharing these photographs with me. I've managed to hook him in, and now I'm planning my options. I can lie, threaten him, or be honest.

'Jake,' I say, leaning against the bench with the portfolio of his work at my fingertips. 'Jake, I'm going to be honest with you.'

I feel his body stiffen, and he glances at Peter, who remains silently at my side.

'The original shah's dagger was stolen and whoever stole it had a replica made by you. The replica is used as a talisman by a group of drug dealers who hook in young kids to swear allegiance to it. They then sell drugs on the street. A group of these kids are known as the *Parks* – they're incredible athletes who run, jump, and scale walls, and fly off buildings with incredible style, grace, and ease—'

'Parkour?' Jake asks, and I nod.

'Yes. They're appearing in a new film by Sandra Worthington, due for release next year – we met them on set in Morocco. They were desperately trying to distance themselves from this drugs gang culture, but when they returned to England, one of the boys, Ali, was taken by the drugs gang and beaten. He managed to escape, but then he killed himself – he jumped off Tower Bridge.'

'I think I saw that on the news.' Jake rubs his chin thoughtfully.

'We know the drug leader who inducted these kids, who are often poor and from deprived city areas, but we need to find the top cult leader, the person who is in charge – and we believe that the person who had this dagger commissioned will help us find that cult leader.'

It is only a small lie, a subtle twist at the end so that Jake will not realise he's giving away a name that would have serious repercussions.

'I doubt that the person you're talking about would be involved in anything like that,' Jake replies eventually.

He reaches for the portfolio, closes the pages, and zips it shut.

'Did you meet him face to face?'

'No.'

'Why do you think that he wouldn't be involved in anything like this?'

Jake shakes his head. 'I can't tell you any more, I'm sorry.'

'Me too, Jake. You see, the thing is, we are from Europol. The name I gave you – Joachin Abascal – is our chief inspector, and we wanted to get this sorted out before the Met police raided here – your studio – and pulled it all apart.' I cast my arms wide dramatically. 'I can stop them from ruining your business and your life. They will assume that as you're not forthcoming with a name that perhaps you are somehow involved in this drugs operation—'

'But I'm not.'

'But they don't know that. All I need is a name, Jake. It's as simple as that.'

Jake shakes his head.

'Okay, I'll call Chief Inspector Mulhoon right now. He's from the Metropolitan Police, and he'll be down here like a shot.'

I reach for my phone, dial a number, and as it begins to ring, Jake holds out his hand.

'Stop! I've seen that chief inspector on the news. He was on the other night after a raid on a warehouse somewhere outside London.'

'That's the one.' I stop the call and place the phone in my pocket. 'Well?'

Jake takes a deep breath. 'I never met them. It was all done by email—'

'So, how did they get the original dagger to you?'

'They left it on the doorstep, phoned me, and I picked it up from outside my front door.'

'That was a risk. Anyone could have picked it up, no?'

'There's a recess in the brickwork, not seen by people walking past, and the small garden at the front helps, but they said they'd wait across the road.'

'So, you did see them?'

'No.'

'So, this person left the original dagger with you and came back to collect the replica and the original when?'

'This all happened last year, maybe eighteen months ago – I guess it took about three weeks to make them.'

'Them?'

'I made two.'

'They asked for two replicas?' I can't hide the surprise in my voice.

Jake nods. 'I left them outside, and they collected them, and the money was wired to my account.'

'What's his name?' I ask.

He pauses, then asks, 'Will I have to provide evidence of the financial transactions?'

'Not if you give me a name. We can take it from there.'

I don't tell him how easy it will be for Peter to hack into his account and find the person's bank details once we have a name.

'I don't want this in the newspapers.'

'Trust me,' I purr. 'No one else needs to know.'

He bites his lower lip and then says, 'Her name is Liz Hunt.'

* * *

I'm leaning over Tower Bridge. The street is busy, and I wander along the road, gazing down into the dark water of the Thames, thinking about Ali and how, just over two weeks ago, we were in Morocco.

I think of his smiling face when he bought his pilot's flying jacket and how proud he was that he had bargained with the stallholder in the Kasbah and accepted the Moorish hospitality of mint tea.

I knew Ali didn't want to kill himself, and Monika had confirmed that. Although he had jumped from the bridge, he hadn't been able to see a way forward, a way out of his dilemma. He'd met someone who he'd trusted – Raymond says it wasn't him, but who was it?

I've a couple of hours to kill while Peter meets Bill for a lunchtime drink, but before we parted, he ran a scan on Raymond Harris's staff – there was no one by the name of Liz Hunt.

'Email me the list, and I'll take a look at it this afternoon,' I'd said.

Now I was looking forward to getting back to the apartment and taking a closer look. There were five female staff and six males, plus several volunteers. It would take Peter longer to check Jake's accounts, and that's assuming Liz Hunt hadn't used a different name and bank account.

I walk south over the bridge, leaving the illuminated Tower of London behind me.

My phone rings and I pause to look at the caller ID.

'Hi, Joachin,' I answer.

'Mulhoon just called me to say that you picked up Adam and

Monika earlier today.'

'Yes, we had to, Joachin. They needed our help.'

'That's fine, Mikky. I understand. The chief inspector is taking personal responsibility for their safety. He appreciates what you did, and now we must leave it to the Met police to sort out.'

'They were worried; the Asian was hanging around the estate. He's recruiting again.'

'Yes, Mulhoon told me.'

'That Asian is brazen.'

'Mulhoon assures me that the police are extra vigilant. They have more officers patrolling and looking out for him. The Met police will find him very shortly. I'm sure of it. They are only one day away from the election, and it's in their interest to find him. The Met is dealing with it. They want to get an arrest before the election.'

I sigh. 'I can imagine, but I wish it wasn't about making the prime minister look good. I wish it were because they want to catch him.'

A gust of cold wind catches me around my face, and so I pull up the collar of my jacket. On Southwark Embankment, the Christmas market stalls glisten brightly, cider and wafts of street food; sweet waffles, burgers, and hot dogs reach me and my stomach gurgles with hunger.

'They do, Mikky. Believe me. Mulhoon doesn't take it lightly that he lost two undercover cops.'

I lean on the wall, surveying the scene below. Couples, families, students, and lovers are walking, chatting, and laughing, and I reply, 'I think there's a traitor in the police, or it's one of Raymond Harris's employees playing a double game.' I walk on, and then pause at the traffic lights and wait to cross the busy road. 'Ali went to Raymond Harris's constituency the night he came back from Morocco. He was there for ten or fifteen minutes. Raymond denies that he was there, but Peter and I think Ali confided in someone and that person then told the Asian. The Asian knew exactly where to find Ali. He picked him up. They beat him, but Ali managed to escape. Monika, one of the other *Parks*, told us that Ali wanted to tell the police everything. And we believe that after Ali realised he'd been betrayed, then he knew there was no escape. There was no one else he could rely on – no one else he could trust.'

'Who was in Raymond's office that night?'

'I don't know, but we do have a lead for the dagger. We know who made a replica dagger that they use as a talisman.' I look both ways and begin to cross the road.

'Which is what Mulhoon wanted you to find out.'

'Yes, and now we're in a position to tell him.'

I step onto the pavement and move out of the way of a commuter dashing for his train.

'You have a name?'

'Yes—'

There's a sharp pain in my right rib. A hand grabs my phone. Another hand grabs my shoulder, and a syringe is aimed at my throat. My legs collapse, and my body goes limp. A second person grabs me by the waist. I've been drugged and I'm dragged to a car, where my head hits the leather seat and, as I lose consciousness, I see the grinning face of the Turk.

Chapter 15

"But from each crime are born bullets that will one day seek out in you where the heart lies."
Pablo Neruda

I don't know how much time has passed. I'm tied in a small and confined place, and I'm suffocating. It's hard to breathe, and my body won't move. I'm moving in a vehicle – probably a car – and I feel sick. I close my eyes, conscious of motion and darkness. My head is blank. I can't concentrate.

Much later, the car stops.

The boot opens, and my eyes are dazzled with bright lights – a torch? Flashlights? Strong hands pull me roughly from the car. We're beside a canal. Regent's Canal? Camden Lock?

Suddenly, my clothes are ripped and torn from my body. I can't resist them. I have no strength. My body can barely remain upright. I'm vaguely aware of the presence of two men wearing black, with their hoods up, as they work methodically, stripping off my jacket, my boots, and my underwear. They throw them into the canal, and it's only when the smaller man faces me and rips off his balaclava that I see it's him – the Asian.

I watch him hurl my phone deep into the water. It's the

only tracking signal that Peter has and a wave of fear ripples through me.

He nods at the man beside me. The Turk, who I'd kicked in the balls and who had raped and drugged Monika, pushes me hard, face first, into the back of the car. I'm lying down, unable to look out of the window, and the leather seat is cold on my skin.

The Turk ties my hands professionally with thick rope, and when I tug at the knots, my arms are weak, and he smacks me on the back of my head.

My scream is muffled against the cold leather, and I close my eyes.

We drive and drive until suddenly, maybe hours later, we stop driving.

There is no movement, then I'm pulled quickly out of the car by my feet and effortlessly lifted up by someone.

It's dark, I can't focus, and I want to be sick.

He carries me like a baby. I'm cold. Rain falls on my naked body, and within seconds, I'm wet, and the wind whips my skin raw.

The man stumbles, and I hear the scraping of a door, then we're inside somewhere vast but dark. Voices echo, but I can't make sense of any of their words.

He leaves me on the floor, where it's dusty, damp, and cold. It smells of rotting fish, and I gag. I groan and try to move, but I can't, and my body begins to shudder. I'm shaking and trembling, and his fingers grab my wrists. He unties them and my ankles, but then I'm tied again and I'm spreadeagled and naked. Then suddenly, I'm hoisted into the air, winched up from the ground, and my arms are yanked apart.

I scream.

The pain makes me pass out, and when I come around, my head has dropped onto my naked chest, and my toes are dangling a few inches from the floor. A flashlight shines behind me.

I shiver; cold, vulnerable, frightened.

'So, Mikky dos Santos ...' The Asian's voice is measured, and he sounds excited. 'The last time you were very fortunate to escape from me. Falling back over the edge of the building, as if you were going to die. You knew there was a safety net, a stunt mattress, to save your life. It was very clever of you to lead me up there, but you made a big mistake. Do you want to know what it was?'

I don't reply, and he gives a signal to someone behind me, and my arms are stretched further apart.

I scream.

'Do you want to know?'

I nod.

'I can't hear you ...'

I croak. 'Yes.'

'You see, I wanted to believe you – all this talk of stealing a valuable dagger. I thought we could be friends, negotiate a deal—' He moves closer and the dagger glints in the beam of light from the flash lamp. I glance around me. We're in a disused warehouse, and I spy a broken window high up. The smell of rotting fish is overwhelming, and I cough and spit on the floor.

'I hope you weren't aiming for me, Mikky?' He trails the dagger across my naked breasts. 'Nice tattoos. Very religious. I hope your God can save you? But no one knows where you are.'

To the left side of me, the Turk laughs; his hand touches my left cheek, but I pull away, which makes his laugh louder.

'We have plenty of time, Mikky. I'm in no hurry. You'll be my play toy once the Turk has finished with you.' The Asian steps away from me. 'So, who are you working for?' The Asian circles me, tapping the dagger against the palm of his hand at regular intervals, as if it's to a beat he's singing in his head.

'Water, please ... have water?' I croak.

'No.'

He leans forward and places the tip of the dagger at the base of my throat. I'm reminded of its sharpness. If I move, it will pierce my skin. I will die.

'Who are you working for?'

'Europol.' I'm conscious of my blood trickling down my skin.

The Asian frowns. 'Europol?' He moves away, considering my reply, tapping the flat blade of the dagger against his hand.

I add huskily, 'It's the dagger ... cultural artefact. Stolen.'

'You mean this old thing?' The Asian raises the knife in front of my face, and shouts, 'THIS?'

'Yes, it's worth $3.3 million.'

The Asian laughs.

The Turk moves to get a better look at the dagger.

'You're lying.'

'Look at the inscription.' I cough. I can hardly hear my voice, but I watch as the two men peer at the engraving. The Asian turns it toward the light, where a large fly is hovering aimlessly above us.

'Where did you get it?' I ask.

The Asian doesn't reply, but the Turk says to him, 'Could it be that valuable? Let me look at it.' His hands are massive by comparison.

'Where did you get it?' the Turk asks. 'From the boss?'

'Of course,' the Asian replies, then he turns to me. 'You want the dagger?'

'Yeah.' My arms are searing in agony, straining at their sockets, and my back and legs hurt. I'm going to pass out. 'Please let me down.'

'If it's worth that amount of money, we could sell it,' the Turk says excitedly. 'We could keep it.'

'You could get a replica made. I can help you. Please let me down ...'

The Turk steps forward with the dagger in his hand. The blade is inches from my naked vagina.

'I'm going to cut you,' he whispers.

'No! Please!' I wriggle my hips to pull away, but then he grabs me from behind. I'm caught in his grasp. My naked body pushed against his chest, his breath against my stomach.

'I'm going to—'

His legs buckle from under him, and he falls to the floor. The dagger clatters on the concrete floor.

'What did you do?' The Asian moves quickly, bending to pick up the knife and, crouching low, he looks around. The warehouse is empty and silent, apart from the wind wailing through the broken windows.

My throat is dry, and I lick my lips. I'm swaying. I'm in pain. And, at my feet, the Turk is lying face down on the ground.

'I didn't do anything—'

The Asian moves quickly, and raising the blade, he lunges forward. The glittering knife coming closer, I close my eyes, but suddenly there's a light thud, and then his body crumples.

He lies soundlessly at my feet.

I can't see anything, and I'm shaking so hard that I'm almost rattling. My teeth are moving against each other, chattering uncontrollably.

I hear soft sounds. There's movement, and I steel myself, looking in one direction and then the next. Tears begin to trickle down my face.

A soft voice says, 'You're okay. You're safe.'

There's a black uniform. A gun. Then more uniforms.

Someone grabs me by the waist and shouts, 'I've got her. She's alive.'

The pulley is released and my arms go slack. I collapse on the floor, sobbing. Someone places a warm, clean blanket over my shoulder. 'Mikky?'

'Peter?' I find his shoulders and throw my aching arms around his neck.

'It's alright. You're safe.'

'But, but ... you ... found me?'

'Of course.' I recognise his familiar smile and short beard as he holds me tightly, kneeling on the cold cement floor. 'Can you walk? It stinks down here.'

'Yes.' I try to stand with his help but then my legs buckle.

He catches me. 'That's a feeble excuse for me to carry you.' He lifts me effortlessly into his arms. 'There's an ambulance outside.'

'How did you ...' I don't finish the sentence. I pass out.

* * *

When I come round, I'm conscious of a paramedic leaning over me. I'm in an ambulance and Peter is sitting beside me.

'She seems okay.' The paramedic moves away. 'Paracetamol will help with the pain.'

'I thought she'd be fine.' Peter stands up. 'Put these clothes on,' he says to me.

I struggle into a dark shirt and trousers that are far too big for me, but he throws me a belt to tie around my waist.

'Shoes?' I ask.

'Trainers, but they're probably on the large side.' He tosses them at me. 'The female shooter is a size larger than you.'

I glance at him but say nothing.

'Mulhoon is outside,' he says.

The paramedic opens the door and Peter helps me out.

'Such a gentleman.'

'Here.' He thrusts a bottle of water at me and hands me two white tablets. 'For the pain.'

'Thanks,' I say, sipping gratefully, my throat soothed, and the sensations begin to return to my arms and legs. I walk slowly beside Peter, taking in my surroundings. It's a massive unused warehouse near the coast. Around us are fields and marshes.

'Where are we?' I ask.

'Suffolk.'

Two ambulances, SWAT police vans, and searchlights light up the area. Inside the warehouse, the forensic team have already begun their jobs. The bodies of the Asian and the Turk are where they fell.

The police forensic team haven't touched the dagger. It's still lying on the floor. Away from the crime scene, Mulhoon stands to one side in discussion with a female officer.

Peter says, 'There will be evidence of your blood on the blade, plus we have the video evidence that we took from the fly drone.'

'Fly?' I vaguely remember a fly hovering over us.

'We used it to see what was going on inside.'

'I thought only the military used mini-drones that small? Was that your idea?'

He grins. 'We were lucky. It can be noisy, but with the wind howling through the broken windows, they didn't hear it. I think there'll be a very clear picture of what went on.'

'Peter, it was like something out of the SAS. So calm and controlled, the way they shot them both. They didn't know what happened. What hit them.'

'One of the best SWAT teams in the world.'

I stare at him.

'What's bothering you?' Peter moves closer to me.

'You came here with the police to rescue me?'

'Yes.'

'How did you find me?' I ask. 'How did you know where I was? They stripped me and threw my clothes and iPhone into the canal.'

'I'll tell you later. Just don't be mad at me.'

I link my arm through his and watch Mulhoon approaching us.

'You're a magician; how could I possibly be angry with you, my saviour?'

* * *

It takes time to bring Mulhoon and his team up to date while a search team, including tracker dogs, as well as white-suited forensic scientists, scan the warehouse; bagging and tagging items for evidence, and marking areas with various cordons. I watch people go backwards and forwards to different vans and cars.

Eventually, I'm allowed to sit in Peter's van. I climb wearily inside, and I pull his thick coat over my body and yawn.

Peter starts the van's engine. 'Mulhoon has said we can go, and I told him we'd be at the flat if he needs anything else.'

'Okay,' I whisper.

My eyes are already closing, and I'm happy to doze as Peter drives us back to the safety of London and Josephine's loft apartment.

I wake as we're on the outskirts of London. It's almost seven, and Peter turns on the radio for the news.

There's an interview with the chief inspector, and with the election tomorrow, he's emphasising the importance of the death of the two drugs gang leaders – an Asian and a Turk. He emphasises the positive effect it could have on the existing government, and he hints that a statement will be made shortly by the prime minister.

Peter pulls the van into the underground parking space and kills the engine, and I stare at him. 'We haven't got the main man.' I pull off my seat belt and Peter turns to open the van door.

'The thing is,' I continue, unwrapping myself from Peter's coat and handing it back to him, 'is that whoever arranged for the daggers to be replicated is behind this whole operation – and responsible for the main drug-smuggling ring.'

'Mikky, that's enough!'

'Did you tell Mulhoon about Ali visiting Raymond Harris's office?' I ask.

'No.'

'Why not?'

'There wasn't time. We were focusing on the Asian and the Turk, but I suggested we meet him tomorrow for a proper debrief after you've had a good rest.'

'Good idea. I want a hot bath, to rid my head of the images of those two awful men, and a decent drink.'

'Then we must phone Joachin.'

'Then we must phone Joachin,' I echo, and I link my arm through his and allow him to guide me upstairs to the safety of Josephine's apartment.

* * *

I'm running a bath when Peter appears, and by the look on his face I know there's something wrong.

'You did WHAT?' I say when he confesses to me.

'Come on, Mikky,' Peter urges me. 'Don't be angry. You promised!'

'I can't believe it! I'm furious with you, Peter!'

'Shush, Mikky. Don't make a fuss – it would be a criminal offence; you know it would be. You have to pretend you're okay with it and that it was part of our plan.'

'You could go to prison for what you did to me.'

'Look, I did it because I made a promise to Joachin and Josephine that I wouldn't let you out of my sight.'

'But you can't do this – that,' I hiss angrily, pulling my bathrobe across my body. 'Is nothing sacred?'

'Pull open your gown,' Peter whispers, 'and turn around.'

'You HAVE to be joking!'

He giggles.

'Stop laughing at me!'

'Sorry! I'm not laughing at you, but your face is a picture, Mikky. You've never been so angry with me.'

'How would you feel if you had been tagged like a dog?' I

turn my back to him and lower the dressing gown to my waist.

'You haven't been tagged, Mikky. All I did was insert a bar code chip under your skin. There it is, look!'

I look in the bathroom mirror and then I turn to look over my shoulder and run my finger over the fading scab at the top of my buttock. 'I can't feel anything.'

'It's the size of a grain of rice. I can get it out, but I think we should leave it until the police have examined you. They might need proof.'

'Tracked like a dog,' I hiss, pulling my gown back over my shoulders and tying the belt securely.

'This is the world of spying, Mikky. Soon, everyone will have them. They will help all sorts of people; you know, parents who want to keep track of their children, and also for the elderly – people with dementia who go missing from care homes—'

'You are seriously morally and ethically nuts!'

'Mikky!'

'Would you put one in your child – in Zofia?'

'Er, well no, probably not.'

'Well, then.' I turn my back and reach for my wine glass.

'Please, Mikky, pretend to the police – and Joachin – that you knew all about it. And remember, the Asian and the Turk did throw your clothes and phone into the river. If I hadn't put it under your skin, then I'd never have found you—'

'Don't get all pious with me. You're behaving like you're infallible, like you're the Almighty.'

He holds up his hands. 'I'm sorry but ... well, I'm not sorry!'

'When did you do it?'

'The other night, after you'd – we'd – had a few drinks.'

'You did it deliberately?'

He looks sheepish, so I add, 'You planned it! You took

advantage of me?'

'You were in a drunken sleep. It's quick and easy to do, and I took all precautions. It's easier than getting a tattoo, and I made sure I cleaned the cut to avoid infection.'

'I have a vague memory of waking up with a small scratch. How did you know it would work?' I ask.

'I checked a couple of times, to make sure. But I couldn't take any more risks, Mikky. Not after the last time, when you jumped off that building. I'd never forgive myself if something happened to you. I was too late to save you the last time ...' His voice trails off, and that's when I see the guilt and sadness in his eyes.

'Oh, Peter.' I reach up and throw my arms around his neck and give him the biggest hug.

'I'm sorry,' he whispers.

'Thank you.'

* * *

Peter cooks pasta and meatballs, and we enjoy a few glasses of Rioja. I'm sitting on the sofa in clean jeans and a T-shirt when we Skype Joachin.

'It was a precaution,' Peter explains. 'We both knew how ruthless both of the men were, and we didn't want to take any chances. Just in case ...'

He goes on to explain how he had gone for a lunchtime drink with Bill when Joachin had called him.

'Mikky didn't answer her phone when I checked the last location of it.' Peter's face is serious. 'The bar code implant was activated. I located Mikky, and I assumed she was in a car or van and heading away from London, so I called Mulhoon.

I told him the Asian had taken Mikky and I was able to track them. He activated his SWAT team immediately. I used the tracking gear in my van while Bill flew the helicopter at a discreet distance and we found the Asian's car. Bill followed him in the air while I followed on the road.'

'To Suffolk.'

'Yes.'

'Mulhoon's team arrived within minutes. Bill and I stayed well back and let them deal with the rescue mission.'

'Good!'

'Are you okay, Mikky?' Joachin asks, regarding me thoughtfully.

'I'm fine; thank you.'

'The chief inspector seems happy.' Peter smiles at the screen.

'Yes. I spoke to Mulhoon, and he said that the prime minister is also relieved.'

'Maybe he might phone you?' I say. 'He might like to thank you for deploying your team—'

'Mikky! I didn't encourage you, and I won't pretend I did. I don't like either of you flouting my orders. We are going to have to review our situation. We can't work on this basis, with the two of you doing what you want to without any regard for the law or jurisdiction, and the unfortunate position in which you place me. You were fortunate this time, Mikky. You're like a cat with nine lives, although I suspect that you must have used them all up by now.'

The irony in his tone doesn't fool me, but I smile anyway. 'Peter and I are a good team.'

Joachin gazes at the screen. His dark eyes seem to penetrate through the lens. 'And now it's over. All done. Finished.'

'There's one more thing,' I say, and cough to clear my voice. 'The thing is, is that we don't have the ringleader. The person who started this gang – the one who organised the oath to the dagger, and the person whose idea it was to recruit these kids. That person is still out there – and they will find another psychopath like the Asian to do their bidding, and to terrorise the children and force them again into working in drugs rings.'

Joachin doesn't blink. He continues to stare at the screen until I say to Peter, 'Have we lost the connection? Is the screen frozen?'

'No,' Joachin replies. 'I'm still here. I'm listening.'

I grin. 'Sorry, Joachin! But we do have a lead,' I say.

'What's the lead?' asks Joachin.

'We believe that Ali went to Raymond's office the night he died, and that he was there for maybe ten to fifteen minutes. Ali met someone who betrayed him because a car was waiting outside, and we believe the Asian picked him up. But Ali managed to escape. The problem was, he knew that no one would believe his story. He also knew that the Asian would kill him. He had nowhere to go, no one to turn to, and that's why he killed himself. Our theory is that the person he spoke to was in a position of authority ...'

'He had Matt?'

'I don't think Matt could have saved him. Not that night.' I rub my eyes. It still upset me to speak about Ali.

'Do you think Raymond Harris is involved? Joachin asks.

'When I asked him, he denied it—'

'But,' Peter interjects, 'it can't be a coincidence that the Asian knew exactly where to find Mikky. Raymond could have tipped the Asian off. I think he might have told the Asian and he started following her – he might have started tailing her after we left Dixon House.'

'You'll have to speak to Mulhoon and turn over *all* the evidence that you have—'

'I can't,' Peter replies. 'I can't show them evidence because the CCTV footage wasn't obtained legally.'

'Oh, for heaven's sake!' splutters Joachin. 'Don't you two understand that you can't go around stealing CCTV and following people, let alone accusing them of serious crimes—'

'The thing is, Joachin, the craftsman who made the dagger – he made *two* that were the same.'

'So, the dagger that the Asian had obviously wasn't the real one?'

'No, but it was modelled on the original.'

Joachin sighs and frowns. 'This is very confusing. Are you telling me there are three daggers?'

I nod. 'The craftsman was asked to make two replicas.'

Joachin rubs his temple, dragging his thumb across the skin. 'So, you think someone stole the authentic dagger and took it to a craftsman and asked them to make two replicas, then put the original dagger back into Jeffrey Bonnington's collection?'

I smile.

'You seriously expect me to believe that there are two replica daggers?' Joachin stares at me. 'And that the original was stolen from Jeffrey Bonnington's secure collection that he has hidden somewhere in the world and that two replicas were made, and the authentic dagger was then returned to his collection – all without him knowing?'

'That's how the craftsman would have got the level of detail, and that's how the head person convinced the Asian. You see, I think that the dagger the Asian had the first time, the one that I stole, *was* the original. It was different to the one that he had today. The engraving wasn't as neat, the inscription was bigger, and the font was larger.'

'How is that possible?' Joachin asks.

I shrug. 'I don't know. Unless he or someone swapped it.'

'There are three daggers, and no one knows which is the original?' he says.

'It does seem a little far-fetched,' I agree.

'Unless Jeffrey Bonnington is involved.' Peter leans closer to the screen.

'This is ludicrous!' Joachin explodes. 'Why on earth would he be involved? The man's a successful multimillionaire and sits on the board of one of the most important pharmaceutical companies in the world.'

'They're all drugs,' I mumble. 'Whichever way you look at it!'

'Impossible.' Joachin shakes his head.

Peter replies, 'I suppose it does seem a bit crazy.'

'Look, we have to follow the evidence, so let's see where it takes us. We know that Jeffrey Bonnington has a massive property portfolio, and according to Raymond Harris, the building Sandra has been using for filming is prime real estate. If it's sold to a company who builds luxury housing and homes for wealthy Russians, or if it gets sold to the local government for social housing – either way, this affects the voting public. It could sway elections. Raymond Harris could gain voters if the block is made into apartments for the homeless or anyone under the poverty level. His stance on this has made him *very* popular.'

'And the opposition?' Joachin asks.

'The other political party obviously want the rich and wealthy investors in their area – for the rich man's vote.'

'Could this be linked to why Bonnington has invested in Dixon House?' Peter asks. 'Do you think Matt could be involved?'

I say, 'I have brought Matt up to date with everything, including my conversations with Raymond and Mulhoon. We've kept him in the picture the whole time.'

Peter looks at me. 'I can't believe Matt would be involved. He loves those kids – the *Parks* – all of them.'

Joachin says, 'You can't trust anyone.'

'So, what's the next step?' I ask. 'Do we have your permission to find Liz Hunt?'

'I checked the database of Raymond's staff and none match that name.' Peter taps the stubs of his finger against the table.

'I think we need to go back to Jeffrey Bonnington.' I stare at Joachin, waiting for him to explode, but instead, he answers cautiously.

'The elections are tomorrow. The government don't want a scandal, but I guess that's what Mulhoon asked you to do. Tread carefully ...'

'Because you tread on my dreams,' Peter recites Yeats's poem, and I giggle.

* * *

I stand at the window, staring out across the river and the illuminated London skyline. There's something both exciting yet weirdly frightening about cities, the thrill of so many different buildings, architecture, colours, people – life. Cities seem to pulsate, but I know the evil that lurks under the glamour of the tourist sites, in the backstreets behind the neon signs. Behind each expensive restaurant is a dark alleyway filled with trash, rats, and fear.

I think about how I was tied up by the Asian and the Turk, and it's only by repeating the images in my head – of them falling, shot dead – that convince me I'm safe.

I sit on the sofa and watch Peter type away on the keyboard. He looks tired, and periodically he stretches his neck and his shoulders, so I pick up my phone and dial Monika's number. She answers on the third ring.

'Hi, are you okay?' I ask.

'Yeah, and you?'

'Fine.'

'I want to tell you some good news, Monika, in case you didn't see the news on TV. We caught the bad guys – the awful ones that hurt you, the Turk and the Asian.'

'Really?'

'Yes. It's all over.'

'Will they go to prison?'

'They're both dead.'

She gasps, and I imagine her covering her mouth.

I add, 'It will be on the Internet news. It happened in Suffolk this afternoon.'

'Good. I'm pleased they're dead.'

'You must know that the law will win, Monika, you must know that. You must believe that there are good people who will help you and protect you.'

'Matt's good. He spoke to Adam's foster parents, and they have said I can stay here, with them and Adam. They're lovely.'

'Good. I'm pleased.'

'I was looking at training today. Marjorie, Adam's foster mother, was helping me look at nursing and stuff.'

I smile. 'So, you're thinking of a career in nursing again?'

'Yeah, I think I'll be eligible for a bursary.'

'Fantastic, Monika. That's excellent news. You can turn your life around. It will be a challenge, but it will also be an amazing opportunity.'

'Yeah, I think I'll like it.'

'How's Adam?'

'He's okay. But he's talking about joining the army. He wants to be like Peter.'

'Oh?'

'Yeah, but I don't want him going off to wars and doing dangerous stuff. He's way too emotional. He's also really talented like as an artist. Can you speak to him sometime and persuade him that the army isn't for him?'

'I'll ask Peter to talk to him, how's that?' I suggest.

'Cool, thanks.'

We speak for a little longer, and when I hang up, I call across to where Peter is still at the table working.

'Liz Hunt is just a name. It could belong to any volunteer, male or female.'

'That's the worrying thing,' he replies.

* * *

I pour myself another glass of wine.

In the corner of the room, the TV is on mute, but the ten o'clock news is showing pictures of the warehouse where I was held captive earlier this afternoon.

I turn up the volume. Then there are a few images of the Turk – it turns out he was a wanted armed criminal. The news channel then shows pictures of the Asian. The newsreader goes on to say how the two men were trapped in a warehouse in Suffolk and shot by police. My name and Peter's have been deliberately kept out of the news, but the politicians are delighted with the rapid police response team.

'What's bothering you, Mikky? Are you frightened after what happened today, and you don't want to go to bed?'

'No, I'm thinking about the craftsman. We could hack into his account and find out who paid him for the daggers?'

Peter sits back, folds his arms across his chest, and regards me thoughtfully for a while. 'I did, and it's not there.'

I smile. 'You already looked?'

Peter nods seriously. 'I've also been onto Martin McVey's Bond Street and mobile banking, and there's nothing.'

I sit down at the table opposite him. 'What about email? They must have had some form of communication?'

'Just checking now, but there's a lot of emails to trawl through.'

'Just supposing the original dagger was stolen and replicated, it wouldn't be easy breaking into a property owned by Jeffrey Bonnington, would it?'

'You mean a London property?'

I smile. 'You've checked, haven't you? Does he have one?'

'He has a home in Holland Park.' Peter returns my smile. 'What do you think I've been doing for the past few hours?'

'Don't be smug!' I punch his arm.

Peter laughs.

'Do you think Jeffrey Bonnington is in on it? Could he have lent the dagger to someone?'

'Someone he trusts?' Peter shakes his head. 'I don't know.'

'Or maybe he got the replicas made himself?'

'Why?'

'To encourage the cult. I don't know, perhaps to stir up

303

trouble, to create a dangerous underworld that would have a knock-on effect with the local property market?'

'Just to help Raymond Harris and his political career? What's the point? What does Jeffrey Bonnington get out of it?' Peter asks, shaking his head dismissively.

'Circumstances can be deceiving.'

'But he's a multimillionaire, Mikky. What's in it for him? He's not going to risk jail, is he?'

'No,' I muse. 'But there must be a common link, or else how did whoever it was manage to get hold of the dagger?'

'Mikky, remember it's only you who has been clever enough to put that thought process together. The Met police have no idea that the authentic dagger is worth $3.3 million.'

'Do you think we should have told Mulhoon today?'

'Mikky, you were in no fit state to think and speak rationally earlier today. Let's sleep on it, and we can tell Mulhoon in the morning. Maybe we need his help to get through to Jeffrey Bonnington.'

'Great!' I smile. 'That's a positive plan. At last. Now I can sleep.' I walk past Peter and kiss the top of his head on my way to the bedroom. 'Night, night, my angel.'

Chapter 16

"Crime has no color. Crime has no type. Crime has no gender. The reason why crime doesn't end. It is being categorized to certain individuals that people who really commit it, get away with it, right under our noses."
De philosopher DJ Kyos

The following morning, I shower and dress in my familiar jeans, T-shirt, hoodie, and biker's boots. My body is sore, my arms and legs ache, and my shoulders and neck feel as though they have been squeezed in a steel vice.

I swallow two paracetamols with orange juice, followed by a strong coffee.

Peter is already in his familiar position at the table.

'It's election day,' he announces, nodding at the television.

'I'm fed up with them all.' I reach for the remote and mute the sound. 'Liz Hunt,' I mull the words over, running the name over my tongue like a fine wine. 'Where else can we check her out?'

'I've done my best, Mikky. But there are no leads.'

'Liz Hunt. Peter – why does that name sound familiar to me?'

'I don't know; maybe it's because it's been going around in

your head?'

'Liz Hunt could be a cover name for anyone. It's a wild thought, but could Raymond be having an affair?'

'If he was, I think the press would be onto that by now.'

'We need to be able to tie up Liz Hunt with Raymond's office; and tell me something else, Peter – why did she have *two* replicas made? And, assuming the original is in Jeffrey Bonnington's collection, and one replica is with the police, where is the second one?'

Peter lifts the mug of coffee I slide over to him to take a sip.

I muddle through my thoughts, thinking out loud. 'I know, Peter, I know! Liz Hunt stole the original dagger and then replaced it with a fake, and the second fake dagger she gave to the Asian. Which means she still has the original shah's dagger. Why would she replace it? What do you think?'

'I think you're on the right track.'

'She's a thief? Like me?'

'You're not a thief anymore.'

'What are you doing?' I ask.

'Scanning Liz Hunt in the criminal underworld to see if she has a record.'

'Do you want to know what I'm thinking?'

'It's a false identity?' He grins.

'What?'

'Well, of course that isn't her real name, but I'm thinking – what if she did steal the dagger and Jeffrey Bonnington isn't aware that it's stolen?'

'Or maybe he lent it to her?' Peter suggests.

'You're right, Peter. There's only one way to find out. I'm going to phone him.'

I scroll through my contact list and find his private phone

number that Marina Thoss gave to me. I'd used it to arrange our meeting in Basel. The ringing tone echoes in the room, and I'm surprised when he answers it.

'Jeffrey Bonnington?' I ask.

'Yes.'

'Mikky dos Santo, we met in Basel last week.'

'Yes.'

'I'm sorry to bother you; I know that you're in the Caribbean, but I have one question for you regarding the shah's dagger—'

'Where are you?' he interrupts angrily.

'In London.'

'So am I, I arrived last night, and you were right – the shah's dagger is missing!'

* * *

It doesn't take Peter long to find Jeffrey Bonnington's house in Holland Park. It's a large, impressive three-storey townhouse with a black front door and brass knocker. We climb the steps to the front door and survey the cul-de-sac below us with approval.

'This is probably worth £10 million,' Peter whispers, as the door opens.

'Come in, come in.' Jeffrey Bonnington looks flustered and quite relieved to see us. 'I've delayed calling the police until you came, but I went into my study this morning ... Look, come and see.'

We follow Jeffrey Bonnington's rotund figure as he marches down the polished oak floor toward a room lined with antique books and display cases containing an assortment of lethal-looking weapons.

'Don't look so surprised! I'm not a murderer, just a collector.'

He stands at an old cabinet, pulls down the door, and reaches inside, and I take the opportunity to glance at Peter, who is already sizing up the room. I know he's checking the security, but there appear to be secure locks on the windows and discreet wall cameras.

'The alarm system is linked directly to the local police,' he says, looking at Peter, and then he hands me the shah's dagger. 'But it hasn't gone off.'

'Well? What do you think?'

I turn the sharp weapon carefully in my hands, aware of the curve of the sharp blade and the gemstone handle. I read the inscription that I've memorised, and I'm also familiar with the emblems and font sizes, and after a thorough inspection, I look back at Jeffrey Bonnington.

'It's not the original.'

'I know it isn't. I just wanted you to tell me that.' He sighs and puffs out his cheeks.

'Have you got insurance?' asks Peter, who's never appreciated the amount art collectors pay. He stands at the window and looks down into the small, secluded, landscaped garden.

'It's not about the money. I want to know who's stolen it!' Jeffrey growls.

He opens his palm, and I return the replica dagger carefully to him. It might not be the original, but it's still lethal. He places it back inside the drawer and turns a small key, which he puts in his waistcoat pocket when he's finished.

'How could they have got in?' I ask.

'It all looks secure.' Peter studies the small garden. 'No windows were broken. No sign of forced entry.'

'It is secure. No one could possibly have got in. It's more secure than any Swiss bank. It's impossible to get in here.'

'Perhaps not.' Peter stares back at Jeffrey Bonnington.

'Did you ever lend it to anyone?' I ask.

'Lend it? Absolutely not. And, besides, if I had, I'd make sure I jolly well got the original back again. This is a fake. A good one, but nevertheless, a worthless fake.'

Peter turns from the window. 'I thought you told us you were going to the Caribbean for Christmas?'

'I was, I am, but ... well, quite frankly, you worried me. So, I decided to call in here on my way. This is my London residence. Then I saw last night on television about some drugs gang members having been shot, and I thought there might be some truth to what you told me.'

'How often do you come here?' I ask.

'A few weeks in the spring and again in the summer. I intend to spend more time here now I'm cutting down on my meetings in Switzerland. I'm not working as much – but what does that have to do with anything? Me being here or not hasn't made any difference, has it?! I'm going to call the police.'

'Do you know anyone called Liz Hunt?' I ask.

Jeffrey Bonnington shakes his head slowly.

'Liz Hunt? I don't think so ...'

'Perhaps you should call Chief Inspector Mulhoon,' Peter says. 'I think you need to tell the police exactly what's happened, but unfortunately, because we are with Europol, we have no jurisdiction over anything that happens here. In fact, Mr Bonnington, because you reported us the last time we met, we are in serious trouble with the Met.'

Jeffrey Bonnington looks surprised and then hurt. 'I didn't

309

mean anything by it. It was just an unusual set of circumstances and … and … well, I'm sorry.'

I tap Jeffrey Bonnington on the arm. 'If we can help you, we
will, but Peter is right. You need to call the police.'

As if by telepathic agreement, Peter and I begin to walk to
the front door and Jeffrey Bonnington follows behind us.

At the front door, I stop and hold out my hand. 'I'm sorry
we couldn't help you more.'

Jeffrey Bonnington looks confused, and his palm is warm
and dry when he shakes my hand. He seems visibly upset, and
I wonder if it's because he loved the shah's dagger, or because
he realises someone has stolen $3.3 million from him.

We are halfway down the steps to where our van is parked
when he calls out, 'Liz Hunt?'

I pause on the steps and turn.

'That couldn't be in any way related to my niece?'

'Your niece?'

'Well, it's a long shot, really. My sister's daughter …'

I walk back up the steps.

'Where does she live?'

'My sister Linda and I fell out years ago. She was very angry
when my father left me as the sole inheritor of the family
property. She was married twice, and her last husband was
called Hunter. She passed away several years ago, maybe
fifteen years ago? And I met her daughter for the first time
at Linda's funeral. We didn't have much in common, but the
resentment was still there, so I wanted to make it up to her. I
invited her and her husband for a holiday to Switzerland. She's
also visited me here a few times when we've been in London.'
He sighs. 'But then our relationship seemed to fall apart, and
we saw less and less of each other. I do what I can, of course—'

'Do you mean financially?'

'Well, sort of, yes. She married a politician a few years ago, a junior minister, and he works with the homeless people. I never had much time for any of it myself. If you want a job, go out and get one; I said it to her once and she was furious. I've never lived on handouts—'

'And her name is Liz Hunt?'

'Her name *was* Hunter, and as far as I remember, her middle name is Elizabeth – Liz. She used it all the time before she got married. Now she uses Arlene – Arlene Harris.'

* * *

'I'll drive,' I say, opening the van door. 'You find out what Raymond Harris is doing today.'

Beside me, Peter fastens his seat belt and glances at his watch. 'I'd imagine he'll have gone early to the polling station with his wife, then they'll probably wait at home until the results start coming through later tonight.'

'Liz Hunt,' I say to Peter, 'is Arlene Elizabeth Harris – née Hunter. I googled her before I visited her at her home. Why didn't I remember?'

'Don't beat yourself up, Mikky.'

'Call Mulhoon and get him to meet us at Raymond's house.'

I drive quickly, but my arms are still sore from yesterday and my back aches. I drive in silence until Peter has finished the call.

'I can't believe she's behind it all. Why?' I complain. 'Why did she do it?'

'That's what we will have to ask her.'

Peter stares ahead out of the window, and we drive the rest

of the way in silence, both deep in thought.

I can't drive fast enough as I try to work out what would have possessed a politician's wife to get mixed up with the Asian and the countless deaths of innocent, vulnerable children.

* * *

Chief Inspector Mulhoon climbs out of the parked car, leaving two uniformed police officers inside to wait for him. It's a wintery December day, and I shiver as we meet at the entrance of Raymond Harris's house. Although it's mid-morning, the lights are glowing on the porch, and the brightly lit Christmas tree in the window looks welcoming.

'Snow is forecast at the weekend.' Peter stretches out his hand. 'Thank you for meeting us, Chief Inspector.'

Mulhoon nods and addresses me. 'Are you alright, Mikky?'

'Much better.' I smile brightly.

'What's this all about?' he asks. 'We were having a debrief this morning.'

'We'll tell you inside.'

'Let's go.' Peter rings the bell.

Arlene opens the front door, and her doll-like face has the same expression as it had the last time – mild surprise and a hint of a smile.

'Is your husband in?' Peter asks.

'He's swamped. It's an important day.'

Mulhoon steps forward. 'Hello, Arlene, can you tell him we'd just like ten minutes of his time. It's freezing out here.'

'Of course, sorry, Chief Inspector, I didn't see it was you, come in.'

When she speaks, her features remain frozen in the same

place; the result of botox, lip enhancement, and heavy make-up.

She stands aside to let us pass, and as we stand awkwardly in the hallway, I smell alcohol on her breath.

'Go through to the lounge, and I'll tell Raymond you're here.'

In the lounge, the chief inspector stands beside the fireplace and rubs his hands at the open flames. Peter sits on a yellow and black patterned chaise longue and crosses his legs, and I stand at the window and watch a robin bobbing along the fence, scavenging for food and twittering happily.

'Mulhoon?' Raymond strides into the lounge smiling, but his step falters when he sees Peter and me at the window. 'Er, hello everyone?'

I move over to greet him.

'We've met before, Raymond. I'm Mikky dos Santos, and this is my colleague Peter.'

Raymond looks at Peter, but neither men make an effort to shake hands. 'What's going on?' he asks.

Arlene hovers at the doorway, and I walk toward her.

'Please come in, Arlene. There are no secrets. Sit down there.' I take charge and indicate for them both to sit together on the sofa. Raymond is reluctant to be bossed around in his own house, so he remains standing.

'What's this about?' He looks at Mulhoon.

'Have you voted this morning?' Peter asks.

Raymond looks bemused. 'Yes, we both walked down to the polling station at nine.'

Peter nods.

'Is this to do with the election?' Raymond looks at Mulhoon for support.

'Sort of, but it's more to do with the events from yesterday.'

'Yesterday?' Raymond straightens his back.

'The Asian,' Mulhoon says.

'And the Turk,' I add.

'They were both killed.' Peter stands up.

'Ah yes. I saw that on the news. It looked a very nasty operation and you did well. The night before the election, too, that must have given the prime minister a boost; he was certainly milking it for all it was worth last night. The TV channels couldn't get enough of him.'

'Like you the night Ali died.' My face remains expressionless. My sarcasm is lost on him.

'What do you mean?'

'You hardly mentioned Ali after he died. The Dixon Trust had looked after him, Matt had been instrumental in getting him help, away from the drugs gangs, but you ignored all that. Instead, you chose to focus on arguing about who was buying the empty apartment block that Sandra Worthington was filming in. You were more obsessed about it being sold to wealthy Russian oligarchs who wouldn't vote for you—'

'That's not true.'

'It's no secret that you wanted if for social housing so that you'd have more voters at the next election.'

'That's a ridiculous idea.'

I smile. 'The good news is that we're not here to talk about the election and your track record.'

'No? Well, that's ... good.' Raymond shifts uncomfortably but still refuses to sit beside his wife. Instead he remains, standing awkwardly, looking at Mulhoon for support.

I reach into my bag and pull out the dagger, lent to me this morning by Jeffrey Bonnington once the real identity of Liz

Hunt became clear to us. I place it on their coffee table in the centre of the room.

Raymond Harris stares at it.

Arlene blinks.

Mulhoon steps away from the fire.

'This is the shah's dagger that the gang leaders, who were shot yesterday, used as a talisman to frighten and intimidate their gangs. They preyed on lonely, isolated, and vulnerable children. They befriended kids, sometimes as young as ten or eleven years old. They'd buy them chips or sweets, talk to them, pretend to care, and take them shopping. They made them feel wanted, and they'd lure them into a false friendship, encouraging them into this cult, where they'd swear to protect each other. They were family. They'd never grass. The leaders pretended to make them feel safe, but what they did was to get the kids involved in selling drugs, making money, and sometimes they'd even have to prove themselves by maiming and killing others. Cheffing—'

'That's when they stab each other,' Peter explains.

'With this?' Raymond asks, leaning forward. 'Can I pick it up?'

'Be careful. It's very sharp,' Peter warns.

'Have you seen it before?' I ask.

Raymond shakes his head. 'No, but it looks interesting – valuable?'

'We'll come back to that,' I reply.

'What does all this have to do with me? Is this about the Dixon Trust?'

'What about you, Arlene? Have you seen this dagger before?'

She shakes her head but doesn't look at Raymond, who is examining it and reading the inscription on the side of the blade.

Mulhoon watches them and continues to warm his backside against the fire, bouncing up and down on his heels.

'Three weeks ago, Chief Inspector Mulhoon asked me to find this dagger. He believed that if we found it, it would help lead us to find the cult members and, more importantly, the head of the gang here in Islington. He'd already lost two undercover police officers, and he didn't want to risk any more lives.'

Mulhoon says, 'I've just remembered, Raymond, I told you I was sending in two of my men undercover at that fundraising night you did.'

'Yes, yes, I think you did.' Raymond frowns.

'Did you tell anyone else?' Mulhoon asks.

Raymond shakes his head and then looks at Arlene, but she's staring down at the table.

I continue speaking, 'This – the shah's dagger – is worth over $3.3 million.'

'My goodness.' Raymond places the dagger back on the table as if it's red hot, and then straightens up suddenly, smiling.

'And we found the gang leaders who were killed yesterday.'

'That's excellent news. So, we can all be reassured that the Asian, and the Turk, no longer rule the drugs gangs in Islington. Excellent! The children will be safe. That's fantastic news.' Raymond beams around the room at that moment as if he's campaigning for the election.

'Well, it's not that simple.' I stare at him and his smile fades. 'The thing is, is that this dagger became an important symbol – a weapon of fear. All the cult members had a tattoo of this dagger just here, under their heart.' I point at my chest. 'But the other point is that the Asian had no idea it was such a valuable dagger. It looks expensive, and that made him happy

...' I pause.

'Where did he get it?' Raymond asks.

'That's what we need to find out. Did the Asian steal it, or did someone give it to him? Where did he get it?'

Arlene focuses on her gripped hands, as if she's in silent prayer.

'This morning, a private collector who bought it at auction for $3.3 million contacted us. This is the one from his collection.'

'Really!' Raymond looks aghast.

Mulhoon shifts uncomfortably on his toes, frowning. He knows that the dagger found at the crime scene yesterday is still in police custody.

'There has to be a link between the private collector and the Asian, or someone who had the opportunity to steal the shah's dagger and make not just one – but *two* – replicas.'

'Two?' Raymond frowns.

Chief Inspector Mulhoon stops rocking.

'Yes. The one that we recovered yesterday in Suffolk that the Asian had in his possession, and this one.' I point to the one on the table. 'We borrowed this earlier this morning from the private collector because – unfortunately – this is a replica.'

'A replica?' Raymond stares at the dagger before adding, 'So where is the original dagger?'

The silence in the room is broken only by a hissing log that crackles, breaks away, and crashes into the ash. Mulhoon glances down at the fire.

Peter stands up. 'I think your wife knows the answer to that,' he says.

'Arlene?' Raymond stares at his wife.

Arlene shakes her head but refuses to look up.

317

I say, 'I believe that by the time the Met have searched this house, and taken a statement from the craftsman in Camden who made the *two* replicas, and checked the bank transfers for payment, and also asked the private collector for a statement, in which he will say that for two weeks Arlene had a key and access to his property, and to his collection—'

'What?' Raymond steps back in surprise.

'That's NOT true!' Arlene grabs the dagger and leaps up. She waves it threateningly at my face. 'YOU know NOTHING!'

I back away.

'HE OWED ME.' She waves the dagger and approaches me menacingly. She hisses, 'What do you know? You have no idea. You meddle. You pry. You judge. You're a nobody. I could buy and sell you. I—' Peter's arm crashes down on her wrist.

Arlene screams, and the dagger drops on the carpet. I bend down and retrieve the dagger as Arlene nurses her hand.

Raymond moves protectively to stand beside her. 'Are you alright—'

'STAY away from ME!' she shouts.

'Arlene? Is this all true?'

'The private collector is Jeffrey Bonnington.' I pass the dagger to Mulhoon. 'He's Arlene's uncle. He had a problem a few years ago when his cleaner was ill. Arlene offered to find him a new one. And, as he was in Switzerland at the time and keen to build a relationship with his estranged niece, he remembers giving Arlene the keys to his house in Holland Park.'

Raymond stares at his wife. 'Is this true?'

'He deserved it.'

'He trusted you. He's your uncle!'

Arlene's facial expression hasn't changed, but now her eyes

are angry. 'He STOLE from us,' Arlene spits. 'He took it all from my mother – she got NOTHING!'

'That's not the point,' I say. 'The point is, is that Arlene encouraged the cult – this gang crime. She recruited the Asian, and under Arlene's instruction, he recruited children from the area. She wanted him to intimidate the kids from the estates. She created the fear, through the Asian and the Turk.'

'Arlene?!' Raymond cries.

I continue, 'After the raid near the canal, when the Asian chased me off the top of the high-rise building, the Asian came back to the area, and he hung around the estate again, intimidating the kids. He did it so that you, Raymond – through the Dixon Trust – would continue to publicly fight against crime, to keep the area free of drugs and gangs – basically to make you look good in the public eye.'

'Is this true, Arlene?' Raymond asks. 'Did you know him? YOU knew the Asian?'

Arlene doesn't speak. Instead, she holds her sore wrist under her arm.

Looking at Mulhoon, I say, 'We have proof that Ali – one of the *Parks* – went to your constituency offices between five and five-thirty the night he came back from Morocco – the night he died. He wanted to speak to someone he could trust. Someone in a stronger position than Matt. Because, although Matt is kind and good, he doesn't have any power. He went looking for Raymond. But you weren't in your office that afternoon, yet by coincidence, Arlene was there. When Ali telephoned, she told him to come to the office. She offered to help him. Ali *trusted* her. He believed that Arlene would tell her husband everything and help him.

'But she didn't. Because, before Ali arrived at the office,

319

Arlene had called the Asian. He waited outside for her instructions. Had Ali not said anything incriminating, she might have
let him go. But because he was ready to tell the police about
the Asian and the initiation ceremony, Arlene knew she had
to do something. She couldn't let Ali tell the police about the
dagger, the cult, the tattoos, or the Asian. So, when Ali told
her that he wanted to tell the police everything – because he
wanted to join the Met – Arlene had Ali followed. She didn't
want Ali telling the police everything he knew about the gang.
She didn't want the Asian to be caught.'

The room is silent.

Raymond slowly digests the information and I wonder if it
has crossed his mind before.

'Was Arlene in your office that afternoon?' Peter asks. 'If
you can't remember, don't worry. It will be easy to check the
phone records. There will be someone who might remember
Arlene was there.'

'Well, my secretary, Pat, he would know ...'

Mulhoon says, 'We will check.'

'I remember ... that night, we were going out for dinner ...'
Raymond stares at Peter and then covers his face with his
hands. 'Oh no, Arlene, what have you done?' he whispers.

I face Arlene and look her in the eyes. 'She murdered Ali,
that's what she's done, as she has done with so many of the
children from the estates.'

Raymond shakes his head in denial. 'This is impossible.
Arlene. Please. Tell me it isn't TRUE!' he shouts. 'You couldn't
be that STUPID!'

'I did it for you, don't you understand?' she spits. 'It's
always about YOU and your political career. It's what YOU
wanted.'

Mulhoon pulls his phone from his pocket and steps out of the lounge and into the hallway, leaving the door open, where I hear him speaking into his phone.

Raymond continues, 'It's not what I wanted. There's no way I wanted you to ... do ... any of this.'

'You like being the hero. The man who saves the day—'

'But—'

'But what?' she says. Her doll-like facial expression is still unchanged, still a polite and surprised smile.

'I never wanted, expected, you to do any of this—' Raymond collapses onto the sofa with his head in his hands. 'They'll crucify me! The press will eat me alive. I'll never survive this.'

Arlene sits beside him. 'They won't. I'll be here with you.'

'You're delusional, Arlene. You're completely insane.' He visibly recoils and pulls away from her.

Mulhoon walks in with the two uniformed officers, who had been waiting in the car. One of them pulls out handcuffs and clips them swiftly around Arlene's wrists.

Over her shoulder, I smile at Peter and he winks back at me.

* * *

A week later, and six days before Christmas, it's a bitterly cold December day, but inside the chapel of the crematorium it's warm and, overpoweringly, it smells of lilies.

The pews are full, and people are even standing at the back. I recognise the *Parks* and greet Monika and Adam, and Lisa and Joe, with a quick hug.

Mustafa, Ali's father, is in the front row with friends and family, and I assume it's Ali's mother on the other side of the aisle, at the front, who cries throughout the short service.

Peter stands beside me as we listen to the tributes spoken by Matt in a solemn and sad tone. He talks about the change parkour has made to all of their lives and how the Dixon Trust will continue to be a place of shelter in the turbulent world in which we live. He briefly mentions the government, and he hopes that the prime minister will abide by his pledge to keep the streets safe, increase policing, and invest in those who need help and care. Ali, he tells everyone, wanted to be a policeman. He was a fine, honest, reliable, and trustworthy young man.

His family should be proud.

Ali's mother sobs loudly.

Claudia, radiant and dressed in a peacock-coloured silk dress and matching turban, dabs at her eyes. Her beautiful black face crumples as she wipes away a tear.

The music is soulful and melancholy, chosen by the *Parks*, and I swallow hard and grip my hands into fists, digging my nails into my skin.

When a large screen comes to life at the front, the room is hushed, and the video I made of the *Parks* in Morocco and photographs of Ali bring his memory to life. The final shot is of him standing proudly in his flying jacket; his hair on top brushed forward and cut in a fohawk taper, buzzed around the ears and dropped down to the neck. He was a handsome young man who wanted to do the right thing.

If he hadn't gone to Raymond's office, we wouldn't have had the CCTV evidence that he met Arlene – nor would we have matched his phone calls to Raymond's office. Mulhoon's diligent team of officers found phone records and his secretary Pat remembered leaving Arlene alone in the office. It wasn't anything unusual; she often helped out. It was unlucky for Ali

322

that she was there. The police also found the original dagger hidden in the bedroom of their Islington home, as well as receipts for the two replicas from the craftsman in Camden.

Arlene told Mulhoon that she had wanted to replace the original in her uncle's collection but that she had become muddled. Arlene was devious and dangerous, but I wonder if alcohol had played a part in her confusion.

I gaze up at the screen. If it weren't for Ali, we wouldn't have continued our investigation. It was his memory and his determination that had kept us all strong.

I wipe a tear from my eye, and Peter reaches out for my hand. His solid reassurance makes me feel safe, and I straighten my back and take a deep breath.

Ali has saved the lives of many, many children. He has helped the Met, and I do not doubt that he would have made an excellent police officer.

As Ali's image on the screen fades, and the coffin gradually disappears, I know I'll never forget Ali nor any of the *Parks*. When I look across at Monika and see her tear-stained face, I understand that she is just one person, of the thousands, who will have a new chance in life. Wherever life takes her, she will be better and stronger for having known Ali, and Matt, and her other friends – the *Parks*.

The disappointment that Marco has been delayed in Croatia, and Stella and her family are staying in India, and I'm not seeing Peter's wife and daughter, pale by comparison to these troubled lives. And, unlike Ali, I would still see my loved ones again next year.

* * *

It's the day before Christmas Eve, and I'm on the train to Salisbury, heading to Blessinghurst Manor feeling exhausted, happy, and excited. I've been delayed in London by Chief Inspector Mulhoon. Two days ago, Peter left for Scotland and I agreed to go through the evidence and our statements one last time.

Marco flew back to England late last night, and I can't wait to see him. He's promised me that he has organised a turkey and the necessary food for the holidays, but I don't care. I know we can shop later today or tomorrow. There's still time. I just want to be with the man I love and share Christmas with him.

The train slows. I look out of the carriage window expecting to see his tanned, happy, and smiling face waiting for me, but as I step down from the train with my case and backpack, he's not there.

The platform is almost empty, and I'm gazing around wondering where he could be and hoping nothing has happened. He couldn't have forgotten I was arriving. I'd called him early this morning, and he said he had lots of jobs to do and he'd see me later. I assumed he'd be here to meet me.

'Mikky!' I turn at the sound of my name and the familiar voice. 'Sorry I'm late, darling; I couldn't find parking.'

'Josephine?' I can barely hide my surprise as she pulls me into her arms and we hug tightly. 'What are you doing here? Why didn't you tell me?'

'Simon and I came back yesterday. You've been through a difficult time, and I wanted to see you. Besides, I thought it would be a surprise.'

'How lovely!' I can't stop hugging her. 'This is amazing!'

'Marco had a problem with the boiler, so he's with maintenance men, and Simon has offered to help him—'

'Simon?' I laugh as we head toward her car, parked at the front of the station. 'What does he know about DIY?'

Josephine laughs. 'Exactly! That's what I said. Pop your bags in the car. I want to hear everything.'

'What's wrong with the boiler?'

'No hot water, but Marco said he'd fix it or we can move into a local hotel.'

Disappointed at the thought of spending Christmas in a hotel, I throw my bags into the boot of the Volvo and sit happily in the front beside Josephine.

'I've been looking forward to our first Christmas at Bless-inghust Manor. Is it bad?'

'What?'

'With no hot water?'

Josephine regards me carefully. 'Pretty bad, but it will be alright. Marco, as you know, only arrived back yesterday, so he's doing his best.'

I nod and remain thoughtful as Josephine pulls the car into the traffic. I'm thinking of earlier trips to Salisbury when Marco's sister, Stella, had been admitted to hospital, eighteen months ago. It had led me on a quest to find Marco, her elusive brother. I'd finally managed to track him down in Croatia. We fell in love almost immediately, and when he turned up in Sardinia to trap his brother in a plan to win back the family estate and save the family heirlooms, I'd been surprised at our feelings. We didn't want to let each other go, and I'd agreed, last year, to return to Blessinghurst Manor for his fiftieth birthday.

'And how's Peter?' Josephine asks, as we head to the main road and follow the signs to the New Forest, one of England's most picturesque landmarks, with its wild ponies, pretty villages, and views to the South Coast.

'He met Aniela and Zofia a few days ago. They've gone to Scotland to see an aunt of his.'

'Are they coming down here?'

'Peter said they'll spend Christmas in Scotland. He thinks it will be more festive.'

'Are you alright?'

I feel Josephine's gaze on me.

'To be honest, I'm really upset. I wanted to see Aniela and meet Zofia. She looks so gorgeous on Zoom. She's beautiful.'

'Oh, that's a shame, Mikky, but never mind. You'll meet up one day.'

'What about Glorietta and Bruno?' I ask.

'They're in Lake Como for Christmas. Don't look so gloomy, Mikky.' She laughs. 'At least you and Marco will be at home for Christmas together.'

'His sister Stella was supposed to fly over, but then they had to cancel. Her husband is a doctor and he's working—'

'Oh, never mind, Mikky. Maybe next year we can organise something bigger. So, tell me, what happened about that dagger you had to find, was it difficult?'

I smile. 'It was a piece of cake.'

I guess she won't have seen the English news in America, so I gloss over the details.

'And what about that politician?' she asks. 'Raymond Harris. I saw him on the news the day after the election. I thought the prime minister was very gracious to him. It wasn't his fault, was it? He didn't have a clue what his wife was up to, did he?'

I shake my head and look out at the darkening sky, only the Christmas lights cheering the otherwise gloomy road. 'She used the Asian to put together a network of vulnerable children to supply drugs – and all out of Islington – so that her husband would be seen as the local hero and saviour.'

'Like in the book *The Three-Body Problem*?' Josephine says.

'You've read it?' I can't hide the surprise in my voice.

'Where the Chinese save the planet from aliens and everyone is happy, not knowing they'd triggered the problem in the first place?'

'Exactly.' I smile.

'She seems delusional but dangerous. So, the Asian followed you?'

'Raymond told her I was snooping around and we think he followed me from Dixon House, and when we went to the craftsman who made the daggers, then Arlene knew she had a problem. She wanted me out of the way.'

'But at least something good came out of it all with the *Parks*?'

'Absolutely. They're incredible, Josephine. I'd like you to meet Matt one day. He runs Dixon House and is instrumental in working with the kids and the local communities. He's hoping that parkour training will take off and become relevant to more kids like Ali and the other *Parks*. It gives them a sense of pride.'

'And the original dagger, did you find it?'

'Mulhoon found it. Arlene had it upstairs in her bedroom, would you believe?'

'She sounds a little crazy.'

'She made a statement, and she's confessed. She kept the original dagger worth over $3 million dollars as an investment for her retirement. She believed that Jeffrey Bonnington, her long-lost uncle, who she met for the first time at her mother's

327

funeral, owed it to her. He'd inherited all the family wealth and she had grown up in relative poverty. She'd also signed a prenuptial agreement that if she and Raymond ever divorced, she'd get nothing.'

'It was her financial security?'

'She felt it was her birthright.'

'How did she meet the Asian?'

'She said she met him at a local gym. They went and had a lunchtime drink and they had an affair. He probably gave her the attention that Raymond never had the time to dedicate to her.'

'Raymond Harris? Well, I guess his political career is over?'

'Time will tell. He's working with Matt and trying to help the Dixon Trust. His heart was always in Dixon House and, presumably, Jeffrey Bonnington is still supporting the Dixon Trust financially.'

'That's kind of him.'

'Yes.'

'He must be delighted with you for returning his dagger?'

'He was pleased. He invited Peter and me for dinner last week.'

'You have been busy in London.' She smiles.

'It was Ali's funeral, and then I promised I'd take the *Parks* out for dinner and give them a preview of the documentary.'

'So, you finished it? I'd love to see it.' She sounds genuinely excited for me.

'You will. It will be on TV in the New Year. Sandra Worthington made it all possible. She's been very supportive.'

'I met her at an awards evening once. She was a splendid person. I'll look forward to meeting her again, one day.'

'I'd like you to meet the *Parks*, too.'

'I'd like that.'

Josephine turns the car into the long driveway of the Chedwell family estate, Blessinghurst Manor, and I take a breath. It looks different since I came here last year. It's almost dark – the December light has faded. My tummy begins somersaults at the thought of seeing Marco.

'Excited?' Josephine grins.

'Very.'

She turns off the track and veers away from the main house toward the cottages: Buttery Cottage, Stable Cottage, and Dairy Cottage.

'Where are you going? It's that way.'

I point to the main house, lit up and welcoming, and the two Christmas trees standing at the entrance, decorated with pretty white festive lights.

'Trust me. I know where I'm going.'

She parks the car outside Dairy Cottage, where I stayed on my first visit, when I'd been employed as a curator to document the Chedwell family treasures, and she throws open the car door. 'Come on. I've got a surprise for you.'

'I stayed in Dairy Cottage. Marco used to live here before his brother framed him and tried to get him sent to prison,' I say, climbing out of the car. 'Stella had Buttery Cottage,' I add.

'She still does, and Joe and Tina have Stable Cottage now.'

'You're very well informed, Josephine.'

'Marco has guests staying in the main house on the estate – you know, the one that Roberto lived in with his wife and Megan.'

'Guests?'

'Well, I suppose Simon and I are hardly guests,' she says with a laugh. 'We're family.'

329

I step inside Dairy Cottage, and it's how I remembered; the open lounge-diner is warm and the log burner is welcoming. Teacups and home-made cakes, including Sandy's home-made carrot cake, have been laid out on the counter. I imagine Sandy's happiness running the estate cafe with Marco back at home. A bucket of ice is holding a chilled bottle of Dom Perignon Vintage.

Josephine turns to face me. She can hardly contain her excitement.

'What's going on?' I ask.

'Come upstairs, Mikky. I want to show you something.'

Intrigued, I follow her up the narrow staircase. She stands aside to let me enter the main bedroom before her.

Hanging on the wardrobe door is the most beautiful dress I've ever seen – a low-cut, Cinderella-style dress that seems to shimmer like tiny golden, glittering stars, in the glow of the bedside lamps.

I reach out, surprised at the softness of the satin and silk. 'It's beautiful,' I whisper.

'I had it made for you,' she says.

'For me?'

'Yes.'

'And these?' I point at a polished pair of my favourite biker boots.

'It's what you said you wanted to get married in. Today is your wedding day, Mikky.'

I stare at her, but she doesn't stop smiling.

'Where's Marco?' I ask.

'Waiting for you in the main room at the Manor.'

'And the broken boiler?'

'It's all been an elaborate surprise. Marco flew back a week

330

ago,' Josephine continues speaking, not pausing for breath. 'He's with all the other guests; everything is arranged and—'

'What other guests?'

'Well, I think you'd better get dressed and come and see for yourself; they're all waiting for us.'

'Really?'

'I promise.'

* * *

We walk along the illuminated garden path, decorated especially with thousands of Christmas lights and little lanterns hung over our heads, to the Manor house.

'It's like a film,' I whisper, conscious of the beautiful golden gown that fits me perfectly.

'It's a fairy tale, my darling. You deserve the happy ending of a princess.'

'Did Marco arrange all this?'

'With a little help.'

'Did you even go to Miami?'

'Er, well, we went for a few days, but Marco needed help to organise all this – Simon and I couldn't wait to get back from Miami. Marco loves you with all his heart.'

'Is this why you told me to go to the hairdressers and get my nails done in London?'

Josephine laughs.

Inside the Manor, a stranger in a three-piece grey, pin-striped suit smiles at us. His blond hair is gelled into a quiff and he claps his hands in delight.

'Hello, Treynor,' Josephine calls happily.

'I'm Treynor, welcome to your wedding, Mikky. You look

gorgeous. I've heard so much about you, and I'm so excited. The guests and,' he grins, 'your future husband are all waiting for you.'

I stare at him, unable to speak, the realisation of this event dawning on me.

It's my wedding day.

Treynor turns to Josephine. 'If you'd like to go inside and take your seat?'

Josephine nods; dressed in a peach suit, she's stunningly beautiful, and I realise how fortunate I am. I reach out.

'Wait! Aren't you going to give me away?'

'I ... I didn't know if you'd want me to—'

'I'd be honoured, Josephine. You're my mama, aren't you?' I pull her closer to me.

'I didn't want to presume.'

'Why? That's not like you!' I joke, and wipe a tear from her eye.

She smiles. 'I'm so proud of you.'

'I know.'

'This is the best day ever,' she says. 'I love you.'

'I love you, too.'

'Are you ready, ladies?' asks Treynor.

'Yes, I'm ready.' I turn to Josephine. 'Thank goodness you poured me a glass of champagne. Look, my hands are shaking.'

Josephine giggles and I can't stop grinning, although my tummy is fluttering wildly.

'Follow me,' Treynor says; he swings his hips when he walks, and when I laugh, hysteria rises in my throat. He sashays toward the main lounge and, very dramatically, pushes open both doors and announces grandly, 'The bride.'

My laughter dies in my throat as we pause to take in the

perfect scene before us; the roaring fires, two stunning Norwegian Firs rising to the ceiling, golden lights, candles, and a massive array of blue irises.

Glorietta, at the front of the room, is facing us. Wearing a cream dress that contrasts with her suave Mediterranean complexion, and her dark hair pulled into a chignon, she begins to sing. Pitch-perfect, the note is melodious and breathtaking as it swells, filling the room.

She.

Written and sung by Charles Aznavour and Herbert Kretzmer, and later recorded by Elvis Costello for the film *Notting Hill*, it is one of my favourite songs.

'*She may be the face I can't forget ...*' Glorietta's soft voice is filled with love and emotion.

Josephine takes my arm, but my step falters. Marco is waiting for me. He's wearing a tailored dinner suit, white jacket, and golden bow tie. His tanned face crinkles in an excited smile, and I know it's a scene I'll never forget.

I slow my pace, determined to enjoy and remember every moment; every face and every friend gathered here to help us celebrate. We walk, mother and daughter, along the aisle and I glance at each row of chairs, as I walk toward the handsome man waiting for me. Marco – my future husband.

'*She may be the song that summer sings ...*'

I stop in surprise when I see my lovely friend Javier, now a world-famous artist living in South America. He was my flatmate in London five years ago when I was about to steal Vermeer's *The Concert*. But then Josephine came into our lives, pretending she needed her portrait painted by him on the pretence of finding me. Javier, still attractive, smiles and raises his hand to blow me a kiss. Beside him, his handsome partner Oscar beams happily.

Next to them are my good friend Dolores – my ex-art teacher from Madrid – and her beautiful granddaughter Maria, who looks serene and stunning in a simple red dress. With them is Sandy, who runs the estate coffee shop, and a few of the estate workers.

On the other side of the aisle, Alexandros stands proudly with his son Milos and daughter Dorika. I'd taken over the job that their mother had set out to do, and returned a valuable Torah to the Kahal Shalom Synagogue in Rhodes after her tragic and untimely death. I blow Dorika a kiss, and she blows one back to me.

Josephine giggles.

Inspector Joachin García Abascal, my boss and friend, smiles at me, and I assume that the petite brunette with the pretty smile at his side is his wife, Maria. Chief Inspector Mulhoon stands with them. He must have known all along about the wedding plans and he deliberately kept me in London. I can't help but smile at their duplicity.

In front of them, Monika, Adam, Joe, and Lisa are dressed in their most elegant suits. For the first time since I saw them in Morocco, the *Parks* look relaxed and happy. Monika's hair is tied in colourful braids and Adam's hair has been cut in a fashionable buzz cut.

Sandra Worthington, the film director, looks dazzling in green chiffon, and Claudia, wearing a purple robe and matching turban, looks exotically sophisticated. With them – and it only dawns on me now – Keith and Matt are in matching tuxedos and bow ties. I'd never realised they were an item. They're smiling, fashionable and smart, and I'm filled with a sense of hope for the future.

'*She may be the reason I survive ... The why and wherefore I'm alive ...*'

I glance at the best man standing beside my future husband. Peter, the ex-SAS hero who saved my life. He returns my smile. My friend for life. I'd been thrilled when the two men in my life had become best friends, and developed a common interest in gadgets and technology. Behind Peter, his wife Aniela is holding their three-month-old baby Zofia. They hadn't gone to Scotland at all. That had all been another ploy arranged by this lovely group of family and friends.

Behind them is Marco's friend and business partner, Lorenzo, and his daughter Franchi, who I'd last seen in Sardinia. Curly haired with sparkling blue eyes, I guess Lorenzo is too shy to be the best man. Franchi, who manages her father's beach bar, is wearing a purple dress and has dyed her hair shocking pink. She's with Mario her boyfriend, who has tied his long hair back into a ponytail. They had been instrumental in nursing Marco back to health and helping him trap his brother Roberto in an elaborate plot to find the family jewellery and in particular the rare and valuable necklace the *Ruby Pear*.

On the other side of the aisle, Stella – Marco's sister – is dressed in a stunning red traditional Indian sari and is with her husband Gurjit. Their daughter Tina and her husband Joe, also wearing traditional Indian suits, were married here eighteen months ago, before I met Marco – I laugh in delight. They, too, had tricked me in saying they would stay in India for Christmas and, in the front row, Rosa Chedwell, Marco's mother, looks radiant in a classic grey and pink suit.

I smile at Glorietta Bareldo. My friend and the world-famous soprano, here with her loving husband, Bruno, who gives me a gallant bow with a nod of his head and a cheeky wink.

'She may be the reason I survive ...'

I kiss Josephine's cheeks, and she takes her place beside Simon, her partner – and my oldest friend – who beams happily at me.

'Me, I'll take her laughter and her tears ... And make them all my souvenirs ...'

I'm overwhelmed. Never could I have imagined, growing up, that I would be so lucky to have a wonderful family, amazing friends, and a man like Marco who loved me. Standing side by side, I look into his eyes, and like mine, they fill with tears.

'For where she goes, I've got to be ... The meaning of my life is she ...' Glorietta's voice fades.

'You look beautiful,' Marco whispers.

I grin at him, unable to speak, his fingers brushing mine.

'Surprised?' he asks.

I wipe my eyes before taking a deep breath. 'Surprisingly, speechless.'

This is my life. This is my forever.

He.

THE END.

Janet Pywell's Books:

Mikky dos Santos Thrillers:
Golden Icon – *The Prequel*
Masterpiece
Book of Hours
Stolen Script
Faking Game
Truthful Lies
Broken Windows

Boxsets
Volume 1 – Masterpiece, Book of Hours & Stolen Script
Volume 2 – Faking Game, Truthful Lies & Broken Windows

Other Books by Janet Pywell:
Red Shoes and Other Short Stories
Bedtime Reads
Ellie Bravo

For more information visit:
website: www.janetpywell.com
blog: janetpywellauthor.wordpress.com

All books are available online and can be ordered through major book stores.

If you enjoy my books then please do leave a review from wherever you purchased the book. Your opinion is important to me. I read them all. It also helps other readers to find my work.

Thank you.

Ronda George Thriller

Ronda George, a well-known private chef to celebrities and royalty, is employed by wealthy international businessman Friedrich Schiltz to celebrate his second wife's birthday in Scotland with their family and close friends.

But, unknown to anyone, Ronda's ex boyfriend has left – taking her life savings – and now she's lost all her confidence.

When Inspector Joachim García Abascal asks for Ronda's help to be his 'eyes and ears' in the spectacular Calder Castle in Aberdeen – she can't say no.

Coping with her past demons, Ronda spies on the family members hiding dark secrets. Siblings from both of Herr Schiltz's marriages have separate agendas. His first wife was murdered five years ago and when the murder weapon, a missing gun, appears – the stakes are raised and no one can be trusted.

Could its sudden appearance be related to a valuable diamond ring?

Who is hiding the deadliest secret of all?

About the Author

Janet lived in Spain and worked in the travel and tourism industry for over twenty years. She managed her own marketing company in Northern Ireland, where she studied for her MA in Creative Writing at the Seamus Heaney Centre at Queen's University Belfast. She uses her experiences of living and travelling abroad and knowledge of locations as an integral part of the scenes in her novels.

To add authenticity to her novels, Janet has studied a variety of courses including, Shipwrecks and Submerged Worlds, Antiquities Trafficking and Art Crime, and Forensic Psychology. She combines her passion for writing, history, and cultural heritage, and loves to see people maintain deep-rooted traditions. Her exciting international crime thrillers are expertly researched and keep you turning the pages.

As well as working on her next book, Janet is also a lecturer at Canterbury Christ Church University on the Creative and Professional Writing course.

You can connect with me on:

- http://www.janetpywell.com
- https://twitter.com/JanPywellAuthor
- https://www.facebook.com/JanetPywell7227
- https://janetpywellauthor.wordpress.com
- https://payhip.com/JanetPywell

Subscribe to my newsletter:

- https://www.subscribepage.com/janetpywell

Printed in Poland
by Amazon Fulfillment
Poland Sp. z o.o., Wrocław

59034032R00197